Retreat
A Story Of 1918

Retreat

A Story Of 1918

Charles R. Benstead

Introduction by
Dr Hugh Cecil

Methuen

Published by Methuen in 2018

1

Methuen
Orchard House
Railway Street
Slingsby
York YO62 4AN

Text Copyright © Charles R. Benstead Estate 2018
Introduction © Dr Hugh Cecil

Moral rights have been asserted

First published by Methuen in 1930

All rights reserved
Without limiting the rights under copyright reserved above,
no part of this publication may be reproduced, stored in
or introduced into a retrieval system, or transmitted,
in any form or by any means (electronic, mechanical,
photocopying, recording or otherwise), without the
prior written permission of the both the copyright
owners and the above publisher of this book.

A CIP catalogue record for this book is available from
the British Library

ISBN: 978 0 413 77809 3

Typeset by SX Composing DTP, Rayleigh, Essex
Printed and bound in Great Britain by Clays Ltd, St Ives Plc

This book is sold subject to the condition that it shall not, by way of trade or otherwise, be lent, resold, hired out or otherwise circulated in any form of binding or cover other than that in which it is published and without a similar condition, including this condition, being imposed on the subsequent purchaser.

www.methuen.co.uk

TO
THE REVEREND
R. M. NICHOLLS
CHAPLAIN, ROYAL NAVY
IN RESPECT AND AFFECTION

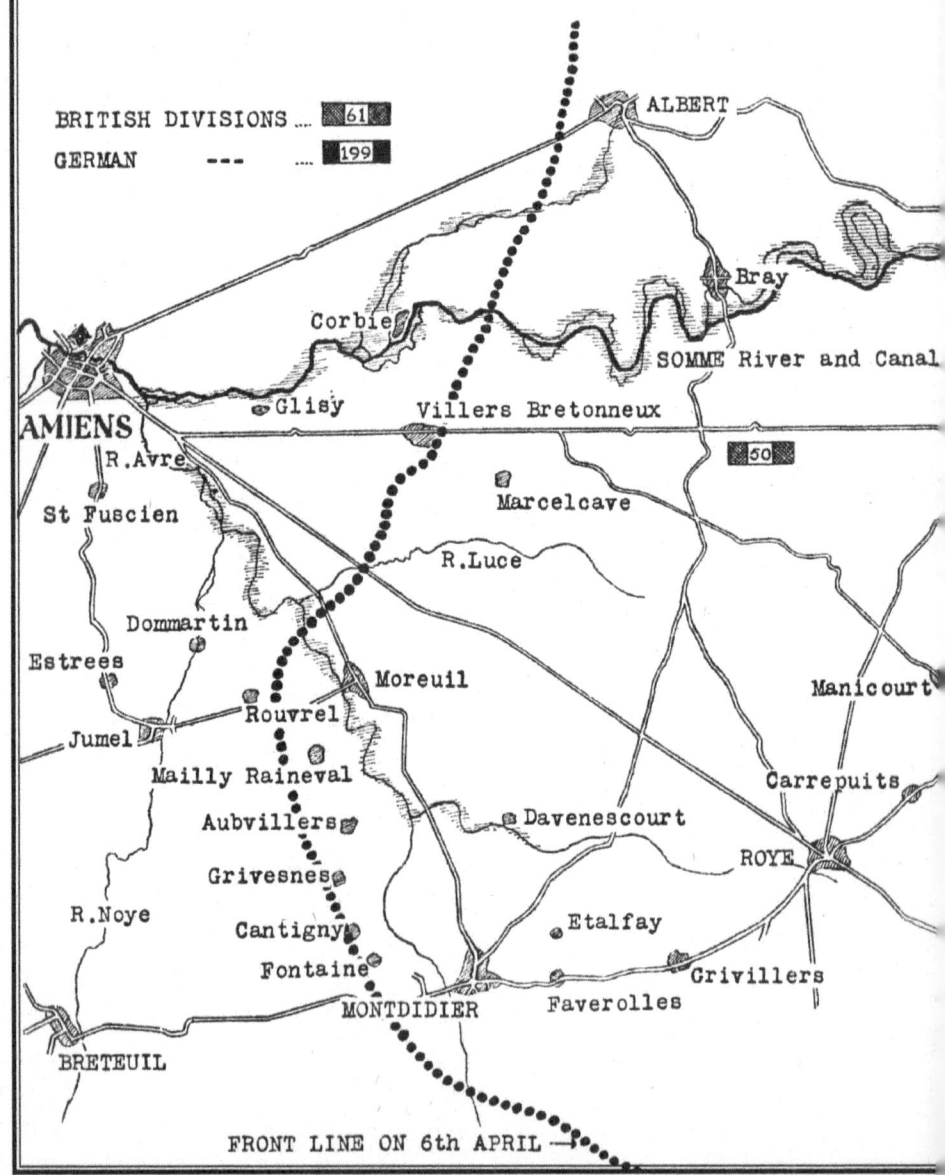

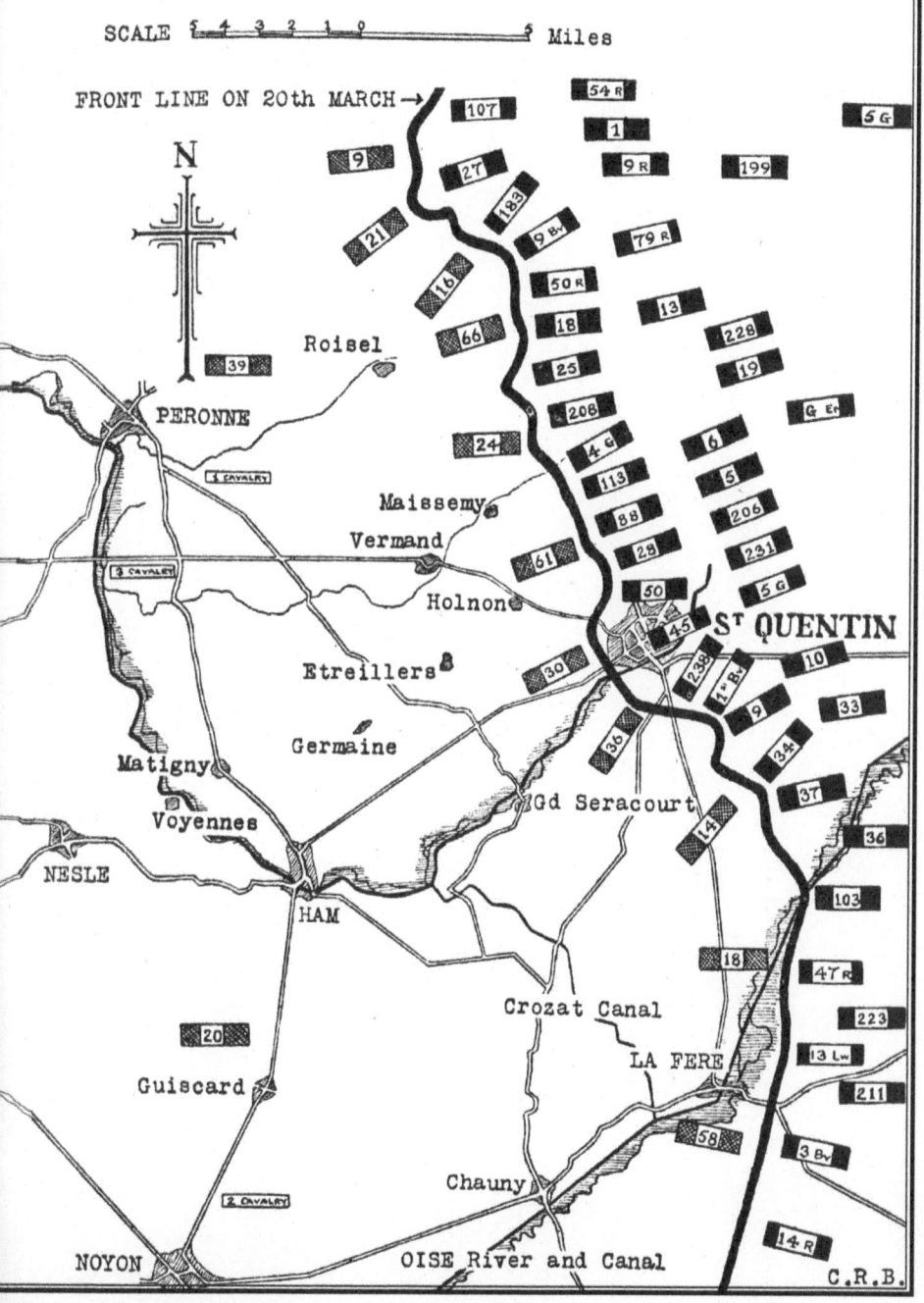

CONTENTS

CHAPTER

	Introduction	xi
	Glossary	xxx
I.	Night	1
II.	Dawn	29
III.	Escape	59
IV.	Finding A Billet	91
V.	Lasting The Course	145
VI.	Starting Afresh	177
VII.	Shepherding The Flock	199
VIII.	Comforting The Dying	227
IX.	Burying The Dead	246
X.	Eclipse	284
XI.	Epitaph	308

INTRODUCTION

Retreat, a Story of 1918, C. R. Benstead's dramatic and harrowing novel chronicling an army padre's psychological collapse, appeared in 1930. By the later twenties the trend in British First World War fiction had changed from being generally positive to becoming disenchanted, as in *All Quiet on the Western Front*. *Retreat* embraces both views. It is a terrible indictment of the struggle and puts no romantic gloss on it, but neither does it depict Britain's aims as futile, and it places the highest value on courage, discipline, and devotion to duty.

It is at once the painful tale of personal disintegration under the stress of battle and army life and a graphic eyewitness account of the March 1918 retreat of the British Fifth Army before an overwhelming German assault. Its wider message is the inadequacy of orthodox religion for soldiers at the front; but it also reflects on the nature of war, its cruelty and injustice, and how it tests a man's character. Captain Cheyne, the brigade adjutant who envies Padre Warne his religious faith, is worn out by years of service and close to breaking yet somehow holds together because he is fundamentally unselfish. Padre Warne, for all his religious fervour, is egotistical and vain and cannot bear the blows to his self-esteem when fear grips him and when the colossal impact of the enemy attack annihilates his personal significance.

The story of Warne's humiliation invites comparison with that of Colley, the young Anglican parson in *Rites of Passage,* William Golding's 1980 Booker Prize—winning historical novel. Both clerics lose the will to live, shamed—in the case of *Retreat* by failure of nerve in battle and in the other by sexual disgrace—but above all because their religious message is spurned. At the start of the First World War, the churches' leaders were full of hope that dedicated work by their chaplains at the front would yield a huge harvest of converts, and during the period 1914—18 over three thousand British clergy joined the Army Chaplains' Service. But by 1918 a man like Warne, with lofty missionary expectations, had become a rarity among army padres, who generally resigned themselves to the less spiritual, though commendable role assigned to them by the military authorities. The authorities, having initially regarded chaplains as nuisances to be kept well behind the lines, decided that they had after all a use in maintaining morale. This function the chaplains sought to fulfil, often heroically—by accompanying the men, unarmed, into battle and helping hard-pressed medical teams to rescue and tend the wounded—and more generally by writing to the bereaved, running errands, brewing tea, dispensing cigarettes, and exchanging cheerful gossip with lonely sentries. Three were awarded the Victoria Cross, the supreme award for courage; and over two hundred, the Military Cross. One hundred and seventy chaplains were wounded, and eighty-eight were killed in battle or died of illness contracted through sharing the hardships of men far younger than themselves.

INTRODUCTION

Many chaplains experienced a deepening of their faith and received a salutary shock to their more self-righteous preconceptions, but as in the fictional case of Warne, the demands of the job proved an unbearable strain for those who were psychologically ill-suited to the war machine. Spiritual guidance tended to be unwelcome, as were religious services, except by the pious. What most soldiers seemed to prefer in the way of religion, if any at all, was that dispensed by the Y.M.C.A. behind the lines—informal affairs with familiar hymns such as they might have sung at football matches. Above all they resented "church parade" with its enforced attendance, fully turned out and, in the earlier stages of the war, carrying their rifles, at formal morning services to hear improving sermons delivered by noncombatant clerics. Many padres, aware of this ill feeling, disliked the institution, but the military authorities favoured it as being in the army spirit regardless of its emptiness. In *Retreat* Warne is reduced to accepting church parade as the only way he can offer religion to his supposed "flock."

Warne is in many ways less of an old-fashioned figure than he seems. His pacifism belongs to the future as well as the past. His indignation at the reduction of the pastoral role to mundane tasks and, at best, simplified religion is paralleled today by clergy who are impatient with "common religion" limited to rites of passage, such as marriage, and to services that are also family occasions, as at Christmas. It is not these scruples alone, however, but Warne's lack of a common touch and his revulsion from the coarsening of fibre essential to soldiers' survival that isolate him.

The author of *Retreat*, Captain Charles Richard "Jack" Benstead, was destined to serve in both world wars. Born on 21

April 1896, he attended the County School in Cambridge, his hometown, and St. Catharine's College, Cambridge University, where, in 1915, he passed part one of the Mathematics Tripos. Nearly six feet six inches tall,[1] he was striking in appearance, with clear-cut, aquiline features and an alert, sardonic look. His diaries, memoirs, and letters reveal him as quick witted, not easily intimidated, humane, imaginative, and eager for experience.[2]

In outlook Benstead was typical of the generation that volunteered for the army between 1914 and 1916 and believed profoundly in their country's cause, in Britain's empire, and in the values that upheld them. They had grown up on a diet of Rudyard Kipling, and *Retreat*, indeed, owes much to that author's influence: the youthful Dalgith (who is Benstead's protagonist); Cheyne, the former planter from Fiji; O'Reilly, the clear-eyed Irish doctor; and the invincible Colonel Metcalfe all seem like characters from Kipling. But they are not mere literary creations—they are drawn directly from the author's memories of his brigade in March 1918. Cheyne was modelled on Captain A. G. "Sambo" Cowling, M.C.,[3] a peacetime schoolteacher from South Africa; O'Reilly on Captain J. T. O'Boyle, M.D.; and Colonel Metcalfe on Lieutenant Colonel H. Rowan-Robinson, D.S.O. M.C.[4] They represented a strain of the British psyche of that time that was at one level conventional and disciplined, at another ruggedly individualistic and critical of authority—but always devoted to the task at hand. It was a type dominant in British public and social life up to the mid-1960s but now in eclipse.

Early in 1916, at the age of nineteen, Benstead entered the army and began training for the Royal Garrison Artillery. The

INTRODUCTION

R.G.A. was the heavy artillery, supposedly the less dashing arm of the gunners, relying more on motor transport and having less to do with horses than the Royal Horse Artillery (the senior arm) or the Royal Field Artillery. This did not worry Benstead as he liked neither riding (and falling off) horses nor the business of grooming them.

Keen and efficient—and helped by his mathematical education—Benstead was singled out for a commission. In late October 1916, trained only in elementary gunnery and riding and not in command, he was packed off with scores of other officers to replace casualties of the Somme battle, which was then drawing to a close. He joined 20 Siege Battery (in the Fifth Army), which consisted of four eight-inch howitzers (not horse-drawn) weighing fourteen tons apiece—adapted from obsolete six-inch naval guns and just about capable of lobbing a two-hundred-pound shell some ten thousand yards. These "museum pieces," which he found squatting "like enormous toads" by the roadside at Pozières on the Albert-Bapaume road, were "naked to the winds of heaven and German reconnaissance aircraft.

... There was not a man to be seen. There was only the grave of a village, its solitude and its silence." He was told to forget all the theory he had been taught in England and simply use his common-sense.[5]

He spent six hundred out of the following seven hundred and fifty days in the line—a common experience among artillerymen, who were usually not relieved during the battles because, unlike the infantry, they were not required to man the forward trenches or to go "over the top." So while spared the worst of the fighting, gunners endured more prolonged stress. The strain was especially felt by forward observation officers and signallers, who, as Benstead's novel graphically illustrates, occupied vulnerable vantage points, well out into no-man's land, to locate enemy guns and assess the effect of their own batteries' gunfire. During the five months he spent near Pozières, Benstead began to learn from a fellow subaltern, Lieutenant Villiers, "stout, bucolic and imperturbable,"[6] how to be an officer. Long afterwards, in his unpublished memoir, Benstead confessed his private fears of being buried alive, but during that freezing winter he impressed Villiers with his coolness and competence in forward observation posts.

In April 1917 Benstead's battery was drawn into much heavier fighting, near Arras. The British forces were supporting a new French offensive, masterminded by General Robert Georges Nivelle, which, that eloquent general boasted to his allies, would assuredly win the war. It failed ignominiously. Mutinies spread widely throughout the French divisions in the line. The British army was left to shoulder the burden. Many more casualties followed. The day after Benstead's twenty-first birthday, he was felled by a shell and, suffering from shock, was withdrawn from his duties as forward observation officer. However, he swallowed down a sedative, potassium bromide salts, and went back into the line. Near Vimy Ridge he was grazed by a German shell splinter that, as he said, finally took the edge off his youthful martial ardour. He went on ten days' leave to England but suffered the frontline veteran's inability to communicate with civilians back at home. On his return he wrote, "The nearer I drew to Arras, the nearer I drew to normality."[7]

He came back to a much changed unit: 20 Siege was now a six-gun battery with a new commander and two extra officers.

INTRODUCTION

It was re-equipped with brand new, lighter, and more efficient howitzers. Once again Benstead was forward observation officer, this time in the vile inferno of Monchy-le-Preux and later at Ypres. Their new group commander kept them hard at "counter-battery" work, engaging and silencing enemy guns harassing the British lines and reinforcing the batteries' cohesion as a fighting unit. "Just a chance handful of young men, of no pretensions or consequence," as Benstead described his own battery, "with Harding, a bank clerk, directing us in the task of producing our own little oasis of order in this devil's lunatic asylum."[8]

Later in the year, by October 1917, as the third battle of Ypres drew to a close with its grisly weeks round Passchendaele, the numbers killed and wounded in Benstead's battery had exceeded those of its original establishment. Ypres III was above all a battle of guns against guns and, proportionately, the artillery casualties were higher than those of the infantry. He saw many dreadful scenes—especially when a direct hit on his battery from a German 4.2 salvo left one of the sergeants terribly mangled and begging to be shot but alive for five hours. To make matters worse, the battery commander—the model for Major Tansley in *Retreat*—was continuously drunk or in a state of "funk" and would skulk for hours in the battery command post. Benstead and other officers, sometimes under fire and without sleep for as much as forty-eight hours, struggled to keep guns from sinking into the mud, and to cross rivers with artillery, horses, men, and limbers flying all over the place.[9]

Balancing these Dantesque visions of horror and degradation was the inspiring figure of brigade padre Fleming, tall, never without his black Cossack helmet, respirator, and staff, and never "talking religion"—his serenity was proof enough of his faith. On one occasion, when the shelling was very heavy, Fleming pressed his helmet on Benstead, who was bareheaded, with a warm-hearted "your need is greater than mine"[10]—a very different spirit from that shown by the tremulous, self-absorbed Padre Warne of *Retreat*. Benstead himself was recommended for the Military Cross and in December was mentioned in despatches for gallant and distinguished services in the field.

In late December, Benstead left his battery to join the Fourteenth Brigade, R.G.A., where he became group orderly officer under Lieutenant Colonel H. Rowan-Robinson. This remarkable man visited the line constantly: a model of how a senior officer should conduct himself. He never looked for trouble, Benstead recalled, "but strode into it looking for something else. . . . I've always said that anyone who kept his end up with Colonel Rowan-Robinson as long as I did, earned at least a Ro-Ro survivor's medal."[11] Eventually the Fourteenth Brigade, numbering temporarily by 20 March 1918 some twenty-five heavy guns, joined General Sir Ivor Maxse's Eighteenth Corps opposite St. Quentin in preparation for the enemy attack on the Somme front, which from early March had been expected daily.

Till then the opposing sides in their trenches on the western front seemed to be locked into a fourth year of stalemate. The French army had been on the defensive since their defeats and mutinies in the spring of 1917, while Britain's expeditionary force had sustained an estimated eight hundred thousand casualties in the same year. It was the Germans, despite widespread civilian demoralization and a deteriorating industrial and communications infrastructure, who now came

INTRODUCTION

within sight of winning. In the east their peace treaty with the Russian Bolsheviks on 3 March gave them potential control of a vast area, including the rich grainfields of the Ukraine and the oil wells of the Transcaucasus. With the end of fighting in that theatre, they were also able to transfer immediately more than forty of their divisions to the western front, giving them superiority for several months, before the American forces—only one of whose divisions was yet battle-ready—could arrive in numbers. Now were the best moments and the last chances for Germany to achieve victory.

General Erich Ludendorff, chief strategist of the German high command, decided to attack the British front at its weakest spot—close to the point where the French and British trenches met and in the region of the 1916 Somme battle near St. Quentin. From there up to Arras, further north, the British lines were manned by General Sir Hubert Gough's Fifth Army (including, at the time, Maxse's Eighteenth Corps and Benstead's own brigade) and by General Sir Julian Byng's Third Army. Against twenty-six British and French divisions Ludendorff concentrated a force nearly three times that size and huge quantities of guns, giving a similar superiority in artillery. The German forces were trained in recently developed infantry tactics involving small units of crack troops equipped to penetrate rapidly their opponents' lines in depth and to destroy their communications while conventional troops took out enemy strong points.

Despite Ludendorff's efforts at secrecy, it would have been incredible if the German preparations had gone unnoticed by the British and French, who attempted to prepare a counter-strategy, but it was quite inadequate. Gough and the Fifth Army were the victims of a prolonged conflict between the British commander in chief, Sir Douglas Haig, and the British prime minister, David Lloyd George, who was horrified by the huge manpower losses on the western front and anxious to keep troops back from it, fearing that they would be wasted on further indecisive bloodbaths like Passchendaele. A substantial force remained in Italy. Meanwhile, over the New Year, British forces had to be rationalized: 141 battalions were disbanded, and divisional strength was reduced from 12 to 9 battalions per division, with no prospect of quick restoration. The Inter-Allied Supreme War Council, a newly appointed body at Versailles with executive military powers, had plans to withdraw further troops from the British Expeditionary Force to become part of a large "general reserve" that could be deployed as the council might decide. At the same time Haig, against his advice, had been required to take over an additional twenty-five miles of line from the French. The result was that the British trenches were undermanned and their defences overstretched. Lloyd George, who took the French military view that any German offensive would be chiefly against the French lines further south in Champagne, ignored Haig's warnings of a massive March attack at St. Quentin.

Gough, like Haig, expected the attack on the Somme, but both men underestimated the resourcefulness and fighting power of their enemy. For blocking any attack in strength, Gough relied on massing most of his available troops close to the front line, where they were vulnerable to artillery and easily outmanœuvered by the new German tactics. He was ill prepared for the kind of flexible strategy—defence in depth—that recent fighting around Ypres should have taught him. Nonetheless he cannot bear the whole blame for what followed.

INTRODUCTION

What followed came close to being a total disaster for the Allies. On 21 March the Germans, aided by fog that concealed their attack and blinded British artillery, shattered the British front line with a million shells and isolated Fifth Army units from one another and from command headquarters. Benstead's account in his private diary over the days that followed gives a vivid picture of the army's frantic withdrawal through a countryside deserted by its French inhabitants: like Dalgith in *Retreat*, he had a narrow escape when a shell splinter whizzed between his legs. The following day he and Brigade Adjutant Sambo Cowling were temporarily cut off from the rest of their brigade, which fell back, hanging on to as many guns as it could, behind the Somme canal. On 23 March he witnessed "a wild stampede down the road to Roye" thanks to a rumour, supposedly started by a German agent, that enemy cavalry was close on their heels. On 24 March one of the brigade's gunners was shot accidentally by "some idiot" from his own side. On 25 March Benstead spent a night at Roye in a mansion that caught fire; on 26 March it was discovered, as the brigade withdrew further west to Montdidier, that most batteries had not received any command to retire, and as orders had been given that no batteries should retire without direct orders, "we stood a good chance of losing our batteries." At the same time the French on their right flank were beginning to retreat, firing on the Germans as they fell back. Looting, especially of wine, became general, with Benstead himself securing burgundy for his comrades. For a while the Fourteenth Brigade prepared to make a stand at Montdidier alongside the French Fifty-sixth Division, but orders came to avoid being separated from their own forces and to retreat a further fifteen miles. The next day the enemy advance largely petered out. By then the brigade had at last reached inhabited regions, with the prospect of food and billets, although cottagers at the village of Mailly refused Benstead entry until he started to break down the door.[12]

In those few days the Germans had pushed the Allied line back forty miles along a fifty-mile-wide front. Since their advance from Mons in 1914, it was their biggest single victory over the British, who by 5 April had lost an estimated 1,000 guns and suffered around 178,000 casualties. The situation was saved on the northern flank, where the Third Army rallied. Meanwhile courage and good leadership at the platoon, company, and battalion levels, as described in *Retreat*, had rescued the Fifth Army from actual defeat, despite panic and confusion. After a week the now over-extended German armies were running out of steam, enabling their opponents to halt their advance with reinforcements and prevent a breakthrough to the key railway junction at Amiens and beyond. Gough was made a scapegoat, many felt unfairly, when Haig relieved him of his command—but no heads rolled in London.

At this juncture Haig himself accepted a unified Allied forces command under the resourceful French leadership of Marshal Ferdinand Foch; and although the Germans continued to score spectacular victories in Flanders and against French lines on the Aisne, they repeated the mistake of over-extending themselves and found themselves losing far more men than they could afford, whereas Britain and France were confident in the knowledge that their own losses would shortly be made up by a massive American presence. Besides, by July the French were equipped with hundreds of fast Renault tanks, while the British Expeditionary Force lined up that summer was the most formidable military machine of the entire war. Reinforced by thousands of fresh troops, trained in the newest tactics involving sophisticated interaction between infantry and artillery, and also with a highly effective tank force, it was described by one articulate junior infantry officer, the poet Richard Aldington, as "abrupt, huge, hairy, testicular."[13] By mid-August, Germany's defeat was inevitable.

Benstead's brigade continued to fight in the Somme region throughout the spring and summer. Many of the incidents described so graphically in the novel, such as the wounding of an elderly Frenchwoman and the deaths of two young officers that much distressed Padre Warne, were recollections from that time.[14] Benstead had an exceptionally accurate memory. Long afterwards, in the 1960s, he was able to identify on his war maps the precise locations of German targets, his own observation post, and his own gun battery near Villers-Bretonneux.[15]

In July he was finally awarded the Military Cross so often promised him. In mid-October, as part of the general Allied advance, the brigade moved northeast. Eventually it took a part, described in his memoir as "insignificant," in the struggle to gain and cross the Sambre-Oise canal. It was during this, the last major Allied offensive leading to the end of the war, that Wilfred Owen, M.C., a subaltern with the Second Manchesters and later rated Britain's finest war poet, lost his life.

Early in 1919 Benstead was demobilized, returning to his interrupted studies at Cambridge, where he also played cricket for the university. In September 1922 he joined the Royal Navy as an instructor lieutenant. Rising over the next twelve years to the rank of instructor lieutenant-commander, he served on a succession of battleships—*Hood, Emperor of India, Rodney,* and *Royal Oak*—and during the first three years of the Second World War on the aircraft carriers *Courageous* and *Furious*. By 1945 he held the rank of instructor captain, with responsibilities in the Pacific fleet, and he remained in the navy until 1947. That year he went back, as steward, to his old college, St. Catharine's, where he is remembered as supervising "with a very light touch"[16] the university's sporting magazine, *Light Blue,* and as being a genial host to athletic stars visiting Cambridge. He combined these duties with those of senior proctor responsible for undergraduate discipline until his eventual retirement. On 3 July 1980, at age eighty-four, he died in a nursing home near the village of Henley-in-Arden, which straddles the ancient "Heart of England Way," in deepest Shakespeare country. His wife and two children survived him.

During his naval service he became a prolific author. Seven of his books were about seafaring, weather, and the navy. Others included two volumes on his beloved Cambridge, a light-hearted guide to drinking, and the translation of a French novel by Edouard Peisson based on the story of the *Titanic*. His writings were informative and witty, displaying a wide sympathy and an eye for unusual detail.

His biggest success was *Retreat,* which was also published in the United States and was reprinted in 1937. The English clergy reacted sharply to the novel, indignant, as Benstead put it, that he had "trodden on the tail of the ecclesiastical cassock."[17] In the *Daily Telegraph*, the Reverend P. B. "Tubby" Clayton, founder of the British army Christian organization Toc H, found the book's dialogue excessively coarse, though he thought it otherwise good.[18] Other clerics were reluctant to believe that such a weak man as Padre Warne would ever have been passed for service by the Army Chaplains' Department or could even have succeeded in the sleepiest and least exacting of parishes. One scandalized library committee ordered their copy of *Retreat* to be burned. There were those who felt the novel's treatment of a priest's sufferings to be unduly callous; but in fact Benstead was far from contemptuous of religion, only convinced that it did not mix with war. *Retreat* itself is dedicated to a naval padre, the Reverend R. M. Nicholls.

There was also talk of *Retreat* being libellous, it being widely assumed that Padre Warne had been drawn from life. In Parliament a member asked whether Benstead, as a lieutenant-commander in the Royal Navy, had not broken service regulations in writing about a fellow officer in this way. Benstead always maintained that Warne was pure invention— the Fourteenth Brigade had no chaplain during the March retreat—and that for anyone who had been in the line, Warne's painful predicament was quite easy enough to visualize without need for a real-life model: "A chaplain on a battlefield was in an impossible position, and, without some earthly compromise to sustain him, would surely go mad if faced with war at its lunatic worst. So I dropped such an imaginary chaplain into the line just before the balloon went up at St Quentin, followed him through the 5th Army's retreat as I had known it, and let him go mad."[19]

It is likely, however, that Benstead drew on some personal recollection, just as he did in describing his other fellow officers and the heroic Padre Fleming, whom he actually mentioned by name in the novel. Encounters with two padres in 1918 furnished ingredients for the Warne story. The first was the Reverend John Fish, who, like Warne, made an unheralded and unwelcome arrival at the front, in this case on 5 March, "temporarily attached to 14th Brigade Headquarters as there was a lack of accommodation at 65th Brigade";[20] but Fish was only with them for a day or two and temperamentally was the very opposite of Warne. After the war the principal chaplain of the British armies in France wrote of him: "In every way suitable for duty as an Army chaplain . . . has done splendid service in the line."[21]

Closer to Warne in personality was the Reverend George James Jarvis (1886—1962), vicar of St. Clement's, Bristol, from 1916—22, who became Fourteenth Brigade chaplain on 24 April 1918. In early May, Benstead described in his private diary going to Villers-Bretonneux with the new padre on an early morning ride—Jarvis's first visit to the line proper. Benstead's comment—"He formed a good psychological study,"[22]—is significant particularly in the light of a similar episode ("Show him the war, eh?") described in *Retreat*. Jarvis was gassed in mid-August 1918 and evacuated with pneumonia from France on 22 October 1918. In January 1919, still ill, he applied to the military authorities and the chaplain general to leave the service and was subsequently involved in unsatisfactory correspondence with a reluctant War Office over back pay owed to him. The tone of his letters is querulous, not unjustifiably so, but certainly in character with Warne. Like Warne, Jarvis seems to have wavered for many months over his decision to join the forces as a padre. In September 1915, at age twenty-nine, he had taken the medical test for service and was pronounced fit, but he did not sign up for a temporary chaplaincy with the forces until March 1918. Unlike Warne however, he recovered from his ordeal as fully as many who

INTRODUCTION

went through the inferno of the western front and remained an active priest for the next thirty years. In November 1931 an Army Council official issued a brief report on his career as army chaplain: "I am to state that his record and services were satisfactory"—not the glowing testimonial that Fish received but presumably sufficient to fend off any rumour that might have identified Jarvis with Warne.[23]

Whether or not the character of Warne was based on any direct observation, the Fourteenth Brigade's diaries, army service records, and Benstead's papers generally confirm *Retreat* as being absolutely authentic in its details. Praise for its force and vividness came from war veterans, such as Edward Shanks in the *New Statesman,* who were also exacting critics.[24] Some rated it as one of the best war books of its time: "The great achievement of the book is the natural way in which the writer takes us from the lonely afflicted Warne to brilliantly described scenes on the battlefield or to the brigade office," wrote the *Times Literary Supplement's* reviewer;[25] while in the *Guardian,* one of the leading Anglican papers, a churchman formerly in the army asserted with conviction: "here is something that is well worthy of a place alongside *All Quiet on the Western Front.*"[26]

Notes

1. See National Archives Kew (hereinafter cited as "NA"), WO 339/ 66179, C. R. Benstead, personal service record.
2. See University of Leeds, Brotherton Library, Liddle Collection (hereinafter cited as "Leeds, LC"), C. R. Benstead wartime diaries and letters; and St. Catharine's College Cambridge Archive, C. R. Benstead unpublished

memoir, "The Garlands Wither." My grateful thanks to J. N. C. Benstead and the Benstead Estate for permission to quote here from this memoir and from other papers of C. R. Benstead, and also to Sir John Baker, St. Catharine's Cambridge; the staff at Leeds University Library (Liddle Collection); and Gary Wragg, the Milestones Museum, Basingstoke, for their help.

3. NA, WO 339/92376, A. G. Cowling, personal service record.
4. NA, W095/468, 14th Bde RGA Diary, February—March 1918.
5. Benstead, "The Garlands Wither."
6. Ibid.
7. Ibid.
8. Ibid.
9. Leeds, LC, C. R. Benstead diaries, 28 September— 29 October 1917.
10. Benstead, "The Garlands Wither."
11. Ibid.
12. Leeds, LC, C. R. Benstead diaries, 21—27 March 1918.
13. Harry Ransom Humanities Research Center, University of Texas, Austin, Mss Flint, R. Aldington to F. S. Flint (letter), 15 September 1918.
14. Leeds, LC, C. R. Benstead diaries, 30 April and 25 May 1918.
15. I am grateful to J. N. C. Benstead for this information.
16. John Britten, "The Story of Light Blue: The Magazine of Cambridge University Sport," Emmanuel College Web site, http://www.emma.cam.ac.uk/collegelife/magazine/ (accessed 28 January 2008).
17. Benstead, "The Garlands Wither."

INTRODUCTION

18. Rev. P. B. Clayton, review of *Retreat,* by Charles R. Benstead, *Daily Telegraph,* 7 February 1930 (press cutting, R. S. Blaker papers, MS. Eng. Lett., Box c. 559, Bodleian Library, Oxford).
19. Benstead, "The Garlands Wither."
20. NA, W095/468, 14th Bde RGA Diary, 5 March 1918 (recorded by C. R. Benstead as orderly officer).
21. NA, WO 374/24367, personal service records of Rev. Thomas Fish, letter dated 16 May 1919.
22. Leeds, LC, C. R. Benstead diaries, 7 May 1918.
23. NA, W0374/37176 personal service records of Rev. G. J. Jarvis.
24. Edward Shanks, review of *Retreat,* by Charles R. Benstead, *New Statesman,* 25 January 1930, 504.
25. Unsigned review of *Retreat,* by Charles R. Benstead, *Times Literary Supplement,* 6 February 1930, 98.
26. "One Who Was There," review of *Retreat,* by Charles R. Benstead, *Guardian, the Church Newspaper,* 17 January 1930, 50.

GLOSSARY

ALL HIGHEST IN POTSDAM Kaiser Wilhelm II.

A.P.M. Assistant provost-marshal, the senior officer in the lower echelons of the military police.

ARMSTRONG HUT Prefabricated collapsible canvas and wood hut used by the British army.

A.S.C. Army Service Corps.

B.C. POST Battery command post.

BRITISH WARM British officer's knee-length, heavy greatcoat, manufactured by firm of Crombie.

CATS Traction vehicles with caterpillar tracks—for all siege artillery larger than the six-inch howitzers and other than the sixty-pound guns.

CHASSEUR DIVISION Crack French infantry division selected from young, tough men.

CHLORIDE OF LIME Compound used as disinfectant in the trenches.

CLYDESDALES Heavy draft horses used to drag the sixty-pound guns.

CORPS H.A. Heavy artillery.

GLOSSARY

D.C.M. Distinguished Conduct Medal; a medal (like the Military Medal) awarded to men in the ranks and, as such, more highly esteemed among the men as a mark of bravery than the Military Cross, which was then for officers only.

Derby scheme Before the much disputed introduction of a compulsory military service system in 1916 to replace the voluntary system, a compromise arrangement was introduced by Lord Derby, director-general of recruitment, whereby potential recruits could "attest," in advance, their willingness to serve if called on to do so, with the government undertaking to call on married men last.

D.R. Despatch rider.

D.S.O. Distinguished Service Order; a medal awarded to junior officers for outstanding courage and to more senior officers for organizational competence—though after 1917 only given to those serving under fire.

Eight-inch howitzer British short-barreled weapon, firing heavy, low-velocity shells with a steep trajectory, suitable for attacking trenches or fortifications.

Five-nine German 5.9-inch (15 cm) heavy howitzer, with a hundred-pound shell and maximum range five and a half miles.

F.O.O. Forward observation officer; the officer who, from an observation post forward of the guns, was responsible for reporting via signal wires on the accuracy of his battery's fire and the location of enemy guns.

Four-two German 4.2-inch howitzer.

F.W.D. Four-wheel drive lorry designed specifically for towing artillery (i.e., the six-inch howitzers and their crews).

RETREAT

G.H.Q. General headquarters.

GOUGH, GENERAL SIR HUBERT Gough (1870-1963) **was** commander of British Fifth Army, October 1916—March 1918.

G.S. WAGON General service wagon, usually drawn by mules.

HAIG, GENERAL SIR DOUGLAS Haig (1861-1928) was commander in chief of the British Expeditionary Force from December 1915 till the end of the war.

HAIRIES Large transport horses used by the British artillery.

"HIGHTY, TIDDLE-Y-IGHTY, CARRY ME BACK TO BLIGHTY" Line from the popular song "Take Me Back to Dear Old Blighty"; "Blighty," meaning the U.K., was a British Indian army expression, deriving from the Hindustani word "belaiti" meaning "home." "A Blighty touch" was a wound bad enough to send a soldier back to Britain, welcome after a long time in the trenches.

KIRSCHNER The popular European illustrator Raphael Kirschner's studies of smart and sassy young women were among the favoured pinups of the wartime period.

M.C. Military Cross, British army award for gallantry, dating from 1914, given to warrant officers and commissioned officers of the rank of captain and below. Since 1993 awarded to other ranks as well.

M.P.S. Member of the Pharmaceutical Society, founded 1841, acquired the title "Royal" in 1988.

NAPOO! GOODBYE! From the French phrase "Il n'y a plus!," as in the popular wartime song "Goodbyee" (the soldiers' version): "If a four-point-two / Drops the shite on you, / Napoo, toodleoo, goodbyee!"

GLOSSARY

N.C.O. Noncommissioned officer (i.e., a sergeant or a corporal).

Nissen hut Prefabricated single-story hut of corrugated steel bent into tunnel shape and closed at both ends with masonry walls; developed in 1916 by Col. Peter Nissen for accommodation and shelter.

O.C. Officer commanding.

O Pip Observation post.

Orderly Officer Officer representing the commanding officer and responsible for supervising the feeding of the brigade, seeing that the brigade understood its orders, and setting an example of smartness and readiness for action.

P.B.I. "Poor Bloody Infantry"—British foot soldiers, the equivalent expression to French "poilu" and German "Landser."

Pemberton-Billing case Notorious trial in 1918. Noel Pemberton-Billing, the ultrapatriotic member of Parliament and editor of *Vigilante,* was prosecuted for criminal libel for alleging that the Canadian-born dancer Maud Allan and the impresario Jack Grein were sexual perverts in the pay of the Germans because they had put on a production of Oscar Wilde's banned *Salomé* at a private theatre club. In the perfervid mood of the time, the popular Billing's acquittal that summer was not surprising.

R.A.M.C. Royal Army Medical Corps.

Royal Garrison Artillery (R.G.A.) Heavy "siege" artillery, as opposed to the Royal Field Artillery, which was equipped with lighter 18-pound field guns and 4.5-inch howitzers.

Siege park Depot, well behind the lines, for reserves of R.G.A. lorries and artillery.

SIX-INCH HOWITZER British weapon, a smaller version of the eight-inch howitzer (see above).

SIXTY-POUNDER Long-barrelled British gun, with a high velocity sixty-pound shell and a maximum range of six miles.

SOS LINES, FIRE ON "Save Our Souls"—emergency signal; fire called down by infantry as final defence against attack. There was usually a prearranged signal by infantry from the trenches to call an instant artillery barrage on no-man's land or an enemy's frontline trenches.

SUFFRAGETTES BURNED PILLAR-BOXES AND REFUSED TO EAT, ETC. Militant activists of the women's suffrage movement intensified their campaign in the years before the 1914—18 war. Tactics included arson attacks on mailboxes and on houses as well as hunger strikes if sent to prison.

30 CWT Thirty hundredweight; a British lorry, with an open cab and a four-cylinder engine, for carrying ammunition, technical equipment, and general stores. It was manufactured by Guys Motors, Wolverhampton, U.K., under the Ministry of Munitions.

3 TON THORNEYCROFT Even more robust than the "30 cwt," thousands of Thorneycroft 3 and 4 ton open-cab Type J general purpose lorries were delivered for use by the British army in World War I.

TWELVE-INCH HOWITZER British weapon that fired 850-pound shells, with a maximum range eight and a half miles.

ULSTER The possibility of civil war between Protestant Ulster and the Catholic south in Ireland (still then part of Great Britain) loomed larger on the British political horizon in early 1914 than the prospect of a continental war.

GLOSSARY

Viti Levu The largest of the Fiji Islands, which were a colony of the British Empire from 1874 until 1970, when they were granted independence as the Republic of the Fiji Islands.

War Council at Versailles Inter-Allied Supreme War Council, set up in the autumn of 1917 to coordinate war strategy and planning and consisting of Allied ministers and army representatives. Also used by the British prime minister, Lloyd George, to wrest control of British military strategy away from the British military high command, which he mistrusted.

CHAPTER I

NIGHT

(I)

'Perhaps you'd care to sit in front, Padre?'

The question, indifferently propounded, required no answer. Already, in the short space of four days in France, the man to whom it was addressed had come to recognize its kind, and along with it the kindly solicitude reserved for his cloth. Or was it tolerance? The suspicion obtruded, but he could not be sure. It did so now, and he looked round quickly but then only in time to observe the speaker, a tall, spare officer, muffled to his eyes in scarf and British Warm, motion a companion with a quiet: 'Come on, Wood. We'll squat behind.'

They were gone before the Reverend Elliot Warne could so much as say 'Thank you'—two dark shadows that merged into the blackness of the March night. For a while he listened to them scrambling over the lorry's tail-board, and the corners of his mouth screwed themselves into a wry little smile as he wondered whether it were possible that he really looked as green as he felt. He could only suppose that he did. Still, it was a consoling thought that this state could not last for ever: the green would wear off soon enough when once he joined his unit, which, please God, would not be long now. Once settled he would be able to measure himself against this bewildering life he had so recently elected to lead, and, he devoutly hoped, regain a little of his vanished ability to behave more like a beneficed clergyman, which he was, instead of a fledgeling curate in his first diaconate, which he had been twenty years earlier. At present he was thinking at least one minute astern of everybody.

'If you'll jump up 'ere, Sir, I'll throw this sack over yer knees.'

Warne managed to achieve a mumbled: 'Yes, yes. Er—yes. Thanks,' as he obediently clambered into the front seat of the lorry, and while he sat there with the driver fussily tucking the sack about his legs, he could not help reflecting that this single-minute phase-difference was a piece of presumptuous flattery: half an hour was nearer the interval.

'It ain't much, Sir, but it's better than nuffin',' the driver said, giving Warne's thigh just such a pat as a nurse may bestow upon a child in a perambulator, and, having paused long enough to light a cigarette, and yell to his mate in the back of the lorry, proceeded to 'rev' up his engine and start with a gigantic crashing of gears. Warne made no attempt at competing.

'If you're joining the Brigade, Sir, you'll be the Reverend Wade's relief?'

The driver's curiosity was nobly restrained, and Warne came near to laughing as, in reply, he scored his first success in anticipation: 'I am—and I've not been out before.'

Why was it every one asked him that fool question? Just as if it were not sufficiently obvious that he had only been in the country five minutes? Still, he had cut that bit of ground from under the driver's feet, but he could wish the fellow would gasp his astonishment with less obvious satisfaction. Actually, though Warne did not know this, no trace of astonishment sullied the purity of that long-drawn 'Ah!' The driver, who deemed himself to have acquired the art of fading away in preference to dying abruptly, was merely indulging the veteran's privilege in the presence of a youngster, in the war sense, who had not.

'Then, Sir,' he added with a sort of luscious smacking of the lips, 'I don't mind tellin' you as you'll be just in time for Jerry's push. It's about due.'

'So I believe.'

This was triumph. Not every day did a man journey 'up the line,' and who was to say that he ever recaptured those sensations of foreboding and exhilaration which must, Warne was sure, have marked the first? For himself Warne was certain that nothing again could be quite like this. Foreboding, exhilaration—yes. He was filled with both these all right. Hence his assumption of pride in the nonchalance with which he had been able to cloak his reply. It was quite the best he had so far accomplished, and he had been trying hard ever since the transport had set him ashore at Havre.

But nonchalant speech remained only a mask, and, though he fortunately did not know, it deceived nobody. What lay behind, and beneath his genuine and justifiable excitement, was a host of lively apprehensions that seemed to grow appreciably livelier at every reference to this impending offensive, and they combined into a sensation he had never before experienced and one he found difficult to describe. It did not hurt, or appal, or even frighten: it merely threw a cold and blighting shadow over the brain so that he felt, at times, mentally empty.

'So I believe,' he muttered again, more to himself than the driver, and stared ahead as if he might see in the strip of road, discernible only as a ribbon of blackness paler than the rest, something of what lay in store when the future became the present and foreboding changed to reality. And unconsciously he clenched his gloved hands over his thighs exactly as men do over the arms of a dentist's chair.

The driver, having no such inhibitions, merely said: 'Yuh!' and turned his attention to the lorry, which demanded it. For the lorry was of the '30 cwt' type, and speedy. Moreover, it carried no lights, and the enveloping darkness hung like a pall over the stretch of country between Ham and its lordly neighbour, St. Quentin. There was no moon. Overhead pale stars pointed a slate-coloured sky. And some detached portion of Warne marvelled how the man kept his dashing vehicle to the barely visible road.

So for a mile or more they drove in silence, Warne with his fears and fancies, the driver with his cigarette. And from time to time when he glanced at the fellow, the fitful glowing of that cigarette would reveal to Warne a Rembrandtian picture of a face, ruddy and deeply furrowed beneath a flat steel helmet. There were saturnine twists about it as well, and the mouth was curled in half-humorous disgust. Warne had the feeling that he might be in part responsible.

But he did not care. What a lorry driver thought of him to-night was of no account. Nothing mattered—apart, of course, from the reason of his being where he was, and that constrained him to savour his 'cocktail' experience with a distinct and more than slightly morbid impatience. The blackness, with its sense of clinging suffocation; the rushing wind that lashed his face and, penetrating his muffler, stung his ears with icy breath; the pulsating clatter of this strange lorry; the ceaseless expectation of disaster in a roadside ditch; the still crowding and bewildering impressions born of that long meandering from the heights of Harfleur to the railhead at Ham; and above everything, dominating it so that even weariness was held in check, the knowledge that somewhere in front of him lay 'the line' and all it so terribly signified—these things formed the ingredients of that cocktail, and it made a heady draught. It touched the imagination, and under its stimulus his tiredness took on the flavour of romance. It was the stuff of heroes, at any rate.

But cocktails are only a prelude at the best of times, and to-night Warne considered he had sipped enough. He wanted to be in at the feast, and the feast was to be found with his unit, nowhere else.

They had told him at the base—they, of course, speaking through the mouth of an insignificant and bespectacled khaki-clad clerk in a Nissen hut—that he was 'for the 200th Brigade, Royal Garrison Artillery,' and the appointment had come to him as something of a shock. He had always regarded the Artillery as a noisy and unavoidable background to the panorama of War, but what sort of life gunners led and how precisely they sickened and died, he could not for the life of him say. Never once had he associated himself with this mighty and, when all was said and done, highly romantic arm of the fighting forces—a curious omission, as he had reflected immediately, because a gunner was undoubtedly possessed of a soul no less than any one else.

'They're down South—with the Fifth Army,' the clerk had added, speaking of the Brigade.

So for two and a half days he had travelled in a train of incredible length and slowness, and in that period had covered a distance which normally takes a few hours, cross-country though it is. And at each halt he had told himself that he was one more step nearer *his* unit, so that long before he had arrived at railhead he had become almost affectionate in his attitude towards them, and when not marvelling at his novel surroundings he was wrapt in visionary dreams of well-doing on the Brigade's behalf. Easter was at hand; Good Friday in a few days. What celebrations then! What a message he would bring! And all beneath the menacing shadow of the guns, and battle, and death.

In these moments of untrammelled enthusiasm he was, indeed, something more than a mere Chaplain: he was the incarnation of his Faith, and that Faith had withstood the buffeting of three terrible years when, with a sympathy all too acute, he had looked upon the world in its agony. There was still much he did not understand, but on these points he sheltered behind his Faith, consoling himself in terms that meant, simply: 'God knows His own business best.'

Fortified thus he had continued to labour unceasingly in the service of God and also the King, staunch in his belief that their causes were identical. That God might conceivably—to put it bluntly—back the other side (as, indeed, the other side were emphatic in proclaiming) never for a moment occurred to him, and with passionate sincerity he prayed for the Divine Light to shine in German Darkness and so illume German Souls that German Armies made speed to surrender to the victorious Allies in token of their penitence.

And now his destiny, which was God's will, was bearing him inexorably onward. Even this terrifying dash through the night would end somewhere, and in that spot, wherever it

NIGHT

was, he would find himself expected and his own unit awaiting him. Nor was he to be disappointed, for only that afternoon Lieutenant (Acting Captain) Michael Cheyne, Adjutant of the 200th Brigade, Royal Garrison Artillery, had received notification of the appointment. But on one account Warne was sadly in error, for whereas he pictured himself, albeit most modestly, in the role of a spiritual saviour welcomed by an ecstatic people crying out for salvation, Cheyne, having read the appointment, had tossed it to the Brigade Orderly Officer with the pungent comment: 'Oh hell! Here's another bloody parson.' And Cheyne did not usually swear, certainly not for the sake of swearing.

(2)

The lorry had left the main Ham-St. Quentin road and was picking its way through Etreillers when the raid began—the raid that was destined to stand forth as a supreme gesture of contempt on the part of a doomed army for its executioners, and, at the time, to verify beyond doubt the imminence of the German blow. It was Gough snapping his fingers under Ludendorff's nose.

But neither Warne nor the driver knew this, and the driver, being essentially war-wise, promptly slowed down and stopped, the better to diagnose the racket; while his passenger, seeing war for the first time, even if from a distance, stared with wide-eyed fascination into a night that was now dancing with the flashes of guns. Away to the east semicircles of light were springing fitfully about the crests of ridges, throwing into momentary silhouette the jagged skeleton of a village. The banging and booming woke a hundred echoes, and the sharper detonations of nearer guns smote gustily upon his ear drums.

'Ours,' diagnosed the driver, and the lorry ground forward again, bearing now a breathless acolyte to the Altar of War. And it might have been noticed that Warne's lips were parted slightly, and that his eyes were shining with a new light; for he was seeing the Glory of the Lord in the stabbing flashes of the guns, and the first swift alarm had vanished from his heart. But it was a puny affair, really—that raid.

The firing quickly died down, and the black pall of silence and mystery fell once more over the land, so that Warne, deprived of the fascination of those dancing lights, was left to shiver and wonder. Some day—how near he mercifully did not know—he would be less of a spectator and more of a performer. How would he shape then? That was the question. Joyfully he told himself that he had not been afraid to-night, and took heart—precisely as men had been doing for the last three and a half years. But later, this offensive . . .

Just short of Villecholes the lorry turned towards St. Quentin and after a short run drew up by the roadside.

'Two—owe—owe Brigade, Sir,' muttered the driver. 'In the quarry, Sir. I've got to take the other two orficers on a bit farver.'

Warne's heart beat a little faster as he climbed stiffly down from his seat.

(3)

The Brigade to which Warne had been posted had little to distinguish it from its neighbours, apart from its Colonel. It was just a solid British unit composed ordinarily of four solid

British batteries recruited, originally, in four distinct comers of the Kingdom. But now, in the March of '18, after months of continually draining out the old blood and assimilating fresh, they could no more have been tied down to separate localities than their officers could have been rated to any particular class, except, perhaps, the all-embracing middle. They were, in fact, just British. And to them came Warne on the very eve of Ludendorff's offensive.

There was one battery of eight-inch howitzers, and three more of six-inch. Attached were a six-gun battery of horse-drawn sixty-pounders and a couple of twelve-inch howitzers that squatted like two enormous toads too fat to move and, once in position, were taken or handed over by Brigades as part of the countryside. And these guns were dotted, either in sections or batteries, over the entire sweep from Maissemy to Holnon, and 914, the eight-inch, temporarily detached, were as far removed as Grand Seracourt. Such was the distribution. It was eloquent revelation of the Fifth Army's meagre resources.

Headquarters resided fairly comfortably in a chalk quarry off the Holnon road, just short of the wood of that name. Batteries resided scarcely less comfortably—for March had been exceptionally dry—in sunken roads, valleys, and the wood itself. And all dwelt in the prophylactic odour of chloride of lime. For, on the orders of a politician who chose to ignore the protests and override the recommendations of G.H.Q. itself, the line had been extended south to Barisis and fourteen miles taken over from the French—fourteen miles, so the Brigade Orderly Officer put it, of open latrine. Only a few weeks had passed since the extension had been made, but in that time the ground had been cleansed, neat little canvas shelters had sprung up where none before had been, and everywhere they bellied out and thrashed in the wind like the sails of the old wooden walls, and every bit as British. And immense, quantities of chloride of lime had been scattered around—principally, the troops thought, in the drinking water.

During the first three weeks of March, indeed, this chemical troubled the Brigade far more than any German attention or threat of attention, for the enemy remained gratifyingly quiet along the whole front and refused to reveal his massing strength however galling the fire that nightly blew up his dumps of ammunition, destroyed his roads and, it was earnestly hoped, his transport and his troops. And as for the threatened offensive, the Brigade were almost tired of hearing about it.

Early in February Sir Douglas Haig himself had told them it was coming, and had given them details with a simple directness that left them under no illusions about what they were in for; they just had to make the best of a bad job, as they had done in the past, and, he felt confident, they would do in the future. All this at an inspection.

And once in the line the fact was further impressed upon them. Daily the Corps to which they belonged reminded them, and lest sufficient heed should not be paid and they should be found wanting in the hour of trial, the Corps Heavy Artillery Commander issued a Defence Scheme, the like of which had never been seen before. It never has since. Amendments, amendments to amendments, amendments to amended amendments, and so on unto the third and fourth generations, then additions, next cancellations—all cascaded from Corps Headquarters like a river in spate. Thus watered, the original scheme expanded in documentary volume even as the ill weed grows in spring, which indeed it was, and ere long it assumed the dimensions of an old-fashioned family Bible. The Orderly Officer vowed that only a concordance was necessary to complete the analogy. And this was no idle jest, for not even its perpetrator could find his way about its pages, and it lay there, a dead thing, stifled beneath the weight of its own amendments. So he who had made it scrapped it and started another. Fortunately for the safety of the Corps, and indirectly the Allied cause, this one never had time to bloom: the Germans attacked while it was still young. But whatever it did apart from driving Cheyne to distraction, it prevented the Brigade from losing sight of the coming offensive.

Then, too, the daily Press had warned them in terms that even the restricted intelligence of a soldier could grasp. Whenever they picked up a paper they read of endless streams of troops pouring over from the lately-collapsed Russian front for no other purpose than that of exterminating them.

And last of all the Germans themselves had said so, by word and deed, in spite of the illusion of secrecy which Ludendorff chose to preserve and flatter himself that he kept. German prisoners, like any other prisoners, could not keep their mouths shut, and the caterpillar tracks of massing transport were every bit as visible to an aerial observer as railway lines to a man on a station platform. Day, hour, place—all were known. But so unfortunate was our national reputation that nobody would believe us, and to the very last the French General Staff clung to the notion that *they* were to be the chosen victims of the All Highest in Potsdam, and the War Council at Versailles hearkened not to the voice of a wonderfully accurate British

Intelligence Service that cried vainly in a wilderness of political intrigue and international prejudice. Nor did the politician at home, for he, having extended the British front, kept the troops necessary to hold it massed in idleness on the Norfolk coast.

For the 200th Brigade, however, sufficient unto the day was the chloride of lime.

(4)

Fate is notoriously capricious. It is therefore not surprising to find that she put Warne's nose quite out of joint at the start by introducing him to his unit in the only set of circumstances his imagination had not foreseen, and provided for, on the journey up from the base. He simply had not conceived a situation wherein he arrived unheralded and unsung at one o'clock in the morning.

Before him lay all the elements of drama, but he could not see them; he was far too ignorant of military life in the field, as well as the crisis then developing.

Three officers paused in their work and looked up as the orderly, who had appeared from nowhere and taken charge of Warne, opened the rough wooden door and ushered him into the Brigade office. The gentle draught of cold night air set half a dozen candles guttering and a host of shadows dancing on the walls of pitprops and nine-by-two timber. Trench maps and papers fluttered at a dozen points. But Warne had no eyes for so novel a scene. He was concerned only with a brief yet vivid impression wherein he saw himself as unwanted, as intruding upon his own unit. It was only an impression, and he could not be sure. Indeed it was gone almost as quickly as it had assailed him, and he was telling himself that his pent excitement had made him hyper-sensitive. It was disappointing, without a doubt, this frosty reception, but it was entirely natural: no man butting in upon strangers at one o'clock in the morning had a right to expect his arrival to be the signal for exuberant felicitation, especially when this offensive . . . Again he experienced that cold shadow across his brain.

He found his voice at last, and after a final blink to accustom himself to the light, stammered rather than said: 'I'm—er—Warne.'

'Warne. Ah, yes. You were expected to-day.'

The grey-haired, grey-moustached, middle-aged Colonel who spoke, held out his hand in friendly welcome. 'My name's Metcalfe. This is my Adjutant, Cheyne.'

Warne breathed again, and turned to be introduced. Somehow this efficient-looking soldier made him feel surprisingly at home.

Cheyne proved to be a lean-faced clean-shaven Captain of about thirty, but his age eluded Warne. Hair, already grey flecked, was receding at the temples, and there was a curious quality about the skin, a sort of sun-baked dryness, due, though Warne did not know it, to long years of residence in Viti Levu, that made him look older than he was without entirely concealing the remains of his youth. He wore just the ordinary khaki tunic and breeches, and the purple and white of the Military Cross ribbon provided the only splash of colour about him. He looked to Warne as if he might have been khaki all through.

The Colonel went on: 'My Orderly Officer—Dalgith.'

And here Warne confronted youth, bright-eyed, brown as

a berry, and almost chubby. For Dalgith had been a modest eighteen at the outbreak of war, and in spite of Arras and Third Ypres still preserved more than a touch of his earlier bloom. Like Colonel Metcalfe he wore a belted trench coat and a steel helmet, for the pair, returning from a final round of the batteries, had reached the office but a few minutes before Warne.

That was Dalgith, and Warne liked him, even as he found himself liking the Colonel and Cheyne. There was something so very calm and reassuring about them, especially to one whose mind insisted upon viewing everything against the disturbing background of an enemy offensive.

And they, on their side, noted a travel-stained and pathetically earnest priest, obviously new to the game he was going to play, and it occurred to both the Colonel and Cheyne that he knew precious little of what the game involved. In 1914 Warne had been thirty-eight and had looked thirty-two. Now, four years later, he looked at least forty-eight. These figures, and what they signified, were naturally hidden from that appraising trio of gunners, but they did see in his tired lined face something of the spiritual fineness and resolution which had once made men say of Warne that he was far too good for this world. Both qualities were there still, but the ageing interval of war had imposed its own special mark.

Introductions completed, the Colonel played the stock opening gambit. 'Been out before?'

Warne smiled, and said he hadn't.

'H'm!'

There was a wealth of expression in the Colonel's barely audible comment, but none of the lorry driver's complacency.

NIGHT

It was essentially sympathetic. Only Dalgith recalled the lorry driver, and he gasped: 'Poor devil!' Whereat all three laughed, and even the waiting orderly hid a grin.

'You see,' the Colonel explained, clucking merrily: 'this German offensive you've probably heard so much about is due'—he glanced at his wrist watch and saw that the hour was after midnight—'this morning, at dawn.'

'Dawn!'

'Yes. About five o'clock. And it's now one-fifteen,' chuckled Dalgith. He turned to the orderly. 'Bell, get the Padre's valise down to my place.' And a gentle guttering of candles proclaimed Bell's departure.

Warne merely strove to ascertain whether he had heard aright. His valise! Did these men actually expect him to sleep now, when at dawn... Merciful God! It was as if the entire background against which he had projected his thoughts had suddenly leapt to the front, and was rushing down upon him, poising itself like some gigantic wave gathering itself up to break. Then he would be engulfed. And yet these men could laugh!

The Colonel was speaking. He forced himself to listen.

'I must apologize for the shortcomings of your reception, Padre. I'm afraid we can offer you nothing more than whisky. If you'd care——'

'Thanks,' said Warne. 'I think I will. A little.' He loathed whisky as a drink, deeming it not far removed from an emetic, but it seemed the courteous thing to accept it. Besides, it might steady his nerves.

'It'll brace you after your journey, Padre,' said Dalgith as he uncorked a bottle of White Horse. 'Say when!'

'Whoa, stop!'

'Nonsense, Padre. You'll never taste that amount in the chloride of lime.'

Warne sighed. Dalgith had his way.

'Any for you, Sir? No need to ask Uncle. He's been a confirmed toper ever since your missionaries converted the Fijians, Padre. Well, here's how, everybody.'

They lifted their glasses, and Warne noted that, in spite of Dalgith's protestation, his alone was anywhere near full.

'Your health, Padre,' said the Colonel.

'And success to our arms at dawn,' he replied. A happy sentiment. He congratulated himself.

But the Colonel drily said: 'Yes, quite,' and turned to his whisky. Warne realized then that he had little cause for self-congratulation. To hide his confusion he strove to drain his own emetic spirit at a draught, but failed, breaking down with a tyro's spluttering.

'It is pretty foul, isn't it?' grinned Dalgith. 'Only the Doc's chloride of lime, of course. You'll get used to it after a bit—that's if Jerry allows us to stay.'

Allows us to stay! So that was what they thought. The offensive loomed up again, displacing all else.

'You expect then—this offensive——' he faltered.

'Oh, that!' Dalgith answered. 'Well, the Old Hun will offense, I suppose.'

And Warne had the curious impression that Dalgith was riding him off from a subject that was not discussed in the way of ordinary conversation. Yet even so he could not restrain himself. Something more than curiosity impelled him to: 'But ourselves—what do we do?'

NIGHT

'Ask Uncle.' Dalgith nodded at Cheyne. 'He knows. Nobody else does. He's really quite clever though he has spent most of his life in a grass hut.'

Cheyne ignored the sally. He was drumming with his finger tips on the map spread out on the table where he stood. Had he observed this, Warne might not have made his helpless little gesture which asked as clearly as any words if anyone cared what happened. As it was the Colonel laughed shortly. 'We have a Defence Scheme, Padre. It's rather complicated—too much so for rapid explanation. That's all.'

Then a telephone bell rang out imperatively, and Cheyne picked up the handpiece.

'Adjutant speaking. Two—owe—owe Brigade.... Yes, Sir... yes... yes... I see. Thanks. Hold on, Sir. The Colonel's here. He may want you.'

He lowered the mouthpiece, placing his hand over the cup, and turned to Colonel Metcalfe.

'Brigade Major, Sir. He says that Jerry's queueing up. The Warwicks took specimen prisoners from half a dozen battalions in the raid just now, so it looks pretty definite—no mistake in the date. You wish to speak to him?'

'No. Just say we're ready. All moves completed.'

Cheyne did so, and rang off, saying, rather grimly, as he put back the receiver: 'Well, that's that.' And for a moment nobody spoke.

It was a commonplace action, a trite remark; but there was finality in it, and it tore the scales from Warne's eyes so that he saw for the first time things as they were, and the discovery frightened him. He felt like a trapped animal, and the future held no escape. He just had to go through with it. That was why

Dalgith had attempted to ride him off. His brain seemed to be freezing. It was all numb. It would not work.

Then, quite suddenly, he became aware of his heart: it was beating with an agitation strangely muffled and yet pronounced. The very air he breathed was stifling. It was electric with a quality of impending crisis. And dully, in the middle of it all, he wondered what he would do, how he would acquit himself when the crash came.

He looked round at his brother officers in turn. Cheyne was drumming again with his finger tips on the map. Both he and Dalgith were staring at Colonel Metcalfe who, in that moment, seemed to Warne to have grown, to have become a dominating personality. Warne stared at him too, and felt obscurely comforted.

'Is there nothing *I* can do?' he asked, and there was more than a hint of wistful pleading in his voice.

The spell was broken.

'Do, eh?' the Colonel reflected. 'I don't think so, Padre. In fact, there's nothing—not yet, at any rate.'

He stirred himself. 'There's no point in asking you to stay here now, Padre. Best get some sleep while you can. Dalgith will show you your dug-out. Good-night.'

Over Warne's shoulder Dalgith said: 'Come on, Padre,' and in the same breath to his Colonel: 'Back in a minute, Sir.'

And so it happened that before the astonished Warne knew what was taking place, Dalgith was warning him to mind the office step. Voices came to him as he went out, and he heard Cheyne telling the Colonel that all communication had been tested through with the new positions, and that counter preparation . . . He lost the rest, but what he heard was sufficient.

NIGHT

It dawned upon him then that he had been dismissed. There was nothing he could do! The supreme moment was at hand, and he a cypher! He had not pictured himself thus, but a little reflection quickly showed him the futility of picturing himself as anything else. There didn't seem to be much room for non-combatants now. The Colonel had been right, but Warne found it in his heart to wish that the Colonel's method had been a trifle less—well, abrupt.

(5)

Out in the quarry Dalgith led the way by steep and treacherous paths with the aid of an electric torch, and coming to a timbered cabin-like shelter cut in the base of a towering wall of chalk, there lit a candle. Warne, still mentally dazed by the cumulative shock of his reception and its culminating dismissal, indifferently noted that rough planks and pitprops framed and supported roof and sides, and that a box at the far end served as a dressing-table for the two occupants. On this Dalgith set the candle. Two bunks, fashioned of wire netting, were fitted one along each side, and on the right hand one Warne recognized his own valise with blankets turned back ready for him. Sleep to-night, he thought!

'Yours,' said Dalgith, pointing. 'My servant's looking after you *pro tem*. Bell. You'll find him a good 'un. A laird or something in real life.' And pulling off his trench coat Dalgith flopped on the other bunk, a very tired young man.

Warne copied him, unloading haversack, respirator and British Warm.

'I should keep that handy,' observed Dalgith, indicating the respirator. 'You'll probably want it in the morning. You know how to use it?'

Warne nodded.

'Best keep it by your pillow,' Dalgith counselled.

'Yes, yes. Certainly.'

He sat down, and Dalgith regarded him curiously. 'You're all right, I take it. Nothing I can do for you, or anything you want to know?'

'Know!' Warne's voice sounded like a feeble echo. Then, as if on the rebound and in one passionate blurt: 'But what's going to happen when——'

He sought for a word, waving one hand in the air.

'When the balloon goes up, eh?' Dalgith smiled wearily.

'Yes.'

'God knows. I don't.'

'But surely we're ready?' This was almost a cry. 'We appear to have known it was coming.'

'Ready! I suppose we are.' Dalgith thought of his own recent and frantic effort to secure from Corps Dumps the material needed for the still half-completed defences of the Battle Zone. 'I suppose we're as ready as it's humanly possible for anyone to be—with the time and material at our disposal. If you'd been with us any time you'd know too that the Bullock—that's the Colonel—is not given to leaving undone those things he ought to have done.'

The answer was the reverse of reassuring. Warne had to know more. 'But your opinion. What do *you* think?'

'I don't.' Dalgith summoned up a tired grin. 'All I know is that we're outweighted right along the line. Jerry's stiff with guns—got some thirty-two batteries tucked into one little loop of a few acres this side of the canal. His back areas are thick with dumps and massing transport. And half Germany seems to have quartered itself in the villages behind St. Quentin. On our side we've a few depleted divisions in the process of internal reorganization—being cut down to a ten battalion strength. Each is holding between five and seven thousand yards of front, and is supported by a ludicrously inadequate supply of artillery. That's the situation without any frills. You can form what opinion you like from it. Last February Haig told us himself we were for it. That's his opinion. You can have it for what it's worth, and I hope it won't disturb your sleep!'

'Sleep!' Warne made a little noise of acute dismay. 'I shall not sleep. I shall pray to God——'

Dalgith slid down from his bunk and yawned pointedly. 'I must be getting back to the office. Anything you want? Got a battle bowler? This quarry 'll be strafed from the word "go."'

Warne forgot his intended prayer and stared at him blankly. A battle bowler?

'A tin hat—steel helmet. No?' Dalgith sounded faintly irritable.

'Oh, that. No. I haven't one.'

'Right. I'll bring one back with me. I've got to go up to the office before I turn in. Lord, but I'm tired.'

He crossed the tiny shelter and pulled back the blanket that served as the door. 'I shouldn't undress altogether if I were you. Blessed is he that keepeth his garments lest he walk naked, you know.' And with that he passed into the night, leaving Warne to make what he could of a situation which was completely and utterly beyond him.

For a minute or two Warne did nothing. He stood there, staring fixedly at the smoking candle stuck high in its bottle neck, and striving to steady his racing thoughts, and he did not move until he chanced to catch his reflection in Dalgith's shaving mirror. Then, rather to his surprise and considerably to his relief, he noted that he still looked sane, whatever he felt.

After that he took out his case and from it a cigarette, lit it and sat down again on his bunk, And as he smoked there gathered above him in the airless shelter a thin blue haze that slowly eddied and thickened. He grew strangely placid.

(6)

The Colonel was gone. Dalgith and Cheyne were alone in the office, too weary even to spar—their customary exercise in conversation.

'You'd better get your head down for an hour of two, Young'un. I'll hang on to the phone.'

Dalgith looked at the older man gratefully. 'Do you mind?'

A mirthless laugh, but no answer. Dalgith understood.

Cheyne said, indifferently: 'Rough luck on the priest,'

'Or us?' muttered Dalgith.

'Like that, is it?'

'Well, don't you?'

Their eyes met, and agreed. Words were unnecessary.

But some faint protesting sense of fair play stirred in Cheyne, prompting him to add: 'Still, five minutes chinning with a tired man over a glass of poison—that's hardly the best criterion.'

'Perhaps not. But there're other things. His attitude, for example. Fancy drinking success to our arms at dawn! What's he take us for?'

NIGHT

'Oh, he'll soon find his feet.'

'H'm!' And again their eyes met.

'I wish old Wade hadn't gone sick,' was Cheyne's only comment. It embraced everything. There was no more to be said.

Dalgith rose to go. 'I've got to find him a battle bowler before I turn in. You staying here?'

'Yes.'

'Good night.'

'Good night.'

The door closed behind Dalgith.

(7)

Dalgith stopped. He had not gone a dozen paces, but the quarry somehow seemed different. The night air struck unusually chill, far more than it had done half an hour before. The chill was so obvious indeed, that he sought for an explanation. And when the beam of his torch, directed upwards, lost itself in faintly wreathing mists and, like the headlamps of a car in fog, revealed a glistening curtain of cotton wool slowly drifting into the quarry, he muttered an oath, for he knew that the Fifth Army had been blinded.

'That,' he said to himself, 'has just about torn it. And the wind's dropped too.'

(8)

Inside the office Cheyne did not move. He remained as he had been when talking to Dalgith—half sitting on the edge of the table by the telephone, one foot planted firmly on the ground and taking his weight, the other raised above and swinging gently from the knee. But his head sank forward when Dalgith had gone, and he thrust his hands in his breeches pockets. It was not an attitude of any soldierly elegance, but it was comfortable, relaxed; and it suited his mood, for now that all had been done he felt curiously weak and deflated. The grind and worry of the past month; the ceaseless and fruitless winnowing of that infernal Defence Scheme—well, it was over now. Only remained the waiting.

He glanced at his wrist watch. Another three hours. His mood veered with the realization, driving beads of sweat to his forehead so that he wondered whether he was ill and not merely suffering from cold feet. It would certainly be a relief when the show started. Cute wheeze of the Colonel's—shifting those guns from known positions to the hilltops. They ought to last a bit longer there with only the area strafe to knock 'em out . . .

A candle suddenly extinguished itself. The stump, melted by the hot glass of the neck, slipped down into the bottle with a faint splutter and a curling spiral of smoke. It roused him, and he noted that he would have to replace the others before dawn. Dawn—and bloody hell let loose! He concluded that he was getting too old for the game, or had experienced too much of it. Two years of foot-slogging in the P.B.I. before he took a commission in the Gunners—it was a long time reckoned in periods of Loos and the Somme. Dangerously long. It made the whisky-bottle look too inviting. And he gave a short, mocking laugh as he thrust back into his pocket the hand that had betrayed him. But his eyes remained riveted to that bottle of White Horse. Its fascination was beyond him to break.

NIGHT

After that Cheyne fought with himself.

Three o'clock found him sitting by the telephone, his head resting upon his folded arms, a queer smile twisting his lips. He was not asleep. He was too distraught for that. For him was the vigil of the dawn.

The Colonel detected a faint reek of whisky when he returned to the office soon after four, and on the chalky planks underfoot there were stains imperfectly dried; also a few tell-tale splinters of glass in odd corners, as if a tumbler had been violently thrown and some of the splinters overlooked. He noticed, too, that the bottle of whisky had gone. (It was lying uncorked at the bottom of a pit whither Cheyne had flung it.) But he said nothing. Sympathy and condemnation were alike useless here. Rest was the only cure for fraying nerves, and of that he saw no prospect whatsoever.

(9)

The air in the little shelter was thick with tobacco smoke when the cigarette came to an end and Warne threw aside the stub. He felt quite tranquil now, not merely resigned, and he was seeing something of what he must do. It astonished him, this strange serenity of mind, especially by contrast with his earlier tension, but it filled him with a great hope. It was an omen.

He had, as it were, become detached from himself, and looking round he saw that he could expect no detailed assistance from either Cheyne or Dalgith, and certainly not the Colonel. This was obvious and natural: they had their own urgent jobs. Indeed, it said much for their fundamental kindliness that they had turned aside at all at this juncture, though in doing so, he had to admit, they had done no more and no less than everybody else he had so far encountered in France. People seemed to make him comfortable as a matter of course, and then leave him while they went their several ways. There was that lorry driver and the sack; and before that the tall, spare officer and his companion—Wood, wasn't the name?—at railhead, who had resigned their claim to the front and, he gathered, tolerable seat. Finally Dalgith. The boy was tired out and perhaps a little impatient on that account if no other, but he had been wonderfully considerate. Funny, too, that he should have quoted Revelations on the eve of Armageddon.

Warne got up and pulled aside the gas blanket in order to free the shelter from its cloud of smoke, and he stood there for some minutes, leaning against the post and staring into the night. There were no stars now, but the white of the chalk imparted a sort of opaqueness to the night, and there was not a sound to break the silence that brooded over the land. Mystery lurked in the cold damp air, but there was peace, and it seemed to him incredible that a few miles to the east German Divisions were marching westward and forming up preparatory to—what? The whole future resolved itself into one vast question mark.

No, whatever the answer was, his duty was clear enough, and his face was shining with a new light, or rather an old one, which the anguish born of the War had extinguished, as he backed into the shelter and allowed the blanket to fall. For the supreme consummation of his work as God's minister was at hand. He had obliterated self.

But the mist began to steal into the quarry as he fumbled in the head of his valise among his socks and shirts and towels, for all his faith in the righteousness of the Allied Cause.

He found what he wanted after a short search. It was a small wafer box, or pyx, that he had used on the few occasions when he had been summoned to the bedside of the dying. He would use it again now, for Dawn spelt Armageddon, and Armageddon spelt Death and Maiming. This was no time for dogmatic argument about Reservation. Men would soon stand in need of the Blessed Sacrament. Let him not deny it them for the sake of a quibble.

But how to obtain the wafer? He had not so much as a slice of bread. And for a moment he stood in sad perplexity, striving to think of a solution.

Ah! He had it. In his haversack were his iron rations of bully beef and biscuits given him at Havre, and an unexpected fount of humour bubbled to life as he fingered the metal-like square so aptly labelled 'iron.' It was terrible fare for a dying man, but it was all he could manage.

And so, in that cabin-like shelter, before the little ivory cross which he had set amid Dalgith's shaving tackle upon that upturned box, Warne took and broke an Army biscuit—a matter which involved him in a most unpriestly display of physical strength—and having consecrated it, placed it in the pyx. For safety he put the pyx in his haversack.

After that he rested his wrists upon the edge of this strange altar and bowed his head into cupped hands, while he prayed that God would forgive, strengthen and protect His servants here in the hour of their peril, but if it should be His Will so to order them that they perished, then His Everlasting Mercy...

Warne was still there when Dalgith returned, and it chanced that the candle, from its perch in the whisky-bottle, threw the shadow of the cross over the fair, bowed head, so that Dalgith, inconsequent pagan, stopped short in his stride and stared with mouth agape.

Warne never stirred, and when Dalgith moved he trod carefully lest he should disturb the kneeling priest. Very carefully, too, he hung up the steel helmet he had brought with him, and arranged Warne's respirator so as to be ready for instant use. Then, with an uncomprehending shake of his head, he pulled off belt and jacket, placed his own respirator by the air-cushion that served him as a pillow, slipped off boots and leggings, and finally rolled on his bunk and into his blankets with the one sweeping movement which months of practice alone can perfect.

'Dawn,' he told himself. 'That means, with luck, a couple of hours' sleep.'

A glance at Warne and then a mouth-splitting yawn. Five minutes later he was sleeping as peacefully as if man had ever loved his neighbour as himself and Nations knew not the meaning of War.

The older man was still praying.

CHAPTER II

DAWN

(I)

Warne slept. Some time elapsed before he did so, and at least an hour slipped by after he had crawled between his pair of stiff, wiry blankets before those fleeting snatches of half-consciousness told him that the accumulated fatigue of his journey was going to outweigh even the menace of the dawn. He had left the candle burning, for somehow its yellow rays seemed enormously comforting. They fell upon Dalgith, lying with an arm outstretched beneath his head like a child, and upon the little ivory cross rising on its plinth of ebony from the litter of a bachelor's dressing-table, and they showed him that he was not alone.

Occasionally a rat scurried softly beneath his bunk, and the medley of tiny sounds that made up the noises of the night would break upon his reverie, recalling him to the present with a jerk; but for the most part he heard nothing; he was concerned only with the part he was to play in the future, and his one dread was that he should fail his trust. And so, in a slowly deadening turmoil of conjecture, of mingled fear and faith, drowsiness came creeping in, weighing down the lids of eyes that still gazed upon the cross. Gradually his breathing deepened. He slept.

And when, soon after four, an orderly stole in and called Dalgith, he was still asleep, and Dalgith rubbed his eyes, dressed and went out adjusting his respirator at the 'alert,' unobserved by any one save the rat cornered beneath his bunk. Nor did he wake when the candle gave out, plunging the shelter in blackness.

But he was not entirely at rest, inert though his body lay, for imagination insisted upon working that ivory cross into strange and disturbing fantasy, and linking it with visions of that other Cross which stood on Calvary. And all the while he saw it through a murky darkness that seethed with the nameless terrors of the dawn, so that once or twice he tossed uneasily in his sleep.

(2)

It was large now, the Cross, very large, and he could vaguely discern the crowds which surged about it—bearded men who gesticulated wildly and wore a sort of caftan with their billowing robes. But he could not be certain of anything because the sky was black and thunder pealed incessantly. Of lightning there was never a flash to reveal what lay about him. Instead the darkness grew more intense, blotting out the Cross, the struggling crowd. Only the thunder remained.

And then he knew that this was no dream thunder. The darkness was that of his blanketed shelter; the thunder that of the guns. Fearfully he stared at his watch. The hour was 4.40. It was dawn at last.

He did not move at once. For fully a minute he lay back in his bunk, desperate in his endeavour to force himself to think, but obsessed and frozen to inaction by the roar. The very air of the shelter was vibrant. And then, in one overwhelming flood, came the desire for company, a craving for the companionship of man. He could think only of Dalgith, and the boy's name broke from his lips in a hoarse cry of fear, the fear of being alone. And he was alone—in the pitch blackness of the shelter, and though he was spared the knowledge till later, the most devastating bombardment in history. He discovered the first when, in a sort of hysterical frenzy, he struck a match and saw at a glance that both Dalgith and the candle were gone.

Terror seized him, such terror as he had never known before in his life. Without waiting to pull on his boots or his gas-mask, or even to button up his braces, he thrust out of the shelter into the quarry. Cold, smoky mist met him. He might have stepped into a wall of cotton-wool, dirty and wet. He could see nothing, only hear, and out in the open the thunder was redoubled. But he blundered on a few paces till his foot warned him of the sloping edge of a pit within the quarry, and then some secondary instinct of caution stayed him.

Out here, too, once his ears became attuned, he could detect the detail of the undying thunder, could pick out the drumming of distant guns, the shriek and whistle of countless projectiles hurtling overhead, and the crash and scatter of others exploding he knew not where. But he did not recognize them as such. All, to him, united in one ear-filling roar.

And then something appeared to detach itself from this canopy of din, something that was sinister and personal, that came with a sibilant hissing curiously separate from the rest of the chorus. It seemed to be rushing upon him with the speed of an express train.

RETREAT

It was, in fact, his first shell, and it arrived with all the paralysing directness of such. He had the momentary impression that some immense incubus was bearing down upon him and that within a space of time too minute for measurement he would be crushed out of existence, and he and his universe would be shattered to dust—all this, while the hissing swelled in a deafening crescendo that itself threatened to stun him.

He fell on his knees and buried his face in his hands. And the shell, one from a 'five-nine' howitzer, screamed into the pit on whose brink he knelt, and meeting the firm chalk detonated with that rending, tearing crash which men have learned to fear.

Chalk rained upon him, buffeting his head and body so that he thought the end had come, and called upon his God. But he was unhurt. Actually the lip protected him from flying splinters. And then, as suddenly as it had begun, the torrent of chalk ceased. Rather to his astonishment he found he was still alive, that the thunder was still going on, that the smoking darkness was still a blind pall. Also he found he was still alone, and helpless, except for the instinct of self-preservation, and that drove him back to the shelter.

(3)

For two hours the storm had been raging. Daylight had come, yet darkness might well have remained, for mist, dun-coloured with smoke and gas, shrouded the land and filled the quarry, blinding the scattered groups of defenders along that attenuated Fifth Army front and masking their fire as with a shield. Men, whose sole chance of successful resistance depended upon a reasonable visibility and a field of fire, thus found the enemy on top of them before they could fire a shot. But, until the enemy advanced, hard on the heels of his barrage, the rain of shells never slackened; the roar went on; and even in the converted lime-kiln which, under the lee of a wall of chalk, sheltered the Brigade Headquarters Staff, men had to raise their voices in order to be heard. They did not speak much, however, and then only in curt phrases answering curt questions, based on surmise for the most part.

Occasionally a runner would stagger in from the outer world, breathless and scared. One, having removed his respirator, revealed a face the colour of a dirty peony. Another, at the opposite end of the scale, resembled an unwashed turnip. And all spoke jerkily, as men do under stress. At these times a stir of expectancy would pass round the little Headquarters, only to die away again when the same old news was repeated. All communication shot to ribbons. No word from Forward Observation Officers since dawn. Guns firing blindly on S. O. S. lines while enemy shells took a steady drain on the gunners. No sign of the enemy infantry, our own infantry, or anything else. Only fog.

'Not worth the risk of a man's life sending it,' muttered Cheyne after the fourth repetition.

No one commented.

Presently Keller, the Brigade Signals Officer, a thick set and burly subaltern, emerged from the mists and stared about him as if surprised to find himself where he was, rather as a drowning man might look if he suddenly felt solid ground beneath his feet after he had given up all hope of reaching it. Then he saluted and reported the utter impossibility of establishing any sort of communication with the rear.

The Colonel nodded. Keller sat down and pushed back his steel helmet. His hand wandered across his forehead. He looked curiously limp. Nobody said anything. They merely settled down for another wait. And thus the morning wore slowly by.

Towards breakfast-time, as it should have been, there came a lull. The German guns ceased to pound the quarry itself and lifted on to other targets. And in this respite—only temporary as it turned out—Bell, steel-helmeted, his respirator mouthpiece held between his teeth, ducked into the shelter bringing a jug of tea and a basin of sugar. He stood them down, went out, and almost immediately returned again with cups and a punctured tin of Nestlé's milk. He counted the cups and looked round.

'You'll be wanting an extra for Padre Warne, Sir,' he said to Dalgith. 'I'll fetch it.'

'Warne? Who's Warne?'

O'Reilly, the Irish doctor, Captain R.A.M.C., a beefy man, fat to the point of obesity, with a button-like nose centred in a round red face, asked the question indifferently.

Nobody answered. Like O'Reilly, Keller had been in his bunk asleep when the newcomer had arrived, and did not so much as know he was joining, let alone had joined. But in the minds of Cheyne and Dalgith there was something akin to dismay: they had entirely forgotten the poor old priest.

In the puzzled silence that followed each searched the other for an explanation.

The Colonel interrupted: 'Is he anywhere about?'

Nobody knew.

'Find him, somebody.'

There was only one person to do that, and as Colonel Metcalfe reverted to his pensive study of a map, Dalgith grinned sheepishly at Cheyne and departed, mildly distressed at his own negligence. He stopped for a moment at the entrance in order to adjust his respirator and sniff suspiciously at the fog.

The others settled down to tea.

'He's a good lad, is Bell,' remarked Cheyne, and surprised himself by wondering whether the Reverend Elliot Warne would ever be half as useful. Somehow he didn't think he would.

(4)

Warne was still in the shelter. Dalgith found him upon his bunk, crouched there in an extremity of terror that bordered on paralysis, his head thrust quite unnecessarily in a gas-mask. And because Dalgith was still a youth and just about as unappreciative of a sensitive nature as a healthy young hedonist can be, the discovery of Warne's mental state shocked him not a little. It forced contrasts upon him, all gravely to the detriment of Warne's fair name. But a point he missed: neither the Colonel, nor Cheyne, nor O'Reilly, nor Keller, nor he himself was fresh to the turmoil of battle. Also they had not been left alone for well over three hours in the vibrant blackness of what threatened every minute to be a tomb, this after a particularly intimate introduction to a 'five-nine' howitzer shell. Dalgith did not think of these things, for, truth to tell, he was not disposed to think clearly about anything while his senses were semi-stunned by the din. Instead, with feelings that united pity and disgust with a definite contriteness of spirit, he placed his torch in a position where it would light up the palsied figure, and prepared to get him away.

RETREAT

He had to do everything. He dressed him and buttoned up his braces. He knelt down and forced on his boots. He had to fix the strap of his helmet and even shove the mouthpiece of his respirator in his teeth. And when he had finished he took him by the arm and more or less dragged him away.

The moment was unfortunate. The Germans, who were plastering the countryside with a fine liberality, switching about and concentrating upon everything that suggested a target, elected to favour the quarry with another burst, though luckily for the men sheltering there the shooting, being from guns necessarily unregistered and therefore erratic in the extreme, missed the target just as often as they found it.

A lump of chalk, flung from a distance, struck Warne a clanging blow on the helmet, knocking it over his eyes. A splinter of shell buried itself at his feet with a thud audible above the din. He made a whimpering noise and stopped. Dalgith dragged at him, shouting to him that he must keep going. Warne barely heard. For, with a sensation of cold emptiness at the pit of his stomach, he was experiencing yet again that impression of imminent death. Shrieking and tearing the weight was pressing down. Soon it would strike and crush him. And when Dalgith yelled at him, bidding him get down in the name of Christ, the faint piping cry that was Dalgith's voice began only to lose itself in the roar.

Vaguely Warne knew that two arms gripped him round the knees, lifted him off his feet and flung him flat, but he had no recollection of being shaken by the fall. For the shriek had passed its crescendo, had ceased to belong to this world. Seconds had stretched to eternities. Something was about to snap, and then there would be oblivion.

He felt himself laughing at the sight of the Brigade office sailing skyward on the fringe of a belching cloud of smoke.

With lumps of timber clattering round, with the whine of splinters, jagged lumps of burning metal, adding yet another note to the general din, and amid the smacking and thudding of these lumps as they buried themselves in the chalk, Dalgith went at the double for the kiln, half-dragging, half-carrying a semi-fainting man.

(5)

Dalgith's arrival with Warne caused a stir in the kiln that brought O'Reilly's bulk sliding hurriedly from its perch on the rough plank table.

'Stopped a bit?' There was anxiety in his wheezing voice.

'No. Wind up.'

'That all?'

O'Reilly's interest waned. 'Shove him on this chair.'

Keller made way, and both he and the Doctor looked thoughtfully down at the white staring face of the priest they were seeing for the first time. Keller saw only a frightened man, and thought of himself. But the Doctor saw further, detecting that most pitiful of all men, the craven who fought with his pride.

'He's certainly got 'em,' he reflected. 'Badly. Too sensitive. Too much of a saint for this game.' Then aloud: 'Any tea left in that jug, Keller?'

There was. A draining. Lukewarm unpalatable stuff, reeking of chloride of lime. Warne's hand shook as he clutched at the cup.

Then Dalgith found a hunk of bread and smarmed jam over it. Warne took it gratefully. He was biting it when a large shell, arriving at an oblique angle, skimmed the protecting wall of chalk behind the kiln and burst outside the entrance with an appalling crash. Away went the candles, plunging them in darkness. Acrid smoke spewed in upon them. Nuggets of chalk hurtled through the narrow doorway in a seemingly solid shower. Men stumbled and fell, and called out. Something heavy struck Warne, sweeping him and his chair over sideways. He opened his mouth to cry, but no word would come. He appeared to be dissolving into the smoky blackness. It was alive with suppressed noises, with the gasping and panting of struggling men. This, he told himself, was the end.

'Strike a match, somebody.'

The Colonel's voice cut like a lash. The struggling ceased. Cheyne, lying on his back, contrived to pull out a box and strike a match. The Colonel passed him a candle. They sorted themselves out.

Dalgith said: 'Thank you, George. If you remove your knee from my belly I really shall be more comfortable.'

He gave a little gasp of relief as Keller scrambled to his feet. He then detached himself from Warne and the chair, started to apologize, saw the futility of wasting words, and motioned O'Reilly. Together they righted the chair and lifted Warne on to it. The Colonel gave him one searching glance and turned away: he had no time for passengers now.

For the morning was drawing on. It stood to reason that the German infantry attack was developing, which meant that some quick decisions would soon be required. But what to decide, and when? Fog; isolation; complete absence of any information on which to work. It was difficult. He forgot about Warne.

He turned to his Adjutant. 'I shall be going round batteries. I'll take Dalgith.'

Dalgith heard, and went cold inside.

The Colonel continued: 'Meanwhile get this to 836 by runner.'

Cheyne said: 'Yes, Sir,' and took up a signal pad.

Another shell, similar to the one that had just skimmed the wall of chalk, burst on top of it, right on the lip, sending down a shower of lumps. Several bounced into the kiln.

'Tell them,' the Colonel said, 'to expect me in a half-hour's time.'

Cheyne said: 'Yes, Sir,' and noted down the instruction, one half of his brain attending to what he wrote, the other half speculating upon the probable bursting-point of the next shell from that particular German gun. No technical knowledge was needed for him to see that, unless the gunlayer altered his range or deflection, it was highly probable the shell would catch the kiln.

Even Warne in some instinctive way saw this, and nerves, already corkscrewed under the strain, received a further twist, He sat there, rigid and bent, his hands gripping his knees. Soon he would go mad. Nothing would matter then.

'Keller.'

The Colonel called his Signals Officer. 'I want you to make another attempt at getting Corps.'

'Yes, Sir.'

Keller heard a thin noise which he assumed was his voice. The Colonel looked at him curiously.

'At once.'

'Yes, Sir.'

His voice was firmer this time. He adjusted his mask and went. Warne, watching him, saw him disappear into the mists as the third shell burst with a smother of grey-white smoke well beyond the kiln.

Dalgith muttered: 'Thank God he's switching about.'

Warne stirred. He did not know what Dalgith meant, but he did know that a reprieve had been granted. He reacted accordingly. The sudden releasing of the tension threw him completely off his mental balance. He was concerned only with an enormous desire to talk. To talk, talk and go on talking. If he could do that he felt he would be all right. But to whom could he talk? O'Reilly's back was towards him; Dalgith and Cheyne were grouped with the Colonel.

His hand wandered out towards O'Reilly, pawing the air and making little ineffective stabs as if afraid to go the few extra inches and attract the Doctor's attention. His jaw worked, mouthing unspoken words. But nobody observed him, and just as suddenly as he had experienced this overwhelming urge to talk, to expand, to make contact with others, he shrank back into himself, seeing himself as the craven, stricken as the result. And this was because some returning sense of appreciation permitted him to see things, even if vaguely, as they were.

He was glad then that he had not spoken, and that nobody had attempted to speak to him. He now craved for solitude, wherein no one might see his shame. Once there he might even think again, for at present he couldn't. The sick tumult of shaken nerves saw to that. They made him dizzy, uncertain of what he was doing. Only one thing was definite, and with elbows resting on his thighs, he buried his face in his cupped hands lest any one should see that he was on the verge of howling.

Then, for no obvious reason, he remembered his God, and silently prayed that he might be given another chance. Afterwards he felt more composed. If only this stabbing thunder would stop, he might even save a little from the present wreck.

(6)

Keller experienced some success at his second attempt, and by running out fresh wire from the quarry, contrived to thread his way between shelled areas until he came within sight of Villeveque, at which point he rang up to say that heavy shelling of the crossroads and neighbourhood would compel him to make a detour of the village. Once beyond the shelling he hoped to pick up the Corps line which, with luck, ought to be still intact to the westward.

This was news. The promise of communication with the rear decided Colonel Metcalfe to delay his tour of the batteries until he had heard what Corps had to say, and so he waited. It seemed then to Warne that a new expectancy added itself to the tension in the kiln. After all these hours the isolation of the little Headquarters was about to end. The outer world, from which they had been separated by a curtain of fire since dawn, was going to speak. What would it have to say?

Keller rang up again to tell them he was now beyond Villeveque, and as far as he could see the line was apparently O.K. He could not, however, raise Corps, which looked as if there was a solitary break somewhere ahead. He was pushing on as quickly as possible and ought to have found it by——

The line suddenly went dead.

RETREAT

Two or three ineffectual attempts at getting Keller, and Cheyne tossed aside the useless receiver. He spoke wearily, as if nothing mattered. 'No good, Sir. Diss again between here and Keller. Probably where that shelling's just started.'

He nodded towards the road that skirted the quarry and across which Keller had run his line.

The Colonel gave it a quick glance. There was, he thought, a chance. Also Keller's work was promising. It could not be abandoned. He turned to his Orderly Officer,

Take a linesman and do what you can with that wire.'

Dalgith said: 'Yes, Sir,' rather as Keller had done.

A covey of shells, all high explosive, went crashing about the road as he made to start, and between the silhouette of his bent figure and the brickwork of the entrance, Warne could see from where he was sitting right through into the sun-tinted mists beyond. Grey-white smoke was spewing along, blotting out what the thinning fog revealed. The place had become a spouting inferno.

And then the psychologist in him, reasserting itself, made him suddenly conscious that he was witnessing drama—insignificant, admittedly, alongside the major tragedy being enacted over the Fifth Army front, but nevertheless complete in itself. For when Dalgith crouched in the entrance to that kiln, it seemed to Warne that a blind was momentarily reft from the window of a boy's soul, and it was as if he were enabled to peep into hidden recesses and read a secret there before the blind fell again. And the secret he read brought a new shame to his torment.

Only for the briefest fraction of a second did Dalgith hesitate, but in that time Warne obtained the curious and vivid impression that a tremor shook the boy's body. It came and went in a flash, and almost without apparent pause Dalgith was striding away head-down into the smoke. But the interval had been long enough. The blind had been withdrawn, and Warne had seen.

After that Warne forgot himself for the first time that day.

He moved his position slightly so that he could follow Dalgith, and soon afterwards picked him out, a dim doubled-up figure that, dogged by another, strode rapidly on to the road. The two separated. A shell burst between them and the kiln so that the smoke of it blotted them out, and when it drifted clear he saw them again, each dragging together the end of a severed wire. He watched them kneel as they made the join, and then saw them start off again.

A couple of shells, this time beyond them. They went on, seemingly indifferent. Again they separated, seeking the ends of another break, and they were barely a hundred yards from the kiln.

And then Warne saw both Dalgith and the linesman fling themselves flat. Immediately a fountain of dirt spouted from where they had fallen. Smoke billowed out, hiding everything, and Warne started from his chair. He wanted to shout at the others, to tell them that a man had been killed, but their very remoteness froze the words on his lips. Wildly he told himself that Dalgith's fate meant nothing to these men. They were inhuman. Horror wrote itself on his face, causing Cheyne, who chanced to look his way, to ask if anything were the matter.

'Matter!' he cried. 'Dalgith—out there!'

Cheyne laughed, shortly. 'Oh, Dalgith. He can look after himself.' He turned away. The episode was dismissed.

But not for Warne. A fascination, morbid and horrible, gripped him. His eyes were drawn to the tragedy that imagination was so vividly painting. He could not tear them away though he dreaded what he might see. Only the Doctor took any notice of him, and he watched him out of professional curiosity.

Warne made out a figure moving through the smoke. It stooped. It lifted another, struggling with it back towards the quarry. It drew near. Warne prayed that it might be Dalgith as he strove to penetrate the veil of haze.

It was.

Dalgith himself appeared soon afterwards and spoke to the Doctor. 'Spine smashed, I think. I've left him with Redley.'

O'Reilly got up and went out, his medical haversack swinging from his shoulder.

Dalgith said to the Colonel: 'I'll have another go, Sir,' He spoke in a low voice, and glancing down, saw blood on one of his hands. He wiped it carelessly upon a handkerchief. Warne shuddered. It seemed that Dalgith, too, was numbered with the rest, He vaguely saw that there were factors in the situation he did not understand. He was curious to see whether Colonel Metcalfe would send Dalgith out again.

Colonel Metcalfe did not. He told Dalgith to remain behind with Cheyne. He himself was going round batteries now. He would take one of the servants—Bell. And a few minutes later he went, unmindful of shell-fire, to direct in person as far as he could the units of his scattered command from which he had been so long cut off. Warne wondered then whether the Colonel was quite so inhuman as he had thought.

(7)

Five hours had passed since the bombardment started. The mist was thinning, though still thick enough to blind the defenders, and between the widely-separated lines of redoubts the Germans were pressing forward unmolested in numbers that made loss of direction impossible. But the shelling continued in front of them. The great leap forward of German guns, with its consequent respite for those who were left of Gough's Army, had yet to come.

Colonel Metcalfe made no attempt at taking cover. It was not that he scorned such action: he merely saw that it was useless. So he strode across-country, direct from battery to battery, a slightly hunched figure that limped a trifle from an early wound and used a walking-stick with methodical deliberation. He neither ducked nor dodged nor sought the passing security of a shell-hole, and the occasions were many when he might, without damaging his reputation, have done so.

Twenty yards behind Gunner Bell followed, less sedately. Bell's attention was divided equally between the striding figure in front of him, and the shrieking, whistling shells that crashed all too frequently about his path. In his 'other-rankish' way he was unsure which was the worse. So he ducked and he dodged, and twice he flung himself flat only to scramble up shamefacedly and hurry on, immensely thankful that the Colonel had not chanced to turn and see him. He was breathless, not from walking, though the Colonel was a fast walker, but from sheer agitation.

Once a small shell burst ahead of him, and he saw his Colonel crumple and slide several yards down the slope they were traversing, just as if a Titan's breath had puffed aside the frail body of a man. But when he had blundered to the Colonel's side, he found him already stirring. Without a word the Colonel picked himself up, found his walking-stick, and went on. Nothing might have happened. Bell paid even less attention to the shelling after that.

In 748 a Cockney bombardier paused to stare at the visitor, and, while drawing the sleeve of his tunic across his sweating forehead, grunted: 'Gawd! Little Percy finks 'e's strollin' darn Piccadilly,' and then collapsed in a heap over the trail of his sixty-pounder with a hole behind his ear and half a pound of hot jagged steel in his brain.

When the Colonel had gone, the harassed Battery Commander noticed that the rate of fire had perceptibly increased without any exhortation on his part and in spite of depleted gun-crews.

Colonel Metcalfe arrived in 679's position just after No. 3 gun had received a direct hit from a 'five-nine' and the whole of its detachment had been laid out. Cartridges had caught alight as well, and flaming cordite was driving back those who sought to enter the pit. The tiny mist-filled valley where the guns were reeked with gas. Men were running about, ghost-like, except for their shouts and curses. Two other guns were firing intermittently. There was confusion everywhere.

The Colonel eyed them for half a minute unobserved, and then a hulking gunner, fully a head taller than himself, came stumbling by. He stopped the man peremptorily, bidding him tell the Major of the battery that the Brigade Commander was there.

'Eh!' said the man. 'Who're you?' He sounded more dazed

than deliberately offensive. His attitude as he looked down upon the Colonel was puzzled rather than insolent.

The Colonel said: 'Salute!'

The word rasped out, making the fellow jump.

'Salute, do you hear me?'

This time the Colonel's voice carried above the din to the burning gun-pit, and startled men into silence even there. The fellow's hand rose shakily to his helmet.

'That's not a salute. Stand properly to attention. Close those heels.'

A shell burst in the position, near enough to shower turf about them. The man would have flinched but he dared not.

'Salute again.'

He did so.

'Now tell Major Tansley that Colonel Metcalfe wishes to see him. Double.'

The fellow blundered off, only too thankful to escape. The Colonel strolled across to the wrecked and smoking pit. The cordite flames were dying away, but whatever would burn in the pit was burning. Several fuse boxes were on fire. If the heat set off the fuses and possibly a shell or two . . .

'Earth on those boxes, Sergeant,' he said. 'Get bights on those cases and drag them clear.'

Within a minute the danger was past. The Colonel watched the Sergeant and his party approvingly.

'Sir,' whispered a voice at his shoulder.

He turned. 'Ah, Tansley. A bad business this. Who's in charge here—your Section Commander? I don't see him.'

Major Tansley, an easy-going Territorial Officer, more suited to a Federation Meeting than a battlefield, stammered something about a shortage of officers. The Colonel cut him short, curtly reminding him that he had a Captain and three other officers, excluding the F.O.O. Where were they?

Major Tansley thought——

'You think, do you?' breathed the Colonel, icily.

'You don't by any chance *know?*'

Frankly the Major did not. He had been hugging the security of his B. C. Post, slender though it was, for most of the time since dawn. But he could not say so.

A couple of 'five-nines' bracketed the guns, exploding noisily, and he broke into a gentle sweat as a deep-drawn 'Aah!' forced itself from clenched teeth. The Colonel's face might have been carved from granite.

Major Tansley remembered then. He was certain that Captain Maclachlan had gone with a party down the valley to bring up ammunition from the temporary dump they had made last night. He had probably taken a subaltern with him.

'Probably!'

The Colonel's tone was sufficient. It vested the word with a significance which reft away the last trace of the Major's composure. He faltered that he had been in the B.C. Post.

'When your place was out here by that gun,' the Colonel thundered, his stick pointing straight at the still smoking pit. 'I'll look into this afterwards,' he added.

The Colonel, who had deliberately led Major Tansley clear of his men, now turned back, making for a gun that had been silent all the while he had been in the position. It fired almost as he reached it, and a subaltern darted away, heading for the pit that had been destroyed. In his haste he narrowly escaped running heavily into the Colonel, but seeing him in time, pulled up short and saluted. He was a young fellow, rather wild-eyed and exhausted, and there was a trickle of blood down his left cheek, which he had wiped into a sticky smear.

'You haven't been firing for some time, have you, Nash?' The Colonel put his question gently.

Nash spoke jerkily. 'No, Sir. Tube jammed in lock. Just freed her. All right now.'

'Good.'

'I was just going along to No. 3, Sir.'

The Colonel nodded and turned away. He was sorely tempted to smile. He wondered whether Tansley's skin was thick enough to withstand the inadvertent taunt.

He strolled down the line of guns, Tansley slinking behind him, Bell following, discreetly distant. The German shelling lifted on to the far slope of the valley. He concluded that the infantry attack must be well advanced. Yet there was no hint of rifle fire going on in front. Nor had there been all the morning. He wondered what it meant, and passed on his way.

At 836 he asked to be introduced to the two officers who had joined early that morning, and learned that one had been killed at the very start of the bombardment. With the other he chatted with the same easy friendliness as he might have employed in his wife's drawing-room in Cadogan Place, and Second-Lieutenant Kenneth Wood ceased trying to find out whether he was standing on his head or his heels and lost his immense and, he devoutly hoped, secret terrors in respectful amazement.

But 836 needed no particular exhortation. Collett, their Major, had them well in hand and was driving them hard. So the Colonel did not stay long.

As he left the position, a weary gunner, nursing a bloody sleeve but still carrying on, said to his mate:

'Lumme! I wouldn't be in that bastard's shoes for a pint o' hops.'

He referred to Gunner Bell.

(8)

Back in the quarry Dalgith and Cheyne spent silent minutes. For a time neither spoke, because neither wanted to. Cheyne nursed his useless telephone and wondered what was going to happen next, and, more particularly, what he was going to do about it when it did. The burden of responsibility promised to unsettle him completely. Dalgith, the unfettered junior, related his body in utter weariness on the table, and cared very little what happened. But obscure in his corner and thankful to be so, Warne sat and watched, still mentally breathless, woefully hesitant and tremendously ashamed. Neither Cheyne nor Dalgith appeared to be aware of his existence.

After a while Cheyne went and stood in the entrance to the kiln, and remarked, more to himself than to Dalgith: 'Mist's thinning a good deal. Shelling's dying down too.'

Another pause, and then he turned back. 'Well, he's either bust through by now or he hasn't. The question's which.'

Warne heard him with a sudden and sickening qualm.

Dalgith stirred himself: 'If he has we're for it, though I suppose we're damn lucky we didn't have to start scratch. God knows what's happened to the O. Pip parties.'

'Probably all wiped out at the start.' Cheyne was quite dispassionate. Warne looked at him as if he were a devil straight from hell.

'Yes.' Dalgith spoke thoughtfully. 'Young Beecher was up in front of Fresnoy, I believe. Only got married last month.'

They laughed, grim mirthless sounds, and Warne, not understanding this puzzling Army habit of disguise, experienced a revulsion that was almost physical.

'I wish to God somebody would tell us something,' Cheyne said. 'This waiting's getting me down.'

'Yes,' said Dalgith again, and relapsed into silence.

It occurred to Warne then that he was judging hastily.

Ten minutes later a runner came. Cheyne, having read the scribbled message, gave vent to an exclamation and followed it with a quick: 'Jerry's in front of 748 down the road. Carless is keeping him off with his Lewis guns. He wants to know what to do.'

He laughed. 'I'm damned if I know. Do you?'

Dalgith made a helpless gesture. Warne had the sensation of something clutching at his heart. He strained forward, half rose from his chair, as he stared at Cheyne with mouth agape.

Cheyne did not even see him. He was thinking, hard, and wishing heartily that his Colonel had not chosen this moment to vanish into the blue. He swung round upon the runner. 'Colonel Metcalfe been to the battery before you started?'

'Yes, Sir. Half-hour before, at least.'

'And where he is now God knows,' muttered Cheyne.

Then he wrote rapidly on a message form. 'Give this to Major Carless.'

The man saluted and went.

'And that's about torn it,' said Cheyne. He spoke casually enough, but to Warne a judge might have been pronouncing a death sentence.

RETREAT

But when Cheyne next spoke, the very gravity of his voice steadied Warne. There was born in him a new respect for this quiet, thoughtful, even if inhuman adjutant.

'Look here, Young'un. It's pretty obvious we can't stay here with Jerry up the road for certain and possibly all round us as well. So I've told Carless to send all runners to Germaine—our Battle Zone Headquarters. If he's forced to abandon his guns he's to fall back there after destroying them. Meanwhile he's to hang on if he can. From what I know of the old Hun he'll stop in front of the first piece of resistance and sit there till he can stage a pukka attack. So if Carless can hang on till nightfall and we can get up a couple of "cats" or F.W.D.'s he may yet succeed in getting his guns away. I don't see what else I could have told him. We'll have to send a D.R. to Siege Park. He ought to get through without difficulty now, though if Pryor had an atom of gumsh——'

'Or the guts of a louse,' put in Dalgith.

'Yes. Or that. He'd certainly have got in touch with us by now.'

'I'll get Hart on it right away,' said Dalgith, leaving the kiln.

'If only Keller would get through,' muttered Cheyne. He lit a cigarette, started pacing the tiny floor space, and stopped short in front of Warne. He appeared momentarily confused.

'I'm sorry, Padre. I'm afraid I'd clean forgotten you were there.'

At least, Warne thought, he's honest about it.

'Have one,' Cheyne urged. 'They're a rare steadier for the nerves.'

Warne took the cigarette gratefully, for this unexpected overture touched him in a way he would not have thought possible. It suddenly revealed Cheyne as a human being, and this knowledge in turn released an emotional whirlwind. All the pent-up stresses of the past six hours broke loose in reactionary waves of gratitude. Dimly Warne saw himself rounding off his earlier display with a woman's hysterics. With a terrific effort he braced himself against it. 'I suppose I have made a fair-sized fool of myself,' he said, and stared out of the kiln at the filtering sunlight.

Cheyne eyed him with misgivings born of a very lively hatred of anything even allied to the 'touching,' and shuffled uneasily. 'Not in the least. You haven't a monopoly of nerves, Padre. Not by a long chalk. Most of us get 'em sooner or later.' He laughed, and thought of his own, worn perilously thin after three years of it.

And Warne, though he wondered how much of this was merely polite palliative, felt marvellously relieved. This man, he sensed, understood. He took strength from the knowledge, and got up. 'I'm all right now,' he said. 'I—well, I'll try to make amends.'

'Sentimental old fool,' thought Cheyne. He was heartily glad when Dalgith came.

Dalgith ducked into the kiln, gabbling as he went. 'Office a wreck. Both battery cars completely bitched. Hullo, Padre! I didn't see you'd come to life again. I should go out and get a breath of fresh air. Shelling's stopped. Sun's out. Mist's practically gone.'

'Yes,' said Warne. 'I——'

His voice trailed away as he saw that Dalgith had eyes for no one but Cheyne. He felt vaguely hurt.

'The old Ford is still intact. Also the '30 cwt'. Hart's chasing Siege Park. Dalton's loading the '30 cwt'. No sign of Jerry . . .'

Another runner came in, this time from 679, and Cheyne said: 'Thank God, here's something at last. We shall know now.'

He tore open the envelope and hurriedly snatched out its contents. For a moment he stared. Then he swore, "Pon my bloody oath, look at this!' And he held up a slip of pencilled paper. There were columns of figures on it. 'Daily ammunition return! Expenditure up to 10 a.m. to-day. Tansley must have gone stark raving mad.'

He stopped, remembering the orderly.

'Has Colonel Metcalfe been to you yet?'

'Yes, Sir. Some time ago. Just after No. 3 gun was hit.'

'Hm. He hasn't been back?'

'No, Sir.'

'What sort of time have you had?'

The runner embarked upon a disjointed story which Cheyne pieced together with fair accuracy. At the end Cheyne said: 'Right. Go an' get some grub and then get back. No answer.'

When the man had gone he said to Dalgith: 'Tansley's a bloody fool at the best of times. Looks as if the Bullock's been shaking him and this bit of humbug is an effort at saving his face with a pose of superefficiency. Efficiency,——!' He employed a common but indelicate expression that shocked Warne, and followed it with: 'It's enough to make God Himself swear.'

Warne got up again and went out. He could not stand this talk. Also it appeared that he did not count. And so, emerging from the kiln, he saw the quarry for the first time. He was amazed.

Overhead the sky glistened, a cloudless expanse of palest blue. The chalk cliffs of the quarry were white and dazzling between slashes of clear-cut shadow, like the bastions of some fairy castle. It caught the imagination, and beneath its spell the long neglected fields with their freshly-turned spotting of craters took on the fantasy of a lunar landscape, preposterously green instead of blue. And even down in the tree-grown marshes of the tiny Cologne River, and in the yellow decaying ruins of Vermand, he beheld beauty.

The stifling hours of nightmare were past. He had broken surface, as it were, and could breathe again. He was back in God's daylight. Darkness, destruction, and now the calm sunshine of a perfect Spring day. It was bewildering, but it was marvellous.

He drank in great draughts of air, only to pause, disturbed by the curious tang. The discovery restored him in part to the realities of the situation, for this devil's breath shouted of war, of the Germans, and with something of a shock he recalled what Cheyne had said. The Germans were there, over that ridge, less than a mile away. With a queer fluttering of still-unsteady nerves he sought to locate the khaki lines of British infantry, but saw none—only a small party of men straggling over the crest that screened the quarry. The fluttering increased.

The men stumbled into the quarry, and he beheld them as they were—forty hungry British gunners, dirty and unshaven, red-eyed with gas, a few roughly bandaged with shell-dressings, others coughing and making dry scraping noises in their throats. Many dropped wearily to the ground as they halted. Some began searching aimlessly for food. And as he watched them a voice whispered to Warne, telling him that there before him was a portion of the flock he had come to tend. Somehow he did not know how to begin, and he envied Cheyne.

Cheyne was talking to the solitary officer with the party, and fragments of conversation floated up to Warne.

'Hullo, Nash. Bad time?'

'Pretty bloody.'

'So I expect. Colonel been up?'

'Yes, twice. Came back again. He's there now. Jerry's occupied the ridge in front of the position.' Nash spoke mechanically, without interest, as a sleep-walker might talk.

'I see. And you?'

'He's sent us back for a breather. We're to hold ourselves in readiness to get the guns away as soon as it gets dark. He's organizing some sort of defensive line with our Lewis-gun sections and what's left of the P.B.I. Over the crest here.'

He jerked his head towards the ridge in front of the quarry, and it seemed to Warne that he had not the strength to support the weight of his helmet.

With a queer reflective grin distorting his blood-smeared face, Nash added half to himself: 'Nice job it will be tonight—I don't think.' He was, indeed, too weary to be more than trite.

Further talk, much of its meaning entirely lost to Warne, whose brain at this stage could cope with one idea at a time and no more; and then the party picked itself up and trudged on. Warne beheld them go with feelings something akin to dismay, and voiced them to Dalgith.

'Then he *has* broken through!'

'Looks like it,' said Dalgith, and hurried along, ironically wondering if this fool of a parson was always going to be so quick in the up-take.

Bewildered, once again fearful, and bitterly conscious of his own supreme unimportance, Warne accosted Cheyne. But Cheyne was busy, searching among the wreckage of what had been the Brigade office, and did not so much as glance up.

'Cheyne!'

It was a low pleading cry for companionship,

'Cheyne!'

'Eh! What's that?' Cheyne looked up quickly. 'Oh, you, is it?' He bent again to his task.

'I—I——'

But Warne had no words in his vocabulary for an occasion like this. Faltering an apology and knowing that he had been hurt as never before in his life, he slowly swung on his heel and climbed back into the open. Cheyne went on rummaging among the wreckage.

With a heart of lead and a feeling of vast emptiness in his brain, Warne looked round the quarry. Men had emerged from their burrows in the chalk. A burly sergeant wearing the blue and white brassard of the Signals Corps, was directing the loading of stores into a small lorry. Warne recognized it as the one he had driven in the previous night, and caught sight of the saturnine driver. Two batmen were approaching with valises, roughly rolled and strapped. Indifferently he saw his own— saw it hurled into the lorry.

So they were going to—retreat. Somehow the word stuck.

(9)

There were men with rifles. Dalgith himself with one. Then Dalgith and Cheyne in conference. Next decision.

The decision Warne sensed, for Dalgith straightway called him over to the lorry and bundled him unceremoniously on the tail-board. The lorry started. Dalgith waved a valedictory hand. The driver swung his clattering vehicle on to the road, dodged a succession of very new shell-holes, reached the cross roads by the river, and then turned west.

Looking back, Warne could just see Dalgith leading a line of men up the ridge. They were moving east, in single file. For them the battle had hardly begun. For himself—safety with the stores! He whose ambitions had soared so high and so recently. His soul cried out at the ignominy.

CHAPTER III

ESCAPE

(I)

They fought. In those dark and fateful days of March and April in 1918 the men of Gough's Army fought as a British Army has seldom fought or been called upon to fight. And when the German avalanche bore them down they fell back, fighting still, and their dead remained as their memorial. Day followed day, each one a sleepless nightmare, and men knew not the meaning of respite. And that 'over-insured' line, so disturbingly thin at the start, grew hourly thinner as it stretched to conform with the westward bulge.

But it held. Such breaks as occurred were patched up again by men, long exhausted, who called upon themselves for yet another miracle of endurance, and the Germans never broke through. Students of the War are still asking why.

And because brave men did all this, because at the cost of their lives they redeemed the folly of a politician, that same politician repaid his debt by saying, in effect: 'They ran away.'

The Germans—and they should know—did not support this calumny either at the time or afterwards. On the contrary they paid their tribute to the resistance offered them, and Hindenburg himself even went out of his way to assure a bunch of dejected British officers, garnered in front of St. Quentin on the morning of the 21st, that they had no cause for feeling ashamed of themselves. He called them 'gentlemen,' too, a courtesy omitted by the gallant politician who—so rumour persistently states—has yet to learn the meaning of the word.

(2)

Warne spent the night of the 21st-22nd March in a dilapidated farm-house which had somehow survived the wholesale destruction of property that had marked the German retreat to the Hindenburg Line in the Spring of 1917. It was a dirty place, with floors of brick and broken windows that previous occupants had blocked with paper and sacking. Plaster was peeling from greying walls, and it smelt of age, bad sanitation, stale rations, and the indefinable stench of decay. But to Warne it was a resting-place with a roof.

Late that night a servant had set out his valise in the corner of one of the two habitable rooms, and he lay there, rolled in a blanket and clothed except for his boots and jacket, and listening to a steady hum of voices that talked mysteriously of caterpillars and F.W.D.s. The telephone, which Keller had at last succeeded in connecting with Corps, kept up an almost incessant tinkle. After a time he slept.

For Dalgith had laughed and said: 'Take my tip, Padre, and sleep while you've got the chance.'

'And you?' he had replied.

Oh, me!' Dalgith had summoned up a weary grin and turned away with a shrug.

So he had accepted his dismissal and gone—like a small

boy, he thought, sent to bed to be out of the way. He had not the energy left to protest.

Prior to that Dalgith had tossed him a haversack, saying: 'Yours, I believe. I'd stuff it with grub. May come in useful if Jerry gets us on the run.'

And the first thing Warne had found inside had been the pyx. Stuff it with grub! It was a terrible reminder.

(3)

He woke up while it was still dark, painfully conscious of the cold brick floor. To his surprise he caught the sound of a voice in the neighbouring room, and after a moment's listening recognized it as Cheyne's. It rang, too, with all the exasperation of extreme weariness. Warne had never heard its like.

'I've told you already, Sir, those two caterpillars are dud. Both knocked out by shell-fire. And they're the only two that have come anywhere near us.'

A pause.

'It's no good telling me that, Sir. I know you've sent a couple of cats, and if Siege Park or somebody say they've sent a couple more they're wrong. They're referring to the same two which you sent. And those two are dead—direct hits on both. That's plain enough, surely! You've got to send us some more if we're going to get away.' . . .

'Get in touch with Siege Park! How on earth should I know where they are? That's your pigeon. One of our most reliable D. R.s spent over two hours looking for 'em this afternoon and couldn't find 'em. They didn't tell us a word where they were going, let alone ask us what we want. And it was their business to come to us. They're there to shift us, not themselves. Seems to me they just beat it with every damn' lorry they could find as soon as the balloon went up.'

The Brigade Major at the Corps end of the line considered a moment before replying. He liked Cheyne and he sympathized with him. He also struggled in the throes of an organization which had failed. And fatigue had made him almost as touchy as Cheyne. . . . Rowing was no good. He'd try the Colonel.

'Colonel Metcalfe there by any chance?'

'No, Sir. He's with the batteries. I'm all alone.'

'Right-o. Sorry to keep on worrying you. Yours is the only line working. I'll do all I can for you.'

'Well, Sir. Unless you can raise something on wheels that will pull a gun, we're stuck—or most of us are. And that's all there is about it.'

Warne heard the telephone handpiece drop heavily into its bracket, as if hurled there in disgust, and then he looked at his watch, luminous in the dark. The hour was after two. He was too sleepy to appreciate what he had heard. He slept again. And it so chanced that even as he dozed off, Second-Lieutenant Ernest Nash started to lead his rescue party into the tiny valley where five abandoned six-inch howitzers stood in line with the wreckage of a sixth.

(4)

Nash had made the final arrangements with his Captain shortly before midnight, in the open fields in front of the quarry.

Maclachlan, a Dundee solicitor, grey, lantern, terse and completely devoid of frills in any shape or form, had eyed his subaltern suspiciously and said: 'I'll bring up the F.W.D.s. You wait here till I send the word, and then get your party down to the position and limber up. By the time you're ready the F.W.D.s will be there. You take charge of the first pair and get 'em away. I'll look after the remainder.'

'No,' said Nash. 'I'll take the last lot.'

'Why?' Maclachlan was still puzzled. Nash seemed a bit queer. He wondered if that scratch on the head had anything to do with it.

'It's only fair. You'll probably be blown to hell getting 'em there.' Nash sounded sullen, defiant.

'Possibly, but all the same I'll bring up the rear,'

'Toss you for it.'

Maclachlan laughed softly. Best humour him, he thought. 'Right. Heads you go first. Tails I do.'

He spun a coin. Both started forward, craning down to see whom Fate had chosen, and Nash caught his breath slightly as Maclachlan's torch lit up the coin. It was tails.

Nash felt suddenly cold, and fumbled at the collar of his trench-coat, only to find it tightly buttoned already.

'I'm still open to change,' said Maclachlan.

'No.'

The answer came as a fierce hiss, such as overwrought men employ when they drive themselves beyond the limits of safety lest they should fail altogether.

Maclachlan went, stumbling away in the darkness. Nash remained, immobile, staring.... This, he thought, must be premonition. He shivered.

After that he started with brutal deliberation to go through his pockets, taking out a number of letters. There was one from the head-master of the very ordinary secondary school where, until a year ago, he had been a master. Another from an admiring scholar who still saw him as a hero. (A slow smile curled on his lips as he recognized the lad's atrocious writing.) There were three from his young wife, and on one, he knew, the baby scrawl of a guided hand.

He spared nothing. He could not read them: it was too dark. Without taking them from their envelopes he tore them into scraps, and ground the heap into the soft earth under-heel.

Then he looked round at his men, dim shapes with here and there a glowing point of a cigarette. The low murmur of their voices came to him, and he wondered what they were talking about, if they knew what lay ahead of them, and if they realized that 'forlorn' was a very mild description of their enterprise.

But it mattered not. Nothing mattered—really. Might as well get killed now and be done with it, as hang on a few weeks, months, or may be years, and get killed then. But why get killed at all? Why was it necessary? Why was he fighting somebody he'd never seen and against whom he had not the faintest trace of animosity? What was the War about?. God knew. He didn't. Did anybody? He doubted it. No, the War had grown too big. It was now merely a costly, cruel and monstrously inefficient depopulator. And at this exact moment those responsible for its fashioning were sleeping on their spring mattresses and swan's-down pillows, while he . . .

He settled down on the damp grass to wait, pulled out a cigarette and lit it, and adjusted his helmet so that it no longer pressed against the plaster-covered scratch on his scalp. He became resigned after a while, and idly watched the smoke coiling into the still night air.

ESCAPE

Came the runner from Maclachlan, gliding up like a ghost from another world.

Maclachlan was ready, but instead of five F. W. D. s he had only two lorries. Two guns behind each and a third behind one if possible. After that trust in God.

Nash's mouth wreathed itself in a cynical smile as he roused himself. The message was Maclachlan all over.

'Sergeant Price!'

'Sir.' Price's voice boomed softly in the dark. He had been a cattle drover before the War.

'All cigarettes out. Pass the word along to follow me. You bring up the rear. Once in the valley carry on as arranged. And for God's sake go quietly.'

'Yes, Sir.'

Nash started towards the German line. Dark shadows picked their way after him. For the guns lay in the valley, and while daylight lasted Briton and German had watched them from opposite crests, each daring the other to move. Tomorrow, the German thought, those guns would be his. Till then they could remain where they were. They were quite safe.

Maclachlan and the local Company Commander, looking down from their side, had been inclined to agree, but, acceding to Maclachlan's request, the Company Commander had pushed out patrols as soon as darkness had fallen, and in the numerous shell-holes pitting the valley's side, they had established themselves beyond the line of guns. This, at any rate, would prevent the rescue party from being rushed without warning.

Nash reached the guns. His party, a bare score of tired men, silently spread themselves between the first two guns.

Somebody tripped over an obstruction and cursed. A tittering laugh followed, telling of nerves stretched to breaking point. Nash breathed an oath. After that the darkness became full of heavy sound, of stertorous breathing and suppressed curses, of the clanking of metal against metal, and the plodding of heavy boots in the soft, muddy ground. Inch by inch the howitzers were extracted from their pits.

And then Nash caught the distant purr of engines. The secret was out. 'Now,' he thought, grimly detached, 'for merry hell!'

'Party on to Four. Remainder stand by to limber up.'

The men bent to the work. Two guns were ready in a trice, and then Nash had the impression of complete unreality. For it did not need the roaring engines of two Thorneycroft lorries to tell the Germans that something was, afoot. It merely confirmed their suspicions, and they were ready. Before the two lorries, running in reverse, were half-way to the guns brisk rifle fire was crackling from the German line, directed into the black channel of the valley. A machine gun joined in, sweeping along. Another followed. And still more. Then patrols pushed out, only to meet stubborn British posts who refused to budge. Soon, within a hundred yards of the labouring gunners, a lively fight was in progress.

'Never mind that, never mind it!'

Nash knew that he was tearing round and shouting like a man demented, and yet all the while he was saying to himself: 'You're getting rattled. You're getting rattled, and you're done for if you do.'

The first lorry careered madly past him in reverse. The other lurched to a standstill as Maclachlan sprang out of the murk, shouting.

The sound of the rich northern accent steadied Nash. He bawled to his Sergeant to stand by to limber. The Sergeant was already at work.

The firing increased tenfold. Bullets zipped through the fabric of the lorry.

A man was struck in the arm. The sudden pain caused him to cry out, and he stepped back, clutching the wound and gasping. Then, without any warning, he laughed stridently and shouted: 'Clicked at last, by God! A Blighty touch all right this time.' After that he performed an absurdly clumsy step dance and then disappeared singing in the darkness. Nash just caught the words: 'Highty, tiddle-y-ighty, carry me back to Blighty——'

The first casualty.

Before the two howitzers had been limbered behind the single lorry, three more men had been hit.

'Stand clear. Right away.'

It was Maclachlan bawling at the driver above the din. The lorry began to grind forward, protesting against its iniquitous load. Its wheels slipped in the soft ground in spite of their chains.

'Shove behind, you God-forsaken lunatics. Shove behind. You're not a set of statues. Shove—shove——'

The men rallied round, urged on by Nash. The lorry gathered speed. She was off.

Maclachlan stopped just long enough to shout in his ear: 'Good-bye, Nash. Don't attempt the fifth. Lorry won't take more than two. Best o' luck.'

He set off after the lorry. Somehow Nash retained the impression that Maclachlan's face was strangely twisted.

Next instant an infantry subaltern was crying out with

breathless gasps in his ear: 'I can't hold 'em much longer. Are you finished?'

'Finished!' Nash stared at the fellow and laughed, a mad, insane cackle. But he checked himself: 'No. For God's sake hang on. We've two more yet. Possibly three.'

The subaltern groaned, and started back to his men. Nash saw him crawling up the bank on all fours.

German field-guns now began firing, sending salvoes blindly into the valley, though, fortunately, on the far side for the most part. Nash guessed what it meant. Fortunately, too, the swathes of bullets from the German machine-guns were also ill-directed. They passed high, so that it seemed to Nash as if a solid sheet of metal whistled and hissed above his head. He had only to stretch up his hand to touch it. In a detached way he was thankful for the convexity of the hillside which protected them.

His foot struck against something soft as he made his way to the other lorry, and he stumbled across a body. Even in the darkness the back seemed familiar. Then he saw the Sergeant's stripes on the arms. He started to roll the body over, but stopped when he saw the face. He shuddered.

After that something began to beat a queer tattoo in his brain, and the look on his face grew oddly triumphant. There came to him an exaltation that rose above even fear.

He heard men working on No. 6 gun, and shouted to them to leave it and get 4 and 5 out first. Six lumbering shapes blundered by, and the seventh, who carried a handspike, just sagged at the knees and sat down in front of him. He recognized his Corporal, the last of his N.C.O.s.

He leapt into No. 4 pit, goading his men on with curses that rose above the uproar. They responded. The gun was tethered behind the lorry.

'No. 5,' he roared.

Half-way to the pit some cautionary sense warned him that the posts were giving way. He dissolved in indecision. Should he cut and run with the third gun, or risk it and try for another? The firing had stopped too. It was ominous.

Came the cries of the man who had carried the handspike. 'Glory be to God! Glory be to God, brother! Glory be——'

The dim outline of the dying man held him. He wanted to stop his ears.

But another voice broke across the crying. It said: 'Altogether now, lads. He-eave.'

'Glory be——'

A rattling sound. The dying man gave a convulsive shiver. He was dead,

'Steady, lads. Steady. All together, he-eave.'

The voice was more than a tonic to Nash. He wondered which of the men it was. By God, the fellow deserved a D.C.M.! And by God he should have it. Five gun was as good as saved. He'd have six if he had to carry it himself.

Once again Nash forgot himself. He was goading his men in the pit. They had the gun out. It was limbered behind the other. Now for the sixth.

'Come on,' he roared, and met the infantry subaltern.

'Get out, man, get out!'

The subaltern waved his arms wildly and blundered on. Pale-faced infantrymen ducked and fired and fell back across the valley, and the lorry driver settled matters for Nash by crashing in the gear and lurching off down towards the road.

Nash screwed himself up a further peg.

'Beat it, lads. Leave everything. Make for the road.'

A dozen bewildered gunners started off in the wake of the lorry.

Shots rang out. Nash saw the stabs of flame. Two men fell. One said: 'Oo—oo—a-ah!' The other said nothing.

Nash made out the dim silhouettes of German helmets against the sky. He came up to the fallen pair. One did not move. The other lay writhing. Several men stopped, hesitating whether to go on or stay and carry the wounded man.

'Go on,' Nash screamed. 'Get out.'

They went. He made to lift the fellow, but before he could bend he cried out. He was conscious of another stab of flame and, simultaneously, a violent blow on the shoulder. He clenched his teeth, but a groan forced its way out as he broke into a tottering run after the lorry, holding his useless arm to his side as he went.

The lorry won through to the road as the first had done, chiefly because the valley swung westward and away from the Germans. And once on the road men scrambled into it, laughing and shouting from sheer nervous reaction.

'Four of 'em, the little beauties,' roared a voice.

'Four of 'em, and that God-damned bahstud of a Fritzy sittin' on their muzzles.'

The fellow lit a crumpled cigarette and carelessly flung aside the match. Instantly the whole body of the lorry was wreathed in smoky flame. Men, laughing a second before, flung themselves over the tail board in frenzied terror.

'Earth, you bloody fools! Earth on it.'

The weak, pain-wracked voice rose to a feeble scream

as Nash staggered up to the lorry. 'Earth, you sods!' Then a cracked inhuman cackle. 'Earth, sods, earth. Put earth on it, earth—on—it.'

His serviceable arm traced out a whirling sweep against the sky. He fell. And even as his very brain seemed to explode in one mighty sheet of flaming darkness within his head, he knew that he had won.

A petrol can, punctured early on and remaining unnoticed, had flooded the floor. The match, carelessly thrown, had done the rest. But, quickly though the handfuls of mud and dirt had extinguished the flames, the German machine-gunners had found a target. Bullets whistled and sung. Many drilled neat round holes in the woodwork and fabric. But only one found a human billet. That passed clean through the brain of Second-Lieutenant Ernest Nash.

They left him where he fell, and it so chanced that as the lorry rattled and bumped in its mad scurry to safety, Cheyne petulantly explained over the telephone: 'I told you *that* two hours ago, Sir. *We have not got two caterpillars that will work.* All we've got is a few odd lorries scrounged from anywhere, and batteries are doing the best they can with *them*. They can't do more.'

Warne slept.

(5)

Drab daylight was stealing through the room when he awoke. Voices sounded beyond the frail partition. A telephone bell rang.

He recalled everything, and with a distinct sense of shame, not untinged with remorse, he hastened to get up. He felt that he had deserted them. But, reason demanded, what could he have done had he stayed up all night? Nothing, as far as he could see; absolutely nothing. And was he ever to do anything?

Then breakfast, a scrambling affair of greasy bacon and stale bread, with mugs of tea, piping hot, sweet and strong and richly comforting in the cold of the early morning—a breakfast to which he came as a man moving painfully through a dream world, unsure of himself, unsure of his purpose, and doubly unsure of his reception. Yet this was, indeed, his first meal with his own unit—a tired and lowly Headquarters staff, unshaven and silent, grouped about a clothless dirty table on boxes and broken chairs, anything that would support their aching bodies. And looking round at the nodding listless Keller, at the massive O'Reilly who, with a calm indifference obviously superior to life's mischances, placidly mopped bacon fat with a piece of fingered bread; at Dalgith, a tired-out schoolboy; at Cheyne, lean-faced, pensive, bright-eyed with the fatigue of two nights without sleep; at the Colonel, greyer, more steely than Warne had ever thought possible in a man—looking round at them he knew a return of the old heartfelt longing to serve, to do something for these weary men who belonged to him. And for a whole second his determination flared.

It was Dalgith's greeting that quenched it. Dalgith said, with what effort Warne mercifully did not know: 'Hullo, Padre! Had a good sleep?'

Nothing more, but it was enough. Nobody spoke.

Bell, in shirt sleeves and braces, pushed a box to the table and brought him bacon on a chipped enamel plate. Tea followed and every one went on sipping and eating until almost tearfully he told himself that he need never have been there.

And he did *so* want to talk, to find out what was happening, to comfort—but no, these men did not require *his* sort of comfort. He sought to make an opening, but found that his very tongue refused its office.

He turned to the bacon. He could understand that.

Eight o'clock found him alone with Cheyne and still no wiser, though before the little party had dispersed after breakfast he had played the rôle of avid listener to much laconic and incomprehensible reference. Some caused him to prick his ears in disturbing wonder.

'Any orders about 990, Sir?' Cheyne had said, and the Colonel had not replied at once. Then: 'No. Hear what Corps have to say, and if they cannot help——'

He left the sentence incomplete, finding it distasteful. Cheyne understood. His silence was more expressive than words.

'You'll find me at 679 if you want me,' the Colonel said, and calling Dalgith, went out, alert, tireless, stiffly erect.

O'Reilly looked at Cheyne inquiringly: '990? That's the new mob at Vaux, isn't it?'

Cheyne replied dully. He was too tired for casual conversation. 'Yes. They're just out from home. Under our orders temporarily. Don't think they've fired a shot yet.'

'Tough.'

'Aye.' He stared moodily at the peeling walls. 'It's being let down by that bloody Siege Park that gets me—and the Bullock. Though what else you can expect if you won't allow a Brigade Commander to control his own transport, God knows.'

He was speaking more to himself than to O'Reilly, rambling on in a manner that aroused O'Reilly's professional curiosity. Cheyne had sunk down on a chair and was leaning forward, a hand gripping each knee, his body rocking gently to and fro as he stared fixedly at the opposite wall.

The Doctor looked at him thoughtfully. His lips pursed. He stroked his bristled chin. He could do no more.

Cheyne went on, still mumbling to himself: 'But I wouldn't be in Mr. Bloody Cholmondeley Pryor's boots the next time old Metcalfe sees him. My God, I wouldn't!...Though the slimy——will probably hide behind his A.S.C. boss and get away with it.'

O'Reilly thought it time to chip in. 'Any news of 'em?'

Cheyne started. 'Oh—eh—news! Not a word. Vanished into thin air.'

'Hm.'

The Doctor considered a moment, surveying two immense putteed legs the while. The tape of one he adjusted. He glanced covertly, first at Cheyne and then at Warne, as he did so. 'Warne,' he thought, 'needs rest. Cheyne wants sleep as well. Both, at the present rate, are heading straight for a nervous breakdown.' And then, acutely aware of his own utter helplessness, he asked himself what he could do. The answer was nothing.

'Must have another look at Maclachlan,' he said, and stuffed away his pipe.

'Bad?'

Cheyne did not look up. His voice sounded dead.

''Fraid he'll have to go. Just missed the groin. Nothing serious if treated properly, but——'

O'Reilly shrugged massive shoulders. A faint smile curled on Cheyne's lips. 'Wants to carry on, does he?' Then, relapsing again to semi-audibility: 'My God! Give me his chance and see where I'd be. Carry on hell!'

O'Reilly swung round. He faced Cheyne squarely. 'What the devil do you think you're doing now?'

'Going dotty, probably.'

The answer was wild and hoarse.

'Don't be a bloody fool. Brace up, man. Surely you've been a couple of nights without sleep before?'

Cheyne looked up, taken aback by the ringing scorn. This time he spoke quietly. 'Too often. That's the trouble. A year or two ago—but it's no good talking about that. . . . You were saying?'

'About Maclachlan.' O'Reilly watched Cheyne narrowly. 'He insisted on remaining.'

'Quite understand that. Tansley's an utter dud.'

The answer sounded normal enough, and O'Reilly was reassured. 'Ought to have chucked his hand in as soon as ever he was hit,' he observed, still watching.

'Why didn't he?'

'Something about a rendezvous with Nash.'

'Oh, that.'

'Yes. I couldn't quite make it out, but I gather he thought the lorries couldn't get there without him, so he took 'em.'

'He would.' Cheyne grinned, knowing Maclachlan. 'How's he taking it?'

O' Reilly, satisfied at last that it was safe for him to go, said: 'So-so. He's a bit cut up about Nash, of course.'

'So I should think.'

O'Reilly sauntered out, saying: 'I'd get in a drop of shut-eye, if I were you.'

Cheyne stared after him for a moment, and then said:

'Sleep, huh! What a hope!' And he looked so feverish and old, as he sat there, that Warne was both shocked and distressed.

Their eyes chanced to meet, but there was no response in Cheyne's, no gleam of friendliness or even resentment. He just saw, and muttered: 'Hullo, Padre! Getting on all right?'

Getting on! All the cynic in Warne, though there was but little, laughed riotously. Getting on, indeed! Had he not the evidence of his own eyes that Cheyne was physically incapable of joking he would have resented the remark as an extremely untimely jest. As it was, the sight of Cheyne's limp sagging body touched some spring of tenderness and sympathy that bore him to the side of this sleepless adjutant exactly as he would have gone to a sick man.

'Cheyne,' he said.

Cheyne looked up again. A ghost of a smile flitted across his face. 'Anything I can do for you?'

'Do for me! It's the other way round, Cheyne. It's what can I do for you?'

Warne's voice had risen. There was a trembling insistence about it that roused Cheyne, and his tired upturned face puckered slightly as he echoed: 'You do something for us, eh! It's very good of you, Padre, but——'

'But what?'

There was none of the suppliant about Warne now. The question had all the ring of a challenge, and Cheyne groaned to himself. Why, oh why, must the fellow come that stuff over him at this of all impossible moments?

He contrived to answer: 'I don't think there is any——' and averted his eyes.

'Nonsense, Cheyne. Nonsense.'

Warne dragged up a box. He sat down, leaning forward, straining, as if held back by some invisible leash. He was hatless, and the tall furrowed dome of his forehead reminded Cheyne, absurdly enough, of a washer-woman's scrubbing board. He wanted to laugh. Warne's voice came to him distantly.

'Listen, Cheyne. ' It was terribly earnest. 'You're tired out. So are you all. I alone am comparatively fresh. There must be dozens of jobs I can do to help you—apart from the spiritual side of my duties——'

'Eh, what's that? I'm sorry, Padre, I missed you.' Cheyne sounded ineffably weary. Warne was too worked up to see an affront. He brushed the interruption aside.

'You must let me help you. I want to. I will——'

'Yes.'

'And I must see my men. I know it's impossible now——'

'Quite.'

'—but at the first opportunity I must do my duty by my Faith.'

'Yes.'

Cheyne felt the deep-set unhappy eyes of the priest peering at him, and sensed the appeal of that taut, straining, eager mind which lay behind them. But the incubus of his weariness was proof against even this. He could *not* interest himself in Warne now. No, not even in God Himself. He wanted to sleep, just sleep, to shut his burning eyes and sink down anywhere. Only let him sleep.

'You, Cheyne—you must help me.'

Oh, God, hadn't the man any savvy at all? Couldn't he *see* that the *time* was all wrong.

Almost angrily Cheyne turned upon his tormentor. 'Have you considered exactly what you can do when you *have* established that contact with the men which, I take it, is your aim?'

RETREAT

The irony was lost to Warne. He laughed. 'Thought what I can do! Man, I've thought of nothing else for the last three years.'

'And you came because you fancied——'

'Because I fancied! Cheyne, you blaspheme. I came because God called me.'

Cheyne's gesture was nondescript. It might have expressed doubt. It might have embodied distaste. It certainly told of a man tired out in body and mind, too fatigued to bother with a priest's illusions.

'To what?' he said, icily remote.

'To tend the sick, comfort the dying, to hearten—' Warne trailed off into a feeble stricken cry. 'Cheyne, you're laughing at me!'

And Cheyne was. He could not help doing so. He was thinking of yesterday, of the quarry. And with the greatest difficulty he restrained himself from shouting: 'Have a banana!' or 'Stuff a sock in it!'—the only two replies that seemed adequate. But a glance at Warne's face, with half-incredulous horror written in every line of it, steadied him. Something told him he had made more than a mistake: he had wounded a sensitive man's pride—a pride, too, already bruised and aching.

He said: 'I'm sorry, Padre. Forgive me. We're both of us a trifle off colour. Things will straighten themselves out soon, and then we shall see where we are. You'll always find difficulties. I'll help all I can, and I—I—well, I hope you'll never be disappointed.'

But it was too late. The wound required other salve than words, and Warne, feeling mentally numb, got up and went out. He had received a lesson. Now he had to digest it.

ESCAPE

For a time he stood in the broken doorway, irresolute, unable to think. Sunlight streamed about the tiny derelict courtyard, whitening mottled walls, casting strong shadows, and striking warm and comforting where it fell. Behind him the telephone bell rang, and he heard Cheyne's voice,

'Hullo! ... Yes, yes. Cheyne speaking ... Nothing doing. I see. ... Yes, it can't be helped. ... No, I suppose not. Good-bye.'

'Hart!'

Cheyne shouted huskily, and a midget despatch-rider came from an outhouse. He brushed by Warne without taking any particular notice.

'You called, Sir?'

'Oh, Hart. You know 990, the six-inch gun crowd?'

'Yessir.'

'Right. Take this note.'

'Very good, Sir.'

Hart saluted and went. A pause to adjust the chin strap of his helmet, and then he mounted his Douglas machine which had been standing by the door, and lurched over the uneven courtyard to the road.

Watching him, Warne thought: 'That man is probably a motor mechanic by trade, a man of little or no education. Yet he has a definite job. He is serving his King, and indirectly his God. I, on the other hand, with all my education, can do neither.'

He argued so dispassionately that he surprised himself.

(6)

Half an hour later the Captain in charge of the detached section of 990 Siege Battery at Vaux took a last look at his brand new guns, and then proceeded to blow them up by the simple expedient of ramming a fused shell down the muzzle and firing another in the normal way, with the assistance of a lanyard of inordinate length, of course. And when he chanced to overhear his gunlayer growl: 'This is all about a bloomin' war, I'm——if it ain't!' he felt inclined to agree.

(7)

They did not remain long in Germaine. The decision that led to the blowing-up of those two six-inch long-range guns was merely the prelude to further retreat. The centre was giving. Both flanks had gone. Hourly the situation grew more precarious. The Battle Zone positions were untenable. Back to the line running north and south through Matigny, and there hold on. Thus said the orders. And, as before, Warne went first in their execution, taking with him the crumbled ruins of his earlier hopes.

'Mayn't I stay with you?' he had pleaded when Dalgith had bundled him into the store-laden '30 cwt'.

But Dalgith had merely grinned, saying he was damn' lucky to be getting out of it so easily. And vexation had struggled with despair as the lorry bore him away to safety with the stores—unwanted still, an impediment.

To make matters worse Warne found himself alongside the same saturnine driver who had driven him the other night from Ham, and far from finding the man a friendly companion; Warne deemed him definitely repulsive. The Rembrandtian picture he had carried away with him that night had faded in the broad light of day. The man struck him as being merely coarse and garrulous, talking glibly of the tragedy of the last twenty-four hours with a complete lack of what to Warne was ordinary decent feeling. So Warne sat there, hating the man for his attitude and yet greedily drinking in the tit-bits of information offered.

It was, however, no palliative to realize that this uncouth Army Service Corps private knew far more of current events than he did, a Chaplain at Headquarters. It struck him as being all wrong, palpably and insultingly wrong, and he resented it. But he learned from the driver what he did not know before— that at least half the Brigade had got away; nobody quite knew how, but they had. 748 in particular had 'copped it crool.'

The driver didn't think old Jerry could do it—shift us like this. No, that he didn't. Strike him pink if he did! But wouldn't old Jerry, the——, cop it when our reserves came up. Proper root in the——he'd get. That 'ud larn the——.

To Warne the lorry driver's language was a lesson in itself, a revelation of current Army phraseology and thought. Not even his lively abhorrence of the terms employed, as well as the familiarity and implied disrespect for his cloth, could entirely stifle his growing interest in the man. Sleepy old Bidderwill, set in the prim determinate landscape of southern Cambridgeshire, had never produced this type. It savoured too much of the football fan, of the fellow who invariably said 'we' when he meant 'they.' Not an attractive type. And he wondered what measure of success he would obtain when he met it in his capacity as a priest of God.

'By the way,' he asked. 'What's your name?'

'Bass, Sir. Harry Bass. Good ol' English that, Sir. Bit beery, p'raps, as my ol' missus says on a Saturday night when I comes 'ome wiv a skinful. "Bass," she says, determined like, "it's Bass yer nime is and it's Bass yer filled wiv."'

'Yes, yes. Any children?'

'Five. An' the eldest, that's young 'Erb, is just joined the Boy Scouts. A rare 'un is our 'Erb, Proper Bass. As my ol' missus——'

'Yes, yes. Quite. You're Church of England, I suppose?'

'Eh! Church o' England. Would that be the sime as C. o' E.?'

Warne groaned in spirit. He had to look twice at the man before he was convinced that the query was genuine. 'Yes,' he said, dully. 'It's meant to be the same.'

'If you're typical of my flock,' he thought, 'God help me.'

He said no more. Cheyne had been right. He could do nothing as yet. Later perhaps——

They drove on, Harry Bass in cheerful but mystified silence.

On the edge of the village the passed a bunch of gunners labouring with drag ropes to haul a six-inch howitzer from its temporary emplacement by the roadside, and the sight of these sweating grunting men both intensified Warne's determination to push ahead with his priestly duties, and revealed to him, according to his own interpretation, how vitally urgent and necessary those duties were.

'I,' he told himself, with a definite pang of shame, 'am the priest passing by on the other side. But later——'

It was no longer 'perhaps.'

Were not those men *his* just as much as that profane young officer's? Indeed they were—as much and a thousand times more. What mattered a gun beside man's immortal soul? And there was pride as well as distress welling within him as he looked down upon the two lines of faces that rose and fell together as tired bodies heaved on the ropes, for he saw them dull, almost devoid of ordinary human expression, unshaven and dirty—just so many blanks; but they were his to tend. Hearten the weary! Cheyne had laughed at that. Cheyne would have to be taught. Why had he come to France if not to——

'Crikey, Sir! Look at that!'

There was ironical dismay in Bass's voice as his elbow delivered a most disrespectful nudge to attract Warne's attention.

'Two six-inch 'ows tied to a nordinary three-ton Thorneycroft. It's come to that, 'as it?'

Slowly the '30 cwt' picked its way past the lorry in question and its tail of limbered howitzers. Warne said nothing. There are times when the turmoil of the spirit crowds out the power of speech. This was one.

Clear of the guns the lorry quickened and rattled along at a good pace for half a mile. Then it had to slow down again while it passed a battalion of infantry moving up, the last of the local reserves. It was just an ordinary English County battalion which had started life as a 'K' formation and now was mostly conscript, and somehow the idea that these men were going into action, many to certain death, caught Warne's imagination in much the same way as the perspiring gunners had done, causing him to stare at the long lines of shuffling laden men with a tenderness and compassion that were just as creditable as they were wasted and out of place.

Cogs in the war machine! How the trite old metaphor sprang to mind! It couldn't be bettered. Cogs, insignificant cogs, purposely fashioned so small that a few hundreds more or less made no appreciable difference to the machine. Only as units they counted—a thousand at a time. And only when the unit ceased to exist as a fighting entity did they affect the running of the machine.

And what uniformity! No individuality left. All dressed alike and reduced to the common level of khaki. All, except the occasional Lewis gunners, carrying their rifles slung over the shoulder in exactly the same way. All slightly bowed under the weight of standard equipment. All silent—moodily silent. Only the shuffling tramp of their boots sounded above the clatter of the lorry's engine. And their faces—all dull and expressionless like the gunners', only clean and shaven whereas the gunners' were grimed and bristled. Old faces, young faces—all set like masks, so that no man might see what premonitions were at work within.

'That,' he told himself, as if correcting an impression, 'is the way men march to battle.'

His distress and his determination grew with the discovery.

'They don't sing now as they used-ter,' Bass knowingly remarked. 'Not like they did in '16 afore the Somme. Not so much gas in 'em——'

'I would to God there wasn't so much in you,' breathed Warne.

Bass fell into sulky silence. 'I'd never 'a' thought it, ' he mused. 'The pie-faced poop! God rot 'is rabbits, sod 'im.' He stamped savagely upon the accelerator and sent the '30 cwt' racing along past the column.

'Bloody jam-pusher,' muttered an infantryman, and spat the dust from his mouth.

So on across a devastated countryside where Nature, bursting again with new life; was even then repairing the year-old ravages of man. In the wreckage of orchards green buds showed on the branches of fruit trees imperfectly sawn down. There was grass in the ruins of compact little villages.

And with every yard Bass recovered some of his *bonhomie*.

'Jerry did all this,' he suddenly and lightly explained, nodding at the half-healed scars. 'Did it last Spring when 'e 'opped it back to 'is 'indenburg Line so as we should 'ave nowhere ter live. 'E's lucky. I'm blowed if 'e ain't! Won't 'ave anywhere 'imself nah!'

The idea tickled Bass, for he laughed gleefully. But it startled Warne. It made him aware, for the first time, of War's abominable savagery as distinct from its incidental destruction. In the shell-swept battle-zone villages crumble and disappear altogether sometimes. But here he was looking upon a village deliberately destroyed by hand. Houses here had been burnt or gutted. The tiny brick church had been blown up; its slated steeple lay there, still wonderfully preserved, sprawling over a weed-hidden patch of cemetery. A winter's rains had been at work. Frosts had lent a hand. And now Nature herself was healing the ugliness with a mantle of green.

They passed a well, once, no doubt, the centre of village gossip. A large notice board had been posted above it, declaring its water befouled. As a further precaution the top had been roughly covered over with planks.

Then a pond, brown, stagnant and noisome. It seemed to Warne, quite rightly, that a midden had been cast there to pollute it.

'Thorough, ain't 'e?' commented Bass. His aplomb was that of a tourist's guide.

But Warne was beyond appreciating that. He remained silent, for if he had said anything he would have told the fellow to keep quiet in the name of common decency.

All the same it was a marvellous ride. Whatever emotional reactions it provoked in Warne, hypersensitive as he was, it certainly caused him to forget for the time being that haunting fear of shame that was born in the quarry near Villecholes the day before.

(8)

They appeared from nowhere—ten German aeroplanes that came skimming along above the tree tops as if seeking a place to land. Warne caught sight of them first, and clutched Bass's arm, pointing as he did so. And Bass, being experienced in the habits of aircraft, glanced hastily at the twirling, glittering bodies, glimpsed the black crosses of Germany, and gasped out the one pregnant word: 'Jerries!'

Frantically he sought for cover, but not a stick could be seen nearer than a quarter mile, for the lorry chanced to be exposed in the middle of a considerable stretch of open road.

'Oh, Christ!' he groaned, and stopped the lorry so abruptly that Warne was flung against the dash.

Warne recovered himself to find Bass gone. Bass and his mate were in the act of jumping into the shelter of the roadside ditch, and seeing them, Warne cried out. But they furnished no sign of having heard, and he, caught with paralysing dismay, stared helplessly at the raiding Germans. Rifles were now crackling. Several machine guns set up a furious staccato rattle. It seemed to Warne that a thousand rivets were being hammered into steel, and it dawned upon him that these swooping aeroplanes were attacking the infantry battalion the lorry had so recently passed.

ESCAPE

Bass yelled up from the ditch, exhorting him to get down before the raiders came for the lorry. And when Warne failed to move, his voice rose to a hoarse screech. 'Down, you bloody fool! Down! For Chri-sake get *down!*'

But not even abuse could shift Warne then. The fear was upon him. His body was no longer his to control. Fascinated, he could only stare at the 'planes which, tiring of the infantry, or, perchance, finding their reception too warm, had suddenly turned and were diving towards the lorry. A dizzy and stricken brain kept likening them absurdly to wasps—wasps that were going to sting.

Bass said: 'Oh, my Gawd!'—half a groan, half a cry. Both he and his mate pressed themselves into the muddy wall of the ditch. The 'planes came on.

Then, from another region of nowhere, appeared the British Flight, ten glittering biplanes bedecked with rings of red, white and blue.

Warne heard himself shouting exultantly. Bass heard too—something about the Lord God being a shield for His Servant—and peered cautiously over the edge of the ditch.

'Shield be blowed!' he muttered.... 'Crikey!'

For the two flights, each wheeling into formation, had met, and not four hundred yards away the sky was full of darting, diving, twirling aeroplanes. And the sunlight, catching their polished wings, their lean silver bodies, their bright markings, broke into myriad beams. The air seemed full of twisting sparkling jewels. It was fascinating, terrible. To Warne the whole world had suddenly centred itself in that aerial fight.

And behind it all was the droning purr of a score of engines. On top, the furious spitting of machine guns.

RETREAT

Warne took in the entire picture as the fight drifted along. He missed nothing. He could even make out the black knobs that were pilots' heads. And breathlessly he waited and watched.

It happened without any warning, as these things do. Just a burst of black oily smoke and a spurt of yellow flame, and then one of the 'planes was spinning and twisting towards the ground. Flame streamed out behind, and smoke—comet-like. Half-way to earth something fell from it, a spidery cross, black against the shining blue of the sky; and it turned round and round like the spokes of a rimless wheel as it raced the burning 'plane. With sick horror Warne recognized a man, one of God's creatures spread-eagled under gravity, a man who in his last few seconds of life preferred . . .

A cry wrung from his lips, no longer of exultation. He called upon God, even as the driver had done.

Bass, however, paid no heed either to Warne or the hurtling airman. He merely scrambled back into his seat, mumbling the while about something which a detached portion of Warne's brain heard and interpreted as a hint to get out while the going was good.

The lorry raced off. Into a field half a mile distant crashed the luckless instrument of God's purpose, a half-burnt bundle of pulp and broken bones. Seconds afterwards the vehicle of its passing, spinning in a vertical nose dive and trailing flames and sparks, crashed too. More flames. More smoke. A dull report. The fight went on.

'A goner,' commented Bass, unmoved.

Warne found a hoarse choking thing that served as a voice and said: 'Was it—ours?'

Bass shook his head, muttering that he couldn't tell, and Warne knew then that Cheyne had been right on a second count. Something was hammering at his brain, bidding him see for himself what is thought of a man's life. He had not been prepared for this.

But there was far more behind the revelation than a mere lorry driver's callousness, and what it was, aimed at the very core of Warne's faith, a core which had hitherto been cloistered and secure. Therein Warne had enshrined his conception of God Himself, and because he had done this thing he made the common but fatal mistake of believing that others had done it as well. It is therefore not surprising that he saw in the mildly obscene though essentially good-tempered and well-meaning Bass that repellent creation of the Devil, a human being who had not God in his heart.

Had Bass looked at his passenger in that moment he would have surprised a white-faced priest staring at him and shrinking from him with all the fascinated loathing decent men experience when suddenly confronted with the unclean. But the lorry claimed him. He had no time for priests till he slowed down, and that he did not intend doing while a squadron of German fighters was anywhere near. Not he!

And Warne, beneath all his suffocating misery, watched him peering ahead, gripping the wheel, tugging at it, first this way and then the other, to keep the bounding lorry on the road, and asked himself if it could be that all men were like this. Was this man alone, or had War indeed driven God from the hearts of men? Yet this same man, who saw nothing in the destruction of his kind, had called upon God in his extremity. What therefore could God mean to him? What indeed? Was God nothing more than a name? Did God really mean anything to anybody out here in this Devil-ridden land?

Tortured to action by the stress of his own anguish, Warne gripped Bass's sleeve. 'Do you,' he panted, 'believe in God?'

'Me—Gawd!'

The ejaculation was quite spontaneous, and after the briefest glance Bass went on with his driving. But it was enough. In those two short words Warne had found his answer, for it seemed to him that Bass had replied: 'God? Who on earth is He?'

He turned away so that Bass should not be able to see his face.

(9)

Late that evening when the lorry was halted by the roadside, waiting, Bass nudged his mate and indicated Warne standing apart with his sorrow, and said: "E's daft, that cove. Didjer 'ear 'im t'day? Arst me if I believed in Gawd, 'e did!'

And the pair laughed mightily.

CHAPTER IV

FINDING A BILLET

(I)

Heaps of weed-grown rubble; remnants of broken walls; an aerodrome whose deserted hangars loomed against the sunset; a hut, with a piano abandoned in one corner, that a few hours before had been a Flying Officers' Mess; Cheyne washing and laboriously shaving in a mug of cold water; hot tea; a meal of stale bread and yellow jam—these were the impressions that Warne took away from Matigny and carried across the marshes of the Somme into the village of Voyennes.

Jerry had turned their flanks, they told him. It was hold the line of the Somme or——?

So back they went, and Warne went first, perched in the front of the '30 cwt' next to an ogre. And packed into a stream of retreating transport—a medley of mule-drawn G. S. wagons, water-carts, motor cars, lorries, field-cookers, all converging on the bridge at Voyennes—the '30 cwt' forged slowly westward. What was left of the Brigade followed later.

At the bridge a cordon of troops with bayonets that still contrived a menacing glint in the half-light of the dusk, stopped all traffic. An officer, with drawn revolver, questioned the driver—ignoring Warne altogether. Bass's explanation sufficed.

The '30 cwt' was allowed to proceed. The Fifth Army was sorting itself out after Ludendorft's disastrous shuffling.

Then hours of weary waiting at the side of a tree-lined road just short of Voyennes—this, while the gloom deepened and wet mists rose from the marsh.

A chill crept into the air, and Warne grew cold and hungry and still more dispirited. He paced irresolutely up and down in a vain endeavour to get warm, and as he paced he strove to quell the riot of his thoughts. But he could obtain no grip on anything. It was all too novel, too bewildering, and above all too profoundly disturbing. There was nothing on which he could base himself. Like the battle front, the very principles underlying his mode of life were in a state of flux. This waiting about doing nothing was terrible. If he could only act, do something, he felt that he might yet pull through.

Men were trooping by in the darkness: phantom figures that loomed up for a moment and then vanished. And incessantly at first came the jingle of harness, the clatter of hoofs, the rattle of lampless motors, the crunch of boots on the gravelly road. There were muttered curses, imprecations; 'Whoa!' and 'Hup!' and soft encouragement to tired horses from men even more tired; but never a gleam of friendly light. All moved in darkness, a merciful darkness which covered the shattered units of a beaten army so that they might reform and fight again on the morrow.

Only in the east was there light, a reddish glow from Matigny's burning hangars.

Midnight approached. The transport had gone. To Warne the world had become blank and empty, forbidding. He began to long for company, for the reassurance, the sense of security,

FINDING A BILLET

that seemed to envelop the tiny Headquarters. And when, half an hour later, he heard the throbbing inelegant Ford come to a standstill by the '30 cwt', his relief was heartfelt. He stepped forward eagerly as the Colonel got out. Cheyne, Dalgith and O'Reilly followed, dark shadows in the night.

There were greetings poised on Warne's lips when the Colonel spoke, saying: 'Ah, Bass. Mr. Keller been here yet?'

Bass saluted. 'Nosir.'

And then Warne shrank back into the murk, while that little demon of the ego which is man's secret pride, mocked and scourged him with bitter taunts. 'See what you're worth now,' it cried. 'Look at these men, your comrades! Look at them, and see that they prefer to question a foul-mouthed blackguard instead of you. They probably haven't even bothered to note you're here. Observe it well, Elliot Warne. Miss nothing. It will do you good.' Next the still voice of reason: 'Don't be a fool, man. It's quite on the cards they haven't seen you yet. It's dark. 'But,' shrieked the demon in triumph, 'they saw that lorry driver, and if they could do that——'

Dull anger, born of the goading, then took charge, driving him forward again. He heard himself saying with a stiffness and haughtiness that made it difficult for him to recognize his own voice: 'No, Mr. Keller has not been here to my knowledge.'

The remark, with its gratuitous information, already half a minute late, cut across the Colonel's instructions about billets for the night, and in the silence that followed, four pairs of eyes, pale glinting points in the darkness, swung round upon the dim oval of greyness that was the face of a disillusioned priest.

Dalgith spoke first. In weary surprise he said: 'Hullo, Padre! Didn't see you were here.'

RETREAT

'No,' thought Warne, coldly furious. 'Of course you didn't. You'd forgotten I was alive. One day, and that quite soon, you'll learn that I am, even if I have to tell you myself.'

Cheyne, in the last extremity of sleeplessness, wondered: 'Oh, God, and what's happened now!' But O'Reilly saw further. He tried to remember when he last had to deal with a neurasthenic.

The Colonel merely recorded a mental note to attend to his new Chaplain—along with Tansley—when the opportunity offered. Meanwhile——

'Dalgith!'

'Sir?'

'As I was saying——'

(2)

Warne had taken himself apart from the others, and Dalgith, setting off to Voyennes, came upon him.

'Coming?' he said, stopping in the middle of his stride.

'Coming!' Warne echoed.

'Yes. Into Voyennes.' Dalgith sounded just the faintest bit impatient.

Warne smiled sadly, a little inward smile to himself. 'You don't want me, Dalgith,' he said.

'Eh! Don't want you?' There was mystification this time.

'Dalgith. After what happened just now——'

'Oh, cut it, Padre, and come if you're coming.'

Dalgith linked his arm through Warne's. He could not argue. If Warne liked to make a fool of himself, that was Warne's business. He himself was far too weary to cope with melodramatic postures at this hour. He was, indeed, too weary even to fathom the significance of the circumstances that had uprooted the Fifth Army and driven back its centre a dozen miles in a couple of days, let alone indulge in this soul-revealing bunkum.

'Come on,' he urged, and gently pulled at Warne's arm. Warne fell into step beside him.

'Billeting,' he added in explanation, and then, as they trudged along the pale ribbon of road, he forced himself to a palsied eloquence out of sheer pity. 'Didn't think the old Hun could shift us like this——'

The sentiment struck Warne as dimly familiar.

'—Doesn't seem to be anybody behind us.... If we can't hold this river line Heaven knows where we shall stop....'

He went babbling on. He might have been talking to himself. 'We never met with a quarter of the success he's met with already. Took us three months to advance five miles up at Passchendaele.... Still, the French are due to come up from the south and take over. Until they do I suppose we hang on....Hope to God they don't waste time.... We may get some sleep when they come, perhaps.... Don't know how old Cheyne sticks it—three days and well into the third night without a wink.... The Bullock's fresh as paint though he did only get down to it for a couple of hours before the show started.'

He broke into a dry, rattling chuckle. 'If I don't get down to it soon myself I shall be looking at the inside of my lids as I walk along.... Still, how old Cheyne sticks it, I don't know.... Ripe egg, old Cheyne.... Good chap.... How he sticks it I don't know.... I don't know....'

RETREAT

Warne heard but little. He was wrapped in himself.

And so through the moonless night into Voyennes.

In their general destruction of 1917 the Germans had spared Voyennes, a fair-sized village, and used it to accommodate, in addition to its own complement of old men, women and children, refugees from the villages they obliterated in the neighbourhood. It was therefore crowded.

'Good Lord, what's that?'

Dalgith, coming to with a start, tightened his grip on Warne's arm. The action wrenched Warne into the present.

Voices came to them, carried on the night air—a wailing murmur, eerie, disquieting. In genuine perplexity Dalgith muttered: 'What on earth's happening here?'

Then, without warning, they saw. They walked into confusion such as Warne had never dreamed of in his wildest moments. Doddering men—the Germans had taken any passably active left by the French authorities—and distracted women bumped into them, invoked God and the Virgin Mary, and stumbled away almost in the same instant to be lost in the darkness. Children blubbered, whimpered and screamed, or stood with pale gaping faces, too frightened even to cry.

Mattresses, blankets, bedding, hurtled down from upper windows. Men and women staggered from cottages under the burden of tables, chairs, crude family portraits, saucepans, hardware, and anything else they could carry. Others piled the stuff into absurd mountainous heaps on frail handcarts and still frailer perambulators. Grandfather pulled in the shafts; grandmother and daughter pushed behind; granddaughter clung to mother's skirts as mother steadied the top-heavy pile.

FINDING A BILLET

'My God!' breathed Dalgith. 'The poor devils! This is what you call taking up your bed and walking with a vengeance.'

For their cry went up to Heaven. There was not one among their elders who did not talk, talk, talk, and go on talking, no matter what the task. They struggled with their burdens; they jammed together; their carts broke down or toppled over completely; but they never ceased talking. And their words poured out in the high pitched monotone of incipient hysteria.

Dalgith pushed on through the throng. It grew worse.

Then a six-inch gun began firing just outside the village, rending the night with its ear-splitting crack and spilling a momentary flood of yellow light. Men, women, children, houses, handcarts, all leapt into high relief and then fled back into darkness more intense by comparison. Chaos became tinged with panic.

Dalgith, now thoroughly alive to the situation, bawled in Warne's ear, saying that they must get out of the place: no billets there. 'The poor devils are half crazy—and will be wholly soon. They must have been lugged from their beds within the last few minutes and told to leg it.'

The gun fired again. A shrill wailing answered its bark.

'This,' roared Dalgith, 'is what you call confusion worse confounded,' and laughed.

A pace or two further on: 'Can you imagine it happening in England? Do some of the croakers and munition workers good, what?' Again the laugh, Warne heard it faintly, and then with revulsion. A man who could laugh when——

'Oh, my God!'

The exclamation fell from Dalgith's startled lips as the woman seized Warne. She threw her arms about his neck and shrieked at him. Her hair tumbled loose about her shoulders. Wild bulging eyes peered into his. Hot, unwholesome breath fanned his cheeks. And involuntarily he shrank from her as from a pestilence. Vainly he strove to thrust her away. But the white face pressed closer to his, mouthing its torrent of words. Dimly he gathered that he was expected to save her grandmother, her mother, herself, her daughter. He was helpless in her grasp. He felt himself being dragged away by this frenzied woman.

Wildly he called upon Dalgith. His voice was an answering shriek to the woman's.

A mighty bellow sounded in his ear. It said: 'Here, my beldame! Scat! Bunk! Hop it! Vamoose! Napoo! Finis!'

Much grunting. Came Dalgith's voice, strangely earnest: 'Lord, but the wench is strong!'

More grunting; a final heave, and Warne found himself free, saw Dalgith using brute force on the woman as he propelled her into the arms of a helpless and equally distracted old gendarme.

Dalgith was roaring: 'For Christ's sake get to hell out of this. Here, Rudolf! Take her. She's yours.'

A night of tragi-comedy, of which Warne saw only the tragedy. Because of that another nail was driven in the coffin of ambition.

(3)

Brigade Headquarters spent the night in Rouy-le-Petit, since Voyennes proved impossible. They spent it, too, just as they were, lying down on the floor of a small farm-house but lately repaired and made habitable. When they arrived both Madame and Monsieur were there, hastily crowding together a few portable belongings. She offered no objections to their presence. Like Warne she was beyond objecting to anything. She appeared not to see them. Only Monsieur did that, and he kept on touching his grey forelock and mumbling words they could not understand. They did not try.

Keeping up a high-pitched moan, ceaselessly wringing her hands, the old lady wandered to and fro between her couple of rooms, vainly endeavouring to decide what she could carry away, while her aged husband, decrepit and bent, loaded the handcart outside.

'Can't we gag her?' groaned Dalgith, and Warne groaned, too, though for a different reason.

Cheyne entered, walking like a man suffering from locomotor ataxia. Somehow he contrived to reach the opposite corner of the room, and then his knees appeared to sag. He subsided, rather than fell, as a flabby blancmange will subside in hot weather. He lay without moving, curiously twisted and huddled. With a shock Warne realized he was asleep.

Dalgith tore down the blind that shielded the solitary window, and tossed it to Warne, who watched him with a kind of stupefied horror. It crumpled up like a newspaper and rested against his legs.

'Do for a blanket, Padre,' Dalgith muttered, and stretched himself on the floor. He cushioned his head in his arm. He, too, was asleep.

A faint wheeze from O'Reilly: 'Use your haversack for a pillow, Padre. You'll be o' righ——'

Heavy breathing began to fill the tiny French living-room.

From the adjoining one came the continual swish of Madame's skirts and her unceasing moans.

The Colonel, rolled in his trench coat, said: 'Put out the candle when you're ready, Padre.'

And then Warne moved.

He looked round at his companions curled up on the floor, and saw them as so many weary animals seeking rest, indifferent alike to God, Man and the Devil. Two days 'in the line,' and it had come to this! Despairingly he asked himself what would be the end, and found no answer.

He glanced at his watch. The hour was nearly two-thirty. They were moving at dawn.

He blew out the candle and lay down, but he did not sleep. Had Bidderwill's pre-war tranquillity embraced him the cold hard bricks would have kept him awake. As it was, his entire consciousness fell little short of an emotional maelstrom.

If he changed his position once, he did so a hundred times, without securing the relief he sought. A temporary respite and then the cramped, hard pain somewhere else. Soon the cold penetrated into his very bones. . . .

Shortly after five he dozed off. Madame had gone by then. He had listened to the creak of the old handcart and the crunching of its wheels in the stones outside as she and her husband had moved off. The high-pitched moaning had grown fainter and fainter until it had died away altogether.

But he slept only to dream of God's creatures who were spread-eagled under gravity like spokes in a rimless wheel, and rained down from Heaven amid chariots of fire. They crashed about him. Ultimately one fell on him, and he started up with a cry.

FINDING A BILLET

O'Reilly said: 'Time to get up, Padre,' and straightened his back. 'Sleep well?'

He said this, but he saw at a glance that Warne had hardly slept at all. Those dark rings under the eyes. The whole strained expression. That start into wakefulness. . . .

'If you last out the course——' he speculated. 'But what the devil I'm to do with you I don't know.'

'Gets the hip if you're not used to it,' he said.

Warne managed a faint smile.

After that Warne became aware of many things. There was a candle burning in the room, and a wan light stealing through the blindless window. His companions were already up. Keller was shaving. The Colonel and Cheyne were busy over a map. Dalgith was talking to Bell about breakfast.

He became aware, too, of his own leaden heaviness, of a dull pain at the back of the eyes. He felt his brow. It was hot. Only with an effort he got to his feet. O'Reilly brought him some shaving water.

Dalgith, foraging, came upon eggs, and these they had for breakfast. Stiff limbs were stretched; circulation restored; hot tea swallowed. Morale shot up. And before the eggs were eaten, Dalgith was nodding at Warne and saying: 'The bad old man! Heard what he did last night. Got off with a wench!'

Keller guffawed,

'Yes. And if I hadn't been there to stop him he would have got off with her grandmother, her mother, herself, her daughter, her granddaughter, her great——'

Laughter drowned Dalgith who, with admirable solemnity, was counting off the generations on his fingers,

'The old Mormon!'

'But that is so, isn't it, Padre?' persisted Dalgith.

And to his own surprise Warne found himself accepting this untimely ribaldry as part of his new life, It did not pain him, as it would have done overnight. It did not even bore him. It just happened, like rain and sunshine.

He sought for a reply, and hesitated: 'Well—I—hardly——'

'There you are!' shrieked Dalgith triumphantly.

'He can't deny it. He pleads guilty to——'

The Colonel cut in, searching Warne with a glance. 'Come, Padre,' he laughed. 'What's behind all this?'

'Well, I——'

'Fell for a dame,' completed Dalgith.

More laughter, at the end of which Cheyne growled: 'Stow it, you infant.'

O'Reilly, looking at Cheyne, raised an eyebrow.

'I think,' stammered Warne, 'it would be more accurate to say she fell for me.'

'Oh, you naughty old Don Juan!' roared Dalgith.

'Unfrock him,' hooted Keller.

And when Warne gazed appealingly round they laughed the more.

'Take his pulse, Doc,' gurgled Dalgith.

'Perhaps I ought,' reflected O'Reilly.

After that they went out. A beaten army was fighting for its life.

(4)

That day the centre of the Fifth Army stayed the German advance on the banks of the Somme, and with one exception

FINDING A BILLET

Warne did not see his companions again until nightfall. The exception was Keller who arrived hurriedly about midday with Sergeant Dalton and a few signallers, and having extracted a couple of reels of telephone cable from the stores, ordered the '30 cwt' on to Manicourt.

'The old Hun got across at Canizy and Voyennes, but they've driven him back,' he said, and went off with his party.

So Warne clambered into the front seat of the '30 cwt' and took his place alongside the detested Bass; and although Manicourt was not far—barely four miles as the crow flies, and only a mile or two more by the circuitous route through the little town of Nesle which a blown-up bridge imposed—it is conceivable that with any other driver at the wheel he would have extracted some tiny grain of comfort from the journey on that gorgeous spring morning. But he found none. Instead, Bass's almost incessant chatter with its faintly disguised obscenities and its inhuman profanities, bade fair to drive him crazy. Bass, whose attention was held mainly by the road ahead, rarely glanced at him and therefore gabbled away without the slightest thought of the pain he was causing.

Then Nesle, with its cobbled square and irregular houses. It looked peaceful enough when the '30 cwt' drove through, though crowded with a heterogeneous collection of troops, non-combatant for the most part. There were base details of a dozen types, postal and railway formations and such-like, all rooted up from their cushy billets by the enemy's approach.

'Like a lot o' bleedin' sheep without a shepherd, Sir. Aren't they?' growled Bass.

Less than a minute later he was crying: 'Blimee! And by Christ they are!'

Even as sheep grazing in a field will suddenly bolt from a passing train in the direction of imagined safety, so were these khaki-clad civilians stampeded. A great confused noise rose behind the '30 cwt'. There were frantic shouts of warning, cries of 'Run! Run! Cavalry!'

Before Warne could so much as grasp what was happening, the lorry had become an island in a sea of bobbing helmets. Men stumbled, fell, were trampled on.

A General, resplendent in polished Sam Browne and patches, swept by. His arms were waving like flails and he was crying for his horse.

Bass stopped. He took the situation in at a glance and breathed a pregnant: 'Gawd!'

He swung about and opened the small trap in the screen behind his seat: 'Hi, Nobby! Any sign o' them cavalry?'

Warne grasped him by the arm, imploring him to drive on, but Bass appeared not to hear. 'Nobby,' he bawled.

Clark's round blank face framed itself in the trap as Clark himself sprawled across the top of the pile of stores.

'Don't see none,' he grunted. 'Whatcher make on it?'

'Reckon it's a scare, Nobby. Still, best keep those guns 'andy.'

'Yuh.'

The head was withdrawn. The trap closed. Bass started to drive slowly in the wake of the fleeing mob, and as if to register his supreme contempt he spat over the side and said: 'Scabs!'

The flight headed for the neighbouring township of Roye, but Manicourt lay to the north, and when the '30 cwt' came to the fork in the road Bass held on his course regardless of a well-meaning but half-panic-stricken military policeman who tried to shepherd him Roye-wards to safety with the rest.

FINDING A BILLET

'Garn, yer udder-faced rat,' he shouted. 'Whatcher take us for?'

The red-cap leapt from the path of the lorry.

'Bloody cosher,' Bass muttered, and spat again. 'To Maneecort yours truly was told to go, and to Maneecort yours truly is blinkin' well goin'. —— all 'Uns!'

And as the '30 cwt' bounded along the wide open road it bore away a white-faced trembling priest who was too frightened even to pray.

In the deserted ruin that was Manicourt Bass stopped and listened. The day was warm and windless. Sound travelled miles. Away to the east a steady cannonade betokened the battle for the Somme crossings. Somebody might have been thrashing a gigantic drum, so hollow and booming the reports came to ear. At times could be heard a distant rattling.

'Now I wonder,' murmured Bass reflectively, ''oo started that there mary-fon? Bloody 'Un ain't wivin miles o' 'ere.'

He scratched his head, but, no' solution offering itself, gave up the problem. He pulled out a pipe and settled down to a comfortable smoke. As he would have explained, had Warne asked him: 'Orders 'is orders.' No more was necessary. Bass's philosophy of his war-life needed no elaboration.

Warne, on the other hand, had, as yet, no philosophy— nothing except a vast loathing for the Godless man beside him; and with a violence that caused Bass to stare after him with a tolerant though uncomprehending amusement, he scrambled from his seat, and, head down, embarked upon one of those aimless wanderings, which start at a speed but little removed from a run and then slowly slacken to a child's dawdle as the turmoil of the spirit quietens and calms. For the dull heaviness of the early morning had increased to a throbbing ache, so that, after the jolt to his nerves administered in Nesle, he felt physically ill as well as sick at heart. And he scarcely saw the broken walls and grass-grown rubble by which his stumbling footsteps led him.

At times, too, he was torn by spasms of self-recrimination, during which he asked himself wildly for what purpose he had been mad enough to forsake his old life and plunge into this hell of blasphemous indifference. He raved to himself: 'By day I am tied to an ogre; by night to a coterie of pagans. Was it for this I left Bidderwill?'

And over all his thoughts fell the shadow: first the quarry; then that hurtling airman. Oh, God, would he ever forget the sight! Next those frenzied refugees in Voyennes. Now the . . .

Without even being aware that he had wandered round the circumference of a vast circle, he suddenly realized he was back by the '30 cwt'.

Bass, reclining by the roadside after a midday meal, saw him and nudged his mate. 'Nutty!' he said, and jerked his head significantly.

'Yuh.'

Clark eyed the unseeing Warne with a sidelong glance, and spat contemptuously.

'All same,' muttered Bass, 's'pose we must feed the bleeder.'

Because of that he went to the lorry and rummaged out a tin of Maconochie, prized open the lid with his jack-knife, and, having coaxed back to life the embers of the small fire they had made by the roadside, proceeded to heat the ration as best he could. In point of fact he tended it far more carefully than he had done his own half an hour earlier.

FINDING A BILLET

'Wash art that billy, Nobby. There's some more tea in that there bag. We'll make 'Is 'Oliness some fresh.'

Ten minutes later the pair were waiting diligently upon the man they affected to despise, and Bass was saying: ' 'Ave a bite 'o this, Sir. Soon putcher right, won't it, Nobby?'

Clark said: 'Yuh,' and spat.

'Sort'er gets yer darn, all this muckin' abart,' Bass airily explained.

And Warne, startled into shamed astonishment, endeavoured with many and halting phrases to thank them. Bass, however, deprecated the very idea of thanks, and retired abruptly.

So Warne sat on the lorry step and dug into that strange mixture of greasy rice and stringy flesh which passed in wartime as a Maconochie stew, and sipped at the hot strong tea; and between times he reflected that even his judgment of Bass was sadly amiss. Perhaps, he argued, it really would be better if he attempted nothing till—But when? . . .

For the greater part of the afternoon he sat without moving, huddled on the step of the '30 cwt', clasping his arms round his knees and staring with tragic eyes from a face of misery.

At first Bass watched him thoughtfully, and finally observed: 'Ol' Jesus is whatcher call konked art, ain't 'e? . . . 'e was that full o' beans too when I druv him up th' other night. Like an ol' bull when 'e niffs a bit o' cow.'

He shook his head. 'We'll 'ave to dose 'im wiv summat mor'n tea, Nobby.'

'Yuh.'

Clark spat. As an afterthought his slow-moving brain prompted: 'Find the ol' b—— a womun. Do 'im good.'

'Art!'

Bass's dark saturnine face lighted up. 'You bet! 'Member that bit in Ar-meens—just orf Charley's Bar by the c'thedral?'

'Yuh. 'Arf 'our wiv 'er——'

They forgot about Warne in bawdy reminiscence.

(5)

At sunset Dalgith drove up in the Ford, and almost immediately from the opposite direction came Keller, riding a Triumph motor-cycle. Their greetings were brief, perfunctory. To Warne they both appeared exhausted, but he was quite incurious: he was too depressed to bother about other people.

He overheard Dalgith: ' . . . Well, thank Heaven for that. We may at least get a drop of sleep to-night. That Nissen hut over there will do us fine.'

Then: 'Hullo, Padre! Everything O. K. You're looking rather seedy. Oh, George! Can you tap that Corps line? . . .'

The pair wandered off in conference, and Warne, gazing after them, experienced a sort of wistful indignation that started a train of thought of its own.

'*The wisdom of a learned man,*' he mused, '*cometh by opportunity of leisure; and he that hath little business shall become wise.* Can that possibly apply to me? Opportunity of leisure! Little business! Do I therefore become wise? Wise! Me wise!'

He dismissed the thought contemptuously.

Again: '*Be not curious in unnecessary matters; for more things are showed unto thee than men understand.* Including me!' he ironically reflected. 'I would to God I could understand

FINDING A BILLET

anything, let alone what others understand. One day I suppose I shall —when they notice my existence.'

Ten o'clock found them all gathered in that abandoned Nissen hut on the edge of Manicourt, squatting round on the hard bare boards, for it was stripped of furniture, and hungrily devouring the hot mass of beans—with their attendant quarter-inch cube of bacon fat which is the measure of the maker's veracity—that Bell had produced for supper; this with stale bread and hot tea. And it seemed to Warne that, for the first time since he had known them, these men, his brother officers, allowed themselves to relax. They were all tired, woefully so, and Cheyne kept nodding while he ate. They were dishevelled too. Their uniforms cried aloud for a clothes-brush. Their boots were caked with mud. They were still dominated by the situation, it is true, but all the same Warne had the queer fancy that if he could have removed all these outward trappings of circumstance he would have seen his companions for what they really were; and because he sensed this, because he felt in some obscure way that he was indeed one of the family, that he was, in fact, an outsider no longer, he rallied desperately lest the chance should slip by, and turned towards them a simulated normality which triumphed over burning eyes and aching head to such purpose that it bred an interest of its own.

They did not talk much. At first they were too busy eating. And the telephone, which Keller had rigged, interrupted with maddening insistence, so that time after time Cheyne would lean back and answer it, his spoonful of beans poised midway to his mouth; and Warne marvelled at the control he held over his voice.

So from the word dropped here and there he gathered much that he had not known; how the line had stood fast on the banks of the Somme and all that it meant to his own unit. He learned, too, that new guns, to replace those abandoned to the enemy, were already on the way; six were to be picked up in Roye on the morrow. Cheyne said it was pretty good going. Warne considered it a miracle of staff work and marvelled again.

But he learned of things less satisfactory as well; how Dalgith, searching for ammunition that evening in the car, had come across a convoy of lorries laden with officers' kits and mess gear, even to floor boards of Armstrong huts.

'Probably,' Dalgith murmured, 'another Siege Park!'

Then the telephone rang out again, and Cheyne having listened, interpolated a few odd words and replaced the receiver, casually announced: 'Gornall says that Butler's Corps are being pushed back to the south of Ham. Our flank may be in the air at any minute.'

And sensitive though he was to impressions, Warne could detect no change whatsoever in the psychic atmosphere as a result of the news. It remained aloof, detached, coldly matter-of-fact. He recalled that he had seen far more excitement over a weight-guessing competition for a currant cake at his Ladies' Guild. And beneath his own immense trepidations he was amazed.

'But where are all these French johnnies who were supposed to come up when the show started?' Keller suddenly queried.

Dalgith grinned: 'Some of 'em appear to have turned up in Nesle this morning. Grim business altogether, that.'

'You must have seen it all, Padre. Didn't you?' said Cheyne. 'Bass says the '30 cwt' got involved in the stampede.'

FINDING A BILLET

'Yes, I saw it,' Warne slowly answered. 'But what happened—?' It seemed funny that they should ask him this. If they had demanded to know where his heart had been during that five minutes of turmoil, he could have said with truth 'in his mouth,' for so it had seemed; but to say what those swirling helmets had betokened—no. 'Honestly,' he said, 'you know more about it than I do, for I don't even know what started it.'

'What started it!' Cheyne laughed shortly. 'A few French cavalrymen appeared as an advance-guard, and the sight of their light blue uniforms did the rest. A spy or two may have helped. That's all.'

'And then?'

'A sergeant and a few chaps went back and reoccupied the place. Sounds good, that—"reoccupied."'

'I saw a General——'

'Yes. We've heard about him. He'll probably hear about it too!'

Dalgith observed: 'There was all sorts of gubbins, kit and stuff, lying about the road on the Nesle side of Rethonvillers when I came back from Roye. They evidently believed in running light!'

'Not one of our more dignified episodes,' the Colonel dryly remarked, and the subject closed.

Half a minute later the telephone rang again, and as Cheyne picked up the receiver he muttered: 'If this goes on all night, George, there's going to be a curse on your head.' . . .

'Hallo! Yes, Cheyne speaking. . . . No, nothing further. . . . We'll let you know directly anything transpires. . . . No, we've heard nothing about any French division. . . . Absolutely nothing. Good night, Sir.'

He pushed the instrument away as if fearful that his tormentor might get in another burst. He groaned: 'I don't think Gornall understands English. Just the same the other night in Germaine. If I told him once about those two burnt-out caterpillars I told him fifty times. Now it's going to be news of the French.'

He looked helplessly at Dalgith.

'Right; I'll take it,' said Dalgith.

Within five minutes they were all rolled in their coats and blankets for the night, but before then O'Reilly had slipped across to Warne and, bending over him, had advised: 'Swallow a couple of these. Only aspirin. Make you sleep. There's a drop of tea left in this cup to wash 'em down with.'

Warne had taken them gratefully. Somehow there seemed more in the offer than mere aspirin. And finally he dozed off trying vainly to find the clue to the force that bound these five totally dissimilar men into one united whole. Could it be that he was about to be bound with them? His tired, aching brain throbbed with a last wild hope, and then he was asleep. This time not even the hardness of the boards or the continual ringing of the telephone bell could disturb him.

And so the night slipped by. Before the pale dawn had filtered into the hut Dalgith was answering the telephone in his sleep, waking up in the middle of a sentence and wondering what it was all about. For Keller had done his work all too well, and for the second time had given the Corps H. A. its one link with its command. With Cheyne, Dalgith groaned beneath the burden of fruitless reiteration.

Heavy-eyed, more weary, perhaps, than if he had not been lying down at all, he responded to Gornall's breakfast-time query by saying: 'Oh, not so bad, Sir. Bit tired, otherwise——'

He never finished. The handpiece was snatched from him, and it was Colonel Metcalfe who carried on.

'That you, Gornall? . . . Good. . . . Yes, we're perfectly all right. Quite fit. Ready for anything. Good morning.'

He tossed aside the handpiece. It fell with a clatter on the floor. He swung round upon Dalgith.

'Tired! What do you mean by it!' His voice rose to a shout. 'How dare you say we're tired?'

Dalgith quailed visibly. He stammered that he only meant——

'Never you dare say that again—to any one. You understand?'

'Yes, Sir.'

Then, on a lower and more kindly note: 'When the line is restored and stable you may be tired—not before. Don't forget.'

'No, Sir.'

Colonel Metcalfe turned back to the corner from where he had come. 'Bell brought that shaving water yet?'

Warne began to breathe again. 'Is this,' he wondered, 'the reason why Cheyne held out?'

(6)

Warne, who had risen that morning in part if not wholly refreshed, faced the day with a nervous exhilaration which foretold its own doom. Memories of the previous night, of his fancied reception into the bond of fellowship, still lived, and their child was renewed hope—born only to be dashed. For the barrier of the Somme gave. It was turned from the north and the south. And the ever-decreasing remnants of the Fifth Army were falling back once more. Briton and German were again moving slowly westward.

French Divisions hurrying up from the south, four days late, moved westward too, only faster, in spite of their encouraging protestations. Bearded French Generals kissed grimy British subalterns and cried, in effect: 'We are here. The retreat is over. The advance will now begin.'

But the following morning invariably found them several miles further west, for they had not the wherewithal for fighting. They arrived without ammunition, without artillery. They brought only the promise of a support they were unable to give.

To the survivors of Gough's Army, therefore, nothing remained but to hold on as best they could, and hold on they did, in spite of relentless assaults from fresh German Divisions, each one a trained exponent in the art of 'infiltration,' tactics so admirably suited to overcome the resistance of a long-drawn patchy line of exhausted troops. They held on, too—at least, the Headquarters of the 200th Brigade, Royal Garrison Artillery, did—to the Reverend Elliot Warne, and had he been the talisman of ultimate victory to the Allied Cause, they could not have guarded him more closely or kept him in greater safety.

So it came about that, after hours of complete neglect, he was peremptorily told that the line was giving and then bundled into the '30 cwt'.

And it always happened thus. Each day found him sitting alongside Bass, sitting there silent and miserable, a victim of stark disillusion, painfully conscious of his own supreme uselessness, and slowly drifting towards a state of mental inertia. And every evening found him waiting with a helpless resignation by the lorry, waiting there until Dalgith, or Keller, or the Doctor, or even Cheyne, should turn up and find him a meal. In these days he would have gone very hungry indeed had it not been for Bass.

FINDING A BILLET

And all the while he was aware of tremendous happenings going on so near at hand and yet so far away. He sensed that history was being made just beyond his reach, and he was not to see more than a brief occasional snatch, for nearer than the fringe of battle they never allowed him. Even so he grew accustomed to the sporadic booming of guns; he learned to recognize the impatient stutter of machine guns and the uneven crackle of rifle fire. But always these tokens of strife, rang out in the distance. Only at night, as a rule, did he encounter his brother officers, and as for his flock, he rarely saw them at all, and then only as a fleeing spectator.

Life for him, therefore, became and remained episodic, and by comparison, safe. The retreat of the Fifth Army fashioned itself before his eyes as a few vivid pictures cropping up here and there against a background of prosaic travel. When the pictures were revealed, he usually gaped, and not infrequently, was terrified as well. At other times, and because the power of coherent thought was gradually returning to him as the interval from the morning of the 21st lengthened, he reflected upon his position and was, naturally, utterly miserable,

Small wonder that in these days he developed the germ of an infinite sadness which ultimately choked even the fountains of ordinary speech. He grew silent; morosely silent, no longer because he had no one to speak to, but because he no longer wanted to talk.

The day that saw him leave Manicourt also saw a break in the weather. The temperature dropped. Clouds began to drive up from the west until, by the evening, rain had augmented the discomforts of the troops.

He spent a sleepless night of misery in a shed at Carrepuits, while the rain dripped through the roof upon him, and his companions, in utter exhaustion, flung themselves down on the rough dirt floor and slept for the few hours granted to them by a relentless enemy. In the morning he was hustled into the '30 cwt' again and packed off, and such was their preoccupation, they never even told him what was happening. All he managed to glean from their brief jerky talk was that the situation was becoming critical. The French were failing, were falling back without fighting. And he found no comfort in the knowledge.

A last look at the retreating lorry, and Dalgith turned to O'Reilly. He looked old, worn. His whole gait was limp. He said: 'God knows what's the matter with that parson. Sits there looking like a lump of death warmed up. And it's not as if he *does* anything. . . . My Christ, I only wish *I* could sit in a lorry and do————all day!'

'Like that, is it?' muttered O'Reilly.

In the late dusk of that same evening, as dismal and threatening as March could make it, Warne sheltered under the lee of a garden wall on the outskirts of Roye, and Cheyne, driving up in the Ford, was too tired even to think.

'This it?' he said, with a nod at the grey bulk of a house beyond the wall.

Warne started. 'You mean——'

The gesture, the faltering expostulation; it did not need them to tell Cheyne that work still lay before him. A second glance at the house had shown him the storm-rack through its gaping upper windows. The place was a shell.

Indignation flamed. He gave Warne one withering look. It wrung back an answering cry.

'But why, why didn't you tell me, Cheyne? Why——'

FINDING A BILLET

Cheyne, who had turned away, swung round. 'Tell you! Good God, man! Must I tell you that we've got to get some sort of roof over our heads unless we're going to sleep in a downpour. Where's your common sense? Where're your eyes? Only the other day you were howling for a job. There's one—staring you in the face. Find us a billet. You've damn-all to do all day but sit in a lorry.... Bass!'

'Sir!'

'Follow behind the Ford.'

'Yessir.'

How he climbed into the '30 cwt' Warne never knew. All he did know was that he had failed in the one trust left to him. His own words were flung back at him in derision by the man he would have given his right hand to serve.

That night he crept into a room away from the others.

Cheyne had selected a small but well-built house in the tiny 'residential' quarter of Roye. It might have been the home of a prosperous G.P. And there, in the quite modern living-room, his companions had stretched their weary bodies on the floor and pulled off their boots in unfeigned thankfulness.

The French, Warne gathered, had come in force at last. There was to be no more retreat. The Brigade were now under French orders, and were to retire only by the express command of French authority.

'Then for the love of Mike let's hope they put up a better show than they did this morning. Otherwise we shan't... get... much...' Dalgith was asleep.

It was then that Warne had stolen away, and the one memory of the scene which crowded out all others was that of a grey-haired, grey-moustached Colonel standing back to the empty grate, feet apart, hands clasped behind him, head sunk forward the merest trifle, and two fixed and gleaming eyes that saw everything and yet appeared to see nothing. For there was in the spectacle of this rock-like man, some hint of possibilities untapped, of iron determination and inflexible will only now coming into play, and it frightened Warne.

Afterwards, reaction setting in, Warne slept, just as he was except for his boots, on the bare floor of what had once been a maid's bedroom. And he was dreaming of a misty November morning in Bidderwill when O'Reilly shook him by the shoulder. He awakened then to find that the atmosphere of the room was choking, and he saw the beam from O'Reilly's torch cutting out a sharp-edged blue-grey cone in the quietly wreathing smoke.

He cried out, and scrambled up, coughing. O'Reilly took him by the arm and led him downstairs.

At the bottom O'Reilly remembered. 'Got your boots?'

No answer. He shone his torch down on to Warne's bootless feet. 'O'right,' he muttered. 'I'll get 'em.'

After that Warne abandoned himself to the swirling tide of events.

In the sitting-room where O'Reilly had left him, there were flames licking along the ceiling from above the chimney-piece. Bell, whose petrol had started the fire, and another servant were striving to get at the burning beam before the whole house caught. Dalton, the Signalling Sergeant, dashed in with a Pyrene. The fumes became almost unbearable. But they extinguished the flames and incidentally saved a perfectly good house for the Germans to live in and ultimately destroy.

And all the time on the far side of the room, indifferent alike to the smoke and the commotion, Colonel Metcalfe stood

FINDING A BILLET

with his Adjutant and quietly devised plans for extricating the remnants of his Brigade from the disaster which, because a French commander forgot his obligations, threatened to befall.

Three Despatch Riders came, saluted and went. Keller arrived, out of breath, and reported the '30 cwt' ready.

The Colonel nodded. 'Carry on. Wait for us beyond the town. If you lose touch with us, work north-west and report to the nearest British command—not the French.'

'Yes, Sir.'

Keller saluted.

In the passage outside Dalgith was shouting: 'Where's that blighted parson hidden himself?' And Warne heard Keller reply: 'In there—the office.'

The office! The word struck him as uproariously funny. He wanted to laugh, and would have done so had not Dalgith appeared and more or less pulled him away. Instead he mouthed words that Dalgith heard indistinctly and whose meaning he guessed.

'Matter!' he cried. 'The place is damn-nearly surrounded. Bloody French have pushed off without saying a word. That's what's the matter.'

New terrors engulfed Warne. The spectre of capture clutched him with icy fingers. He saw nothing then but the '30 cwt'. He scrambled up, panting. O'Reilly squeezed after him, muttering: 'I'd do my boots up if I were you, Padre.'

Boots! Office! Capture! ... Warne felt his self-control slipping. And then the '30 cwt' leapt into pulsating life. Dalgith stepped back and waved a hand. Keller was already ahead on his Triumph. Bass slammed in the gear. The '30 cwt' gave one bound forward. A minute later it was out of sight.

RETREAT

'Talk-a the bloomin' Fire Brigade!' chuckled Bass.

Dawn had broken with sunshine and clear skies, and soft friendly light filled the quaint old deserted streets. The rattle of a machine-gun rang out, alarmingly close. Keller signalled the lorry to come on. Bass opened the throttle still wider. It crossed the Square at a speed of nearly thirty. . . .

It was clear of Roye and waiting on the Montdidier road a good hour before the net closed completely round the little town and the Germans came through.

But Colonel Metcalfe and the portion of his Brigade that still survived had to be content with a far narrower margin, so narrow indeed that at one time it seemed as if the Germans must win. They had cut the road to Amiens, west of the town. They were creeping up from the south, and pushing in from the east. The way to Montdidier alone was clear, for the moment, and that ran to the south-west. Batteries on the Noyon road therefore had to dash north into Roye and then swing south-west on to the Montdidier road. It was the one way out and the race had to be run. But for the action of a lone French armoured car that sprayed the advancing Germans with its machine-guns while the batteries raced along this northward arm of their course, the result might have been very different.

And while this was going on, while Dalgith and Cheyne were shepherding the odd details and raking together some sort of covering party, on the other side of the town, to the west, Colonel Metcalfe was piloting four six-inch howitzers across a stretch of impossible ground. It survived as the Germans had left it in 1917. Returning civilians and those in Roye had looked at it and shunned it, and found other fields to cultivate. For it was intersected with deep and derelict trenches belonging to the old rear-line defences of 1915 and 1916; it was laced with belts of rusty barbed wire; it was pitted with craters and overgrown with rank vegetation. But the guns had to be taken across it. They could not go west to Amiens, and to go back into Roye meant risking capture from the north, certainly heavy sniping and probable destruction that way.

There were French cavalry, too, similarly cut off, unable to cross this devastated patch. They clung to the heels of the straining, sweating gunners who, inch by inch, and with incredible difficulty, edged their pieces to safety. And many a weary British soldier threw his audience a puzzled glance and wondered why he was left to hack his way through the tangle while a score of Frenchmen sat on their horses *and* never raised a finger to help him. But he laboured doggedly on without complaint, worn-out and hungry though he was, and it was only when he saw his way barred at the very moment safety seemed assured that his spirit faltered and cried out. A great ditch, or it might have been a sunken lane at one time, lay at his feet. He just sank down by his gun.

But within half a minute those same gunners were scattering through the wilderness. They ranged far and near. They bent their aching backs and ripped down baulks and pit-props from the old German dug-outs. Two of their number staggered under the burden of an uprooted telegraph pole. A party even worried along a huge tree trunk. They requisitioned anything that could possibly be employed to bridge that gulf, and they bridged it. And Colonel Metcalfe, standing aside again and searching the country to the north-east through his field-glasses, calculated that he would win through after all.

He nodded approval to the fat and genial Collett—genial still in spite of a week of almost continuous wakefulness—and watched the final adjustments being made to the bridge. It was a rough but solid affair, and he saw no reason why it should not carry the weight of the guns.

He also watched the French cavalry put their horses into the startled gunners and, brushing them aside, race across the bridge at the first moment of its completion, and he heard with sympathy the growl that went up from indignant men who stopped for a moment in order to stare after the retreating horsemen.

'I had an idea,' the Colonel mused, 'that these French reinforcements were supposed to help us.'

Collett, who was feeling a sudden and overwhelming relief, laughed. 'Well, they've certainly tested the bridge!'

'Yes, they've done that, as you say.'

The Colonel spoke absent-mindedly, as if his thoughts were elsewhere, but after a pause he became his normal authoritative self. 'You'll be all right now, Collett. I'll be moving along. You're quite clear about your route?'

'Quite, Sir.'

'Good morning.'

The Colonel scrambled down into the ditch and up the other side, and as he strode away he threw a last glance over his shoulder at the bridge. Two guns were already across. Another was being man-handled on it at the moment. The other stood waiting. It was well. But he wondered. The signs were not good. They were, in fact, ugly. He did not know, of course, that Marshal Petain had ordered the French troops to fall back on Paris, thereby creating the very gap Sir Douglas

Haig was striving to avoid, and that these same French troops were even then carrying out those orders. Nor did he know that he was being left in the gap created. He merely saw the immediate and deduced corollaries. And the immediate was that the line had for the moment ceased to exist. It had to be restored. But how? . . . He wondered again, many things. And at times he stumbled as he walked along, not because the ground was particularly rough, but because he had difficulty in finding sufficient strength to lift one foot in front of the other.

There were more French cavalry to the south-west of Roye, French armoured cars, and French transport pulled by mangy-looking horses yoked in dirty harness; and a French General and his Staff, splendidly immaculate in their sky-blue uniforms. There were British stragglers, too, pitiable objects who could scarcely drag themselves along. Some could not, and had sunk down by the roadside, indifferent to Fate. Others sagged beneath the weight of the rifles they still clung to. And because all these united to obstruct the passage of the '30 cwt', Keller halted nearer to Roye than he had intended. The decision meant a lot to Warne.

It was a beautiful morning. Roye lay less than a mile distant, a squat little town set in a flat expanse of fields. The sun shone mistily over a land in bud. And Warne, looking down the dead-straight, tree-lined road, suddenly thrilled in breathless ecstasy, so that he forgot himself, his sorrows, his shortcomings. He saw only the two sixty-pounders that were sweeping along towards him.

On they came, rattling and bumping, their drivers whipping up the lumbering hairies to a desperate canter. A quick wheel to the left, and the guns were ploughing deep ruts on the soft green turf of a roadside field. Crisp orders. Another wheel. The jingle of harness and the plodding of hoofs. The two guns were abreast. In a second the limbers were free and the horses' away. Lean tapering shells slammed home in the chambers. Breeches shut with a crash. The long grey barrels rose slightly and steadied. Flame, yellow and scorching, leapt from the muzzles. Smoke billowed out in a brown and filmy cloud. A double report, sharp and metallic, struck painfully against his ears. Fumes of cordite assailed him.

And then, amid the banging and the shouting, he beheld a fresh sight—one that roused in him an admiration almost fearful. Colonel Metcalfe was whipping up stragglers at the revolver's point. He might well have been some elemental fury let loose. He stormed and threatened. He caught men by the shoulder and with one seeming flick of his wrist sent them staggering into his growing parade. He kicked men into wakefulness. And beneath the lash of his tongue the exhausted, unshaven, grime-coated, hungry infantrymen, survivors from a dozen different battalions, squared their shoulders and straightened themselves into a couple of heart-wringing lines. And when they were fallen in, he continued to pace up and down before them, crouching a little as if he would spring upon the first man who moved. His blazing eyes swept the ranks from end to end. The point of his revolver punctuated his words.

'Soldiers!' he rasped, and his voice gradually rose in a stinging crescendo. 'You call yourselves soldiers. You're not. You're a rabble, I tell you. A rabble. But you're going to be soldiers. By God you are! And, by God I'll make you, if I have to shoot half of you to do it. You get that? You're soldiers—not a rabble. And you'll march like soldiers—not like a mob. You understand that?'

He paused. His eyes searched each man in turn. Slowly his revolver swung from one to the other. No one moved. A stillness seemed to have fallen on the whole battlefield.

The cold biting voice rang out again: 'And now you'll march down this road as the British Army marches. You get that? . . . Number!'

Hoarse noises rippled down the line, coming from throats that were equally parched with thirst and fear.

'Slope arms! . . . Form fours! . . . As you were! By God, you'll do that properly if I have to keep you here till the Germans are on top of us. Form fours!'

The movement went with some semblance of a click.

'That's better. Right turn! Quick march—and remember the eyes of the French are upon you.'

The little column of scarecrows marched stolidly away. The Colonel slipped his revolver back into its holster. For a minute he said nothing. He just supported himself against a tree, and watched the fruit of his labour—or rather, tried to watch it. Actually he found the whole scene would suddenly lose itself in a vast swimming mist, and then he would have to force himself to see.

'Cheyne,' he said, 'see that those men get some food from Carless.'

'Yes, Sir.'

Colonel Metcalfe went over to the barking sixty-pounders as if nothing untoward had occurred that morning or any other morning. And back on the front of the '30 cwt' O'Reilly muttered: 'Don't know how he does it, Padre. I suppose he has been to sleep since the show started, but *I've* never seen him. . . . I wonder what the old Hun could have thought if he chanced to be watching through a pair of field-glasses?'

And then the '30 cwt' started off, overtaking the little column of infantry; and that was all Fate vouchsafed Warne to see of the War that morning. Once again he found himself borne away to safety with the stores, and to-day the humiliation seemed more acute than usual.

(7)

That day the battle drifted across the old Somme trench-systems of 1915 and '16, and Colonel Metcalfe leisurely withdrew his tiny force down the Roye-Montdidier road, keeping just beyond effective rifle range of the advancing Germans but at the same time subjecting them to a fire so galling that they sent over an aeroplane and did their best to retaliate in kind. As a result he lost a six-inch howitzer, put out of action by a 'four-two' bursting alongside, and several more men. The fire of his other guns, however, went grimly on. As the Germans threatened to close the two foremost guns, he brought them back to a position behind the rearmost two, where they came into action again and remained until the process of leap-frogging had brought them to the front once more.

About noon, while on his way back from a hurried liaison with the Staff of a French Division then arriving at Etalfay, Dalgith surprised Warne sitting by the '30 cwt' as it waited in the shelter of Grivillers.

He looked as he felt, played out; sufficiently so to blind him to the state of others. He said: 'My God, I'm hungry.' And his

FINDING A BILLET

voice sounded husky with a sort of animal longing.

Warne did not so much as glance round. He answered: 'Bass may have some food in the lorry.'

For a moment Dalgith thought: 'And what *is* the matter with the old fool now?' And then, aloud, in a hoarse shout: 'Bass! . . . Clark!'

No answer.

He judged they were scrounging round somewhere, and turned back to Warne: 'Got anything in that haversack, Padre?'

The haversack lay by Warne's side on the grass, where he had put it to ease the burden on his shoulders, and Dalgith picked it up.

'Mind?'

'No. There should be some biscuits down the bottom.'

He sounded remote. He himself wondered idly whether it was his own voice answering. He paid no attention to Dalgith. He had none to spare. In spirit he was over by the spurts of smoke, white and fluffy in the sunlight, that betokened the creeping tide of the German advance, and he was thinking of what he had seen that morning. It wasn't war. Those tragic infantrymen. The Colonel . . . Newspapers never said anything of *this* side. In all his preliminary steeling he had never pictured men driven thus.

Dimly he heard Dalgith crunching away at an army biscuit, and then the casual off-hand observation: 'Nobby box you've got here, Padre. Silver, isn't it? Too good and not big enough to keep biscuits in.'

Nobby box! Keep biscuits in! Memory stirred. Those several words began to weave a pattern in his brain, to call him back to the present and link him with that pagan boy beside him.

With one hand Dalgith was idly fingering the pyx; with the other and nearer one he held the half-eaten portion of biscuit. And even as Warne swung round, he made to bite again.

A moan burst from Warne's lips. He struck at the lifted arm, knocking it down. The biscuit fell unheeded to the ground, and Dalgith recoiled in amazement, crying: 'Here! What the devil!'

He jumped to his feet, and Warne jumped too. They stood facing each other a couple of paces apart. Warne's helmet had fallen off. His hair, unbrushed since the previous morning, stood up in matted peaks. And in half-fearful bewilderment Dalgith stared at the working face, at the wild accusing eyes; and his own lips parted.

'Boy!'—the hoarse trembling thing that was Warne's voice rose to a pitiful cry—'You know not what you do!'

'Eh!' Then: 'Christ!'

For to Dalgith it seemed that a madman had leapt upon him, was beating upon his shoulders, clawing at him. And a spate of entreaty was breaking over him, urging him to his knees.

'Are you mad?' he cried, and retreated still further.

Warne followed, until a chance blow struck the pyx from Dalgith's protecting hand, and it fell with a clink on the hard metalled road. Then he stopped, and the frenzy slipped from him. . . .

There were tears in his eyes as he raised his hands in a last despairing appeal. For a moment his lips quivered. Faltering words hung uncertainly on their brink, and then, no longer able to be contained, welled out in all the fullness of a bleeding heart.

'*The body of Our Lord Jesus Christ which was given for thee, preserve thy body and soul into everlasting life. Take and eat this in remembrance that Christ died for thee, and feed on*——'

He did not finish. He saw that Dalgith had gone. And when, quite mechanically, he bent down to retrieve the pyx, he discovered that he had been standing on the other half of the biscuit—standing there, grinding it to a powder in the dust and grit of the road.

Not twenty yards away, behind the shelter of a broken wall, Bass leered knowingly at his mate. The pantomime was over. They had watched it with more interest than surprise, for it merely strengthened a growing conviction. Bass summarized it in that single look, when, inclining his head towards the unseeing Warne, he said: 'See 'ere, Nobby. Don't you ever dare come relid-jus.' And he solemnly tapped his brow.

'Yuh,' said Clark, and spat.

(8)

Not until the evening sun was throwing long shadows down the Roye-Montdidier road was Dalgith able to solve the riddle of Warne's behaviour. Early in the afternoon he had reported to Colonel Metcalfe the result of his visit to the French Divisional Headquarters. This was merely that the French Commander had expressed himself confident of holding the line of hills to the east of Montdidier against any attack. *'Mes braves chasseurs sont ici,'* Dalgith explained with a tired attempt at mimicry. 'And there they're going to remain—so he says.'

'He didn't say for how long, did he?' the Colonel had commented.

After that the variegated tide of battle had suddenly swirled about them, claiming their undivided attention so that they forgot themselves, their hunger, their fatigue, and thought only in terms of ammunition supply, fields of fire, and lines of retirement. They had, for the time being, given up all hope of advance.

So tea-time came, but no tea; and the long shadows of the trees made a trellis pattern in the golden light. And a stillness seemed to fall upon the battlefield itself. No one fired, Somewhere in the shelter of a skeleton wood to the left of the road a bird sang.

Along the road, heading for Roye, O'Reilly and Dalgith trudged side by side. Dalgith was the bearer of instructions to the leading section of guns, and had asked O'Reilly to go with him. Neither spoke at first, though for utterly different reasons. Both were tired out, leg-weary and weak, though here again with a difference. In comparison with Dalgith, O'Reilly was relatively fresh. But the splendour of the evening claimed Dalgith, transporting him to a time-mellowed manor on the Sussex Downs where in bygone years the trees and the sunlight had weaved the same pattern, spoken the same language—a language which his boyish subconsciousness recognized and understood. Only his aching body moved along the Roye-Montdidier road.

Not so the Doctor. He saw only the dusty road, the gaunt bare trees, and the roadside ditch—convenient cover if the Germans started shelling or sniping. He kept one eye on it. With the other, the link with his detached perceptions, he surveyed the world as it immediately affected him, but with a curiosity essentially languid and not even remotely acquisitive. Emotionally he was dead; incapable of responding to anything not directly physical. He preferred to look upon life from afar, explaining with a half-quizzical humour when taxed with the

FINDING A BILLET

apparent lethargy of his conduct: 'Never meet trouble half-way. Not worth the candle. It'll come soon enough without being met.' And yet he knew all the time that but for this fallacy he would have been, in 1914, something more than a rather bored possessor of a mediocre urban practice.

But if he preferred to look upon life from afar, life did not retaliate by passing him by altogether. Rather did it flow round him and then pass on. He was thus able, quite leisurely, to study it, to observe its strength and its weakness, its pitfalls and problems, and not infrequently its trend; and at odd times he pondered deeply and seriously about what *might* be done. On the border line of action, however, he baulked. Beyond lay trouble.

And therefore, because Dalgith did not speak and he himself had nothing particular to discuss, he thought quite a lot this evening. He thought about the prematurely grown-up youngster at his side; about that new parson fellow, wet as a scrubber if ever man was; about Cheyne and his cracking nerves. Bit of a mystery how the chap had pulled himself together in the last few days when he might well have been expected to cave in completely. Ought to rest before it's too late. But if he rests, thousands of others ought too.... After half a mile of silent trudging he gave it up.

'Topping evening,' he murmured.

Dalgith, from the Chanctonbury Ring, heard distantly. 'Eh!' he said. 'Oh, yes! Topping.'

The Doctor looked at him. 'Tired?'

There was gentle irony in the quite unnecessary question, but Dalgith was still on the Sussex Downs. 'A bit,' he answered.

'Think we shall pull out to-night?'

'Pull out,' he echoed, and the Sussex Downs receded. 'I suppose so. Corps say we do.'

'Corps, eh!'

'Yes, Corps.' The tone was irritable. 'Message from 'em to-day. First for a week, nearly. Or thereabouts. I don't know.'

'Like that, is it?' mused O'Reilly. Aloud: 'Seen the parson since this morning?'

And then Dalgith suddenly laughed. He laughed so raucously that O'Reilly asked him what the devil was the matter.

'Matter,' said Dalgith, the whole of his being now back on the Roye-Montdidier road, 'The parson. He's stark.'

'What, naked?'

'No, you fool. Mad. Raving mad.'

And Dalgith told him all that had occurred.

'Finished up by burbling something about the body of the Lord Jesus and my soul. God knows the connection between the two.'

'Shall I tell you'?'

'You?'

Dalgith peered quickly into the round red face beside him. He found two pig-like eyes regarding him merrily. He said, angrily: 'What the hell——'

Back came the breathy wheeze, its laughter hardly suppressed: 'No, no, Young-un. You've got it wrong. No devil in this. Merely the Holy Sacrament. You evidently began wolfing the bit reserved for the comfort of the dying—though I don't go much on an Army biscuit for that purpose—and he did the only thing he could think of, namely pronounce the necessary incantation over you. You've been in a choir. Surely you ought

FINDING A BILLET

to recognize a chunk of the Communion Service when you hear it?'

'Probably should—Merbecke's setting in F,' Dalgith muttered. Then: 'God's Teeth!'

They walked on, again in silence, each reviewing in his own peculiar light this latest prank of Fate, and they were almost level with their destination when a swelling drone told of an aeroplane's approach. Then Warne and his problem vanished as though it had never been.

The aeroplane was flying low. It looked like a hornet with the tail of a fish, a study in black and red and gleaming white. It buzzed over the heads of the startled gunners, and the 'tac-tac' of its machine gun betrayed its purpose clearly. A flight of bullets came hissing to earth by the tree where Dalgith had sheltered. Within a few yards of him a group of battery signallers cowered in a grass-grown derelict trench of 1916, and borrowing strength from he knew not where, he leapt down into the trench, yelling as he came.

'Shoot, you——! Shoot! For Christ's sake, shoot! Are you all mummified? Shoot back, blast you! Shoot!'

He kicked; he swore; he laid violent hands upon them. But he roused them. He grabbed a rifle himself and started shooting, and when the aeroplane returned on a second dive it was met with a determined though ineffective splutter of rifle fire. Within the space of seconds a nearby rattle told him that the battery Lewis-gun section had come into action.

After that the aeroplane did not venture within rifleshot again, but it began ranging a German battery, and soon there came the ominous tell-tale hiss of approaching howitzer shells. 'Four-twos' detonated in quick succession about the two guns.

Loose earth and stones came rattling down like hail. Then a new noise —the crack of shrapnel bursting in front of the battery. One, straying to the right, emptied its cargo of marble-sized balls of lead over the iron-hard road. They flew off at the oddest of angles and went bouncing in all directions. Several, on the ricochet, their force largely expended, struck O'Reilly stinging blows as he crouched behind a tree from the splinters of 'four-two.' He looked anxiously round for better protection. . . .

Before the guns had been hauled to the road and started on their way to safety, the blue-grey line of German skirmishers was spread across the countryside barely a couple of fields distant, and hastily aimed bullets were speeding the departure of the exhausted gunners.

Once clear of this sniping Collett drew Dalgith aside with a creditable simulation of gravity.

'Look here, young fellow! What do you think you mean by ordering my signallers about as if they were your own, eh? Damn sauce, what?'

But Collett's fat unshaven face split into a grin even as Dalgith searched it for a clue.

'No, I won't report you this time. Lucky you turned up when you did. Wood—he's the new boy—ought to have had them on to that 'plane, but he's still a bit lost, you know. Should turn out all right.'

'I understand,' said Dalgith. But he was thinking of Warne, not Wood.

(9)

By sundown the battle had cleared the zone of crumbling

earthworks and skeleton villages, and men were fighting in country unscarred by war, in fields under cultivation, among houses freshly abandoned by their inhabitants. The retreat had entered upon a new phase.

Night found the Brigade Headquarters grouped in a signalman's hut by the railway at Faverolles. French officers were there, too, from the Chasseur Division that day arrived to cover Montdidier, whom Dalgith had interviewed earlier on.

'If you go,' they said, with many and characteristic gestures of protest, 'we have no artillery. Montdidier falls.'

'Our orders,' replied Colonel Metcalfe, 'tell us to pull out tonight and proceed to the neighbourhood of Davenescourt at once.'

With pointing finger he traced out the fifteen-mile jump to the north, and the British area, that the orders meant.

Whereat the Frenchmen shrugged dapper and perfectly tailored shoulders and started their argument again.

Nevertheless the Brigade went.

'So that's that,' sighed Dalgith when the two Frenchmen had gone. 'Montdidier falls! Old Whiskered Willie has altered his tune since this morning. You ought to have heard him—and seen him. Slobbered like an old cat over these two birds when they took me in to see him. Kissed 'em on both cheeks and stroked 'em. And every one purred. But he shied off me though—like a stag. My bristled dewlap——'

He rambled on, almost inaudibly, rather like a man talking in his sleep, and with very little idea of what he was saying. Only Warne paid any attention. He alone was a spectator.

Dalgith looked as if he might sink to the floor at any moment and stay there, but when Colonel Metcalfe called his name, he jerked himself back to the present.

RETREAT

'Sir?'

'The column will leave as soon as ready. Route—Montdidier, Fontaine, Cantigny, Grivesnes and Aubvillers.'

The Colonel indicated the route on his map.

'I am going ahead with Cheyne. You will look after the column and see that the tail gets formed before it starts, otherwise you'll be strung half over France by daybreak.'

'Yes, Sir.'

When the Colonel had finished and the way was clear, Warne crept from his corner and laid a trembling hand on Dalgith's arm. 'I must come with you to-night. I *must*. You understand?'

Dalgith did not. Nor did he so much as guess at the complexity of forces which moved Warne to such insistence. And Warne himself knew only imperfectly. The fiasco of the Blessed Sacrament had entered too deeply into his soul. He could see nothing clearly. He knew only that he hated this pagan boy with a loathing that came near to being physical, and yet he was drawn to him as to a repentant sinner crying out for salvation.

'You hear me?' he whispered. 'I *must* come with you to-night,'

Strangely affected, Dalgith answered: 'Why, yes! Certainly—if you really want to.'

For a moment he wondered why on earth any man should want to give up the chance of a sleep on the front seat of a '30 cwt' lorry, but only for a moment. He was too tired to think. Also he was still young, and if bothering his head at all about life's riddles, was youthfully dogmatic, because the philosophy of War, in which he had been trained, is necessarily a selfish one. Based on the preservation of self, it ignores the spiritual responses of others. And so it was not until weeks had passed and Cheyne had attended to his education, that Dalgith appreciated the wild clutching hope of restoring, if only in part, a vanished self-esteem, for it was that which really impelled Warne to act as he did that night in Faverolles. Dalgith knew nothing at the time because nothing came of the action. Certainly Warne beheld his flock in various stages of exhaustion, but the sight of them so afflicted merely increased his misery because he could do nothing to lighten their burden. It led to no manifestation such as Dalgith would notice.

Under bleak and frigid stars that pointed a moonless slate-coloured sky, Warne hung on Dalgith's heels while Dalgith shepherded, encouraged and cursed weary men and weary drivers, and, without the curses, weary captains and weary subalterns. And thus, in the darkness, Warne beheld his flock toiling by, the lucky ones in lorries, the unlucky ones anyhow. Men stumbled along with dragging feet that had to be forced step by step. Men forged along like automata, like sleep-walkers, the mind holding the body subconsciously to its course. Every gun had its complement of men huddled grotesquely upon it, inert, sprawling, arms and legs hanging limp, dead to the world, like half-filled sacks carelessly flung. One fellow lay sound asleep along a six-inch draught pole, preserving his balance by an agency known to heaven but not to science.

'Here, Padre! Jump up.'

Dalgith pushed him unceremoniously into the seat alongside the driver of the rearmost lorry, and melted into the night towards the head of the column. They overtook him soon after they had started. He was standing in the road waiting for them, and with a gesture to the driver bidding him do no more than slow down, he half jumped, half fell on the front wing of the lorry. He rolled against the warm pulsating bonnet. His body slid down the curving mudguard until relaxing joints could bend no more. He settled there, a huddled heap of stained khaki. It slowly dawned upon Warne that the boy was asleep.

And thus the 200th Brigade, Royal Garrison Artillery, withdrew from the battle for a few hours. And thus, too, ended a day fateful in European history. For the gap between the two armies had been made, and the gap was widening with every mile the French withdrew on Paris. British troops had to close it, therefore, until Marshal Foch came along to overrule his compatriot. But the only British troops available were the exhausted remnants of Gough's maligned command, and *they* had to close the gap. Incidentally they were not by any means confined to Carey's collection of heroic oddments, as the politician would have one believe—erroneously on a second count, for Grant, not Carey, collected the force that fought at Marcelcave.

Into this gap, too, hurried the 200th Brigade, away from the French area into which they had been carried, and to this day there may be found survivors from the Brigade who, with twinkling eyes and prodigious solemnity, will repeat the words of those French Liaison Officers in Faverolles—'If you go, Montdidier falls'—and will add that the Germans entered the town early the following morning.

Comedy likewise marked their own dash to Davenescourt, though at the time it scarcely showed up in that light. For just beyond Montdidier, on the steep, hedge-lined and narrow road to Fontaine, the column overtook an obstruction looming vaguely large in the darkness. At once the foremost

FINDING A BILLET

lorry stopped, for double-banking in narrow roads was a sin punishable with bombing. The entire column therefore stopped.

Dalgith, who had gone to the head of the column as guide during a halt in Montdidier, just sank forward against the dash. Tansley of 679 gently canted sideways till his body rested on Dalgith's; his head rolled heavily on to Dalgith's shoulder. He broke into faint breathy snores. The driver merely collapsed over his wheel—dead to the world. And everybody in the other lorries not already asleep, fell off too.

In short the whole column slept, and only when Colonel Metcalfe, having returned hurriedly in the Ford seeking his missing Brigade, burst upon them in a storm of fury did they realise they had been sleeping for nigh upon two hours.

They discovered also that they had been waiting behind an empty farm-cart, abandoned by the roadside.

So, under this merciless castigation, the column came to life again, but when Colonel Metcalfe stamped furiously back to his car, he found both Cheyne and the driver fast asleep.

Because of this they did not reach Aubvillers until after 4 a.m.; and by the time they were ready to take up positions about Davenescourt, the Germans had arrived there first.

Later on, when the tide of war was flowing the other way, they laughed. Clucking merrily, the Colonel would murmur: 'Arm-chair critics are so apt to overlook the importance of the trivial in war.'

(10)

Another day had gone, another day of alternating gloom and watery sunshine, of hazardous adventure and inevitable retreat; and now, with approaching night, Warne entered the scattered hamlet of Mailly Raineval.

'That,' he astonished himself by thinking as he observed a trim little one-storied cottage from whose open door fed a bar of yellow light—'That will do for our billet.'

He had forgotten about Cheyne and the question of bidets, but now he saw heaven-sent opportunity, and clutched at it. He felt inordinately pleased. Whole vistas of unexpected triumph opened up. For the Brigade were still toiling down in the river valley, and he had the field to himself.

When the '30 cwt' had parked itself beneath the trees that lined an almost English-looking village green, he dismounted and strolled back, passing and repassing the cottage, eyeing it furtively and spying out its possibilities.

It looked attractive enough, as billets went in his brief experience, and cosy. Only there were people in it—old women who bustled about packing things, and children who, like their elders, chattered shrilly and were for ever calling down torrential rebuke by getting in the way. But every house in Mailly Raineval had its feminine complement, and the problem of taking over an occupied house was not to be avoided. He viewed it from a thousand angles, vainly seeking a solution; and the more he meditated, the more obsessed he became with the sense of his own impotence. But he rallied. He stared up at the darkling sky, and that bolstered up his courage. For raindrops, heavy and deliberate, the presage of downpour, splashed his face, and the black traceries of leafless branches swayed, creaking and rustling, across the leaden grey of the clouds. The wind moaned drearily.

Civilians or no civilians, he told himself, that cottage should shelter the Brigade Headquarters.

It did. The occupation, however, was hardly the triumph of vindication that his overwrought brain had imagined. Nor did he reap the gratitude which his good intentions had genuinely earned.

As Cheyne told him afterwards: 'On occasions like this, Padre, it's only the end that counts. It obscures the means which enable it to be reached. Only when there is no end do people bother about means, and good intentions. It's the old tag, of course—the paving on the road to hell.'

But, at the time, Warne was too alarmed and too distressed to see justification in Cheyne's methods of flagrant housebreaking; alarmed because every instinct bred and nurtured under years of police protection cried out against such action and conjured up the penalties; distressed on account of his own unavoidable participation in the affair and still more so on account of the brutality the episode revealed in a man to whom, in the space of a few days, he had become strangely attached. Then, too, there were the luckless women. A deplorable episode. And one for which he was logically responsible.

For after the Brigade arrived he led Cheyne—with some satisfaction, be it recorded—to the cottage, only to find its windows shuttered, its doors bolted, and all entrance barred. In mild dismay at this unforeseen circumstance, he knocked timidly, and nothing happened. With a sinking heart he knocked louder, and again nothing happened. In desperation he thumped, and still nothing happened. He had failed, as usual. There was no doubt to be entertained on that score. His billet had misfired like the damp squib. And feeling as if he would howl at any moment he turned helplessly to Cheyne.

Tired and wretched, Cheyne mumbled testily: 'You say you saw them inside when you arrived?'

'Yes. They were——'

'Then they must be there now.'

Cheyne paused, thinking. Warne continued to look miserably at him, condemned once more to the role of spectator. A sudden gust drove raindrops noisily against their steel helmets, drove others stingingly against their faces. Water streamed down their trench-coats. A damnable night.

Savagely Cheyne turned to the nearest shutter, and muttering: 'To hell with all this humbug!' shook it with violent hands.

The shutter gave slightly, creaked, and finally a piece came free with a report like a pistol shot. Cheyne staggered back, recovered himself, and advanced again. Affrighted little shrieks sounded from the room behind the broken shutter. Warne looked on aghast.

Cheyne shouted: 'Open that door. Quick. *Tout' suite.*'

Cries of '*Non! Non!*' began to predominate in the medley of noise that came from the bedroom.

Cheyne roared: '*La porte,* blast you! *Ouvrez* the bloody thing. *Tout' suite,* I tell you.'

Then, to the speechless Warne, in a sort of wailing-impotence: 'What the devil *is* that old cow trying to say?'

He attacked again, and this time gave the shutter a tug that threatened to tear out the entire window. The shrieking rose in muffled crescendo. Warne had a vision of cornered mice. But nothing coherent came to him, except the frenzied '*Non! Non!*'

'No, is it!' breathed Cheyne. 'We'll see about that. Madame!' he called. '*Je vous donne* one minute—*une minute—compris?—*

FINDING A BILLET

pour ouvrir la porte. See? . . . Oh hell! How the devil do I tell her I'll knock the bloody thing down if she won't?'

Warne could not assist. His face showed pale and strained in the darkness.'

'*Si vous ne* don't *pas* —oh hell!' Cheyne went on, '*je—je—je frappez la porte par la terre.*'—this in a roar of triumphant conclusion.

The squeaking stopped abruptly. Silence fell, broken only by the hiss of the rain. Warne wrung hands encased in sodden gloves.

Cheyne turned to him almost apologetically, saying; 'I don't think these birds realize that this is a battle area—that Jerry is only the other side of that potty little river, and they'd better leg it while they can. . . . Lord, what a night!'

He shook the water from his helmet and trench-coat much as a hairy retriever does when it leaps from a river to the bank.

'Minute's up, I think.'

Warne found his voice at last. 'You—you *can't*!'

But Cheyne appeared not to hear. He walked calmly to the still-unopened door, eyed his distance, gathered himself, and then delivered a kick with his heel that shivered the lower panel of the frail door from top to bottom.

It was opened before the next blow was necessary.

Maman stood there, candle in hand, a patch-work quilt about her shoulders. Two children clung to her nightdress, peering from the shelter of her bulk. Two other women, with four other children, cowered behind them, and all edged back as Cheyne stepped forward into the mean French living-room. Eyes that were wide with terror searched him, and there was in some of the elder ones a horror that roused in Warne a sense of blushing shame.

But Cheyne, standing there in all his staggering weariness, with water dripping from his helmet and draining from his coat into tiny pools on the brick floor—this Cheyne compelled his admiration.

'*Madame,*' said Cheyne, almost casually, '*votre chambre à coucher—c' est à vous. La salon ici*'—he swept his hand at the room—'*est pour les soldats. Comprenez?*'

Maman did, and nodded, slightly reassured.

'This,' Cheyne continued, producing a ten-franc note—the exchange was 26 to the pound sterling then—'*est pour la petite.*' And he pushed the note into the grubby hand of the nearest child.

For a moment *Maman* stared at Cheyne, thinking him mad; but only for a moment. Almost immediately she snatched the note from the child, saw it was good, palmed it tightly, and stared again.

Cheyne's last effort that night was the smile he contrived for *Maman*, but it set the crown on his work. Five minutes later *Maman* and company were bringing, unasked, blankets and petticoats and all manner of frowsty wrappings to keep warm these brutally benevolent warriors who despised her proffered beds and slept on the cold brick floor.

The household fled with the coming of day, and within forty-eight hours the village was a smoking ruin, blasted by shells from both sides.

CHAPTER V

LASTING THE COURSE

(1)

This incident at Mailly Raineval marked the end of Warne's determination to give expression to that urge to assist his companions which, a few days earlier, hours even, had been so painfully insistent; but it also marked the beginning of another and far more dangerous phase. Tattered nerves, rioting in a tired body, insufficiently controlled by a mind that failed to understand; the suffocating sense of failure bred of tumbled hopes and wrecked aspirations; a groping realization of his own supreme futility—all these began to play their part in framing his reactions to this world of anti-Christ and violence whither he had driven himself.

Driven himself! The knowledge was itself a torment.

At times he looked back upon his life, tracing it forward from that miraculous moment in later adolescence when he had first seen Christianity as a life-giving force, had savoured its idealism, its vitality, and its marvellous promise of hope; when he had first seen in God the sum-total of altruism as well as a personal saviour and a creative fount—from that moment he had been a willing slave to the priesthood, seeing his duty clear and rejoicing in his strength.

Then God had led him to Bidderwill and years of plenty.

RETREAT

He had given of his best, devoting himself without stint to furthering the happiness of others, repaying himself only with the harvest of a well-earned gratitude. So 1914 had dawned, and if suffragettes burned pillar-boxes and refused to eat in order to demonstrate their fitness to govern the country, and if men talked incessantly of Home Rule for Ireland and revolt in Ulster, they did none of these things in Bidderwill. Not until the War came tumbling from a clear sky to shatter his peace of mind, did the bright path of his future divide into a hundred tracks and lose itself in forbidding uncertainty. Daily then, he had sought for a line of action, and had prayed for guidance. But every night when he took his candle, left day in and day out in the one spot reserved for it on the Queen Anne chest in the hall, and mounted the old oak stairs to his raftered bedroom in that beloved rectory—every night was the same torment of indecision; for, although the interpretation of his duty to which he most inclined definitely bound him to his people in this hour of their trial, no less urgent were the importunings of an outraged manhood which ever told him that Bidderwill was no place for a *man* when the country's youth and his own parishioners were flocking to the colours. Soldiers, as well as civilians, stood in need of spiritual consolation, and his place was over there, in France.

Thirty-eight and single. Not young for soldiering but certainly not too old. And there were no compassionate ties. But to join up in any capacity, to go abroad and look with his own eyes on War's bloody harvest—a thousand times he had told himself that he could never do it. With a sort of disgusted loathing of himself he knew at the time that he could not. In those days he recoiled from intimate experience of War in sheer imaginative horror. He shrank from this orgy of slaughter—then, of course, barely begun, and insignificant beside its later dimensions—as from something obscene and foul. And the knowledge of this cowardice had been unceasing torture.

Then he had taken to dreaming, and with mouth parched and gaping, with beads of sweat bedewing his brow, he would start into wakefulness from some hideous nightmare which had planted him down in a foreign field where men fought and fell and died, while he stood by in the grip of his own terror, powerless to stop, to tend or to comfort.

And, as the months dragged by, he had watched the hand of death reach out to his own parish and he had been able to do nothing while it snatched away precious lives he had tended these last six years. Then had bereaved mothers and wives cursed the God whose word he had brought them—the God, so he had told them, of Love, of Charity, of Peace. And he had not known what to do.

So he had gone. For three terrible years he had fought with himself, conquered, and driven himself to France—for what? Wildly he asked himself the question as he surveyed his present lot. Was it for *this* that he had come?

'Kill me, oh God!' he prayed. 'But never let them say I am—unwanted.'

(2)

Curiously enough the day after this prayer wrung itself from his heart, they found him a job which he could, and did for a time, accomplish with success, although its nature was such that the very core of his pride fluttered in protest. Twice a day he nursed bottles of milk extracted from straying cows which Bell had herded together, shaking them until a buttery cream had formed. And they laughingly called him O.C. Dairy until, one morning, he could stomach his fancied degradation no longer. Then he flung the bottle away. The splinter of glass on the brick floor of the cottage where he was, brought Bell hurrying to the room. Bell, however, stopped short on the threshold when he saw a frenzied man kicking fragments of bottle into the uttermost corners of the room. A glance, and he quietly withdrew in search of O'Reilly.

To his particular crony, the Colonel's groom, he subsequently confided his opinion that the Bishop was batchy, with many and eloquent gestures explaining: 'There was the cow juice all over the floor, and him a-laying into the bits of the bottle as they might-a been footballs. Reckon he's daft, Corp., dontcher?'

Corporal Demellweek winked knowingly. 'You just ax Pincher Bass and Nobby 'bout that. Get ol' Pincher ter tell yer 'ow 'is 'Oliness went for 'Is Majesty's Lef-tenant John Ollyfant Dalgith that day Fritzy turfed us out-a Roye. Pukka dust-up it were, and 'Oly Joe a-screaming like one o' them hyenas yer get in Injer.'

'Garn!'

''Onest ter God, Gussy.'

Bell departed in wide-eyed wonder. Corporal Demellweek also, only he went with the set purpose of disseminating this latest exploit of his entertaining chaplain.

But the incident did far more than provide a tit-bit for the delectation of a few weary soldiers: it forced realization upon O'Reilly, compelling him to admit to himself that the period during which he could stand comfortably by and do nothing was drawing rapidly to a close; and beneath the quick breath he drew at the sight of the trampled pool of milk, the scattered glass, and, more particularly, Warne himself, he cursed the priest for thrusting upon him what he regarded as an extra burden.

'Why,' he fumed, 'must he worry *me*? And what the devil is the matter with him?'

But the further sight of the crumpled body sagging in a chair, of the hand and arm hanging limp so that the knuckles rested in the splash of milk, of the haunting expression of unutterable misery in the deep-set staring eyes—this sight wrung pity.

He shook Warne by the shoulder, and not unkindly his wheezy voice rapped out: 'What's the matter now, Warne? Come on. Cough it up.'

He stood back, his brow puckering in great rolls, his bushy eyebrows drawing together in a line. He stroked his chin. But Warne gave him one look, implacably hostile and yet strangely pleading.

'In Christ's name,' O'Reilly wondered, 'what does he mean by that?' Then aloud, after a pause: 'Come on, Warne. Tell me, what *is* upsetting you?'

For answer a gesture which plainly told him to go.

'God blast the fool,' groaned O'Reilly, and turned impatiently away. 'I'm damned if I know what to make of you.'

By the door he stopped and turned round for another look. Warne had given way altogether. His face was hidden in cupped hands. O'Reilly wondered why on earth the man had ever come to France. What had he expected to find? A paradise for parsons? A place more unlike one he found it difficult to conceive.

Sunlight fell in a golden bar across the gloomy cottage-parlour. It was, O'Reilly thought, the only cheerful thing in the place. Why couldn't this fool of a parson get out into it, muck around and do something, instead of acting like an over-sexed schoolgirl in later adolescence? ... He gave it up.

Adjusting his helmet, he stood for a minute in the shelter of the doorway and appraised the situation so far as it concerned himself. Away to the east, just beyond the village, the Germans were striving to force the passage of the Avre. The air throbbed with gunfire. That he did not mind, but he looked anxiously at the eddying smoke-bursts which continually rose above the tops of the cottages opposite, across the road. 'For those shells were obviously meant for the village, Rouvrel, and only the faulty aiming of the German gunners spared him a remarkably unpleasant morning. He was thankful. Then a splinter came whining over and struck the roof above him a sharp rap, and he gave a little shiver at the thought that it might have hit him. Without waiting to see if anything further came over, he put his head down and ambled off towards his tiny aid-post at the end of the village. He had forgotten Warne.

But half-way there he was surprised by the sound of running footfalls, and looking round he was still more surprised to see Warne, bareheaded and wild of eye, rapidly overtaking him.

'You!' he muttered. 'What do you want?'

They stood facing each other in the deserted village, street, between the rows of ill-kept wattle-and-daub cottages, unsavoury middens and stagnant gutters. There was little wind. The whitened walls gleamed and flung back the heat, so that the place smelt warm and fetid. There were fumes of explosive too.

'I'm coming with you.'

'You're not.'

The tone was impatient, rudely so.

Warne said: 'But I must——'

'You get back to the cottage.'

O'Reilly seized Warne by the arm and spun him round. 'You hear? Get back to the cottage, and the next time you come out you wear a gas-mask. Understand?'

More running footsteps. Both turned to see a small bespectacled R.A.M.C. orderly panting breathlessly behind them.

'It's Docwra, Sir,' he stuttered. 'They've just brought him in. Shell-shock, Sir. Clean off his head, Sir. Keeps on shouting that Mr. Dalgith's killed, Sir.'

'O'right, Redley. You get back. I'm coming.'

'Yes, Sir.'

Redley trotted away. Warne caught at O'Reilly's sleeve.

'Dalgith! He said he was——'

'Yes, yes. I heard all that. Now do be a good fellow and do as I tell you. Get back to the cottage. I've got work to do.'

'But haven't *I* any?'

'God knows. I don't. But if you have, for God's sake go and do it, and don't get in the way.'

O'Reilly strode off, leaving Warne rooted to the spot, staring after him, and Warne did not move until a tearing, rending crash followed by a clatter of falling debris warned him of his position. Then he turned slowly round and wandered back to the cottage. For he did not seem to be able to think. Dimly he appreciated that he had been repelled, brusquely thrust aside as being in the way, but that was secondary to the curious feeling of utter emptiness which represented his reaction to the news that Dalgith had been killed. Somehow he had never looked upon Death as an instrument capable of stealing away these men about him. Was it possible that he would have to sit by and watch them disappear one by one, and conjecture who would be the next to go? Perhaps himself. Who could tell?

He felt strangely cold. He remembered seeing a burly young subaltern sit down and howl when it came to the point of returning from leave ... Dalgith was dead.

(3)

During the early part of the afternoon he went out, being unable to endure any longer the solitude of that deserted room. With the exception of Bell, who came in at noon with a slice of bully, two biscuits and a mug of tea, no one had been near him since O'Reilly had left. His nerves, indeed, were so much on edge that only with the greatest difficulty he stopped himself from screaming.

Outside the cottage he stared about him for a moment. The firing had long since died down in the east, though it had not ceased altogether. A few men, British and French troops, were gathered at the end of the street, idly watching the battle front. Then he recognized O'Reilly's comfortable bulk sauntering towards him, and the sight roused him to decision. He turned towards the west.

Only when he was clear of the village did he become aware that he had been running, and the discovery touched a gentle spring of sardonic humour, bidding him laugh at himself for the fool he was. But the mood was transient. It passed quickly, and there remained no comforting offset to his sense of appalling frustration and failure. Let him hide himself away with his God —if He could be found.

Once his rioting thoughts plunged down upon the morning's battle. He dismissed it as a prelude to further retreat, and asked himself why he had ever left Bidderwill.

And so, entirely without any idea of the direction in which his stumbling footsteps were leading him, he wandered over the crest of the high ground that separates the Avre from the Noye, and dropped downhill into Dommartin. There was magic in the air that afternoon. The glory of the Spring was bursting from the woods and the hedgerows. There were birds singing in the soft warm sunshine. But they were not for him. He was deaf to the call. He sought only rest, and peace.

Beyond the river he started climbing the ridge, but he found himself suddenly engulfed in a swirling tide of refugees of the kind he had seen at Voyennes, all struggling uphill with their preposterously-laden handcarts and perambulators. He could not go on. He had to stop and take in the pitiful sight, though it wrung his heart to do so. But horror tinged his emotion when his burning ears finally tuned themselves to the moaning cries of the half-crazy peasants. For old men and older women paused as they passed him just long enough to vent '*Anglais no bon. Anglais no bon.*' And the reproach was terrible.

Finally a wizened hag in rent and dirty black hobbled frantically aside from her precious perambulator, and, shaking her fist in his face, called down vengeance upon the race that had thus abandoned them to the invader. The colour fled from his face, pale though it was already. Pain leapt to his staring eyes. Then indignation. He, an Englishman in the uniform of his country—that he should be held up to execration by the people his country was pouring out its life-blood to save—for whom Dalgith had died.... The witch-like figure of the old women suddenly dissolved in swimming mists.

There were shrill cries which struck through to his brain, stunning him so that he heard them indistinctly. He sensed rather than felt the wild dragging clutches of alien hands. The sunlight was gone, blotted out by a gnarled and knotted forest of waving arms. No longer the sweet air of the Spring. The unsavoury reek of French peasantry filled his nostrils. Faces took shape before him, mouthed horribly for a moment, and then vanished in the swirl. Dimly he knew that he was shouting, striking, beating helplessly against the throng. The pressure grew. A stick clanged on his helmet. Another blow knocked it over his eyes and it fell to the ground. He threw up his hands to protect his head as a woman's hands clawed through his hair. Rough fingernails ploughed furrows down one cheek. Blood started in the wake. Somebody kicked him. He lost his balance. They were dragging him down. He was sinking in a turbulent sea of malodorous black skirts and foul corduroys. He was vaguely conscious of stamping blows. Soon, he knew, he would be suffocated. Noise filled his ears. Dust choked him. A trumpeting mingled with the cries.

And then the sea ebbed suddenly, and strong hands jerked him to his feet while a boyish voice asked cheerfully whether he was hurt. And he, catching together his straggling senses, found himself in the arms of a subaltern. In front of him a dozen sturdy British soldiers were jockeying the crowd away, pressing them back with their rifles. Warne could have wept with relief. Behind him a convoy of lorries was hooting furiously.

Warne said: 'Thank God!' and sank limply against his rescuer. But he pulled himself together again immediately, and the subaltern, relieved of the weight, said: 'All right now?' and then lightly added: 'They weren't half laying about you, Padre, when we came up. What started it?'

But ere Warne could answer, the subaltern turned to his men. 'Shove those wheelbarrows and handcarts into the ditch there. Never mind that old witch.' (Warne recognized with something of a shock the aged woman who had first shaken her fist in his face.) 'Shove her in, too, if she won't budge. These blighters buy up all the road, Padre, don't they? Look at that Pickford's pantechnicon over there! We'll never get by it. Stand round that wagon, lads.'

Warne laughed, a queer crackling thing that caused the subaltern to look back from the wagon with a quick glance. But the subaltern had no time for casual study in psychology. A donkey had taken fright. It was squealing and plunging. Pandemonium, for a moment stilled, was breaking out again.

'*Anglais no bon!*'

The cry went up, relentless, accusing. Warne thought of that night in Mailly Raineval when Cheyne had procured his billet.

'*Anglais no bon*, is it?' breathed the subaltern. Then: 'Hi! You on the lorry! . . .'

He casually turned back to Warne. 'There's too much of this no-bon business, Padre. Do you know they've poured paraffin into most of the wells round here—these people here, our noble allies?. We'll give them something to no-bon about.' And with a smile of grim satisfaction he watched a platoon of men busy themselves on the wretched collection of vehicles, and particularly upon the lumbering over-laden wagon. In a trice they had unharnessed the pathetic, cruelly overworked horse.

RETREAT

Within a minute the wagon was lying on its side in the ditch. Within five minutes the road was clear.

The subaltern's company-commander, who had strolled up from the convoy to ascertain exactly what was happening, said: 'Better let us take you along for a bit—clear of these.'

He nodded towards the stricken refugees.

And so Warne sat on the front of a lorry as far as the eastern side of Dommartin, and then, after hesitatingly thanking his rescuers, he walked slowly back over the ridge towards Rouvrel. His thoughts were a tumult. Nor could he entirely rid himself of that reproachful wailing, *Anglais no bon! Anglais no bon!* It seemed to weave itself into the rhythm of his very footsteps.

But he had not gone half a mile when he encountered more refugees, the belated ones, few in number and scattered. And there were British soldiers with them, all wounded, some so badly that Warne could only wonder how they contrived to walk. Their bloody rags stood out as an accusation against him. He stopped. They trooped slowly by without so much as a glance, for, whatever their hurt, they were doing their best to help others. One, whose head was roughly bound with a shell dressing, still carried his rifle, unusual with a wounded man; but he also carried, on the other shoulder, a pale-faced, frightened kiddie. Several were pushing at the handcarts.

Their silence was itself a reproach.

So they tottered by and were gone, leaving Warne standing by the roadside staring after them, motionless, inexpressibly sad. Till at last a gun boomed loutishly in the distance and called to him, and then he turned, and with bowed head started again for Rouvrel. This time his footsteps lagged more than ever. He was conscious, too, that his cheek was smarting, but physical pain was a distraction to be welcomed rather than avoided during that forty-minute journey.

(4)

Dalgith met him in the doorway of the cottage, and he gasped out: 'Dalgith! You!'

But Dalgith's nerves were also on edge, for that day Dalgith had seen the base of a German 'five-nine' imperfectly guillotine a Frenchman talking to his orderly, a sight which had driven his orderly screaming and raving into the German barrage, shell-shocked out of his senses. After that Dalgith had lain with a half-hundred French riflemen along the edge of a burgeoning copse, while shells shrieked and tore in the trees above them, lopping off whole branches and taking steady toll of the unprotected men beneath. For two galling hours he and they had waited for the barrage to lift and the Germans to come, and he had counted minutes as he peered through the eddying smoke in vain endeavour to glimpse the German lines and ascertain their secret.

Once a cow, mad with fright, charged blindly past the copse, bellowing and foaming at the mouth as it went.

And finally the Germans had come, and *le bon Dieu Boche* had relented, blowing aside the smoke with sudden gusts and revealing the blue-grey line of attackers sweeping down upon them. A deep 'Aah!' of relief broke from the prone French riflemen. A score of weapons levelled and steadied as dirty unshaven cheeks pressed against their stocks. The French Captain, almost incoherent with excitement, shouted, bidding them wait for the word and hold their fire.

Next a mighty rushing overhead, a confused banging in the rear quite distinct from the roar of the German guns, and within the space of seconds the slope opposite the copse, down which the Germans were pressing, was dancing with the splashes of shell-bursts. The 'seventy-fives' had found a target. Exultant shouts rose from parched and cracking throats. . . .

The attack was blotted out.

Because of this, and other things that followed, Dalgith retorted irritably and without understanding in the least what Warne was driving at. 'Yes. It's me. Think it's m'ghost?'

Warne was taken aback. Apologetically he explained: 'They said you were dead.'

'Huh. You're not disappointed, I hope?'

'Don't, Dalgith! Don't! I——'

But Dalgith interrupted. He had noticed Warne's dishevelled clothes, the dust, the tiny clots of dried blood marking four parallel lines down one cheek. Curiosity awoke.

'I'd get some iodine on that face if I were you.'

He laughed shortly and went into the cottage, and Warne, following, overheard him sarcastically observe: ''Nother casualty for you, Doc. The parson!'

The mean, ill-lighted French living-room, with its round black stove and right-angled pipe, its dark boarded walls and smoke-blackened ceiling, stood in gloomy contrast to the mellow sunshine outside, but the spectacle which met Warne's astonished eyes leapt out vividly enough and quelled the dull anger which Dalgith's rudeness had aroused. For Cheyne was lying back on the table, his hands locked beneath his head for a pillow, and a medical orderly was standing by with a steaming bowl into which O'Reilly dipped from time to time as, puffing and wheezing, he dabbed and sponged away at a bloody thigh with cleansing wads of cotton-wool.

Without stopping his work, O'Reilly gave Warne a quick, searching look and dismissed him from mind. The fellow could wait.

Nervously Warne tapped at Dalgith's arm, and when Dalgith turned impatiently upon him, he whispered: 'Is he—bad?'

Dalgith groaned. Warne caught words which sounded like: 'Oh, my God!' And then Dalgith swung away to a nearby chair and dropped heavily on it, allowing his whole body to relax.

O'Reilly, dabbing away at Cheyne's thigh, tossed off-hand advice. 'Get a pull at a whisky bottle.'

Dalgith looked up sideways, scornfully. 'Whisky! Don't know where you think you'll get it.'

'Strong tea, then. Just as good.'

Dalgith muttered: 'I think I will,' and went out, passing within a foot of Warne but never giving him so much as a glance. Half a minute later Warne heard him shouting for Bell and tea, and then a silence fell in the gloomy parlour, a silence broken only by the Doctor's heavy breathing and the tiny splash of water in the bowl as the swabs were extracted. Cheyne lay quite still. He might have been dead, but that his eyes were open and moved occasionally.

Fascinated and fearful, Warne stood by and watched, and felt at the same time utterly useless. Was there, he asked himself, anything that he *could* do? He sought vainly for an answer, for he would not admit the negative.

At last O'Reilly called for dressings, and then Warne beheld a pair of clumsy-looking podgy hands binding up the wound with a deft swiftness that was little short of the incredible. He thought, with bitter amusement, of his own first-aid classes at Bidderwill.

When he had finished O'Reilly stepped back and wiped his hands on a towel. He eyed Cheyne professionally. 'Feeling all right?'

Cheyne stirred. He spoke for the first time since Warne had entered the room. He might have been speaking from a trance, so flat and lifeless was his voice. It said, indifferently: 'Not so bad. Head's pretty foul.'

'That's the crack on your skull, of course.'

O'Reilly finished wiping and tossed the towel to Redley. 'I'll get you sent on to Amiens right away. They'll be able to evacuate you from there.'

'You won't!'

Almost savagely Cheyne flung back the words. He raised himself on one elbow and fairly glared at O'Reilly.

'If you think you're going to send me to England, Doc, you can bloody well think again, and that's all about it.'

His voice trailed off as he sank back on the table.

O'Reilly laughed quietly, grimly. 'We'll see about that.'

'We will.'

Cheyne flared again. 'We will, by God! You let Maclachlan stay when he was far worse than I am, and now you'll let me.'

Whereat O'Reilly laughed again, still more shortly, and, ignoring Cheyne, told Redley to clear a space for a stretcher on top of the stores in the '30 cwt'.

This done, to Cheyne he returned: 'Barely a week ago, my lad, I seem to remember hearing you pray for a Blighty touch—implying that if you got one we shouldn't see you for dust. What about that?'

No answer.

Instead, a silence—sullen and defiant, telling of two wills in conflict. And the scene appeared to change. Every detail of that morning in Germaine came flooding back to Warne. He saw yet again the huddled form of this worn-out young man as it rested there, sunk on a chair, each hand gripping a knee while the trunk rocked gently to and fro. He detected again the utter weariness that hid in the cry which said: 'Give me Maclachlan's chance and see if I'd stay!' And he recalled that when he himself had told his purpose in coming, Cheyne had laughed....

Three men came in with a stretcher. They lifted Cheyne on to it and took him away.

O'Reilly finished lighting a pipe, sucked reflectively and watched. As the party slowly edged through the door, he remarked, as much to himself as to Warne:

'Queer sort of cuss. A queer sort, but a good one. Doesn't talk much. Gets on with the job instead. Got a bit of a past, I should say. Quite well read when you get him going. Been abroad for some years—Fiji or somewhere similarly God-forsaken. Came over in 1914 and joined up in the ranks.'

He stopped. Warne said: 'Yes.' There seemed nothing else for him to say. He could only think of his own war record.

O'Reilly went on, ruminating aloud. 'Ought to send him home, of course—but... Thigh's nothing—mere scratch.... But his nerves are——'

He suddenly remembered Warne, and lowered his pipe. 'Let me look at that face of yours, Padre. Come over by the window.... Hm! Looks like somebody's finger-nails.'

He glanced curiously at Warne. Their eyes met.

Warne said: 'You're right.' It was beyond him to dissemble, even to hide his shame.

'What happened?'

Warne told him, speaking in a voice so low that O'Reilly was hard put to catch the words, and all the time staring from the window at the strip of blue above the roof tops.

O'Reilly did not interrupt. He understood. That young fool Dalgith and the business with the biscuit; the events that preceded it in Roye; a dozen and one episodes hitherto deemed insignificant began to arrange themselves, and the sequence pointed to a possible explanation. Mentally he drew a breath. And when the pathetic recital came to an end, he offered no comment. He muttered: 'This stuff may sting,' and dabbed strong iodine on the furrows that scarred Warne's cheek.

Warne gave a tiny gasp, said: 'Thank you,' and turned away.

O'Reilly thought: 'Poor devil!' and pitied him. He made to offer sympathy, but Dalgith appeared in the doorway and said that the '30 cwt' was ready to move off, adding: 'You'd better go with it as well, Padre.'

So they went, driving off through the mellow evening sunlight while Dalgith remained behind in the cottage to await his Colonel. And it chanced that as he settled himself and loosened his Sam Browne for comfort, the thumb of his right hand slipped into that small 'ticket' pocket normally hidden by the belt. He felt something, hard, irregular. Wondering, he drew it forth. It was Cheyne's collar-stud.

He allowed it to rest in the palm of his hand, and a faint smile twisted his lips as he eyed it.

Time slipped back then. It sped back some hours to a moment when the German attack of the morning had been crushed, but when German guns, as if to wreak vengeance that way, were still scattering their shell about the sunlit fields. He himself stood with Cheyne and Colonel Metcalfe in the roof of a small well-built farm that lay half a mile to the west of the copse from which he had come. Along with the French battalion the Colonel used the place as a temporary head-quarters, for, being on the crest of the ridge, it commanded a wide view of the battlefield, particularly the German lines. So here, for a while, the three of them perched in the roof side by side and watched, until a 'five-nine' crashed without warning through the roof itself. Then he and the Colonel had struggled from the wreckage, as white as millers from the dust and plaster. But Cheyne had not.

He was unconscious. With difficulty they pulled him clear and carried him down, intending to search for and dress his wounds in the cellar. But the French troops, with their advantage of a start, had filled it to overflowing before they arrived, and they were compelled to content themselves with the scanty shelter afforded by the entrance which led down from the courtyard, and to dress Cheyne's wound on the top stairs. In the cramped space available and amid the muck and dirt sticking to his uniform they could only find one.

Between times they watched squealing pigs dashing about the yard, only to fall, give a few convulsive kicks and then lie still as some flying splinter of shell struck home and put them out of their agony. And as the bombardment went steadily on French troops passed up wine from the cellar below. To Dalgith the scene embodied all the elements of insanity.

Nevertheless, though he and the Colonel had between them dressed Cheyne's thigh, they were not satisfied. The deathly pallor of Cheyne's face pointed to another and far more dangerous wound. Dalgith had seen that pallor many times. He knew what it meant, as a rule. So he had taken, Cheyne's collar-stud, remembering that his own was broken and needed replacing, and arguing that Cheyne would probably never require one again.

But Cheyne had merely been stunned. The dented steel of his helmet had saved him. . . .

Idly Dalgith contemplated the stud. It roused no sense of shame though he knew at the back of his mind that decency itself had been outraged, Rather did his conduct quietly amuse him, and cause him to congratulate himself ironically upon the completeness of his emotional detachment in this time of legitimate stress. And his smile broadened as he wondered what a particularly pious aunt of his would say if she knew. And what that fool parson would think. Three years before—but no, that was another epoch, another life. It was too long ago to remember.

(5)

Half an hour later Colonel Metcalfe and Dalgith sat by the table on which O'Reilly had dressed Cheyne's thigh. Neither spoke. The Colonel's right hand was wrapped in a bloody rag. In his left he supported his chin, resting his elbow on the table. Dalgith, similarly relaxed, watched him pensively. Both wore their helmets. Gas-masks were at the alert. Their uniforms were stained and dirty. Dalgith's was torn as well. And over their dark faces dust was caked in patches like a bad make-up.

Not a sound came to them from the outer world. It was the

end of the day. It was the dawn of a new hope. For in the last few hours the situation had developed. French resistance had stiffened miraculously, and those same French divisions who had protested their intentions before Roye and Montdidier and failed so dismally to carry them out, were now fighting with all the temperamental dash and desperate gallantry which had so strikingly been absent from their conduct during that period. That day the German had sought to smash his way across the Avre, and had been fought to a standstill on most of the front. Relief was in sight at last. And it seemed to Colonel Metcalfe that ordinary reaction must succeed and break him down where the accumulated burdens and fatigue of a fortnight's retreat had failed. For the first time since that fateful morning in the quarry at Villecholles he permitted himself to look upon his command as one composed of human beings; and the more he looked the more he wondered whether they could be driven another yard, and if he himself could drive them. More important still, whether he could drive himself.

He glanced at his Orderly Officer. He saw Dalgith's tired, red-rimmed eyes fixed upon him with all the mute devotion of a dog for its master, and for a moment he asked himself what he had done to merit this measure of loyalty from one whom he cursed as often as he praised. Not his ideal of an Orderly Officer, but . . .

He supposed it was this 'but' that had given him such a turn when the boy's raving orderly had rushed back through the barrage shrieking that the boy had been killed. Perhaps some psychic wave pulsed between them in that moment for Dalgith, too, recalled that occasion. But Dalgith saw only a bent, striding figure bearing deliberately down upon the copse—his Colonel who came personally to seek him out amid the aftermath of battle. They had walked back to the farm without saying a word, but there was much Dalgith would have liked to have said, had he been able. Such sentiment does not go easily into words at any time; never into a soldier's vocabulary.

So now, in the cottage, they sat and thought and wondered each in his own way, until a faint whistle caused them both to start. They would have moved then, had they the chance, but the whistle swelled to a screeching roar ere they could so much as leap from their chairs, and it was downwards they went, not of their own volition. For the shell, a 'four-two,' struck the corner of the cottage near the ground, and wrecked it as if a giant had caught up the place and shaken it to pieces. The floor collapsed in a mighty welter of smoke and dust. Furniture, plaster, battens, crockery, tiles—the entire cottage emptied itself on top of them. And they found themselves on the potatoes in the cellar beneath.

When the murk had cleared away sufficiently for them to see, they struggled free.

'I think it's time we went,' was all the comment offered, and the Colonel provided that. Together they hurried down the village street, sheltering by the walls of cottages bathed amber in the light of the westering sun. And thus they completed their retreat.

Almost at the same instant Harry Bass, tiring of the company of, and genuinely desiring to cheer with appropriate expression a speechless Warne at his side in the front of the '30 cwt', ventured to remark upon the beauty of that evening.

'Bit of orl-right, ain't it, Sir? All them bleeders at 'ome is just abart goin't' church nah. Aw!'

He laughed raucously at the fancied joke.
Warne shuddered.

(6)

For the next three days, until that raw and foggy night when the Brigade pulled out to rest and refit, Warne accepted his position with a spiritual numbness that made anything other than a quiet resignation impossible. He was played out. They sent him back to a rear headquarters with Keller and O'Reilly, and there he mooned round, watching his companions come and go in the making of that final effort which was to last them out the course.

Batteries had withdrawn to the Noye valley, and Colonel Metcalfe established himself with his Orderly Officer first in a deserted estaminet at Jumencourt, and then in a farm-house at Estrees. But there was no more retreat.

In a way, and had he been able to discern what was there, these last few days might have been to Warne something of a revelation, for in them were the elements of normality, as far as any life at the front could be termed normal. Scanty though the opportunities for rest were, they were at least sufficient to put some semblance of life into men. Scarecrows they had become, and scarecrows they remained until they went into rest proper. But they slowly began to display those human passions and weaknesses which passing events had for the time being suppressed.

Only once did Warne visit Colonel Metcalfe's personal headquarters amid the batteries, and then he found Dalgith in a mood of friendly benevolence that astonished him. He had last seen the boy standing outside the cottage in Rouvrel as the '30 cwt' had driven off. Now he came upon him in the stables attached to the farm, and for several minutes he stood aside and watched the boy fondling the muzzle of a wise old chestnut that mouthed appealingly for sugar, and he caught snatches of the running comment which passed between the boy and his horse with an appreciation of his own loneliness so acute that he was torn between a longing to rush in also and a protesting sense that if he did he would be intruding upon intimacies that were never to be his.

He edged away, but Dalgith, attracted by the slow movement of the soft brown eyes that languidly followed Warne, turned and saw him before he could escape, and a friendly hail called him back.

'Ah, Padre! Where've you sprung from? Come and look at our nags. You've never seen 'em yet—not properly, that is. Arh! Stop it, you twirp, You've had all you're going to get.'

Dalgith paused to take the horse's head affectionately under his arm, and then continued, stroking away at the velvety muzzle as he spoke:

'A nice beast, Padre. Pulled a milk float in the palmy days of peace. Do you ride?'

It was a new Dalgith. Warne dared to hope that it was the real one. He answered: 'A little. Not much, though,' For in all truth he could raise precious little interest in riding when the souls of a Brigade of men lay abandoned to the devil.

Cheerily Dalgith shot back:. 'You'll have to try my nag. The Beetle. He's got a back like a barrel and a trot as steady as an ordinary gee's canter. Not much to look at, though. Only his nature is beautiful, as you can see.'

Vaguely curious, Warne conjectured aloud: 'But the chance—when do you get it?'

'Buckets. Old Metcalfe's mad keen on horseflesh. Big polo bug in his day—before he got smashed up at Ypres. He'll make some as soon as we get settled. We pull out to-night, you know.'

'I didn't.'

'No!'

'You see, Dalgith, nobody ever tells me anything.'

'But my dear Padre!'

Dalgith stopped. Sad level eyes looked into his. And then, to his secret annoyance, not to say disgust, he suddenly felt extremely uncomfortable, as if, in some obscure way, he had been guilty of not playing the game and had been found out. A pang of genuine regret shot through him, followed by an intense desire to make amends. But how to?

'You have been busy, of course,' Warne muttered.

'I understand.'

'Yes, yes, All the same I—we——'

Helplessly Dalgith floundered.

'Come,' said Warne. 'Let's go indoors.'

Strangely chastened, and feeling not unlike a small delinquent following his master to the mat, Dalgith splashed in Warne's footsteps round the midden and across the reeking courtyard to the house.

On the way they passed a byre where three cows stood placidly munching. Seated on a stool was Gunner Bell, equally placidly milking one.

Dalgith forced a laugh. 'We miss your efforts at butter-making, Padre. Bell hasn't the time to make more than a mouthful. How about having some bottles sent back to——'

Warne had stopped. He faced Dalgith, and Dalgith's voice died away. To himself he cried: 'And what on earth have I done now?'

But the angry flush which had spread over Warne's cheeks faded. His hand, raised in protest, sank again to his side. He said, quietly, a little drearily: 'No, Dalgith. I did not come out here for that.'

He turned and strode on.

A half-stifled 'Good Lord!' escaped from Dalgith. And then he recalled in every detail that incident on the road in Grivillers. The sudden comprehension of the incident left him aghast. 'Poor devil,' he thought.

The poor old devil! God! What he must have suffered.'

They entered the house. More uncomfortable than ever, Dalgith sat down, striving the while to find a way of expressing his contrition. Warne hardly noticed him. He had locked himself away once more with his sorrow. This pagan boy, however well-meaning, he could never help. Colonel Metcalfe could....

In the silence of that farmhouse living-room the idea took shape and blossomed.

Warne stood by the window. Dalgith sat watching him. Outside French reinforcements were trickling past, slouching along in the way that the French had.

When Dalgith's second cigarette had burned away he went over to Warne and said: 'I'm sorry, Padre, about all this business, especially that affair between Roye and Montdidier. I'm afraid——'

It had cost him something of an effort to bring himself to take this plunge, but he was glad, none the less, when Warne cut him short with a low: 'That's all right, Dalgith. That's all right.' The air seemed clearer.

Much relieved, he murmured happily: 'Lord! Won't it be grand to flop down to-night and know that we're not going to be chased away at dawn. And think of the joy of lugging off the old shirt. Mine will soon have grown on me. And do you know, I'm clean through the sole of one boot. I rather envy you, Padre—being able to slide off in that '30 cwt' as soon as the racket started.'

Warne swung back to the window. He bit his lip. Dalgith babbled innocently on.

'All same, Padre, you look pretty done. Bit tough, getting chivvied round from the start, specially if you're not used to it. One of those two birds who came up with you from railhead that night was killed next morning, you know.'

'Killed!'

Dalgith just caught the word. He answered: 'Yes, killed.' And every line in his attitude postulated the question: 'Well, why shouldn't he? Nothing unusual in that, is there?' He eyed Warne with a languid curiosity, sensing rather than seeing that something was wrong, and feeling vaguely resentful at this frustration of sincere effort.

'You're not ill, Padre, are you?' he muttered, voicing a sudden thought.

'Ill!'

Warne started as if stung. He grasped Dalgith by the shoulder. Dalgith made to jerk away but, remembering Grivillers, stood firm.

'Ill!' Warne repeated. 'Only in mind, Dalgith. Only in mind. And then because I find men who are no longer men but beasts. His voice sank to a whisper: 'Have you no decent feeling, Dalgith?'

Dalgith stared. 'Eh! No decent feeling!' he echoed.

'Yes, I repeat it. No decent feeling.'

Warne was now holding on to the window sash with one hand while gripping Dalgith's arm with the other, and thus he remained until Dalgith gently released his arm. Very slowly Dalgith withdrew, leaving Warne by the window. He said: 'I'm sorry, Padre. I fear we see things differently.' In peroration he thought: 'My God, what a turn-out!'

He went over to the round French stove and stood for a while warming himself, back towards it. Warne never moved. Neither spoke. Intensely uncomfortable, Dalgith wondered what on earth was going to happen next. . . .

'Which of the two was it?' Warne put the question quietly, without warning. To Dalgith he had even assumed an air of dignity.

Dalgith had to think before he answered: 'The elder one. I forget his name. Wood is the youngster.'

For a moment Warne looked at him, thinking: 'You forget his name. A brother officer joins you, is killed, and becomes as though he had never been; is just—forgotten. That is all you care—you, a boy, who cannot be more than a year or two older than one you look down upon as a youngster.'

Aloud he said: 'I remember.' Then, as if to himself: 'He was the one who first showed me the front of that '30 cwt'.

He gave a little helpless gesture, and abruptly swung back to the window.

Dalgith thought: 'Oh, Christ! And what have I said now?' Muttering to himself he flopped down on the nearest chair.

He gave up the attempt. Warne would have to run his own course.

After that there was silence again, until Bell came in churning a bottle of milk with much the same action he would have employed had he been playing the concertina. He announced that Captain Pryor had just arrived and was coming in, and Dalgith drew a breath of relief that was almost audible.

'Show him in,' he muttered. 'Show him in.' Anything to offset this blighted parson.

But the command was unnecessary, for Pryor himself appeared magnificently in the doorway ere Bell could depart.

Captain Cholmondeley Pryor belonged to that small and objectionable type of non-fighting soldier that was only tolerated because, to the vulgar and ordinary mind, it was intrinsically, though quite innocently funny. It was a type that bore every mark of fastidious elegance, finding the King's uniform merely a means of flattering adornment. Because of this he did not come into the room immediately, but stood for a space of seconds, attitudinizing with exquisite grace while Warne stared and Dalgith grinned.

The waxed moustache, trimmed to a hair; the lofty gaze; the superb air of imperious condescension; his immaculate tunic; the gleaming lustre of his Sam Browne; the faultless cut and delicate shade of his breeches; the sparkle and gleam of patterned buttons; the shapely calves so splendidly encased in polished leather—these things united in a whole, the like of which Warne had never seen before, not even at home. It was crushing. He felt mean and insignificant in its presence. He gaped slightly.

Dalgith's grin broadened happily. He could not cope with the parson, but this offered no obstacle. 'Come in, Cholmondeley.' (He deliberately pronounced the word as it was spelt.) 'Come right in. You've no idea how glad we are to see you.'

'Don't call me Cholmondeley.'

The tone was icy, faintly tinged with anger.

'Right-ho, Thresher and Glenny. Anything to oblige, my dear Chumley. As I was saying: come right in. You're just in time.'

Pryor did. He swept past the disreputable Bell who stood there waiting patiently to get through the door, and fairly lorded it over his audience. He brushed aside imaginary specks of dust from his sleeve with brown leather gloves.

'For what?' he demanded.

'To catch us before we pull out, dear boy. Old Metcalfe prophesied that we'd see your noble figure precisely half an hour before we did so. He's got you taped all right, m'lad.'

He grinned unfeelingly. A little of Pryor's magnificent composure evaporated. He blustered: 'What do you mean?'

'Tut, tut, Cholmondeley dear! No need to fly off the handle. All you've got to do is pop the other side of that door over there and see. The Colonel's waiting for you. . . . Yes, he wants to know where you and the rest of your blasted Siege Park flicked off to a fortnight ago. Hope you've got the answer ready. So pop along, dear boy, and get it over. Then I'll introduce you to our new Padre.'

'That,' Dalgith explained to Warne as the immaculate back disappeared inside the Colonel's room, 'is our Column Officer from Siege Park. He'll get away with it, of course, on the grounds that no man may serve two bosses, but I'd face another retreat right now before I'd be in his shoes at this instant. Meanwhile, Jerry has the guns.'

His good humour thoroughly restored, Dalgith prattled gaily on while they waited for Pryor to emerge. His commentary ranged far and wide, from the failure of the Siege Park system to the prospects of rest. Half of it was above Warne's head. Most of the other distressed him. Selfishness, callousness, indifference—every sentiment reeked of it. And he knew that the attitude was general, from that blasphemous lorry driver to the Colonel himself. 'Or is it,' he wondered, 'that life is judged by different values and that mine are wrong?'

But he listened without interrupting until Dalgith, seeing another batch of French soldiers straggling along, laughed lightly, saying: 'Ha! A merry quip. You know that all the old dames of the village tipped paraffin down the wells, don't you? Mucked up the lot, every blessed one. And now we, the horrid English, are clearing out, and they and their *braves poilus* will have to go without water or drink the paraffin! Serve 'em damn well right.'

'I won't wait for Pryor,' muttered Warne. 'I think I'll be going.'

He caught up his helmet and hurried from the room, leaving Dalgith in the middle of further comment.

Dalgith gaped slightly, said: 'Gawd!' and then made himself comfortable by the stove. There was nothing else to be done.

(7)

Darkness had fallen. The convoy was ready. In the candle-lit living-room of a cottage Warne stood by the table packing his haversack for the journey. In it, among the fragments of biscuits that filled the bottom, he found the silver pyx, and then his tiny pocket diary. He fingered them both. They touched springs of infinite sadness,

He had intended keeping a small diary, but now something told him that the task was too formidable, even if desirable. It were best that none should know his failure. And with a queer smile playing round the corners of his thin straight lips he idly turned the pages. Daily jottings ran up to the 20th March; then a blank. He turned on.... Yes, that was the day Dalgith had taken the consecrated biscuit, the day when——

For an instant the tiny print blurred and swam before his eyes, and then he turned away, a bowed, drooping figure that stuffed pyx and diary, everything, into the haversack as he went. For Easter had come and gone, unnoticed in the turmoil of the retreat, and the message he had set his heart on giving remained unspoken.

Something told him that it would never be spoken now. He had failed his own God.

Hunched in a stupor of silent misery he was carried out to rest, and his vehicle was the front of the '30 cwt'.

CHAPTER VI

STARTING AFRESH

(1)

Forty-eight hours had passed.

The retreat was over. The Fifth Army had been relieved, its place being taken by the Fourth Army; that is, Rawlinson's Staff had relieved Gough's Staff and, until the Australian Corps came down from the north, the survivors of the Fifth Army went gaily on under a new name—a rich-sounding subtlety that was destined to be repeated in principle and with equal success later in the year when Marshal Foch had to sustain the Allied Offensive with his quite nonexistent reserves. And out of it all, to refit and renew its strength, had crawled what was left of the 200th Brigade, Royal Garrison Artillery, assisted for the first time in its retreat by its Column Officer.

Poix, their orders had said, and to Poix they had struggled—over some twenty-five miles of bad French by-roads—only to learn that some one had blundered; this destination was a mistake. Villeroy was the place, another twenty-five miles further on. Then had come the fog; after that, rain. And when at last they had arrived at Villeroy they had found a Machine Gun Battalion already there and resolutely declining to move. More trouble. More orders. Finally, in the late afternoon of a cold dull April day, they had pulled themselves into Hocquincourt and rest.

Dalgith had settled on the Headquarter's billet, a small lath and plaster cottage fronting a rutty and pot-holed road. This was to provide the 'office,' the mess, and sleeping quarters for Colonel Metcalfe, himself and Cheyne, who, nursing his damaged thigh, had joined them there. Warne, with Keller and O'Reilly, were to sleep out, in a similar cottage a few yards away.

And this arrangement had been decided upon because Dalgith had taken O'Reilly aside and urged: 'Better have the parson along with you. We shall be pretty busy here, clearing up things, and he's rather in the way.'

So the Doctor had nodded, replying: 'All right I'll keep an eye on him. He needs one for a bit.'

Warne had therefore gone to the other cottage. And when they had all stripped off their stinking underclothes and sponged their rotting bodies as clean as they could, they turned in for their first proper sleep for three weeks. Warne took the bed, a mountainous thing where he had to insert his body into a cavern beneath the absurd cushion-like down, scarlet, square and a foot thick in the middle, which rested on top. O'Reilly had insisted on this, explaining in his breathy husky way that their hips were as hard as the boards. Warne was grateful.

Later, from his mattressed heights, he heard, but could not see, this fat middle-aged general practitioner as he wheezed to Keller: 'Boy, between you and me we're damn-lucky. We've at least got our valises. Nobody else in the Brigade's got a thing— 'cept what he stands up in.'

And for the first time Warne beheld his fancied humiliation in another and quite unaccustomed light—that of good fortune. The revelation was dim, but it was obscurely comforting though it did smack of the flesh.

STARTING AFRESH

Then came sounds of O'Reilly's bulk as it slowly insinuated itself between folded blankets. A grunt or two, and: 'That '30 cwt' was a godsend if ever anything was.'

That '30 cwt'! Warne's battered spirit gave a last protesting heave. He would have said—but no, he could say nothing. Somehow the tiny cottage bedroom seemed to be slipping away from him. He was soaring into an oblivion of repose. The Doctor's weary 'Goo-night' came to him from an infinite distance, as from another world. And the last conscious recollection before sleep gathered him, was a recognition of his own good fortune, no longer dim but bright and definite. He had been spared to live.

(2)

Hocquincourt had been long astir when the Brigade roused itself and rubbed the sleep from its eyes. Old women in tight black bodices and flowing black skirts were drawing water from clanking pumps, doddering about chicken-runs with aimless intent, and doing the hundred and one jobs that make up the round of village life. And Warne, standing by the low twisted door of his cottage, and looking down the little hill into the village, experienced the nearest approach to mental peace he had known since landing in France. True, this state of mind was far from absolute, being dull and leaden with terrible undercurrents still running strongly. Yet somehow he felt more free, as if he could breathe again, much as he had done after the bombardment in the quarry.

For in that huge feather bed he had slept as the weariest, and less than half an hour ago he had slid, down from its heights with a satisfaction of well-being that can be realized only by one who has slept in a bed all his life and then been called to sleep all-standing anywhere but in a bed for three weeks on end. It. was as if he had awakened to a new life; as if the weeks he had lived through were unreal, a nightmare, vast and hideous, from which memory shrank. And with this awakening there returned something, if only a trifle, of his old determination; something of the moral courage he had scourged into himself during those three preparatory years at Bidderwill. God, it appeared, had not deserted him after all.

Soft warm sunlight bathed the village as he looked down upon it. Crooked, straggling cottages showed clean and white through budding trees. A creaking farm-cart, caked in mud and drawn by a wise old horse almost as muddy as itself, slowly mounted the hill, Its driver, a wrinkled peasant in blouse and corduroys, touched his cap and showed stumps of yellow teeth as it lumbered by Warne recalled those other peasants in Dommartin, and shook the recollection from him.

At the bottom of the hill villagers were moving about; women in black, mostly, but here and there a man, old and grey-haired. Yet for all this evidence of life there was a strange quality about the place, a quality that reached out and touched him, and that would, at any other time, have made him sad. For there was a sort of brooding solitude, of tragedy even, hanging over the village. He wondered, seeking the cause.

Cheyne appeared from the cottage below him, a worn wreck of a man who hobbled slowly with the aid of two stout sticks, his damaged leg hanging stiffly down from the hip. With him, and lending an arm, came Dalgith. Both were hatless, Cheyne wore slacks. They saw him, and mounted the hill. Warne forgot the village. Here was an advance from the other side. Could it mean that . . .

He waited expectantly,

They reached him. Cheerily, and quite unaffectedly, Dalgith greeted him, 'Hallo, Padre! Had a good sleep?'

Germaine! That farmhouse breakfast! Dalgith greeting him as he came to the table! Hallo, Padre, had a good sleep! The identical words. Was he never to be allowed to forget? Was everything he heard and saw now destined to bring his shame to mind? . . .

He forced himself to affability, answering with a laugh: 'The best ever, thanks. How's the leg, Cheyne?'

'Slow off the mark,' thought Dalgith, and wondered.

But Cheyne merely sighed gently, and addressing nobody in particular, murmured: 'So-so, just so-so.' Then, after a pause: 'How excellent a thing is sleep! One must agree with the worthy Sancho. It does wrap a chap round like a cloak.'

'Stop burbling, for the love of Mike! He gets like this at times, Padre, usually when there's a new moon. Quite harmless, though.'

Dalgith's gaiety was infectious. The War began to recede again. They chatted inconsequently.

Then Cheyne, eyeing the village during a lull, remarked: 'Comic sort of place, really. No middle to its life.'

The War returned. The meaning of this brooding solitude leapt at Warne. He had seen it before in Bidderwill, only he had forgotten that France had bled too. No middle to its life! Youth had gone. Nothing masculine remained between the very old and the very young. There were young women, of course, but not men. The only young men, that is, men between the ages of twenty and forty, were those who had come in the day before and were now stirring, as he could see, outside the odd-shaped barns which appeared to be an indispensable adjunct to every cottage; and these were grey-shirted men in khaki trousers, who strolled unconcernedly to the nearest pump or well and, using their scrounged buckets and pails, proceeded to wash themselves shamelessly before the astonished eyes of gaping grubby little children. These men, he reflected, were *his* flock—turned loose in a village such as this. The reflection was profoundly disturbing.

It occurred also to Cheyne, who smiled faintly and half-apologetically explained: 'After all, it's only as Bacon said, isn't it? Martial men are given to love even as they are given to wine, for perils——'

'Oh Lor! He's off again.' In comic resignation Dalgith turned to Warne. 'What he really wants to say, Padre, is that there'll be dirty work at the cross-roads to-night—and plenty of it!'

Dalgith laughed merrily.

'Come on, Young 'un.' Cheyne's voice was curt. 'Grub's ready by now.'

He started swinging himself down towards the cottage mess, Dalgith at his side. Over his shoulder he called: 'Come on, Padre. You must be hungry too.'

But Warne did not follow immediately. He wanted to be alone for a while to recover from the blunt crudeness of Dalgith's exposition. His duty had taken on a new urgency, and one that refused to be put off. He looked at the retreating pair with troubled eyes, and Cheyne's voice floated up to him as it addressed to Dalgith words that sounded suspiciously like: 'You bloody young fool!' It was no palliative.

STARTING AFRESH

(3)

Breakfast, a late meal that might have passed for lunch had it not been for the eggs and bacon and marmalade, went by in an atmosphere which plainly said: 'This is good.'

There was banter and speculation, mainly about the mail and the possibility of getting a lorry into the Expeditionary Force Canteen at Abbeville; and there was much quiet talk about nothing. But of the War and, in particular, the events of the last three weeks, there was scarcely a word, and then only by indirect reference. Warne listened in mild amazement.

Before the meal was over, he was asking himself whether he had indeed lived through that period. If he had, and these men about him had too, then it was a living blasphemy for him and them to be sitting there as if nothing had happened. It smacked of unreality, of madness, all this talk of Holland's Handy Hams and Prana Sparklets and Tiptree Jams, when the Empire itself was shaking. Was he dreaming now? Or was he merely looking for what he wanted to see, and crying out against what he found? Could it be that these men around him wore masks, that they deliberately shut themselves off from the world? Three at least were grown-up men. *They* must think. But what were their thoughts? Was he ever to know? This indifference—it was all affectation. He somehow felt sure of that. It was just satanic affectation. It couldn't be otherwise. No, no, it couldn't. God so loved the world that He gave . . .

Breakfast, was over. The party was breaking up. Warne prepared to go, back to his billet, for he could think of nowhere else. And he was by the door when the Colonel called him back.

'Ah, Warne!'

He turned. The Colonel was standing, back to the drainpipe stove, sipping a final cup of tea.

'About your work.'

'Yes, Colonel.'

'I have not been able to speak to you before about it.'

'No. I quite understand.'

'I do not think you do. I am not referring to the arrangements you may come to about services. That is a matter entirely between you and the batteries, though it is always well to remember that opportunities are not frequent. It is about your general attitude that I want to talk, for I feel that your ideas of the functions of a Chaplain in the field differ widely from what they are in practice. They are, for the most part, bound up in the man himself. A Chaplain's job——'

Job!, The answer to God's call was a job! A ghost of a smile twisted Warne's lip.

'—is one which the Chaplain has to carve out for himself, and nobody can help him. He will either win the confidence and respect of the men or he won't; there is no half-way measure.'

They were alone now. The others had tactfully withdrawn. And the Colonel, though still impersonal, became even more direct. His words rained down on Warne, stunning him. Two level grey eyes never wavered from him. . . .

'I'm telling you this,' Colonel Metcalfe concluded, 'because from the little I have seen of you since you joined, I gather that you are not only feeling lost, which is to be expected for a while, but also resentful at, apparently, what you imagine to be a lack of confidence placed in you—as, for example, on that night when the Brigade crossed the Somme. Quite candidly, Warne, that is not the right way to start if one day you expect to enjoy the confidence which is bred only by experience. Try to know those about you——'

Know those about you! This was laughable. 'I would to God I could,' Warne breathed.

The Colonel made a tiny gesture of finality. 'Make the attempt. Standards out here are different from those at home. A lot are inflated, a few artificial, but a number are nearer to the absolute than any, I should say, accepted in 1914. When you can distinguish between them you will see what I mean.'

He moved away to the table and set down his cup, adding: 'I should not be in too much of a hurry to. start, Warne. Give things a chance to settle.'

The talk was over. Warne knew that he was dismissed. Mechanically he said: 'Yes.'

He went out. He knew now where he stood. He had to fend for himself, had he? Well, with all respect to Colonel Metcalfe, he ventured that he had realized it already. If anything his pathetic determination increased.

Not too much of a hurry! No, he would not hurry, but there was no reason why he shouldn't wander round batteries and see which was which. Nobody could object to that, he thought. He was, however, astonished to find that they did.

Dalgith, Cheyne, O'Reilly and Keller—the four were lounging against the cottage wall, sunning themselves happily, and to them Warne made his request. Could some one just take him round batteries? They looked at him with mild interest.

'I wouldn't, Padre.' Cheyne shook his head.

'Not to-day. They'll be fearfully busy straightening themselves out.'

But Keller laughingly told him to let the poor devils sleep

in peace. 'Besides'—and this with a knowing wink—'there's a Brigade lorry going to the Abbeville canteen this afternoon after all.'

The other two said nothing, but Cheyne added: 'We'll find somebody to take you round tomorrow.'

'Thanks. Don't trouble. Your convenience.'

Warne smiled, with difficulty, and passed on to his billet.

All four looked after him, still with interest; and when he was out of earshot, O'Reilly murmured; 'Wonder what the Bullock had to tell him? He's a sight different from his predecessor, isn't he?' And involuntarily they compared this frail and troubled scholar with the hale, bald-headed parson of little theology but merry heart and gross appetite, whom he had relieved.

'Wade,' gurgled O'Reilly, 'didn't care two hoots whether the troops worshipped God or Beelzebub so long as he had a comfortable bed and a full belly—and between times a good novel. But a good priest. The troops liked him.'

'They'll never like this one.' On that point Dalgith was emphatic.

'Oh, I don't know. He'll settle down.'

'Everything "settles down" in your philosophy of Life, Doc.,' Cheyne laughed.

O'Reilly grinned. 'That's only the law of mental gravitation, and you mark my words: this fellow'll find his level as soon as we get settled.'

'And if he sinks to the bottom altogether?'

'A possibility. But if he does he drowns. That's all. All the same I don't think he will. I'll put him on to Redley. He used to be a sidesman or something, so they'll be happy together—trying to reconcile this bloody dust-up with the Blessing of

STARTING AFRESH

God. He'll soon collect a band of the devout together. Always happens that way. Seen it so often. A few sheep, a lot of goats. The sheep make up for the goats. If they didn't all the parsons in France who believe in a Personal God would have committed suicide long ago.'

A pause. Then: 'I wonder what the Bullock'll do with Tansley?'

They continued chatting aimlessly till lunch time. They were at rest, and forgot about Warne.

So during the afternoon and evening Warne was left to mooch about the hill top while his flock browsed in the valley, and the delay added foreboding to impatience.

How much the future depended upon this seemingly so unimportant introduction to the batteries, he was almost afraid to contemplate, and even then, if he had, it is doubtful whether he himself appreciated the exact and dangerous extent to which he was clinging to its outcome as a means of wiping out the memory of the last three weeks; for bound up inseparably with that memory was the self-respect of a sensitive man as well as the faith of a priest. So let the door be slammed on those terrible weeks; let it be barred and sealed, and then, perhaps, he might win. His work lay ahead now, and with it the chance of temporal salvation. He had to start afresh. There was nothing else he could do.

(4)

The morrow came—cold and dreary with storms of wind and rain. Nobody did anything for him, and patiently Warne sat in the office, waiting for Cheyne's promise to be fulfilled.

He reminded Cheyne once, and Cheyne assured him that it would be all right. But the afternoon was well advanced before Dalgith, acting as Adjutant during Cheyne's convalescence, threw down his pen, cursed the Army and all its indents, and, as if suddenly remembering Warne, said: 'Come along, Padre. I'll take you along to 836. I've got to see Collett. We'll get some tea there, and go on to the others afterwards.'

But, as things turned out, they did not go elsewhere. Warne found the visit to 836 all too sufficient, and, with a sorry attempt at dissembling which quite failed to deceive Dalgith, he explained that he thought it better not to see everybody at once, lest he should confuse himself unnecessarily. Actually he could not face another mess. He would have been sick if he had.

'But you won't forget Collett, will you?' Dalgith grinned.

'No, I shall not forget him.'

(5)

So that night, when they were comfortably rolled in their blankets on the floor of the office, Dalgith told Cheyne the whole riotous story.

'I really believe,' he said, with many a chuckle in the darkness, 'that old Holy Joe thought 836 were going to rise up and hold a prayer meeting. He sort of preened himself and shot out his tail feathers as we blew up to their pub. But Lord! When we opened the door! You could have cut the fug. And the din! They had a birthday celebration going full bat. So instead of holding his prayer meeting, Holy Joe found himself holding a glass that was never allowed to stay empty, and he just stood there, goggling and soaking whisky. Most of 'em were half shot, and some were completely foxed, and it was just too killing. You ought to have seen the parson's dial when Collett—and you know at the best of times he's like a beer barrel on legs—lurched up with a bottle of Old Orkney in one hand and a glass in the other, and then spilt about a pint in trying to pour it out. It was too perfectly priceless for words.'

'Funny! Hm! It's a queer idea you've got of what's funny, Young 'un.'

Cheyne murmured softly. He was too sleepy to lodge a more telling protest, but he wondered a good deal before he dropped off, and, as far as his sleepiness permitted, he was definitely uneasy about Warne.

(6)

But in the morning Warne was forgotten again, for the two days of rest and utter freedom vouchsafed to the survivors of his Brigade by Colonel Metcalfe had slipped away, and there remained now the strenuous work of reconstruction. The village became a veritable hive of activity—for everyone, so Warne discovered, but himself.

He savoured this bitter truth by midday, and after lunch went for a walk in the hazel woods above the village, mocking himself as he strode along with the knowledge that there, at least, he would not be in the way.

The afternoon was moist and overcast, and the ground underfoot was wet, but he argued that if he walked far enough and fast enough, he might possibly tire himself into forgetfulness. And between times he wondered how his fellow Chaplains fared in this hell of indifference. Could it be that his own shattering experience was typical? Were those tales of splendid doings, those hard-won decorations——

But no, they couldn't be. The mere doubt was a blasphemy, *He* was the failure.... His lips muttered a prayer as he went along.

Yet Cheyne in that cottage at Germaine, and the Colonel only the day before, had hinted at possibilities, at difficulties in his path of which he had never dreamed. Doubt refused to be suppressed.

It is not, therefore, surprising that he returned to Hocquincourt in a mood of the blackest depression, and when, after tea, O'Reilly from sheer pity drew him aside and suggested: 'I don't know what your plans are, Padre, but Wade—that's your predecessor—used to work with Redley, one of my orderlies who's been a sidesman and what not at home. He can put you wise about services, you know,'—he only half-understood that here was someone striving to help him at last.

'Thank you, Doctor,' he muttered. 'Thank you. I'll remember that. Redley.'

'No need to. I'll send him along.'

'Thank you. Thank you. But don't bother. I'll find him.'

And with that he turned and hurried from the cottage. This patronizing solicitude, it was maddening, maddening. He could not stand it.

Miserably he went in search of Redley.

Back in the office O'Reilly, Cheyne, Dalgith and Keller stared blankly at one another for fully half a minute, and then they laughed.

'Thank you, thank you,' mimicked Dalgith. 'Thank you, thank you.' And they laughed the more, till O'Reilly growled in disgust: 'That fellow's just about beginning to feed me up. God! did you see how he sheered off?'

They had, and they agreed in their diverse ways.

And then Cheyne, responding to some more chivalrous urge, retorted that it was grossly unfair to run down a man who was manifestly as green as a cabbage. 'Besides,' he added, 'he couldn't have turned up at a worse moment if he'd tried.'

'Green, maybe, but—' O'Reilly guffawed mightily. He ran through a list of Warne's antics, as he called them, starting in the quarry by Villecholes and finishing in Hocquincourt. He traced the sorry story through St. Germaine to Voyennes, from the Somme to the Avre. And Dalgith interpolated the incident of the pyx. Finally O'Reilly told them of the refugees at Dommartin, and the history of those four parallel scars on Warne's cheek. 'You didn't know that bit, did you?' he concluded, significantly.

It was a damning recital, and it induced silence.

O'Reilly's voice was huskily sympathetic when next he lowered his pipe. 'You see, Cheyne—this parson of ours came out, I should say, thinking he was going to preach a Jehad. All parsons do to a certain extent. And what happens—some of 'em turn into quite good mess caterers, and that's about all. It's terrible when you look at it.'

'And Warne?' said Cheyne, gently.

A puff of smoke. Then: 'Honestly, I don't think he'll ever turn into a decent caterer. He's green, admittedly. But that doesn't make a man a fool if he's not one already. Young Wood, for example—that kid in 836—was green enough, God knows. But he pulled through, and he did see a bit of the War, which is more than the parson has done to date.'

'But what are we going to do about it?'

Cheyne looked inquiringly at the Doctor, but O'Reilly merely shrugged his massive shoulders.

'I dunno,' he reflected. 'Honestly I don't. He scarcely comes within my province. If he did I could evacuate him.... Still, it may come to that later. One never knows. He's too much of a visionary to last this life for long unless he manages to settle down before we go into the line again. Not enough character, guts, or whatever you like to call it. But all the same an interesting subject to watch—a very interesting sub——'

Dalgith nudged Cheyne, saying in loud aside: 'Hark, The Medical Profession reveals itself. Observe its mentality. A chappie with a broken leg is not really a chappie with a broken leg: he's merely a fracture which, inconveniently has a man attached to it.'

'As you say,' gurgled O'Reilly. 'As you say,'

'Thank you, thank you.'

Sufficient unto the day.... The War had yet to engulf Hocquincourt. Various War Correspondents described the spirit of the troops as wonderful.

(7)

Private Bertram Hollis Redley, M.P.S., R.A.M.C., suggested a Church Parade,

In *real* life, as the New Army accurately distinguished between its pre-war and war-time existences, Redley had been a well-to-do chemist in a small way; hence his preference for the Royal Army Medical Corps when the Derby Scheme and a pair of defective eyes enabled him to dodge conscription into a combatant unit and, until he was called up, pose with proper Christian modesty before the local Church Council, of which he was a respected member, as one of England's abundant heroes. But a chemist, who is also a churchwarden, in a market town too, can only look one thing; and that is what he is. No amount of sartorial disguise will conceal it; not even khaki. So when the teeth of the Derby comb finally closed upon him, he continued to peer through ridiculously high-powered spectacles, and, as he had always done in moments of perplexity, when, for example, he had been called upon to decide between the merits of Glauber and Gregory, he continued to stroke an absurdly bushy and greying moustache with ragged drooping ends. His face remained dry and yellow even as a constant association with chemicals had made it; and his expression altered not a whit. It was perpetually lugubrious. But he was a good medical orderly.

Then, too, years of endless and delicate inquiry into the nature of his customer's ailments—and all his customers had been becomingly, not to say provincially, reticent—had given him a counter-manner which was compounded equally of a very earnest desire for knowledge and a keen solicitude for his customer's susceptibilities. To this had been added a trace of that pompous dignity and loftiness of carriage which is the natural perquisite of such people as are to be found in the lesser fraternity of Mayors and Church Councils and, generally, vain men dressed with a little brief authority. Needless to say he possessed a wife, who was inclined to be stout, but was undoubtedly very loving and not a little cowish; and he cherished two daughters as well. Also the family conduct was just as impeccable as their Church attendance was consistently sustained.

In short, therefore, Private Redley carried about with him an atmosphere that was unique even among the collection of labourers, miners, clerks, policemen, mechanics, small shop-keepers and professional men who had left *real* life ultimately to form the personnel of Brigade Headquarters, and who still retained more than a touch of their odd civilian ways.

To him came Warne, a man of no 'atmosphere,' of no personality; only his stricken Faith and a protesting sense of right and wrong which told him that no Chaplain ought to be driven to discussing his work with a Private in the R.A.M.C. But where else, he cried to himself, could he turn?

And as he picked his way cautiously round the huge insanitary midden that blocked the way to Redley's barn, he thought involuntarily of the life he had left, Of Bidderwill's prim cleanliness, its rows of thatched cottages, its weather-worn Church behind the elms, and above all, its invincible Englishness. He wondered involuntarily whether he would ever see them again. Somehow he thought he would not. And this premonition persisted even when Redley had mooted the idea of a full-dress Church Parade.

(8)

So grey days merged into blue as April drew on, and secure in the rustic peace of this Picard village the Brigade quickly reverted again to a fighting unit of unimpaired efficiency, and one, too, with morale magnificently sustained. A couple of days' rest, a good bath in a commandeered bran-tub, and men changed from the ragged collapsing scarecrows they were into clean British soldiers, just as smart and with just so much spring in their steps—or absence of it, a Guardsman would say—as distinguished the Garrison Gunner.

In addition they collected new guns, sent old ones to Ordnance workshops, made up to establishment in missing stores, and assimilated their due portion of the drafts which a panic-stricken politician was rushing from England in order to repair the long-predicted damage resulting from his own misguided strategy.

Then mail began to trickle through, and Warne beheld his companions in a new and unexpected light. He saw that they could be human after all. Cheyne alone kept aloof when the bags arrived, but that, Warne discovered, was because he rarely received anything in them. Both Dalgith and Keller had girls as well as families and friends, and the news that a mail had arrived was sufficient to rouse in them an excitement that could not be concealed. O'Reilly, too, was well-blessed with correspondents.

The first mail, however, was, in a way, a complete fiasco. It contained nothing more than a few newspapers, and when Bell entered and placed the little bundle on the table, there was a general growl of dismay. To Warne especially was the disappointment bitter, for he had yet to receive his first letter in France. The others were naturally experienced enough to hold their hopes and themselves in check, and they did not, as he did, retire to a corner and sit nursing a grievance. They merely cursed a little and opened the papers.

Tired at last of watching, Warne opened one also, and thus it happened that for the next few minutes the silence of the tiny parlour was broken only by the rustling of sheets and the occasional tearing of a wrapper. He read of another world. And he read on, growing more and more engrossed, until Dalgith vented an oath that shocked him to attention. Then, with Cheyne and Keller and O'Reilly, he stared at the boy.

For Dalgith, sitting on the edge of the table, reading, had suddenly cried: 'Christ All Bloody Mighty!' Just that and nothing more, but with a vehemence that was compelling. And they saw him holding the paper at arm's length in front of him, looking at it as if the very print were hypnotic.

He repeated the oath, slowly this time, and on a lower note. And lowering his paper, he caught sight of Warne. He roughly apologized. But in explanation he cried: 'If this isn't the ruddy limit: here we are, getting chased half across France, and all the while those bloody swine at home are going on strike. On *strike,* mark you.... Christ!' he breathed.

He tossed the paper over. 'Read it,' he said, and then, more to himself than to the others: 'Next war I'm going to drive a blasted railway engine or something.... God, it's enough to make a man puke! Talk of stabbing in the back!'

Warne was unsure which was the more disturbing: the news or Dalgith's language.

But these more revealing incidents were very few, and on the whole life sped smoothly along in Hocquincourt. O'Reilly sanctioned a rum-issue on medical grounds. Headquarters extracted a new Sunbeam car from Siege Park, now rediscovered. Cheyne's thigh healed rapidly. Keller found the feminine society necessary for his entertainment. The surrounding country proved delightful for walking and scarcely less so for riding. The War seemed very far away, and, curiously enough, the retreat still farther—presumably because the experience of being soundly thrashed was so unusual that nobody could quite realize that it had occurred. And therefore everybody, less one, contrived to enjoy themselves in several ways. The exception was Warne, who did not enjoy himself at all.

For nobody wanted God in Hocquincourt, except, perhaps, the fat little black-robed *curé* with the flat clerical hat and the round white face, who wandered to and fro from the church at the top of the village; but he and his kind found no place in Warne's orthodoxy. It did not need the intuitive processes of a preternaturally sensitive man to tell Warne this; his own eyes had shown him. On two occasions Dalgith had hurried him round battery messes, and once, in the vain hope that he might penetrate to the men, he had gone alone; and because of this he knew in his heart that he was no nearer establishing that contact he so desired than if he had never come to France.

When he asked Dalgith or Cheyne about the possibility of a Church Parade, they put him off with: 'Oh that, well—must it be next Sunday? Day after tomorrow, you say. A bad time.' Or: 'Sorry, Padre. Could you manage to postpone it? We're fearfully busy. The Colonel's on that inquiry and all this new gear has to be collected.' Or, and this was indeed breath-taking: 'Why not wait till we get in the line again and comfortably settled down?'

Comfortably settled in the line! Then did Warne realize what a business the War had become. It was *normal* to be in the line. Men were not fighting Germany: they were merely doing a job—organizing slaughter, suffering slaughter. This period of refit was an interruption in routine, like the yearly fortnight at Southend or Blackpool.

And so, even in the course of these few days, and just as O'Reilly had predicted, Warne began to take what came as it came because there was nothing else to be done; and when Dalgith or Keller cheerfully hailed him with: 'Ah! Just in time to help with these letters!' or 'Padre, if you're going in the mess you might give those letters the once-over!' he took a part or the whole of the uncensored correspondence and read it through from beginning to end, not because he liked reading other people's private correspondence—which he did not, the idea being repugnant to his sense of decency—but simply because by this means and this means alone he could stifle his aching sense of failure. At least he was doing *something*, for his King if not for his God.

CHAPTER VII

SHEPHERDING THE FLOCK

(I)

The first Sunday of the refit came and went, a day of bright moments with great white clouds sailing majestically across a sky of deepest blue; and it passed by the Brigade unnoticed as a Sunday; In the late afternoon the men played a Soccer match, and Warne, returning from a solitary walk in the woods, heard the raucous shouting which floated up with the wind, and knew not whether to laugh or howl. Yet he had to go. Something drew him to the brow of the hill, and from there he looked down upon this latest caricature of all he held sacred.

For some time he did not move. He just stood there, a prey to mournful, leaden-hearted reverie, a lone bent figure numbered among the most pathetic of all men—those who desire only to do good but cannot, not because their gifts are spurned but because they are merely ignored.

The faint, unmusical tolling of the Church's single bell roused him to a trace of a smile, and in the slowly moving black-garmented men and women, all converging upon the church itself, he saw Bidderwill again, the Bidderwill he had known prior to 1914. But the smile gradually hardened, for this was an alien flock. *His* flock was playing football in the meadow below.

The tolling ceased. The last of the faithful disappeared into the church. The shouting went on, culminating in a derisive roar when a lumbering gunner scored a goal. . . .

By the time Warne had reached the village on his way back to his billet, the football was over. Players and spectators were once more strolling in twos and threes, or gathered in bunches outside their barns, there to loll and jest with the non-churchgoing portion of Plocquincourt's maidenhood. And through the dim evening light Warne strode fiercely by them. Some saluted. Others did not. He noted their indifference with angry resentment.

From several billets came laughter and the sound of mouth-organs, and from one a full-throated song. With rare gusto someone was leading his companions in *Mademoiselle from Armentières*. Every word was distinct, and Warne, with burning ears and amid the hardly-suppressed grins of a khaki audience standing in the road, heard for the first time that verse which dwells so indelicately upon the physiological changes resulting from pregnancy. The men delightedly saluted him.

Furious rather than disgusted, he hurried on, and passing 836's mess he ran into Cheyne, just leaving.

'No, no. I'm not coming in. I—I——'

'If you're not in a hurry I'll walk back with you,' Cheyne answered, for the plight of this urgent, pale-faced man at his side was too compelling to dismiss with a nod: he had to discover the reason. 'I'm afraid I can't hurry, Padre. This leg, you know.'

Warne did not reply, but fell into step with Cheyne. They had not moved a dozen paces when, from down the street, came the final rousing bars of *Mademoiselle*. Cheyne understood.

'They're a quaint lot, aren't they?' he said, for he had to say something.

'Quaint, you call it?' retorted Warne, and bitterness lurked in his voice. 'I should have called it scandalous—filthy.'

Cheyne looked into wild, accusing eyes and said nothing. But he felt extremely uncomfortable. They were, too, passing at the moment a little knot of men joking with a girl in the middle twenties. She was standing arms akimbo, bareheaded, a black shawl carelessly flung about her shoulders, and she was leaning back and laughing with a joyous abandon. Cheyne casually thought she was rather attractive. The men stopped their banter, stiffened and saluted as the pair went by, only to continue their clumsy attempts at making love in a foreign tongue when the pair had passed.

'That,'—and with a backward glance and a gesture Warne indicated the group—'That is what I find in Hocquincourt. Men have more use for a harlot than for a parson.'

This time the bitterness in his voice was no longer veiled.

'My dear Padre!'

Cheyne stared at his companion with an interest suddenly and enormously increased, an interest, too, that was not unmingled with astonishment. Warne's assertion roused a hundred thoughts.

'Oh, don't deny it,' Warne burst out. 'It's true. Those men—yours and mine—prefer a painted woman to communion with God.'

And Cheyne, recalling in one swift flood of memory the solitudes of the Pacific Isles and the woman-hunger of the Army ranks, felt the sting of a partial truth and knew not what to reply. 'Not so fast, Padre,' he muttered. 'I can't keep up this pace.'

'No, you have nothing to answer because there is nothing,' Warne cried, but he slackened his pace. 'It's you and your kind who tolerate this—this—this bestiality. This is the result of all your smug theories of free-will. Have you no moral authority?'

'That, I think,' murmured Cheyne, with a display of outward calm that was quite lost upon Warne, 'is your province.'

'Mine! You tell me that when for the last month you have treated me as if I am so much ullage.'

'But, my dear Padre!'

Warne swept aside the interruption. 'You tell me that after you and your companions have deliberately kept me from my own men, put me off with excuses and pushed me out of the way as a nuisance. Oh, I may be a parson, but I'm not a fool—except, perhaps, to be one.'

Cheyne was nonplussed, and for a moment a wave of contrition stifled impatience. 'I'm sorry, Padre,' he said, and he meant it. 'I'm more sorry than I can say. I didn't realize that you—well, that you felt as you do.'

'Felt!'

Warne broke off, laughing quietly, terribly. Then suddenly: 'To-day is Sunday, the Lord's day. Yet what have we here in this village? Football, obscene choruses, dalliance and licentiousness instead of—'

'Steady, Padre. I can't keep up this pace. My leg, you know. You keep going faster and faster.'

They slackened down once more. They reverted to their argument, and Cheyne protested that Warne's statement was altogether too sweeping. 'Even if these men are guilty of all you say,' he urged, 'it does not mean that they are entirely devoid of what we understand as Christian virtues.'

Cheyne's voice hardened perceptibly as he spoke, but again the implication escaped Warne. 'Most men act foolishly, Padre. Wickedly often. But they're good fellows at the bottom. Ignorance——'

Warne flared. 'Yes. Ignorance. Always ignorance. That is the whole point. Why are they blind? What have you and your people done to enlighten them, you who are set in authority over them? Nothing, I say. Nothing. You worship the Devil, not God.'

'Maybe, Padre. I should prefer to say that they—we—don't worship anything in particular. We merely get on with the job.'

'On with the job!'

'Yes. The job of winning the War. One is apt to lose sight of that'—this almost dryly.

Then, with an earnestness that startled Warne into silence: 'Be a Christian yourself, Padre. Be charitable. These men, whom you choose to condemn at large on the very human failings of the few, are no better and no worse than the rest of the B.E.F.—that is, of British manhood. I did not go through the ranks with my eyes shut, or my ears, and if you, Padre, had ever had any experience of men in the mass, men deprived of women, you'd never say the things you are now saying. Don't you realize that it would be just as unfair for me to condemn the Church you represent on your own personal failure—I say it though it's a hard word—on your own personal failure with us, as it is for you to run down these men because you've heard a few singing a smutty song and seen a few ogling a tart. And this applies just as much to the women. Some of the whitest I've ever met, you'd call scarlet. One saved my life not so many years ago. Shoved herself between me and a Mexican's knife. She was a White Slave! And yet, because you live in another world where these things don't happen, you'd probably be the first to condemn that girl. Your world, I would say, is peopled by saints. The world you're in now is upside down and temporarily mad, but the people in it are human, and that's what you've got to remember. For all their silly ways, these fellows lolling about this street are damn' good chaps. Their language, I know, is filthy, but it means nothing. Padre, just after I joined up, in the ranks, I travelled in a railway carriage with two other fellows newly caught like myself, and I counted the number of times they used the word ——either as a verb or an adjective. Chiefly the latter, of course. In a four-and-a-half-minute run between two stations, they used it ninety-two times, and one, not content with applying it to his father whom he appeared to love quite dearly, applied it also to the girl he was engaged to marry. So when you hear men using obscenities almost every other word, as you certainly will if you ever move among them, just reflect that it is as natural for them to do so as it is for you to pray—and probably just——'

Cheyne broke off abruptly, choking back the stinging commentary that forced itself to his lips; but Warne followed him in thought, and clutching at his arm, moaned rather than said: 'Say it, man. Say it. Say that it probably means just as much.'

'That, Padre,' answered Cheyne, very gently, 'would be untrue—in general.'

'In general! Go on.'

But Cheyne did not wish to go on. He sought for a palliative. 'Would you then have me doubt the sincerity of the entire priesthood? Some, perhaps. But not all. There are definite reflexes to sincerity, especially in prayer.'

'But never by chance God's answer?'

'That I can't say.'

'I can!' Warne's grip tightened fiercely on Cheyne's arm. 'I can. For nigh on four years I prayed as never man prayed before to God. And this is the answer.'

The moaning thing that was Warne's voice terminated in a choking sob, and Warne himself swept his disengaged arm round at the village. The stick he carried went flying. It struck the side of a cottage, but Warne did not notice it. Had not Cheyne stopped him he would have continued unheedingly.

After that Warne made no attempt at renewing the argument. He was more than exhausted by the unaccustomed vigour of his own rebellion, and Cheyne was too perturbed. So they walked in silence for the remainder of the way up the gravelly road to their mess. At the door they stopped.

'Padre,' said Cheyne. 'The other day you asked me about a Church Parade. Would next Sunday do? If so, I'll fix it.'

Warne nodded and passed on to his own billet. For several seconds Cheyne stood watching him, wondering, anxious more than distressed, perplexed more than contrite. But other tasks claimed him, and with a quite involuntary shrug of the shoulders he turned and limped into the mess.

O'Reilly and Dalgith were there, sitting on two hard wooden chairs by the stove, and while throwing aside his British Warm, Cheyne enlightened O'Reilly upon this latest development.

'So he's opened his mouth at last, has he?'

'Yes, he's opened it right enough this time—wide. He simply poured out his soul. Properly rattled. Thinks we're all heathens and have gone to the devil. I don't like it.'

'What? The insinuation?'

'Don't be an idiot. This is serious.'

'For whom?'

'The priest, of course. What are you going to do about it?'

'Me! Nothing. What's the matter with him anyway?'

'Doubt, I should think—with a capital D.'

'Hm. That's hardly my province, though it may mean a bromide.'

'But we can't let him go on like this.'

'Find him a job of work then.'

'I'm going to fix up his Church Parade for next Sunday.'

'I said work.'

'Christ! You are enough to make a saint swear at times, Doc.'

'I should think,' murmured Dalgith, without, however, lifting his eyes from the entrancing issue of *La Vie Parisienne* that engaged his attention, 'I should think Walmisley's anthem would be a good one for him to put on. You know, where it says:

Thou feedest them on the Bread of Tears
  And givest them plenteousness of Tears to drink.

La Vie isn't so good since Kirschner died, is it?'

Cheyne vented a tiny ejaculation of impatience and sought out the latest paper.

(2)

Warne took to the proposed Church Parade much as a repenting suicide catches the rescuer's rope.

He began by borrowing Dalgith's horse with the intention of canvassing batteries daily, morning, noon and night; and refusing the groom that Cheyne offered him, he rode alone, a pathetically earnest middle-aged man (for he now showed considerably more than his years) with none too good a seat on a round-bellied, short-legged chestnut. The Beetle's beautiful nature, as much as anything, contrived to keep Warne in the saddle, but nothing on earth could have lent dignity to the combination.

Like so many people who are unused to horses but riders after a fashion, he rode with short stirrups; which method, aided by a natural timidity, hunched him up and invested him with an air of desperate determination that merely intensified in the onlooker's mind the uncertainty that he would remain for long in the saddle. The whole effect therefore pertained to an Old Master, for there were present all the elements of disproportion and grimness that are the characteristics of the earlier equestrian painters.

Mercifully unaware of this Warne trotted about the village, and because of a curious and undefined respect for the cloth whose significance they ignored, the troops hid their smiles—and some were pretty broad—behind their backs. But one morning while watching him depart, Keller guffawed more loudly than courtesy ordained, and to Warne's tingling ears came the voicing of a general opinion:

"Look at him! Rides like a sack of spuds!'

After that he reverted to walking.

(3)

But although Warne crept nervously into the battery messes, all of them boisterous, and none of them, according to his standards, any too sober; and although he essayed, even more nervously, to penetrate into battery life, hoping thereby to reach the men, he had to admit to himself that his visits, as preparation for a Church Parade, were utterly useless. He saw—and here he quite unconsciously compared with Bidderwill's tested piety—a flock which had been allowed to stray. To him was the task of bringing them back to the fold. But the act of bringing he found impossibly difficult.

For batteries welcomed him, crying: 'Come right in, Padre! Just in time for a spot.' And they did this until he began to wonder when it would not be time for a spot. They forced drink upon him till he thought that another drop would make him sick. They deafened him with their inconsequent pagan babble till his tattered nerves bade him shriek. And when he ventured on the subject of the coming Church Parade, they were no less disconcerting.

'We'll be there, Padre,' they laughed. 'Don't worry about that. Brigade will let us know all details. What about another spot?'

In the face of such overwhelming but quite misdirected zeal for his welfare, he could do nothing, except take spots of Old Orkney, for he had not the personality to make himself understood. Nor had he the strength of mind to avoid this incessant tippling, though he did make one despairing effort after two days of bibulous canvassing with 836. Here Collett proved to be such a benevolent terror, for drink merely intensified his natural and courteous insistence, that Warne took to calling there at tea-time. He then made the disturbing discovery that tea is not the only liquid regularly consumed at this hour.

Yet 836 provided his one solace, for he never entered their mess—a large, stone-flagged, raftered, French living-room—

without seeing young Wood. Memories of that ride through the night from railhead—God! How long ago it seemed!—bound him obscurely to this fresh-complexioned English lad.

Young Wood was the junior subaltern, straight out from England as a casualty reinforcement, and the War had yet to touch him. He was still full of wonder. He never crowded to the front with the whisky, but held back, as if unable to get the hang of his new life; as if, indeed, the desperate devil-may-care *bonhomie* of his companions were a mystery to him, and he feared the revelation to come. Warne knew, and felt acutely, for he saw the tragedy of a soul destined to be led to its doom. But to act, to do anything on the lad's behalf, was just as much beyond him as the refusal of those emetic whiskies. Yet every time he came to the mess Young Wood smiled from the back of the throng, just a shy little wisp of a smile, but it somehow made Warne feel that his visits were not altogether in vain.

(4)

So Warne pottered around Hocquincourt and about his own mess, building all his hopes upon the Church Parade promised for the coming Sunday, and between times watching his brother officers rather as Dives must have watched Lazarus. In a despairing, detached sort of way, as if he knew well enough that nothing would ever come of it, as indeed nothing did, he tried to probe their minds, to get behind their reticences and to understand them, so that they in turn might understand him and realize how much their spiritual welfare still meant to him; for bound up in this he felt there lurked the explanation of his failure.

There was the Colonel, enjoying, if ever man did, each moment of life, nursing his Brigade back to the pink of human efficiency and projecting his personality into every department so that men rarely discussed him but, as Cheyne had done, offered him in affection as the reason for their existence.

Then Cheyne, sober-minded, efficient, half-Colonial. It had taken Warne nearly a month to discover this fact.

Dalgith, on the other hand, fulfilled all the requirements of the young, healthy and care-free. Destined for Cambridge from birth, he had gone up early, at eighteen, and had put in a half-hearted first year before departing with loudly proclaimed joy into the Army. Warne found him pleasant enough, even if a trifle intolerant, and liked him; for there yet remained unmistakable impressions of an earlier gentleness which no amount of War's brutality could erase. A man's wisdom crowded into a boy's mind. The War had done much for Dalgith; too much, Warne sadly reflected. It had killed the image of God in his heart.

In O'Reilly Warne beheld the tragedy of a wasted life, a life devoted to self. Yet, as he knew by his own small experience, O'Reilly was anything but selfish in many ways. The student and psychologist in Warne recognized in O'Reilly all the symptoms of a clever man, but instead of finding that, Warne found a contented one—a man with brains atrophied from lack of will to raise himself from the ruck of a provincial G.P.; a man whose motto was *Mañana*, and who did just so much of his job as would make him comfortable, and, as he himself once expressed it in Warne's presence, 'left God to the parsons.' For him the War meant a change of venue with plenty of whisky and excitement thrown in; nothing more.

SHEPHERDING THE FLOCK

Only in Keller did Warne find evidence of the sensual. Keller was inclined to be loud-voiced, but inclination found expression only when the Colonel was out of earshot. For the same reason he would have worn khaki of unorthodox shades, but he did not. Beefy and brainless, Warne judged him, and with truly Christian charity refrained from more intimate speculation. Actually George Erdelot Keller had passed out of the Shop rather low in a War-time entry, and while there, had favoured the nude as mural decoration. God had forgotten Keller, or vice versa: Warne was uncertain which.

And round him, outside his own mess, Warne beheld Britain's amateur soldiers going quietly—apart from their hectic moments of relaxation—about their unaccustomed jobs. Professional men for the most part, they included lawyers, agents, stockbrokers, schoolmasters, with a fair sprinkling of University and public-school fellows, and one brewer of repute; all it might be said, of the sturdy middle-class, and all gifted with the capacity of thinking soberly if not profoundly. And among them the War was kept in its place, as far as possible, in much the same way as business is left in the office at closing time.

It was this remote and distant attitude towards the War that puzzled Warne more than anything else, for at times he fancied that they banged the office door a little too violently to be in keeping with the nonchalance of their pose. It was as if they were deliberately forcing themselves not to think of the War and what it involved, and their banter often seemed to him to ring false. They wore their indifference as a mask. Behind it, hidden away and never to be divulged, were those secret contacts he sought. He knew they were there because he glimpsed them time and again when some quick gust blew aside the curtain of their reticence. But even as darkness follows the lightning flash, so the curtain would fall again.

These men, Warne grew to understand, would no more have dreamed of discussing the War for the sake of discussion, or have embarked upon one of those scathing dissections and exposures of the Higher Command's popularly imagined ineptitude, than they would have dreamed of calling themselves 'heroes.' They were content to leave both to men who sat in arm-chairs at home. But Warne also came to know that they thought quite a lot, and felt, strongly at times.

He had seen this in Dalgith's outburst over the strike. He saw it again a day or two later when Maclachlan of 679 limped into the office and the talk swung from the subject of casualty reinforcements direct to the ministerial statements on the Fifth Army debacle then appearing in the daily papers.

One lay open on the table, and Maclachlan, catching sight of an offending paragraph, suddenly blurted out:

'God, man! This stuff makes me fair sick.' And he rapped on the paragraph with his knuckles.

He went on: 'You're told to do the impossible, left completely in the lurch and God Himself conspires against you. And then, because you don't do it, in order to save a politician's face the world is told that you ran away.'

Dalgith laughed softly. 'Never mind, Mac. It's —'

'But I do mind! Did *I* run away? Did *Nash* run away? Did *you* run away?'

'I never got the chance!'

'Nash,' said Maclachlan, lowering his voice, 'left a wife and a kiddie. I wrote to her the other day, telling her that he died getting the guns away. I might have said doing a job for which

V.C.s were showered round by the sackful in South Africa. And now she'll read in the paper stuff which implies unmistakably that her husband ran away, and thousands of other women will read that *their* husbands ran away too, when at this very instant German burial parties are at work from St. Quentin to the Avre because they didn't run fast enough. Christ!'

His voice, which had risen in crescendo, died away in muttered profanity, but he apologized when he remembered Warne, standing by the stove.

'I'm sorry, Padre. But this sort of parliamentary stunt, this deliberate lying at the expense of the honour of dead men in order to save one's political face—it gets my goat. . . . I think I'll get the Doc. to look at my leg now I'm here. Know where he is?'

Dalgith thought a moment. 'Having a shut-eye in his billet, I should think. Second cottage up the street. Come back and have a spot when you've done.'

'Thanks. I think I will.'

When Maclachlan had gone, Dalgith turned to Warne, saying: 'He's a good scout—Old Mac. He'll take on 679 in place of Tansley, sure as eggs. The Bullock's going to toss Old Tansley clean over the fence. . . .'

(5)

But if the papers were trying on occasion, to Warne they were as soothing unguent in comparison with the letter mail when it arrived. All England wanted to know exactly what had befallen the Army in France during these dark Spring days, and receiving no satisfactory detail from the Censor, turned promptly to that portion of England resident in France for the information they desired. Mail poured into Hocquincourt, for, as the fighting front stabilized and permitted a harassed yet highly efficient postal service to sort out itself and its letters, past accumulations began to find the Brigade. As a result Bidderwill came very close to its Rector.

Not until he had read through this stream of ill-written correspondence, with its pencilled addresses on cheap village paper, its carefully misspelt wording, and above all its simple directness, was he permitted to realize how deeply he lived in the affection of his parishioners. And yet this knowledge was gall, for there was not one among them who did not see him preaching the Word of God with the same quiet zeal, the same unqualified success, and doing so in the same atmosphere of reciprocated affection as marked his work in Bidderwell.

Jessie Smith, the spinster schoolmistress of the parish, and mighty worker in the name of the Lord, bespectacled, ambitious, forty-three and still hopeful, even came out with: 'The inspiration of your presence, dear Mr. Warne, must be above the price of rubies.' And later on in her letter she delivered herself of: 'How I would love to be with you at your services, just to see the serried ranks of our boys gathering the pearls you cast before them.'

In the same tenor the butcher's wife wrote: 'We are proud to think of our Rector out there in the thick of it, holding up the Cross of Jesus before our boys.

Unfortunately Warne's stomach was not of the kind to digest this surfeit of affection; it lacked the juices of a ready humour. And Bidderwill, instead of providing the soothing palliative and making him laugh, merely added to his depression by making him mentally bilious.

(6)

It remained for Dalgith to remind Warne of the practical side of a Church Parade, when, chancing to meet Warne outside the mess, he said indifferently: '''Bout your show next Sunday, Padre.'

'My what?'

'Your show—the Church Parade. Let me know what arrangements you'd like, won't you? If you want any copies of hymns run off, I'll get Booth, our clerk, to do 'em on the office hectagraph. But I'm afraid we can't run to a drum and a union-jack.' He smiled pleasantly.

'I'll let you know,' returned Warne, vacantly, and Dalgith went his way.

Your Show on Sunday! It had come to that, Warne reflected and mentally retched. Still, he supposed it was all an attitude of mind, and one consistent with everything else. He was sure that Dalgith had not meant to be offensive.

He set off to find Redley.

The same old midden blocked the way to Redley's barn, and the same old cackle of poultry greeted his arrival in the yard; and even as he had done on the occasion of his first visit he thought of Bidderwill. The comparison was involuntary, and its effect was such that he recoiled from his surroundings as from things unclean, as indeed they were.

Not even stolid British soldiers, with all their insular and quaint notions of cleanliness, could purify a French village inside a week, valiantly though they set about the task. Quite unthinkingly they had thrown open windows that were never meant to be opened, windows that shrieked in protest before the onslaught. Deliberately they had enticed the relatively fresh air from outside into corners where lurked the age-old accumulations of stale and sickly fumes. And disdaining the obvious convenience of the many middens, they had built themselves neat little canvas latrines where none had ever existed, and, in general, they had made themselves at once ridiculous and mildly unpopular.

'Come,' he said to Redley. 'I can't stick this muck-heap.' And together they sought the road. Poultry scattered and clucked as they splashed through the brown semi-liquid filth of the yard. Warne casually noticed that it drained into a nearby well.

Redley inquired: 'You have seen Captain Cheyne about the Parade, Sir?' And his manner was so unctuous and diffident that he might have been asking a young and bashful mother whether baby's bowels were open. Looking down, Warne observed that the little man was twining his fingers breast high and peering up expectantly as if some imaginary counter separated him from Warne.

But Warne suppressed his revulsion and said: 'Next Sunday—definitely.'

'Excellent, Sir. Have you decided whether it shall be Matins or Evensong?'

'Matins! Evensong!'

'Yes, Sir.'

Warne did not reply at once. He was looking down the village street and thinking how mean, ugly and piggy it all seemed; so unlike his impression on that morning when he had first stood outside his billet and watched the men cleaning themselves after the retreat. Now his sad grey eyes were noting little groups of soldiers dallying away the time with cards and strange games that were beyond his comprehension. Some were clustered round Hocquincourt's maidenhood. Others were helping the old and decrepit in a dozen odd ways. And when he spoke, Warne had forgotten Redley. His words fell slowly, too, like those of a man describing a vision dimly seen, or a man groping after a truth just out of reach.

'Matins ... Evensong ... Formal service with the lips——'

All the churchwarden in Redley raised its perky head, shocked. 'I beg your pardon, Sir!'

'Lip service from half a thousand men who have forgotten God—half a thousand men ordered to their knees in worship by an authority they cannot refuse. What are Matins, Evensong, to them? Or the Sacrament itself? Nothing. There is no prayer book in existence built for such men as these. For the believer, yes; and the hypocrite. But what is there to offer to men who have wandered? Is there anything in our own prayer book to call them back to God when its own shortcomings have allowed them to drift?'

A scandalized voice protested: 'Sir!'

'There is nothing,' said Warne, and turned to the gaping Redley with a tenderness of feeling that he would have deemed impossible five minutes earlier. With the saddest of smiles he suggested: 'We shall have to turn evangelical, Redley. Revivalist, if you like. Afterwards, perhaps, we may conform in letter as well, I think, as in spirit. Our governance is not elastic enough.

Or was it too elastic?

Strange, how the sight of the village *curé* pottering along in the distance should provoke the comparison it did. Rigidity; iron discipline; a Church run like an Army! Absurd? No, not in the least: Rome did it, and it worked as well as any other method, if not better. The Pope as Chief of God's General Staff: that was the idealistic way of looking at the appointment. Different, however, considerably different from the view of the rank and file who would see God in the person of the Sergeant-Major, somebody much nearer than Pope or Field-Marshal and infinitely more terrible. These villagers in Hocquincourt, if they saw anything at all, as Warne was open to doubt, probably saw God in the person of that rotund little priest with the moon-face and blinking eyes.

The analogy, once started, coursed through Warne's brain much as a large snowball may tumble down a snow-clad hill; at every twist and turn additions presented themselves and were caked on. He saw absolution and indulgences in the light of beers to the sergeant and the consequent forgiveness of less heinous sins. No beer, no palm-oil in any of its hundred forms, meant the straight and narrow path and the watchful eye, with the penance of double fatigue for him who erred. The promise of salvation paired itself so aptly with the promise of promotion to a cushy billet. Then there was hell, or, so he gathered, the guardroom on pay-night. Routine beliefs, as inflexible as regimental tradition though not as the drill book, for General Staffs did have enough sense to revise that and bring it up to date once in a while. And over all the inspiration of fear and the threat of damnation; the shadow of the A.P.M. and the firing-party at dawn.

Yet it worked, for the same reason that the Army worked. And for that reason it would collapse even as the Army would collapse were discipline and the other factor—call it what you will—withdrawn. Back then to barbarism. An argument for discipline certainly.

The black figure of the *curé* vanished, and Warne, faintly horrified by the bitterness of his own reflections, turned for relief to Redley. More safely he began discussing hymns, while a sudden commotion on the midden sent half a dozen fowls into the road, fluttering and clucking about their legs.

Redley was helpful here, and although his training on a Church Council compelled him to discuss for the sake of discussion, his suggestions were sound and based on his own experience in the field. The Brigade dulcitone, a sweetly feeble instrument resembling a midget piano, which had somehow escaped destruction or capture on the 21st March, this, he declared, was useless in the open for a large gathering. Therefore, unless a piano could be found in the village, it were best to have a small choir to lead the singing. He had a few friends in the batteries who would undertake this, provided they knew the hymns.

Finally the pair decided on *Fight the Good Fight, For all the Saints,* in Barnby's rousing and quite unwarrantably scoffed-at setting, and *Onward, Christian Soldiers*—a trio that promised to be sufficiently widely known to ensure success.

When they parted Warne was a little less despondent.

(7)

The following day he spied out a suitable 'stage' for his 'show,' and the word was his own because the cut of Dalgith's careless reference refused to heal. He selected a stretch of verdant meadow where 679's guns stood wheel to wheel, lined in a menacing row. But it was not necessary to look at them. They alone reminded one of the War. And apart from them he felt that God, if anywhere, would be here. Something of the peace of the countryside entered his soul as he looked, and even the brook which swept along between lines of burgeoning willows seemed to babble a message of hope. It caught the sunlight and went its way, a glittering ribbon of happiness. Then there were the birds, nesting in the poplars by the road. They were all with Nature, fresh with renewed life.... No, he would *not* look at the guns.

Afterwards he avoided his brother officers and hid himself in his billet, for he wanted to be alone that he might study the better the fit of Revivalism's mantle. And as he put pencil to paper for his notes, the idea touched a spring of gentle cynicism within him, so that he quietly mocked himself with visions of earlier days at Bidderwill, and still earlier days at Cambridge when, in debate over coffee after hall, youth had once proclaimed a sturdy agnosticism and a sad disregard of the unassimilated evidences of Paley. He had been something of a Revivalist then.

But, though he donned the mantle, it was to God that he aimed to call the erring Brigade, not to Jehovah.

(8)

Meanwhile to the north-east, from Kemmel to Givenchy, the line swayed and bent before Ludendorff's second onslaught, one scarcely less terrific than the first. Once again the fortunes of the Allies hung in the balance and this time a tired Commander-in-Chief addressed himself to his troops, telling them that they had been deliberately selected by the German Command for nothing less than extermination, and that they had to fend for themselves. He concluded magnificently: 'With our backs to the wall, and trusting in the justice of our cause . . .'

Meanwhile, too, Warne had to suffer his own mess.

In a way he knew that his heart, in all its misery and loneliness, was naked in the sight of these men with whom he had to live and eat and sleep, but he knew also that they scarcely bothered to look, that they had 'not time' for such as he. They lived their lives, each his little own, and he had to live his, alone, it seemed, without a friend, even though his heart were a fountain of pain. Cultivate forgetfulness? He couldn't. There was a conspiracy in heaven against him. At every moment, it appeared, he was liable to be brought face to face with the ghosts of the past—a past that was barely a month!—so that in the space of those few days at Hocquincourt, just as he had come to accept events in a stunned and silent indifference, he came to fear the most casual conversation lest a sudden twist of the tongue should evoke those torturing reminders.

One afternoon, for example, he surprised Dalgith with O'Reilly and Cheyne in the mess. They were discussing the distribution of awards.

So liberal, indeed, had been the generosity of the French Command in its rationing of decorations to celebrate their participation in the retreat, that a round handful had percolated through the meshes, notoriously absorbent, of the Higher British Formations and had reached down to the lowly Brigade. A problem arose at once, for heroes had to be found whose heroism admitted of grading. Thus, to the superlatively brave would go a *Croix de Guerre* with, maybe, a Star, while to the ordinarily gallant would go a *Citation*; that is, the satisfying pleasure of beholding his name in a French Divisional Order of the Day. The final say, of course, rested with Colonel Metcalfe, who also had the first as well, and characteristically he divided them all among batteries, retaining for the aggrandisement of his own staff and Headquarters personnel but one *Citation*. To Dalgith, therefore, as Acting-Adjutant during the period of Cheyne's convalescence, fell the unenviable task of finding a candidate to submit for approval; a candidate whose gallantry had been noticeable but not too pronounced. And prolonged reflection did nothing more than increase his perplexity to such an extent that finally he gave up in disgust, and pushing back his chair, flung out: 'Oh hell! Let's give it to the priest.'

Both Cheyne and O'Reilly told him emphatically not to be a fool.

It was soon after this that Warne came in, and the silence that greeted his arrival was more eloquent than words.

'Pray go on,' he said, icily polite. 'Don't mind me.'

Cheyne eyed him thoughtfully. 'We're trying to award a decoration,' he said, quietly. 'Perhaps you can help.'

'And you thought you might give it to me, eh?'

His tone was offensive. He glared angrily at the three men in turn. Dalgith gaped slightly, his eyes round with astonishment. Cheyne offered a prayer for protection against a second deluge of priestly resentment, and looked helplessly at O'Reilly.

'To be quite candid, Padre, your name was mentioned as a possible candidate for this high honour, but your claims, on examination, could not be taken—shall we say—seriously.'

His voice was a husky wheeze, but O'Reilly himself remained blandly composed, and at the end he bent down and quietly knocked out his pipe.

Warne was crushed, annihilated with a snub. Flushing with

anger and chagrin he turned away, forcing from his lips: 'So I should imagine. But pray continue. Pray continue.' And going to the table, he started opening newspapers one after the other, in search of he knew not what.

Cheyne's voice came to him from beyond the barrier of paper: 'To get back to Bell. Why not give it to him?' And Warne, choking with resentment, reflected: 'So they've been comparing me with—with a servant.'

He listened. Cheyne unfolded the claims of Gunner Bell, and they sounded unchallengable. He thought of his own, and how they must have sounded from Dalgith's lips, or O'Reilly's, God! How those men must despise him!

Then there was laughter as O'Reilly intoned a possible wording of the recommendation . . . 'By his unceasing ministrations to the bodily needs of an entire Headquarters Staff, this enterprising Gunner sustained their morale throughout a critical period and so enabled them to extricate themselves and their command from the threat of destruction, and thus permit them to fight another day. How's that?'

More laughter.

Dalgith chortled: 'And don't forget to put in the cows and his butter-making.'

The Continental *Daily Mail* fluttered from Warne's hands. Shame engulfed him. With bowed head he hurried from the room, and ere the door had closed behind him, O'Reilly was growling: 'For the love of Mike, boy, can't you be careful. You can see the man's as touchy as hell, and here you go blurting out the one thing that's certain to catch him on the raw.'

Indignantly Dalgith expostulated that *he* wasn't going to dry-nurse that silly old fool, and if . . .

The window was open, wide; and although Warne did not overhear much as he passed, he heard enough to make his ears burn and his heart change to something worse than lead.

In the solitude of the woods above the village he tried to think of his Church Parade, and after a while found solace in that, but only a little.

(9)

Another day had come, crisp and clear and bright, with a bracing nip in the air when one stood in the shade; and after breakfast Warne conquered his diffidence and unfolded his plans to Dalgith.

Dalgith scribbled down a note, saying: 'Right-o, Padre. I'll shove it in orders. Everything as you say —hymns and all. You shall have copies before zero. Anything else while we're about it? If so, say on. It's your show.'

Show again! But this time the hateful word did not hurt so keenly. Warne sensed behind it the careless phraseology of decentralization. The Church Parade was *his* pigeon, sponsored by Brigade. For that, at least, he supposed he ought to be thankful. The Brigade would certainly not let him down, however they referred to his service; and the knowledge comforted him considerably.

So he borrowed a stick and strode round the batteries with an alertness of step that told of renewed hope, and one by one he canvassed them, outlining his arrangements and almost begging their voluntary patronage. They must not think that because it was an official parade . . .

'We'll be there, Padre,' they laughed, and such was their

indifference, and their creed, that only a few said 'Damn!' beneath their breath.

Hungry from walking, as elated as he could be from the number of spots he had taken and the nearing prospect of some real service to God, Warne entered the mess in search of lunch. But the mess proved to be still the office, as it were; it had yet to revert to the domestic side of its dual function. Bell and the other batmen had yet to lay the table, for the table was spread with a map and over it bent the Colonel, Dalgith and Cheyne.

They glanced at the door as he entered, but continued their conversation. Ends of it floated about Warne. It told of caterpillars and columns and guns. And he, fearing to interrupt, stood there not knowing what to do.

But in the end the Colonel straightened his back, and seeing him still there by the door, announced in that impersonal voice whose significance Warne was already beginning to know so well: 'I'm afraid your service is a wash-out, Warne. We start moving into the line to-morrow.'

Whereat Warne's brain took on a curious numbness, so that he could not think, and he heard Dalgith as from a great distance when, folding up the map, Dalgith said: 'We can't grumble, can we? We've had nine clear days' rest.'

And with that the whole subject of the Church Parade was dismissed. Warne alone thought any more about it, but he was exceptional, being left in the ruins of his hopes. Feeling curiously hollow and empty, as if the bottom had been knocked out of himself as well as his aspirations, he turned to go, without a word. But a hand fell on his arm, restraining him, and with difficulty he focused his eyes upon Cheyne. Gravely tender, Cheyne said: 'I'm sorry.' A pause, then: 'I'll do what I can when we get settled again.'

The hand tightened momentarily on his arm, causing words to stick in his throat. Unable to speak, he touched Cheyne's hand with his own, turned quickly away and went out.

He did not come in to lunch.

CHAPTER VIII

COMFORTING THE DYING

(1)

Warne climbed laboriously down from the front of the '30 cwt'.

He knew exactly what to do now. Every day for the past week the '30 cwt' had decanted him thus into some strange billet and, frequently enough, some equally strange adventure. For the Brigade had been ordered here one day, and there the next. Orders had even been countermanded before they could be carried out. Finally the Germans themselves had settled the Brigade's destination by storming Villers Bretonneux and opening the door to Amiens. True, the Australians, then arriving in force, and the remnants of the British 8th Division had promptly recaptured it and slammed the door shut again, but the frame itself had been weakened and the timbers of the door sprung in the banging. To buttress it up, therefore, went the Brigade, right at the junction of the British and French Armies. (Actually the right of the British were Australians, and to the left of the French were Moroccans.) All of which meant to Warne nothing more than days of anxious idleness in the company of the insufferable Bass, either on the front or by the side of a '30 cwt' lorry, and nights that seemed to be inextricably mixed up with bombs.

RETREAT

Every night, with the rising of the moon (and those crisp spring nights were glorious), giant Gothas circled Amiens, scorning the pencilled beams of the searchlight ring and the streaming tracers that spouted from countless machine-guns; and the crashing explosions of their bombs came to Warne as fearful reminders of the War he had yet to see.

Some nights the bombing was nearer, as at St. Fuscien, and he had been able to detect the roar of falling bricks and debris as some village street was flattened.

And once as he lay rolled in his valise by the roadside, staring at frosty stars and listening to the rhythmic drone of the raider's engine, the raider had spotted the dark smudge of the lorry column drawn up by the silver ribbon of road. A 200 lb. bomb had hurtled right into the middle of it.

Warne had caught his breath in alarm at the first tell-tale swish of the falling canister, and then, before he could voice the cry that rose to his lips, the earth had shaken like a palsied thing, and instinct had made him drag his blankets over his head as some protection against the bruising shower of chalk that rained down in lumps as big as eggs, as bricks, and even footballs. In the morning he had found a boulder as large as a nine-gallon cask within a few feet of his legs, and, not forty yards distant, a conical crater that would have accommodated a motor-bus.

There had been shouts and curses as the men were torn from their sleep, and a voice had called out, asking if any one were damaged. Nobody, apparently, for the cursing had died down as tired men had resettled themselves for slumber. And then he had recognized the voice for it had continued quietly, in mock solemnity and fair imitation of a clerical monotone, but in execrable Scotch:

> 'From all ghaesties and ghoulies,
> From all lang leggity beasties,
> And things that go bump in the night,
> Gude Lord deliver us.'

And Cheyne's voice had tersely growled: 'Dry up, Infant, for God's sake.'

After that peace had come again, and Warne had listened to the receding drone of the raider's engine while a polished moon shone down serenely, coldly aloof. And he had lain awake, marvelling both at the Providence which had so directed the flight of the bomb that it plunged into the one vacant spot in a bivouac a quarter-mile long, and at the mentality of Dalgith who could joke at such a moment....

He had ended by asking himself whether he knew anything at all about Dalgith and the others, and deciding that he didn't, or at least, very little. Joke! They all seemed to joke. At times there was not a grain of responsibility among the whole lot, apart from the Colonel.

The last night at Hocquincourt—Dalgith had joked about even that, a debauch, when those who should have been on their knees asking God for His protection during the coming battle, had preferred to get drunk instead, knowingly and steadily get drunk.

He recalled the scene in his own billet at 3 o'clock in the morning when Keller had lurched in and stumbled against his bed as a preliminary to falling over O'Reilly —himself lying in a semi-drunken stupor—and finally spewing up the contents of an over-taxed stomach. There he had lain until his batman came at six-thirty.

After breakfast he had inquired of Dalgith, who appeared to be slightly less under the weather than either Cheyne or O'Reilly, and Dalgith had winked naughtily and laughed: 'Oh, George! He was only saying a fond good-bye to that sweetie he found in the next village.'

And when he had ventured to deplore, ever so mildly, the overnight debauch, Dalgith had looked at him suspiciously and laughed again. 'Do you know, Padre, the night before we went into the line in that Passchendaele show last year, five of us swiped ten and a half bottles of whisky between 7-30 p.m. and—well, I don't quite know when, but we went in at dawn next morning. We didn't know much about it,' he grinned.

'And last night?'

'Oh, then! That was nothing. Collett had a bit of a newt party. Everyone got pleasantly woozled but nobody passed out completely—'cept young Wood. He was a proper body.'

Something in Warne's face told Dalgith then that he had said the wrong thing, and he hastened to add:

'Though joy reigneth overnight, sorrow cometh in the morning—and, you know, to-morrow we may die!'

He had passed on with a grin, pressing his forehead with his hand.

Yet, when the time had come for the column to move off, bar a certain noticeable listlessness about some of them, and also a slight pallor about the faces, there was little evidence of what had taken place the night before. And the men, so he gathered from Bass's voluble allusions, had been little better than the officers, only quieter.

A village without a middle to its life! Warne had shuddered as he gazed in the direction of Amiens and the bombing.

COMFORTING THE DYING

A week of this treatment had been more than enough, coming, as it did, on top of the Church Parade fiasco; and he made no attempt at competing with it. And so, when the '30 cwt' decanted him at a village called Glisy, he did as experience had taught him; he merely stood aside and waited with all the patience of resignation until some one should come and tell him where to go. On this occasion it was Dalton, the heavy-jowled Signalling Sergeant, who found him in the way.

Dalton was swearing loudly, cursing the driver of another lorry for a fancied dilatoriness, when he noticed Warne, and he interpolated in one breath a blunt: 'Office last 'ouse on the right, Sir, beyond the church,' between his hearty references to wasting the damn day and backing the damn lorry into the damn yard. At times he reverted to the more vulgar expletive.

'Under this arch 'ere,' he barked. 'Look lively!'

Warne was forgotten.

A snug hamlet, Glisy, quite unscarred by War; and Warne felt inclined to like it for itself as he slowly wandered down the street towards the office. There was a newness about it, a red newness of brick houses and tiled roofs, that imparted a colour and warmth never possessed by Hocquincourt. Ugly, yes; but cheerful. And the quintessence of ugliness and cheerfulness was the modern little church with its windows so colourful that yellows and greens betrayed themselves even to an observer on the outside. But there were old cottages, too, with whitewash hiding their wattle and daub, and dark beams holding them together. Here the past gleamed white and stark through the ruddy glow of the present.

Also there were no middens, as far as he could smell; and no people, as far as he could see, except a few Australian soldiers whom he recognized by their turned-up slouch hats. In characteristic attitudes they supported convenient doorposts and stared at him with indifferent aloofness as he passed. Being Australian, they naturally never thought of saluting.

And then, as if in answer to his unspoken query about the absence of villagers, an old woman suddenly emerged from her cottage and hobbled so rashly across his path that he had to swerve in order to avoid a collision. He stammered an apology, knowing well enough that it could not be understood. But the woman merely turned upon him a pair of bloodshot, watery eyes that glared furiously from a skin the colour of leather, a skin where every line and wrinkle stood out clearly, etched in dirt—and spat.

He hurried on, painfully shocked and conscious of that sickly reek of stale food and unwashed flesh which he was beginning to connect with all French cottages and their peasantry.

But the end house proved delightfully fresh and sunny. It stood on a corner and commanded a view of two streets. There was scarcely a sign of its legitimate occupants, for Bell had been loose in its couple of rooms for several hours and had freshened them up as, probably, never before. They were clean, and, at the moment, one of them was sunny as well. In this, the front room, was Cheyne, with maps and correspondence spread over a portable trestle table. Every window was flung open as wide as it would go, and a cool draught swept the place as Warne entered from the road. Papers fluttered. Two or three eddied to the floor, and Cheyne, stooping to pick them up, said: 'Hullo, Padre! Found us all right, I see. This is our temporary H.Q. We're fixing up a mess just down the street, I'll take you along in a minute. Booth!'

The clicking of a typewriter in the adjoining room ceased, and a voice called: 'Sir!' Its owner, wearing glasses and the look of conscious superiority which is permitted to Artillery clerks, stood in the doorway.

Cheyne began: 'Oh, Booth. About that B 213 . . .'

A little heavily Warne settled himself in the patch of sunlight by the window. He was beginning to know Cheyne and his 'minutes'; also his own status in the Brigade, but he did not care to think about that.

He waited, for nearly two hours.

(2)

That evening, just before dinner, there was trouble in Glisy.

It was a glorious evening, too, with the village transfigured in the glow of sunset. Very round and very red, the sun lingered over the roof-tops as if reluctant to destroy so fair a scene, for its amber light flooded the village and mellowed where it fell. Distantly from the wooded marshes of the Somme floated up the lazy cawing of rooks. It was the hour of peace, and Warne, standing with O'Reilly outside the mess and contemplating the empty street, stirred beneath its caress.

He looked out beyond the rows of cottages. He beheld the War as God Himself must have seen it—a mad crusade against a Militarism even madder, or a struggle for the Earthling Rights of Man. How petty, and yet how stupendous it all appeared! The work of a child, appalling in its very futility. A gigantic squandering of human life and riches, as well as time that could never be replaced. And in order to accomplish this thing, men were standing in graves of their own digging when, on this evening above all others, they should have been on their knees thanking God for giving them life.

Warne's soul cried out for a truce to this folly. His heart ached with a yearning for peace, for the old ivy-grown Rectory at Bidderwill and—so traitorous is the urge of self even at these emotional crises—for the little kindnesses, the simple acts of appreciation which told of the love of a people he held in affection. Here, in a world of blasphemy——

'Better wear your tin-hat,' muttered O'Reilly. 'Safer.'

He persuaded a particularly foul briar to draw. There were puffs and wisps of blue-grey smoke, and a soft gurgling. 'Not a bad evening, is it? Something to miss the rain.'

Warne wanted to scream. Not a bad evening! No rain! To be told to wear a cumbersome bowl of painted steel for a hat when God Himself was smiling down from Heaven——

Still, he wore the thing. Looming recollections of a mist-filled quarry stifled rebellion. There was that bomb, too.

They were strolling down the middle of the road when the first shell shrieked into Glisy. It came from a high-velocity gun, with little or no warning of its approach, and it struck a red-bricked cottage some fifty yards ahead. Smoke and dust, a pattern in pink and grey, shot skywards and bellied out, boiling within itself. Followed the clatter and roar of tumbling bricks.

O'Reilly panted, and pulled Warne to the shelter of a doorway. Between breathless gasps he said: 'Worst of these damn villages. They always get strafed.'

O'Reilly turned to his pipe for comfort, but Warne could turn to nothing, for over and above his acute physical fear, he felt that God had deceived him. A cottage lay wrecked down the street, but in Warne's heart lay the wreck of a grand illusion. Not till later was he to gauge the extent. For the moment it sufficed that his heart was hammering a mad tattoo in his throat.

Almost immediately another shell came plunging over them, landing in a garden up the street. A fountain of earth shot into the air, crowning it the spidery shape of a bush. For the space of seconds its black silhouette screened the sun. Then the glowing disk broke through, blood red, terrible in its beauty.

O'Reilly's voice came to him as a far-away muttering. 'Fair devil, isn't it? Got a bracket on us properly.'

O'Reilly looked anxiously round for safer cover. Something in Warne that stood apart noticed that O'Reilly kept knocking away at an empty pipe long after the last shred of tobacco ash had fallen to the ground; and that same detached sense observed that O'Reilly's tongue grew suddenly loose. In a wheezing gabble O'Reilly told him to keep close in, out of the way of bits. 'We'll make a bolt for it as soon as the next pair have landed. Nasty business, this waiting. Nasty business. I don't think a fellow ever gets used to it, really. I myself get the wind up now, after three years of it, just as much as ever I did. A-ah!'

A shattering explosion; moments of eternity, each one pregnant with the fear of death. And then Warne heard O'Reilly's hoarse cry of dismay: 'Somebody's stopped a bit!'

He saw the stumpy form of his companion, his one link with sanity, disappearing into the rose-red pall of dust that hid the street, and impelled by the single swift realization that he was being left alone, he followed, too frightened to know what he was doing.

Then he was in the murk of the explosion. The air was like fog, only it caught the throat, choking, strangely acrid. A thin powder of brickdust and plaster, growing thicker every second, covered the road. Dimly he made out the scattered debris that remained of a cottage. A Titan's hand might have crushed it and flung it aside. But looming in this fog, and among the tangled beams, were Australians. O'Reilly joined them. Grunting and cursing they laboured.

Soon they brought her out—the same old woman whom Warne had come so near to capsizing that afternoon—and they had to kick aside the rubble before they could lay her down upon the road, a limp bundle of clothes almost unrecognizable beneath the smother of plaster and dust. Two red eyes stared fish-like from a face that might have been a mask, so thick was the coating of dust. Two lips slowly mouthed words that refused to come. For the woman was dying, and every instinct born of his creed united to throw Warne at her side, forgetful of self, seeing only the convulsions of a human soul breaking from its earthly fetters and slipping away to God. But those eyes! Despite their glaze they pierced, repelling him even as he made to kneel, so that he had the shocking impression that only her inability to do so prevented her from spitting at him as she had done but a few hours before.

Nevertheless he would have gone, had not O'Reilly pulled him back.

'Get her down to the railway—under that arch.'

O'Reilly addressed the Australians. He appeared not to see Warne, even though he held his arm.

Of his own subsequent movements; of the carrying of that broken body to the shelter of the arch; of the coming of Redley, as comically incongruous as ever, with the medical paraphernalia,—of these things Warne held no clear recollection. Dimly he knew that two more shells plunged harmlessly into Glisy's gardens as the party struck out for safety, but not until the dying woman had been laid by the roadside with her head pillowed in the border of grass, did he regain anything like a grip on himself. Then he noticed that the sun had set behind the western ridge as if in silent protest against man's violation of her glory. Glisy lay deep in shadow. Dust and smoke still lingered over its roofs. A chill had entered the air.

In the enormous thankfulness of his relief at being clear of the shelling, Warne's judgment was necessarily inaccurate, but it gave him a new vision. He now saw gaunt lounging Australians where before he had seen heroism incarnate. He saw them lean as greyhounds, browner than the khaki they wore, hands thrust deep in pockets; and he hated their indifference, their callous contemplation. He saw the stumpy asthmatical O'Reilly, red as a winter berry from exertion, and he knew not what to think. He saw the slow-moving colourless lips of the dying woman, and knew only compassion and tenderness. For he looked beyond the plaster-coated worn-out rag of a skirt, even as he had looked beyond Glisy before the sun had set. He did not see the frayed and bursting bodice for what it was. He looked beyond even the animal pain and hatred that twisted every line in her wrinkled face. He looked beyond all these to where he beheld a daughter of God, and because of this he knelt down at her side, taking her hand in his. With the feeblest of jerks the dying woman pulled back. Even through the film of approaching death her two red eyes glared at him, stabbing him to the heart. The hand he had taken in his slipped through nerveless fingers and dropped to the ground.

O'Reilly grunted:' Leave her alone. These damned old hags are more trouble than they're worth'—and started to rip up her shirt with a penknife, muttering half-audibly as he worked.

'Don't think I can do much for her. . . . Can't see where she's hit. . . . Probably riddled like a sieve. . . . A goner, anyhow. . . . Lucky she's quiet about it. . . . Fair devil when they pass out shrieking. . . .'

Whereupon there came over Warne that curious sensation of mental numbness that he was beginning to recognize from repetition, and to fear the more. It was as if his brain had suddenly stopped working, all except some obscure portion devoted to preservation of self, and this warned him that men went mad in France, that one day his brain might refuse to start working again. And with this mental numbness was the sense of utter helplessness, the impression that some occult force was sapping his will-power while invisible bonds held him in a definite physical restraint. He felt that he could do nothing, not raise even a lone protesting cry when God Himself was blasphemed and men behaved like beasts. He could only stay and hearken, and wonder how it would all end, and that question began to be terribly insistent.

So he did nothing when an Australian behind him vented a joke as obscene as it was out of place. He merely stared down at the mass of petticoats, grey and yellow with dirt, mottled with stains of blood, which were revealed as O'Reilly tore back the ends of skirt. And when the other Australians, with hands in trouser-pockets, looked down with all the detached and slightly superior combination of indifference and interest which is so typical of their race, and thinking the joke a good one, laughed raucously, he still did nothing. As for Redley, the chemist in him permitted a sheepish grin; the churchwarden, however, stifled it with prim disapproval, and the result was far worse than overt laughter. O'Reilly alone remained unmoved, and he continued to slit garment after garment with the blade of his penknife. His distaste was ill-concealed.

Then it was that something deep within Warne cried out, taunting him. 'This,' it said, 'is how you comfort the dying, *you*, who came forth with such high hopes and noble resolves,'

Bare from her waist, the woman lay before them, watching them with glazing eyes even as a wild animal caught in a trap will watch the coming of the trapper. And her lips never ceased their inaudible mouthings. A splinter of shell, it appeared, had pierced her thigh, smashing it high up and tearing it horribly, so that the mere sight of the bloody mess made Warne's stomach retch. Outlines blurred before his eyes as he wrestled with fascination, and he had to support himself on his downstretched arms lest he should plunge head first over the woman's legs. He made awkward pretence at assisting O'Reilly in order to hide his distress. He wondered whether he would end by being sick. . . .

At last O'Reilly pulled back her petticoats and scrambled to his feet, muttering: 'And now what the devil do we do with her?'

No one knew.

But in that moment the Colonel and Dalgith drove up from the river in the car, and Dalgith, coming over, asked: 'What's up? Somebody stopped a packet?'

And O'Reilly answered shortly: 'This old girl here. Can you 'phone Amiens for an ambulance?'

Dalgith thought a moment and looked at the woman. Her

lips still moved, though very slowly now, and her eyes still glared with animal hatred behind their mask of approaching death.

O'Reilly said: 'She won't last much longer. It's a question whether we can get her away before she pops off. Shock——'

The Colonel came up. 'Send my car in. Warne, you take it.' But even as Warne caught his breath at the suggestion, came: 'No, Dalgith.'

The car drove off, taking Dalgith. The Colonel continued his way to the village on foot. And the Australians, now that the entertainment was over and the shelling stopped, sauntered back too. Only the Doctor and his orderly remained with Warne, and O'Reilly wheezed: 'We'll remain with the old girl till Dalgith comes.'

So, under a railway bridge in the gathering dusk, they stood by a dying woman, with Redley a silent figure in the background; and to pass the time O'Reilly discoursed huskily upon the ethics of her death. Such was the extent of Warne's capitulation to circumstance, the discourse ran, for the most part, as a monologue between reflective pulls at the resuscitated briar.

Once, in response to O'Reilly's contention that these old peasant women were little more than animals, Warne protested: 'No, no! They're God's creatures. They're God's creatures.' And his voice rang with such utter weariness that O'Reilly searched him curiously before replying.

'That may be,' he murmured at length. 'That may be. But all the same I doubt whether they've got the intelligence of a good dog. They've lived in one place all their life, worn the same clothes almost as long. They know a world that is bounded by the village church and the back-yard muck-heap, and refuse to admit the existence of any other factors.'

O'Reilly warmed to his argument. 'This old girl here'—he jabbed the mouthpiece of his pipe at her, and he might just as well have plunged it into Warne's heart, the action hurt so—'probably refused to believe there was such a thing as the War, or, if she remembered anything of 1870, thought this dust-up couldn't possibly interfere with *her* little world. Quite possibly she thinks we're Germans. Evidence means nothing to her sort, any more than it does to a British electorate. Both have to learn from bitter experience what five minutes' sober reasoning would have told 'em at the start. And look at the result—trouble all round for every one. Some people in this world ought never to be allowed loose.'

A faint rustling, like that of silken skirts, sounded above them.

O'Reilly glanced upwards involuntarily. 'That means trouble for somebody too—Dalgith's ambulance by the sound of it.'

Came the distant explosion of a shell. 'He's got a hate on the Amiens road now.'

There was much rustling and many crashes during the next half-hour, but neither Warne nor O'Reilly pictured at all accurately the frantic rush of the ambulance. Swaying and bucketing it tore along, Dalgith bent double behind the dash, the driver crouched over the wheel, sensing rather than seeing the way. And when the edge of the road itself suddenly leapt skyward to crash about them with earth and stones and fragments of iron, the ambulance lurched madly from side to side at forty miles an hour while the driver tugged desperately at the wheel and the glass of the windscreen rattled off their bowed helmets. . . .

Dalgith was still a little white about the lips when, leaving the driver to examine the radiator, he came over to O'Reilly, and blood dripped slowly from his hand.

'Bloody windscreen,' he said. 'And all on account of that—— witch there.'

With a few words they lifted the stricken woman on to a stretcher and placed her inside the ambulance. It drove off, heading for Amiens by a safer route.

The old woman was forgotten.

(3)

Over a meal of fried bully that night, Cheyne remarked: 'Suppose this evening's strafe is going to be pretty regular.' And Keller replied: 'Sure to.' A laugh followed, short and rather forced, but no more was said until Colonel Metcalfe had withdrawn. Then Keller laughed again, saying: 'Christ! If old Jerry's going to make a habit of this evening's performance, I shall grow whiskers.'

He got up and foraged out another bottle of whisky.

Before they left the table, Cheyne, Dalgith, O'Reilly and Keller had between them finished the bottle. Only Warne abstained, excusing himself on the plea that whisky overnight gave him a head in the morning. So he sat in one corner, censoring letters, while his companions 'warmed their cold feet,' as Dalgith explained. All the same, Warne noticed that Dalgith drank least. Cheyne and Keller were the offenders.

Warne noticed, too, that Keller particularly grew more bombastic as the night wore on. His conversation was faintly reminiscent of Bass's. O'Reilly merely developed a benevolent cynicism.

COMFORTING THE DYING

Before they dispersed to their scattered billets, Warne was probing his own sanity, asking himself whether he was indeed in France, in a village liable to be obliterated at any minute; and whether that evening he had really seen a broken woman lying at the roadside. Whether two of these men carousing in that cottage parlour had really imperilled their lives on her behalf....

They took him away soon after eleven, back to the office down the street where, in the cellar beneath, his servant had rigged his camp-bed. Cheyne and Dalgith slept there too.

So they passed beneath the void of translucent night that hid Glisy's wounds, and away to the east, from Hamel south to beyond the Bois l'Abbé, white star-lights slowly, silently, rose and fell, showing above the black cliff of the roof-tops as trails of sparks like amber chains that burst, each into a pearl of light. It was all so vague in the village, mysterious and ghostly. And in the west a quarter-moon struggled with a film of cloud, making that ghostly too, while a faint reek of mustard gas gave to the air a tang of bitterness that caught the nostrils like a disinfectant.

To Warne, obsessed with the significance of what he had seen a few hours earlier, this darkened, volcanic vista meant nothing. If it aroused any response at all, it merely increased his impression of unreality. But to Cheyne, influenced by whisky in excess, it presented itself as the very abstract of Life, a Life where men dwelt in cruel malignancy, and where folly ruled in the guise of wisdom. He harkened back to O'Reilly's oft-repeated elucidation of the theological riddle: the possibility of a Christian who did not believe in God. And he asked himself as thousands of other men had done in the extremity of their perplexity: if God existed as a supreme arbiter directly concerned with the minutest portion of embryonic amoeba on this quite undistinguished planet, then why this hellish tumult, this seemingly unending slaughter of innocent, peace-loving lives in a wilderness of warring fools? If Christ died to save the world and succeeded only in part, then surely the bulk sacrifice on the battlefields of the present War would more than save the entire solar system, and, indeed, any world suffering from Earth's decay. It was all so invincibly baffling—not the least point being the wisdom of a Deity Who ordained that a fellow of Warne's calibre should represent His interests in Wartime France, above all impossible places.

Dalgith murmured: 'Topping night, but I don't like this stink of gas.' No more.

They stumbled into the scattered debris of the old woman's cottage. Obviously to Cheyne and Dalgith it was merely an obstruction to be avoided, so much rubble in their path. They side-stepped and passed on, and so did Warne, but in spirit he lingered there for the next two hours,

Lying on his camp-bed, hot, sweaty and woefully uncomfortable, he stared into the darkness and reviewed the whole episode, striving to find good where only evil flourished. Such callous obscenity as the Australians had displayed, such complete lack of ordinary decent feeling, he had never believed possible; and yet with his own eyes he had seen those same men voluntarily at work rescuing that wretched woman at extreme peril to themselves. Greater love hath no man than that he should lay down, or risk his life for another. Did *that* mean anything?

And was not O'Reilly just as bad, or good? Had he not in

principle done just the same things? And was he not every bit as callous?

And what of Dalgith? 'All on account of that——witch.' His bleeding hand. That splintered windscreen. ...

What was the answer to it all? Was it that War had brought out the best and the worst in men simultaneously?

Riddles everywhere, and only one thing certain: his own crass failure. But even that postulated a further question: Was it that men resented God or merely that they resented *him*?

Sleep can be very merciful.

CHAPTER IX

BURYING THE DEAD

(1)

So April slipped into May, and leaves burgeoned on the trees down by the Somme until the whole valley rustled with green. And bordering the great east-west road that runs dead straight, apart from a few kinks, for thirty-three miles, from a suburb of Amiens to Vermand, not far from St. Quentin—bordering this the bare trees clothed themselves and marked the countryside with a thick double line. Shells hurtled into Amiens by day; bombs rained into it by night; and the valleys reverberated with the thunder of their explosions. The northern offensive died down. The Germans gathered themselves for a fresh blow elsewhere, and daily the tension increased. Guns boomed sullenly throughout the twenty-four hours. There was preparation and then counter-preparation, and busy days for every one, except Warne, and he lived on, unwanted and alone in Glisy.

He went about rather as a man dead, moving like a ghost in a world of tense reality. So much was going on around him, so much of tremendous importance to everything he held sacred, and yet nothing touched him, and he in turn could touch nothing. It was all apart from him. Life continued to sweep by on the other side.

Orderlies came and departed from the Brigade office. Despatch riders bounced along the rough village street on snorting Triumphs or purring Douglases. Occasional lorries rumbled in and out again. Even the village as a whole wore a look of importance, for every man in it had a job, and every man went quietly about it. Only Warne hadn't one. Or was it, he wondered, that *his* job was a sinecure?

There were moments, too, during this period, when the Devil beat with terrible cunning against the frail and wearing armour of his Faith, for strive as he might, Warne could not repress these surging blasphemies. Some vital link in his brain would part before long. He knew that, for his soul was already an ache. A vast unfathomable weariness had filled him long ago. But how long? With something of a shock he realized one day that he had not been in France even a couple of months. Yet it seemed like years; long enough, at any rate, he bitterly reflected, to wreck and wreck again every preconceived notion born of his self-immolation at Bidderwill. What were those three tormenting years worth to him now—those three ageing years during which he had wrestled with his fears and prayed for strength, and finally screwed himself, at what cost nobody could ever know, to the pitch necessary to support him along the path of his duty? What had he found after all this? Merely that his God had deserted him; his King had no use for him. Small wonder that his spirit, which had softened rather than hardened under his earlier work in the Ministry, had broken under the strain.

But life had another side to it, one crowded with swift apprehensions when he caught himself speculating upon the chance shell which might put him in the place of that old peasant woman. But these alarms were tempered by a growing and fatalistic indifference. Only when shells were actually shrieking and plunging into the village did this anodyne fail him, and then the cold sweat that moistened his body reflected only too well the terrors that gripped his mind. At other times, in those long intervals often lasting all day, when Glisy lay there curiously peaceful and quiet, he accepted the respite much as a tired and beaten pugilist accepts the respite between rounds. As with the pugilist, his future held no prize, not even hope. Or seemed not to hold.

Often he yearned from the bottom of his heart for the kind of companionship that sustains, and his yearning was all the more poignant because he saw so much replete with that very quality and going on all round him. No previous knowledge of messes and their peculiarities was necessary to tell him that this, the Brigade Mess, the one he had been privileged to join, was truly happy. Strong words meant nothing. Banter was the order of the day. There was never the slightest friction (for the simple reason, unknown to Warne, of course, that Colonel Metcalfe would not have tolerated a disturbing element in his presence for one day) in spite of the utter dissimilarity in age, outlook, personality and experience of individual officers. Even Keller's slightly Hogarthian figure seemed to fit in and fill a gap. And the virile comradeship that knit them together appeared to Warne the most beautiful thing he had so far encountered in France. His one desire was to share in it, for that, he felt, would ultimately lead where he so wanted to go.

Yet, even allowing for the sense of terrible disillusion under which he laboured, he knew that he had only himself to blame for not joining in, for his mess-mates were never stand-offish, and the little irritations they had shown during the retreat had disappeared altogether. Busy they were for certain, but always friendly. But—and herein lay the root cause of his trouble—not once did anyone refer to his duties, his *job* (presumably because they so rarely referred to their own), and it was about his job that he so badly wanted to talk. Until he could, and thereby establish that intimate contact which he yearned for, he perforce had to remain outside the pale—a nonentity, a cypher, miserably inarticulate.

All the same, there were times when his companions nearly drove him frantic. Their inconsequent chatter grated. Their hellish affectation of indifference was an offence against God. And their incessant tippling, breaking at times into scenes that, in Warne's disordered judgment, bordered perilously upon debauch, both shocked and alarmed him. But it was Dalgith who innocently caused him most pain—Dalgith the ex-chorister, for ever bursting into snatches of sacred song; Dalgith swinging into the cottage parlour at lunch time and declaiming boisterously: 'Ho, everyone that thirsteth! Come ye to the waters, and he that hath no money...'; and Dalgith pushing over the whisky bottle and pressing him to 'take a little wine for his stomach's sake.'

Once, during an hour of depression even blacker than usual, an hour when his longing for companionship was nothing less than acute pain, he heard Dalgith's not unpleasant baritone lightly transposing that peculiarly haunting appeal from *The Messiah*:

> *He looked for someone to have pity on him, but there was no one, neither found he any to comfort him.*

On that occasion tears started to his eyes.

Then there was Dalgith singing from Wesley's *Wilderness*: 'And sorrow and sighing shall flee away.'

In truth Dalgith was at times intolerable.

On top of this came letters in steady cascade from Bidderwill, and their number was sufficient to rouse a fire of good-natured chaffing at his expense, and too, no little wonder in both Cheyne and O'Reilly. But how to answer them, how to preserve the illusion of these simple-minded villagers who continued to picture him in France as they had known him in England—how to accomplish this deception Warne had not the faintest idea, short of deliberate lying; and at times he crept down into his cellar bedroom and there, in the gloom, sitting on his camp bed, he buried his face in his hands and clutched at his temples in vain endeavour to stifle the flaming mockery that threatened to scorch up the very fountain of sober thought.

When he remembered to pray, it was to the effect that they, his parishioners, should never know.

To Cheyne, however, he was indebted for a solution of his purely secretarial problem, for Cheyne, eyeing one day the dozen or so unopened letters which Warne had that minute received, all letters whose scrawling addresses and crude pencillings shouted their parochial origin, lightly asked what on earth Warne had to say to the lot in reply.

'Say!' echoed Warne, and laughed shortly. 'I don't know. I would to God I did.'

Cheyne shot him a swift glance. 'Why don't you issue a monthly bulletin, and be done with it?'

'A monthly what?'

'Sort of standard letter to everybody. You could add a small personal note at the bottom of each to suit individual taste.'

To his astonishment Warne discovered that Cheyne was perfectly serious. And then a slow smile curled his lips. 'It could be done,' he said, more to himself than to Cheyne.

'Of course it could be done. Scribble your standard note and give it to Booth, He'll hectagraph fifty or a hundred or whatever number of copies you want. Save you no end of time and trouble.'

'It's certainly an idea. I think I will. Thanks. Thanks.'

He took his letters and went into the sunshine of the dusty village street, intending to read them there. But his wandering, slow though it was, quickly brought him to the wreck of the old peasant woman's cottage, and he stopped, staring thoughtfully at its jagged beams and splintered furnishings. Should he describe *that* in his bulletin?

Bass and his mate sauntered by as he stood there. Both saluted after a fashion, and Bass cheerfully remarked: 'Regular spring-clean of the ol' place, ain't it, Sir?'

They passed on, Clark spitting appreciatively, Bass declaring that Ol' Jesus looked just about as happy as if he had received a slap across the belly with a wet fish.

And back in the office Cheyne suddenly remembered enough to prolong his conversation with the Adjutant of the neighbouring Artillery Brigade immediately to the north of the Somme.

'Oh, by the way, when you come over next, you might bring along your parson. We've a new one who hasn't quite got the hang of things yet.'

'What's up? Too pi?'

'Yes—in a way.'

A faint laugh sounded in the receiver. It seemed to say: 'I could guess that.' But the voice replied: 'Right-o. I see.'

'Well, bring him along—but don't tell him why.'

'Right you are. Bye-bye.'

They rang off.

A little wearily Cheyne set down the handpiece. It was hot in the office, too hot for comfort, and without getting up he slid out of his jacket, letting it fall on the back of the chair. Came the dull thudding explosion of a shell bursting in the ravine just east of the village, and the thought occurred to him that if the German gunners lengthened their range they might easily drop a shell through the open window in front of which he sat. He had thought of that before, many times. The thing was rapidly becoming an obsession, his special fear. It had now reached a stage where it gripped him suddenly while he struggled through the daily pile of indents, ammunition returns, defence schemes, and the host of irritating domestic problems bound up in the Brigade. There was that bloody Tansley business, curse the man. And 3rd Echelon howling for a War Diary covering the period of the retreat. Then blasted French peasants screeching for their almighty francs in compensation for mythical damage. And always those hellish shells. Sooner or later one would cop a billet and flake out everybody in it.... He'd suggest to the Colonel that they moved into the open as soon as the batteries were dug in and settled. The Old Bullock was never stubborn before suggestions even though he was a Regular. Safer in the fields. These bloody villages just asked for it. No point in passing out now, after three years of it. Especially as he had got a reasonably cushy job. He thought of an earlier one, getting through that uncut wire at Loos, and was genuinely surprised a minute later when he passed the back of his hand across his forehead to find it still dry.

After that he got up and crossed to where a bottle of whisky lurked discreetly behind his office stores, and while tossing back a stiff peg of the neat spirit he allowed his memory to reach into the past to other days when columns of tired men, himself among them, used to tramp toward the line singing:

> Take me over the sea
> Where the Allemands can't get at me.
> Oh my, I don't want to die.
> I want to go home.

Go home! My God, did he not! Home! If only to Fiji and coco-nuts. God blast the place! Yet he could still recall that night when he first landed at Suva. He had walked along the coast road where the Grand Hotel now stands, and there the tropic night had drugged his brain. He shut his eyes, the better to call back the scene, his empty glass still in his hand. And he saw it all—the strip of silver that was a beach gleaming in the pearly moonlight beneath the interlacing fronds that drooped from majestic palms; and the sea, a grey silk curtain beneath the stars, was feathered with light by the reef. Spellbound he had stood on the marge of that tropic sea, and had drunk in the warm scented air, telling himself ecstatically that England could produce nothing like this. Within a month he had been crying his eyes out to be home again, in England.

Home! As he stood in that bare office-parlour of a peasant's cottage, Cheyne computed that he had not known the meaning of the word since his father and surviving parent had died in—when was it?—1907. As long ago as that. His maternal uncle had come forward then, loudly proclaiming his desire to give the lad a start in life; actually, Cheyne had since thought, only too anxious to get rid of him. And the start had been in Fiji, distant enough in all truth.

Cheyne's lips twisted in a reminiscent smile as he pondered over this avuncular solicitude. But the business was over now, and for all he knew his uncle might be dead, like his cousins, both killed on the Somme. He might get something back after all. Another of Fate's sardonic little touches!

But this particular touch had taken too long in the making; it had eaten up too large a chunk of Cheyne's allotted span. Youth had passed in the South Seas and solitude, and there was nothing to hold a man in the South Seas. Memory had to go back a bit further, and Cheyne's did, so that across the length of years, came achingly the recollection of old walled-gardens, of tidy lawns, of cedars and rose bushes; of a stone-rimmed pond bespattered with lilies, where as a boy he had never tired of watching the streaks of yellow light that were goldfish. He recalled the hedges of yew with their clematis-covered arches, looking for all the world like quaint little bridges in blue. He saw again the row of great beeches and the solitary huge old oak, the scene of a thousand adventures in acrobatics and torn trouser-seats.... He had been forced to exchange *that* for a grass hut in Levuka, and his uncle called it a start in life! It was. Cheyne did not dispute that. He merely knew that the start had set his footsteps along a path which led to no apparent end, and as he stood there, clutching his empty glass of whisky and staring through the bright rectangle of the open door into the street beyond, he experienced in its acutest form that nostalgia which comes to the wanderer and is all the more terrible because it is only a memory he clings to, a memory of what has ceased to be. He supposed that man's selective instincts became rooted in his native soil, if it were not too stony, and there the spirit turned for consolation when all else failed.

A shell swished over, causing him to start, and half a mile away he watched a cloud of smoke and dust shoot skyward. It hung there for seconds above the houses, and then slowly dissolved, drifting across the polished blue of the sky in a smudge of wreathing black.

He poured himself another whisky before he went back to his chair. From the other room came the click of Booth's typewriter. It spoke of something above war, something that was at least sane.

'A mad world,' he thought. 'Stark, bloody, raving mad.' With an effort he forced himself to his work.

(2)

So Cheyne, in his own extremity, braced his fraying nerves by taking to spirits, and faced the threatening German offensive that way; and round him hovered Warne, who no longer had any nerves to fray. Of the two Cheyne was certainly the more deserving, but Warne could not see that: he was too deeply immersed in self. To him Cheyne was merely the one human being whom he could approach even remotely.

Every morning the Colonel and Dalgith were away, often till late afternoon or even dusk, visiting batteries, observation posts and neighbouring units. O'Reilly had the round of batteries too;

Keller a veritable spider's web of telephonic communications to build up and keep in repair. They all went, therefore, except Cheyne, and he stayed in his office, sitting at his table before that open window, 'running the War,' as, with a wry sort of grin, he used to tell Warne on those not infrequent occasions when Warne, egged on by that desire for companionship, shyly drifted into the office.

But although Warne derived an obscure satisfaction from Cheyne's presence, he never made a confidant of him, partly because Cheyne was always too busy to invite the making, but chiefly because his own intensely English and middle-class reticence held him back from that first difficult approach; and he dreaded anything in the nature of another outburst similar to that one in Hocquincourt. He liked Cheyne, loved him almost, and he knew that Cheyne in part understood him, but Warne continued to hold back in shame. Nevertheless there did spring up between the two, especially on Warne's side, a mute friendship that did something, if only a little, to dispel the clouds of his personal loneliness, although nothing at all to relieve his aching sense of failure. For the slight alleviation he received under that heading he had to thank, curiously enough, the insignificant Redley.

(3)

Brigade Headquarters had been established in Glisy just over a week when to Warne, alone in the cottage parlour that served as the mess and engaged in his one, and hateful, task of reading other men's private correspondence, came Redley. Very earnest, very respectful, but churchwardenish to the tips of his drooping moustache, Redley queried: 'Would it be convenient for me to trouble you for a moment, Sir?' And Warne, genuinely curious, for he had not spoken to Redley since the Church Parade fiasco, murmured: 'By all means, Redley. By all means.'

'Well, Sir'—again the churchwarden speaking—'I was thinking that now, seeing as things are fairly quiet still, we might start our Sunday evening services.'

We might! Sunday evening services! Warne's fountain pen actually slipped from his fingers. The clatter of its fall had the effect of staying Redley. It also permitted Warne to quiet the angry surge of some still-living and outraged feeling. *We* might! *We,* indeed! Who was this little rat to assume collaboration with him? And then, as suddenly, he saw how silly this resentment really was.

'Go on,' he said, and stooping, picked up his pen.

'We might'—-we again!—' start services in the batteries as well. Mr. Wade was not particular about the days, but I myself think Sunday is the best day if possible, don't you, Sir?'

Battery services! Here was news indeed. But why hadn't any one told him before? It was a scandal. It placed him so completely in Redley's hands, and that was the last thing he wanted. And Redley, knowing it, loved it. All his provincial hankering after power of a sort that larger men would scorn to use even if they possessed it, coursed pleasantly through his veins as he stood there looking down into the sad white face of his chaplain. This being so, he did not wait for a reply, but went on:

'If you'll just let me know what time will be convenient for you, I'll have everything ready. Evening, is, of course, the best time for us: most of the linesmen are back by then if nothing is happening. I'll let everybody know, and we can meet in a small barn I've got down the street. There's no need for you to do anything here.' There was emphasis on the *here*, and Redley contrived to convey quite clearly to Warne that he would be seriously in the way if he made the attempt. 'Of course,' Redley went on, 'with the batteries you had better get Captain Cheyne to ring them up and tell them when you're coming.'

It was galling, but Warne managed: 'And you?'

'I shall come with you, Sir. Captain O' Reilly always allowed me to go with Mr. Wade.'

Some ten minutes later when a thoroughly complacent churchwarden in khaki strutted from the room, Warne knew once again that welling desire which hovered between mirth and tears.

(4)

Sunday duly arrived, a mere date to the Brigade as a whole, who did not even know that it was a Sunday. But Warne did, and to him it came as the Lord's Day. Yet he saw it approaching with no very high hope, but rather with a dull curiosity to see what Redley would make of the job.

Actually Redley did his work quite well, for reasons of personal expediency, and he swept out the barn he had chosen, carried down the dulcitone and rigged up an altar before he reported anything to Warne. A looted table, with its red plush cloth, served as the altar; on top of it a box suitably draped with more velvet; and surmounting all, the gleaming ivory crucifix that meant so much to Warne and apparently so little to any one else.

There were no windows in the barn, but the warm rays of the evening sun fell solidly across the benches grouped about the door, and a single beam, from a chink in the wattle wall, struck boldly into the barn itself like some pointing finger, alive and golden with motes of dust. At first it lighted upon the table, leaving a pool of crimson on the plush cloth, but as the evening wore on, it strayed to the ivory cross.

To Warne, in surplice and stole, his cassock over his khaki uniform, it seemed that God Himself had suddenly stepped into the barn, and was bidding him be of good cheer, so that for the moment all the doubts of the last month fell away, leaving him as he had been in the prime of his Faith; and his voice rang with something of his old fervour.

But the arrow of light travelled on, leaving him as he had become in that past month. For the service did little to comfort him, even as a memory: all told there were only eight people there.

They sang *Holy Father, cheer our way,* Redley's choice, and it so chanced that Keller and Dalgith passed down the road at the precise instant the eight were mournfully disputing the pitch of a top E Flat. In genuine astonishment Keller blurted: 'My God! If the old priest isn't earning his pay!'

To his further astonishment Dalgith merely replied: 'Poor devil!'

(5)

Two days later Warne had a visitor, the Chaplain from the neighbouring Brigade. Cheyne's scheme worked excellently, and the meeting was nothing if not casual, although it was with a distinct shock that Warne beheld a Chaplain's uniform: he had temporarily forgotten that he was not alone of the Ministry in France.

Cheyne introduced him. 'This is Warne, our Padre. Mardell, my opposite number. Fraser, yours.'

They shook hands. It was all very much as it should be.

There were just the four of them to tea, and they divided naturally according to their cloth. But it was not till afterwards, when cigarettes were burning, that Warne pressed the opportunity he sensed, as Cheyne intended that he should, and by then Cheyne and Mardell had drifted back to the office. Till this privacy was achieved he perforce had to talk of the commonplace, and do little more than study his guest.

He judged him a man not appreciably younger than himself in years, but ten years his junior in looks. For, indeed, Fraser was tinged with the robust and, quite unconsciously, flaunted his strength. The contrast with Warne was remarkable, and Warne felt it, saying to himself: 'This man lives. He is in touch with life. But I ...'

To that extent Warne was prepared to envy Fraser, or at least to congratulate him, but he sensed all too acutely that the secret of Fraser's quite obvious success would never achieve his own. The general air of self-satisfied well-being that seemed to hang about the man, Warne did not like. He recoiled from it. Yet the man *appeared* decent enough, though devoid of any particular intellectual force. Warne recalled having met the type before.

So they talked on, earnestly, with freedom almost, and Warne learned that Fraser had done over two years in France in various jobs—a Base Hospital one of them. But Fraser hadn't cared for that so much. He preferred the open manly life of the line. The men were so splendid—an honour to be with them, you know. Didn't Warne think it was?

The pair were alone when Fraser delivered himself of this long-accepted truism. They were still at the tea-table, but had pulled their chairs sideways, symmetrical about a corner, and were smoking idly, each supporting his chin with his free hand.

Warne smiled faintly. He quietly marvelled at the man's complacency. 'I take it,' he said, 'you know the ropes sufficiently well by now to—to find your way about, shall I say? It must make things considerably easier.'

'Oh, yes. Things work very smoothly with us.'

'And how exactly would you interpret that?'

'A set routine mainly. And it is surprising how much you can get in without interruption. All done through Mardell officially, of course.'

'And you are satisfied?'

'Indeed I am. Why, last Sunday, for example, I had well over thirty of the Brigade Headquarters. There are barely forty all told.'

'Hm! I had seven.'

'Seven! My dear fellow! Go to your Adjutant. Make your service a parade. Have'm detailed. Seven indeed!'

Fraser laughed with unctuous deprecation of a situation so manifestly absurd and, at the same time, beyond the possibility of his own experience. 'Seven indeed!'

'Yes, seven.'

Warne answered gently, his eyes never wavering from this abomination before him. Then, drawing back ever so slightly: 'All the same, Fraser, I would rather my seven of their own accord, than seven times seven, or seventy, or seven hundred, driven there by compulsion.'

The sudden flame of resentment, of anger, died away.

It was as if a curtain had fallen between them.

(6)

Fraser did not stay long, and when Mardell came back to collect him, Warne did not encourage him to stay. He wanted to be alone, to think, if possible. For that reason he sought his cellar bedroom after a while. Cheyne, already returned to the office, looked up from his table as Warne came in, saying, for the sake of conversation: 'Good chap, Fraser, don't you think? I'm told he gets on very well with his crowd.'

'If he does, then I'm not sure that I want to.'

Cheyne stared incredulously, but Warne continued on, finally to disappear down the cellar steps. And then Cheyne vented a groan, thinking: 'And now, my God, what has he been up to?' But only for a moment. Within a minute he was thinking: 'The lorries that take those six-inch to 836 will have to go on to 679 for those empties. One can also take 836's surplus 106s.'

(7)

That night the Germans bombarded Glisy. They did it methodically, hurling high-explosive shells into the luckless village from midnight to daybreak; and Warne, experiencing for the first time a slow deliberate bombardment, decided with all sincerity, in so far as he was able to decide anything at all, that the hurricane type of the 21st March was preferable: at least that did not deliver one to the hellish torture of waiting. Here, the five-minute intervals between the crashes were eternities of terror. Sweat burst from him, soaking his pyjamas so that, cold and clammy, they stuck to his flesh. No criminal in the condemned cell, in the last moments before execution, ever knew the agony of mind which Warne suffered that night, for the criminal does not suffer repetition every five minutes.

Sleepless from the moment he crawled into his valise, Warne heard the swish and crash of the first shell with a dismay that set his heart hammering in his throat. He could have flown sooner than he could have slept after that; and he dared not move or cry out, though he felt at times that the slender thread of his control would last no longer. For Cheyne and Dalgith lay in that cellar, too, awake, both of them. He could hear them muttering occasionally, cursing the German and all his works. But he could not see Cheyne's drawn face and tautened lips. Nor did he know that Cheyne was breaking his finger-nails on the rough brick floor where he sought to obtain the courage that comes with a grip. And there was nothing to tell him that Dalgith was almost as terror-stricken as himself.

So he cowered beneath his blankets, shrinking into them every time his straining over-wrought fancy warned him of a shell's approach, often as not quite falsely, and finally a hammer seemed to beat against his brain, bludgeoning his senses, so that his entire body became nerveless and he heard the bombardment as a thing infinitely remote. He could not have moved had he been told to do so. He was, for the time being, paralysed.

There were dark rings under his eyes when he got up, and it was only by sheer effort that he forced himself towards the mess.

This pretence at normality, this sitting down to a breakfast of fried bacon after a night such as had gone, when around him the rubble was strewn in the streets and the cottages gaped with fresh and bleeding wounds—it was all mad, mad, and he was going mad too. In another five minutes he would be sitting at a table with a white cloth on it, even if a dirty one, and he would be acting the part of sanity. No, he could not keep it up much longer. A repetition of last night . . .

He entered the mess. With the exception of the Colonel the others were already at breakfast. He sat down, and nobody said a word until Cheyne, quietly, almost listlessly announced: 'There's a job for you this afternoon, Padre.'

Then he looked quickly at Cheyne, for the assertion was so unusual.

'Yes. A couple of chaps in 836—killed last night. You may know them—Wood and Tollemache. Wood's that fair-haired youngster who joined when you did.'

'Wood! Wood!'

The name was a whispered echo from a brain benumbed. Wood, that fair-haired youngster! Too well did Warne remember the boy, the shy, timid smile that was his greeting. Tollemache also, though more remotely, for Tollemache was an older man. Now it was a job for him! Yes, he supposed burying the dead was a parson's job. The blow had fallen at last. He could only wonder why it had never fallen before. Wastage of men had been going on slowly ever since the Brigade had gone into the line, and was still going on, half a dozen here, an odd man there. ' Oh, 914 were shot up a bit last night. Lost a sergeant and three men.' Or: '679 caught it this morning. Several chaps done in.' These and others were the casual references from which he had to glean his information. And he was not encouraged to prowl on his own.

But so far nobody had been killed outright, though a few had died at the Casualty Clearing Station—outside his province. Now God had decided that he should bury Young Wood. Deep within him some outraged sense of justice demanded why.

Between mouthfuls of bacon and sips of tea, Cheyne told him what was to happen, but the forced matter-of-factness of Cheyne's voice was entirely lost upon him. He heard only the words as words. He read into them a significance that was not there.

'Two o'clock this afternoon at the new cemetery they've just started off the main road—opposite the village. . . . Full-dress show. . . . Colonel's going, of course. . . . Parties from all the batteries as well. . . . Principally from their own crowd, though.'

Then, after a pause: 'Hope it keeps fine.'

Hope it keeps fine! Was this a fête or a funeral? Warne groaned in sheer agony of spirit.

Desperately anxious to keep up conversation of some sort, Dalgith broke in with: 'Awfully hard cheese on Young Wood. Only been out a few weeks.' And quite unintentionally he packed into his words all the fancied superiority of the veteran, who never dies but simply fades away, over the novice who obviously lacks the veteran's advantage.

This time Warne nearly screamed. His nerves stood on edge. Something told him to talk, do anything to take his mind from himself. He asked wildly how it happened.

'Happen!' said Cheyne. 'Oh, much the same as it always happens. Just the normal harassing fire, and a bit of it landed on their bivvy. Killed 'em both instantaneously. Collett says you'd hardly know Young Wood, he's so messed up.'

RETREAT

Not once during this recital did Cheyne's voice rise above its dead level of monotony. It rang, indeed, with a weariness of its own. It told of a man forcing himself along subconsciously. He went on with his breakfast as he spoke, not so much as glancing at Warne. Had he have done so he might have stopped short of anatomical detail.

'Don't!'

The cry rang out, shrill and imperative. It woke all three, Cheyne, O'Reilly and Dalgith, to a sudden realization of tragedy. It frightened Keller into staring attention. And all four beheld a man who was half demented.

Pale of face, hardly knowing what he was doing and still less what he was saying, Warne stood before them, gripping the edge of the table as if he were about to fling it aside. Knuckles showed white beneath the tautened skin. He had pushed himself backwards and half-risen from his chair. His voice had swelled to what would have been a scream had it not been so hoarse a thing.

'I can't stand it,' he was choking. 'I can't stand it. You're not human. Your own brothers have been killed and you sit there gloating. You're monsters.'

A dark, angry flush deepened the tan on Cheyne's face. His lips tightened perceptibly. But he said nothing, and when O'Reilly made to get up from his chair he checked him with outstretched arm. Warne did not see this, and flinging out: 'Yes, you're enjoying it. Enjoying it, I say. Laughing when you ought to be mourning the loss of your comrades. The Devil has seized you. You're no longer human. You're monsters, I say. Monsters! Monsters!——'

Flinging this out, Warne hurried from the table, the room and the cottage.

The fall of his canted chair, which overturned with a crash on the stove, brought Bell from the kitchen, seeking the cause.

'The Chaplain,' said Cheyne, quietly resuming his breakfast, 'will not be having anything this morning. You may remove his plate. . . . Also you might take along his gas-mask—that one over there in the corner—and give it him with my compliments.'

When Bell had gone, he muttered: 'Outburst Number Two.' But the incident was not to be dismissed either so easily or so soon. Warne had cast a spell, and although they tried to eat as if nothing had occurred, something had occurred, and that spell was going to remain till someone released it.

That someone turned out to be Dalgith who, breaking surface like a suddenly liberated cork, gasped out: 'Gawd! Fancy Holy Joe flying off the handle like that! Worse than that communion box-up.' Then, in fair imitation: 'You're monsters, I say. Monsters! Monsters! . . . Ooh-er!'

He began laughing gaily, irresponsibly, but Cheyne checked him with a terse: 'For Christ's sake, shove a sock in it.'

'Nerves,' croaked O'Reilly. 'Here, Young'un. Gimme some tea.' He pushed along his cup. 'Looks as if we shall have to get rid of the priest.'

'You think it's the end?'

'I think it will be if he doesn't get his mind off whatever's sitting on it now. You can see for yourself. The fellow's nothing short of an idealist, and, I should say, one of the few orthodox Christians alive. On top of that he's an immense capacity for feeling, and that's the worst complaint of the lot. You can imagine what sort of hell he lives in.'

'Hm. I suppose that's why he manages to read into our most innocuous remarks exactly what we don't intend.'

'A characteristic of most nervous disorders. Something preys on a fellow's mind till it becomes an obsession, and after that everything the fellow sees or does is coloured by it. Warne probably sees us in a red glow. But the point is: reason no longer enters into the question. Like many another man has done in similar circs, he's got it into his head that we're all monsters and that he's a martyr, when all the while we're just ordinary human beings and he's a damned fool. The border-line between martyrdom and folly is very indistinct.'

Dalgith, understanding for the first time much that had been a mystery to him, murmured: 'Poor old priest!'

Keller guffawed, and referred gratuitously to Warne as a silly old b——. With impatience Cheyne broke in, pleading to O'Reilly: 'But what on earth are *we* to do?'

'Fake up a pretext, I suppose.'

'Have to be a pretty good one. I doubt if he could be persuaded to go. From our few talks I gather he had a call to come out here.'

'Ah, well. If he won't he won't. Can't make him.' O'Reilly sounded as if he had lost interest, as indeed he had for the time being, and he thrust out his hand, saying: 'Hurry up with that tea, Young'un. Three lumps. Aren't you ever going to learn?'

The Colonel entered, returning from a visit to 836 whither he had gone as soon as they had telephoned the news of their casualties.

The subject was not resumed.

(8)

It was two o'clock in the afternoon—an afternoon of windy

sunshine and great lumps of swift-moving clouds, snow-white and fleecy. It was a day, too, bursting with life and hope. The very trees by the roadside, the oaks and saplings in the copse at the foot of the tiny burial ground, responded to it and tossed their heads, all fresh and green with crisp young leaves, as if proudly defiant of death. But to Warne, cloaked in all the vestments of his office, a sad, strained figure, pale and haggard, standing by the newly-dug grave, they told of no vernal miracle; their rustling leaves whispered a message of despair.

In a few short weeks those same verdant leaves, now moist with the sap of youth, would be the yellowing victims of autumnal gusts. Another frolic would then be theirs, and finally they would be left to decay in brown-black nastiness, sodden with winter rains. Bare and denuded, the mighty branches that bore them would bend again to the tearing south-westers even as the pate of an old man bends to approaching death. But *their* youth would return again in the spring to cloak them afresh. Man's wouldn't. Daily he journeyed nearer to the end. He had but a short time to live, so he must needs devote all his time, his energy, and his God-given ingenuity to making it shorter still. . . .

Warne looked down from the swaying trees to the stretchers resting at his feet. On them lay the bodies of Wood and Tollemache, each roughly sewn in a blanket.

The scent of freshly-turned earth assailed him, drawing his gaze to the open pit. Into that, he thought, they would soon lower Young Wood.

Round him, grouped in a square, stood the solid ranks of khaki, brown-faced men, bareheaded and dull, indifferent, it seemed, to fate. Only a few of the younger ones *felt*, and then in bewilderment. They reminded him of so many animals newly caught in a trap, for their eyes wandered furtively from him, the white-surpliced priest, symbolical to them of all the fear bound up in religious ignorance, to the dark repellent grave, which, like some foreign railway station, was their starting point for the unknown.

But the others, the older men, had been caught too long to worry about a fate which might at any moment be theirs. They just stood where they were placed, like cattle in a market, dumb and unprotesting. And looking at their stolid faces, Warne felt once again that he wanted to scream. It was terrible, this devilish indifference. It was a blasphemy against the Holy Ghost.

He read the burial service in a voice that was low and barely audible, for the warm breeze from the south caressed his cheeks and carried his voice away, as if saying: 'Let *me* take it. These men don't want to hear you. All this is only a formality meaning nothing to them.' And taking it, the south wind bellied out his surplice in passing.

Years of practice alone enabled him to struggle to the end. His tongue fashioned the words automatically. He kept waking up with a start to discover that his thoughts were still busy with substance already forgotten by those who stood around him.

> 'Yea, though I walk through the valley of the shadow of death I will fear no evil: for Thou art with me; Thy rod and Thy staff comfort me.'

Few heard; fewer still understood. But Warne could not get beyond it. The words wove a pattern in his brain, and though his lips finished the service his brain was occupied only with asking whether those words meant anything. 'The Lord is my Shepherd.' Those blanketed bodies lying lumpishly at his feet. The yawning rapacious grave. . . .

There were no weeping mourners in black grouped about the grave at the end of the service. Half a dozen sharp words of command, a few perfunctory salutes, and the troops marched away, back to the killing; and even before they had gone the corporal in charge of the burial party was growling: 'Look lively there, can't yer? Cover 'em up. We ain't got all the blinkin' night ter do it.' In response the six gunners quickened up, sending a cascade of earth and small stones into the grave with their shovels.

Tears were slowly coursing down Warne's face as he turned away and removed his robes, and that night the troops said among themselves that Holy Joe had a soft heart.

(9)

Back in Glisy, Warne avoided his companions as much as possible, and they, sensing his distress, left him alone. He came into tea and also to supper, but for him these meals were silent and choking. And the reason for this was twofold; some still lingering appreciation of recognized conduct made him ashamed of his outburst at breakfast; and in addition he felt so utterly crushed in spirit that he made no effort to stem his crowding terrors, which, since the afternoon, had become doubly fearful. There was Young Wood now. The boy seemed to be walking with him, to be achieving such a projection of personality that Warne had the vivid and awful impression of being haunted, that if he turned his head quickly he would see the boy standing beside him, smiling shyly at him as when their eyes had first met in Hocquincourt. But Wood lay sewn in a grey Army blanket, a broken corpse beneath the dirt and stones.

At times Warne shook his head as if striving to wake up and free himself from the nightmare world that held him.

It was queer, he told himself, how he should be so taken by this ill-starred youth whom, after all, he barely knew. And as if to cap the telling, something that yet contrived to remain apart from his conscious misery warned him that it was too queer. He thought for a moment of going to O'Reilly, but here obstinate pride stepped in, the blind, unreasoning, foolish pride of the martyr. O'Reilly had been right in his diagnosis.

After supper even the unobservant Keller remarked Warne's depression. Colonel Metcalfe, however, decided on a new Chaplain. For the present, until the military situation clarified, Warne could remain: in whatever way one regarded him, he scarcely affected the fighting efficiency of the Brigade.

And outside the cottage, Warne himself had very little idea of anything until he found that he was standing in the long dry grass that covered the ridge to the west of the village—standing there and staring up towards Villers Bretonneux where, to the extreme edge of the plateau, clung the Australian battalions who barred the way to Amiens. The wind of the afternoon had dropped. The air was warm and scented. A soft haze hung over the horizon. It reminded him of the Royston Downs. But the illusion, with its blessing of relief, was short-lived. A flight of aeroplanes, returning from patrol, came speeding west, recalling to him that terrible occasion when he had first seen war in the air. Their pilots, in sheer *joie de vivre*, swooped and zoomed so that one instant they were flying below the level of the ridge, and a few seconds later they were up aloft, catching the level rays of a sun all but set. Once, in response to some invisible signal, the whole five 'planes in the flight went into a mad whirl of joy, revolving with their propellers just as a shell spins on its axis. And Warne, holding his breath at this exhibition of indefensible foolhardiness (one of the airmen was killed a few days later while endeavouring to dive under a field aerial little bigger than a soccer goal), saw in it only the tragedy of wasted lives—young lives, too, like Wood's.

He spun round as if a bullet had struck him, and then passed a soft, thin hand over his forehead, finding it damp. He had to press firmly in order to keep his hand still. He trembled all over, as if with ague, unable to make out exactly why Young Wood was not really there beside him. He told himself that he was going mad, and his mind gave itself up to malignant anticipation.

With an effort he forced his attention to saner, more substantial things, and turned again to the east. In the middle distance, by the indigo belt that was the Bois l'Abbé, guns were firing, his own guns. Spurts of orange flame kept stabbing the purple dusk, around each flash a dim but growing halo, growing as the darkness gathered. Seconds afterwards came the sullen, loutish boom of the gun.

Up there, he told himself, Young Wood had been killed.

This time a sharp cry broke from his lips as he spun round. It was the cry of one tormented with the spectre of madness, and it drove him down the gentle slope towards Glisy and the company of the living. All the same, he did not see Cheyne, lounging outside the mess as he passed; nor did he hear Cheyne's call. He swept by unheedingly, intent only on reaching his cellar where, in its candle-lit semblance of security, he might share his troubles with his God.

Cheyne watched him with misgiving, and when the stumbling figure had finally disappeared, he suddenly found himself wondering how long it would be before he himself was in the same boat. Another night like the last would just about see him off; certainly it would finish the priest. . . .

Cheyne marvelled at the tranquillity of his own reflections.

God! It was a treat just to lie back and do nothing. A bloody night; a tiring, worrying day. Now . . . He gave himself once more to reverie, content for the while to bathe in the calm clear beauty of the evening. And it was, indeed, the supreme moment of the day. The sun had set. Purple and lilac were colouring the western sky, and the few slated roofs in Glisy that caught the glow, gleamed dully with blues and reds. A solitary chimney, smokeless and gaunt and taller than the rest, gashed the sky with a vertical streak of black, but even that was soft and mellow.

So Cheyne, in his bleached and faded khaki, patched with leather at wrist and elbow, his respirator hanging loosely from his shoulder, his hands thrust deep into breeches-pockets, lolled against the doorpost, entranced, strangely soothed. Bitterness, fatigue, could not live when—what was it?—the Heavens declared the Glory of God and the Firmament showed His Handiwork? . . . Queer business altogether, and always the unanswerable question: What started first, and how?

From the mess behind him came the gusty murmur of voices, punctuated by Keller's belching laughter. Cheyne reflected that Pemberton-Billing and Maud Allan between them might easily keep George hilariously entertained until the end of the War, if he survived it; and somehow this contemplation of Keller wove itself into his reverie. With half cynical amusement it occurred to him that this transparent and continued refusal on the part of the Almighty to employ mankind as the demonstrating vehicle of His Glory, was a revealing example both of the Divine Wisdom and the Divine Opinion. The Heavens declare ... Put Keller, the coarse beetle-browed hedonist, against the Firmament! Small wonder the parson was so taken up with the problem of God's Creatures. They were indeed hard to recognize as such. That old woman here, for instance; the one that was killed.

He allowed his thoughts to evoke the image he had carried away from his one sight of her. She had been shuffling along outside her cottage when he had first arrived in Glisy, and he remembered her as scraggy, dun-coloured and smelly. As a biological specimen she had offered small promise. Humanly she had lived too long. Still, it was bad joss—getting killed like that, almost with the first shot.

He dismissed her from mind, and listened with some faint astonishment to the sound of men's voices that floated to him from down the street, for he recognized the rough melody of a hymn. Correctly he judged that Redley was leading the faithful in prayer. It couldn't be Warne because he was certain that Warne had not left his billet, and, until a footstep sounded behind him and his nostril caught the reek of whisky, he permitted his thoughts to traverse the whole gambit of Warne's debacle.

Lazily he turned towards O'Reilly at his side. O'Reilly said it was a nice evening, and, catching the distant song, breathed huskily his opinion that His Reverence was nothing if not surprising. After this afternoon he would have thought ...

Cheyne enlightened him, saying: 'That's Redley doing a bit on his own. Warne's in his cellar.'

'That's much more like it.'

From the tone of the reply it seemed evident to Cheyne that the subject suited the Doctor's mood. O'Reilly was obviously talkative. (Cheyne hesitated to say 'foxed.') But Cheyne did not mind that. The mote couldn't look sideways at the beam. And with amused tolerance he watched O'Reilly drag forth the faithful pipe.

'You were saying?' he prompted.

'Not saying; I was just thinking that I'm wrong.'

'No! Not really.'

'Yes. I've misjudged His Reverence.'

'Never!'

Cheyne laughed softly, but O'Reilly shook his head, airily sorrowful. 'Yes, I'm afraid I'm wrong.'

'Well? What about it?'

'You see: I thought when we were at that place what you call it—Hocquincourt—I thought the priest would pull round, settle down, you know. But I'm wrong. He won't.'

'That all!'

The revelation, as such, was disappointing. Cheyne felt that he could have told the Doctor that much himself. But O'Reilly slightly bottled was always entertaining. 'Go on,' Cheyne said. 'Tell me more.'

'This afternoon's work has just about finished him.'

'I can believe that.'

'And now he'll just run on till something crops up to push him right over the edge.'

'Such as?'

'A repetition of last night—or worse.'

'The Bullock's getting rid of him.'

'When?'

'Soon as this Tansley business has died down and things have settled generally.'

'Well, pray to the Lord that it *is* soon. That's all.'

'If you think like that about him, why don't you do something for him?'

'Why should I? If he reports sick I will, certainly. But it's not my job to go running about after a man of forty imploring him not to behave like a kid of four. Candidly, he leaves me cold, taken all round. At times he's annoyed me, intensely. At others I've sympathized with him. But as for the other thing——'

A shrug was more expressive than words.

'You see,' he added, 'we all live a life of superlatives now.'

'Superlatives? What on earth have they got to do with Warne?'

Glancing at O'Reilly, Cheyne saw him searching the afterglow as if endeavouring to put his pipe-stem on some critical word. The action was characteristic, and to help him out, Cheyne suggested: 'You mean there's nothing restrained now—no economy of thought, words, feeling, of men even?'

'That's it. No economy. Everything unrestrained.' The pipe stem gave an appreciative wave. 'And our very soulful cleric down there'—he nodded towards Warne's billet—'doesn't happen to be modern. That's all.'

'Well, if that fellow Fraser who came over here yesterday is what you call a modern,' Cheyne answered drily, 'then give me the ancients. I prefer 'em.'

'So do I, but we and they have got to go through with the

job as the job is. Why, look at it! Life's speeded up to such an extent that the old set of adjectives are quite inadequate. *Hectic* degenerated to *tame* in 1914, and *tame* according to war-time standards is the bed-rock level of suicidal monotony. So with people. They speed up too. But along comes a Warne with a mind saturated with inflexible ideas, and the result is a crash. And mark you, all these new evangelicals, steeped in their philosophy of superlatives, will crash too when the old pendulum swings back again to the true.'

'True being 1914 backwards, I suppose.'

'Nearer than 1918 onwards is going to be for a few years.'

'And therefore you suggest that all our judgments are unsound and will be until the world settles itself again.'

The pipe-stem grew animated. 'And it's going to be worse when these lads now bawling about green hills far away'—he jerked the stem-point in the direction of Redley's barn—' get back to their own little green hills, and find the commonplace instead of the superlative.'

Cheyne laughed softly. 'What you ought to blame, Doc., is not the War, but Education,'

'And what is War but an education, and a damn bad one at that?' O'Reilly was almost fierce. 'It makes men think, men who've never thought before, and it makes them think according to standards that are fictitious. We shall reap the result of this starting about five years after peace is signed, and the harvest will be all tares. A little exotic knowledge forced up in a hothouse—that's the product of War.'

'And do you,' murmured Cheyne maliciously, 'consider your own judgment infallible. Can you still maintain a 1914 perspective when, say, you look at Holy Joe?'

'I don't judge the value of Christianity by the failure of a single priest, if that's what you mean.'

'I'm glad. Had you done so I should have been forced to remind you of Fleming, for example.'

Cheyne spoke with quiet feeling, for memory somehow insisted on recalling a grey-haired smiling old man who almost daily, while he lasted, used to come to them, picking his way alone across the horrors of Ypres' battlefield, staff in hand, a black cassock hiding his uniform, and on top of all, steel helmet and gas mask, in order to brighten if only for a few minutes the ghastly existence of those who fought and died in Flanders' mud. A man, that—and a Christian, who never spoke of religion and yet irradiated his Faith.

'And that fellow who's running that rest-house in Poperinghe,' he added.

'Which,' retorted O'Reilly, 'only goes to prove what I've always contended. It's the man that counts in the long run. He is the mouthpiece, the leader. Faith by itself is not enough. Witness Warne. You wouldn't ask a fellow who hasn't the faintest grasp of the elementary principles of arithmetic to run a bank, and yet that is the sort of system tolerated in the Church. As far as I know, the Church is, at present, the only institution on this earth that does not demand of its novices the obvious qualities necessary for the functions they are to fulfil, namely that they should be leaders of men and not sanctimonious parrots. Instead, they give an amiable nonentity, very often a social climber, a few months' theological training, and then shove him in a pulpit there to propound dubious solutions to problems which have been worrying his elders and betters for years. It's not good enough. It's bad for the Church. I'm probably a first class atheist in your reckoning, but I've sufficient savvy left to see that the world would be very much the worse for the collapse of Christianity.'

'That's something, anyway!'

'Yes. And I want you to get hold of it. I'm not carping at the Faith. In essentials and divested of its quackery that's all right. It's the Faithful that get my goat at times.'

He nodded down the street, vaguely indicating Warne's billet and Redley's prayer meeting. 'That pearly-gate dope just makes me sick. Listen to it! ... In the course of the last couple of years I've seen a good many fellows enter 'em—Anglicans, Romans, Baptists, Sectarians, Salvationists and the rest—but I've never seen one in a hurry to go. On the contrary quite a few had to be pushed through. Dying's a pretty grim business when it comes to the point.'

He began quoting from Sankey and Moody:

> *'I should like to die, said Willie,*
> *If my Papa could die too.*
> *But he says he isn't ready:*
> *He's got so much to do.*

'Now tell me, Cheyne. Did you ever come across such utter——as that?'

Cheyne had to admit that he hadn't.

O'Reilly smiled faintly and grew serious. 'No Cheyne, it seems to me that the Church of to-day has lost sight of the moral and economic side of Christ's teaching in a welter of quite irrelevant sacerdotalism. The Ten Commandments don't count so long as some comic vestment isn't worn inside out, or the curate, in a burst of enthusiasm, doesn't forget himself and call the Eucharist by its proper name. Quaint ritual and unsupported dogma will never make a Christian while those Ten Commandments are waiting to be obeyed. By the same token you won't lead men with washy talk of Heaven when the Salvation Army can't frighten them with threats of a fiery hell. There's such a thing as evolution of ideas—conceptions, I should say—as well as anthropoids. Things move. We like to think of them as moving forward, but they may be going back for all we know. Nothing stands still in its conceptions and methods except the Church, and they still try to dose a practical and relatively educated people, already grown used to wireless and flying machines, dose them, if you please, on the fairy tales prepared especially for a set of flea-bitten nomads.'

There fell a silence between them, and when Cheyne answered his voice was thoughtful.

'Maybe, Doc. Maybe. I won't dispute your theology because it follows my own, in part at any rate. Our conception of God is, in the long run, necessarily individual, in much the same way as it is of Time as a Fourth Dimension. It is merely the outcome of religious, which is emotional, experience; and we, being earth-bound, can do no more than make God in Man's image. A poor compliment, really, but unavoidable, the limitations of the human brain being what they are in this year of grace, or evolution. Most people can think only in 'terms of personality. Their religious beliefs must therefore be moulded to that shape, and unless we are prepared to accept the popular dogma, that is as far as we get. All this " No God " talk leads nowhere.'

'Nor does the other stuff.'

'No, Doc. I wouldn't say that. In the present stage of the human mind's development the idea of a Personal God can make a direct and vivid appeal where some impersonal altruistic conception would fail. And that appeal can only be for good. Why then upset it?'

O'Reilly did not reply.

'After all,' said Cheyne, quietly, 'Christianity is the greatest moral force for good the world has ever seen, look at its inspiration how you will.'

The argument was not resumed. Nor, indeed, did they speak again until a faint whine followed by a thudding explosion down by the railway bridge, told them that the night's harassing fire had begun. Then Cheyne suddenly realized that the evening had gone, the glory had faded from the western sky. His thoughts ceased to be tranquil. He muttered: 'I hope to God he keeps those shells down by the railway.'

Another came, the whine of its approach audible in the calm air for nigh on twenty seconds. It struck the last house in the village. They watched the smoke of the explosion slowly dissolve.

'His Reverence,' said O'Reilly, and again the pipe-stem came into play, 'would probably tell us that shell came as a direct warning from Providence that we're thinking blasphemies and talking treason.' He chuckled. 'And all it's done is knock the roof off some poor devil's house.'

Cheyne stirred himself. He forced himself to jocularity. He muttered that he didn't worry so long as Jerry didn't knock the roof off the office. But the affectation was transparent.

'Come,' said O'Reilly. 'Let's get a drink.'

Together the two men turned into the cottage, and as they did so another shell crashed into luckless Glisy.

An hour later O'Reilly and Dalgith between them led

Cheyne back to the office and his cellar. They thought it advisable as the Colonel might have come into the mess. And Dalgith said that there was nothing to worry about since he could look after the 'phone.

But Warne was still awake, reading a paper by candlelight. He did not say anything, however, and Cheyne was persuaded to turn in without a scene. This done, O'Reilly dealt with Warne, for a glance at the grey-lined face, at the haunted eyes staring in terror at the shadow of insanity, was sufficient. He went out and mixed a stiff sleeping draught. He brought it back himself, and to his surprise Warne took it without a word.

CHAPTER X

ECLIPSE

(1)

The next week went by in grilling sunshine and extreme military tension. The German offensive still hung fire, but it never ceased to threaten, and against the day of its coming men laboured to build reserve positions, open up trench lines miles to the west of Amiens, and prepare routes of retreat, presumably, Dalgith argued, because Sir Douglas Haig had definitely stated in what the Army irreverently dubbed his Hot Air Order, that there would be no more retreat. 'Every position must be held to the last man; there must be no retirement. . . .'

Characteristically he summed up the situation by saying that Haig was not such a fool as to be caught with his trousers down.

But Warne—had he been living at the North Pole during the hundred years of peace, he could scarcely have appreciated the military situation less. Time, weather, War in its detail—these things meant nothing to him. He was just waiting for the *end*, whenever and whatever it might be.

Energetic, efficient, but damnably patronizing, Redley raised a churchwardenish head and more or less drove Warne round the batteries, but, although these daily excursions to a certain extent roused Warne from complete inertia, they afforded no comfort spiritually. Nor did he expect any. After the meagre attendance at his own Sunday service he knew within a little what to expect, and therefore it came as no surprise when the largest battery congregation that hearkened to his teaching was under a score. The average was about a dozen, and no officers.

It was this absence of officers, indeed, which constituted the mystery, for among the battery messes there was certainly none of those restraints, intangible yet clogging, which might have been born from some secret antipathy towards his cloth.

'Come back for a drink when you've finished, Padre. Don't forget.'

That was the burden of the refrain that went up in every mess, and it was made with charming ingenuousness and the best of intentions. So, with it ringing mockingly in his ears, he would go to some out-of-the-way corner where Redley had dumped the dulcitone, and there, with a cartridge box for a stool, lead his congregation in prayer and a hymn—only that, for services were necessarily short.

Yet, as he stood before them, bare-headed and erect in surplice and cassock, prayer-book in hand, the novelty of his position never failed to stir him, albeit but faintly, so that he forgot the pathetic insignificance of numbers and allowed his eyes to range over bowed heads to the nearby guns. Then his voice would tremble with a suspicion of its old urgency, and his face would light up, though dimly, with the flame of his old grace; while his heart would swell with the old, old yearning to serve until it seemed that only his rushing out, just as he was, and haling in the unbelievers idling about the position, and in the mess, would stop it from bursting.

With the unerring instinct of their kind, these same unbelievers retaliated by dubbing him 'The Pope.'

(2)

Only once did Warne encounter the disconcerting in these services, and that occurred on his second visit to 836. In the splinter-proof shelter which served as their mess he ventured to deplore ever so gently the absence of officers from church, as he called it.

'What!' roared Collett, happily inebriated. 'You tell me all my officers are heathens?'

The shelter resounded to his laughter.

Shocked and confused, and entirely unable to rid himself of the idea that Young Wood had been living in this same mess only a few days before, Warne stared helplessly at Collett, dimly aware that this fat, jovial, semi-drunken major enjoyed a reputation for gallantry and initiative second to none among the Battery Commanders. The Colonel himself had said so.

Still quaking with mirth, Collett addressed himself to his grinning subalterns. 'Hear that?' he boomed. 'The Padre says you're a pack of heathens made of mud what bow down to wood and stone.'

He paused, puzzling: 'That doesn't sound right, that bit, does it? . . . But never mind. You obey no blinking orders 'cept mine, and I say you're all going to church. Right now. And I'm coming too. No heathens in my battery, Padre. All God-fearing fellows here. Sober, too—no, not sober. Hendry, you little pipsqueak, what you laughing at?'

He turned with Jove-like indignation upon his junior

subaltern. Hendry, a freckled, snub-nosed, straw-coloured young Scot, began: 'Well, Sir——'

'I knew it!' roared Collett. 'I knew it! You want to suggest I'm shot, don't you? I know.' He winked portentously. 'Here, gimme another drink.'

Along came the bottle. Collett replenished, drank deep of the almost undiluted whisky, sighed happily and turned to Warne.

'Ready now, Your Reverence. Lead on.'

It was beyond Warne to protest.

But at the entrance to the shelter Collett stopped, and furnished, had Warne been able to discern it, a glimpse of the self he concealed behind his preposterous air of drunkenness. Quite suddenly, and with no trace of his previous levity, he said: 'You, Spence, and you, Fenley, remain here. Can't put all our eggs in one basket, you know, Padre.'

So at this service Warne presided over five officers and eight other ranks and except for a single resounding belch during the Benediction the Major's conduct was impeccable.

But half an hour later Collett was imploring Cheyne, over the telephone, to have a heart. 'Look here,' he urged, 'this is the second time you let that tame priest of yours loose on us. It's beyond a joke, straight. He lowers our morale. Honestly, that face of his is enough to make a sow litter. For God's sake, Cheyne, tie him up.'

As events transpired, the appeal was unnecessary.

When Warne himself arrived back, he found a letter from his Diocesan Bishop waiting for him, and after reading it he had the queer impression that a voice had spoken to him from another world—a world he was forgetting.

And there was one passage, too, which moved him poignantly in spite of his misery. It came near the end and read:

RETREAT

'I doubt not that you are finding, as other men have found, your new life strange and, perhaps disappointing, even discouraging. If so, and you feel the burden more than you can bear, write to me, should you care to, and permit an old man to share that burden. It is only the privilege of my age to ask this favour, and indeed, there is little else I can do.

'My son, God calls us along difficult paths, where the stones cut and the pitfalls bruise, where Satan himself lies in wait at every turn. Such a path I think you are treading now. I would therefore say this: when you see men in the guise of beasts, remember that they are still God's children. War may scourge and disfigure, but it touches only the body. The soul remains. See that you tend it well.

'May the blessing of God be with you, and may He protect you and bring you safely back to us.'

But it was too late. Nobody could share Warne's burden now. He was waiting for the end. And the end started to come that night.

(3)

It began with a scare. Scouts, taking a last flight over the German lines before darkness set in, were surprised to see large bodies of German troops moving westward towards the line. This fact, duly reported, 'released a balloon.' It took the Colonel, accompanied by Dalgith, away on a thorough inspection of those defensive arrangements which, so everybody thought, were to be tested in earnest at dawn. It sent Keller, supperless, chasing his emergency communications. Cheyne, O'Reilly and Warne were left, and they, apart from their men, had the village to themselves, for

ECLIPSE

the Australian troops had been withdrawn several days before, after the first night's shelling. And when 'five-nines' began to fall at steady intervals into the village, both Cheyne and O'Reilly betook themselves hurriedly to the office cellar.

'Not that it'll stop a pipsqueak,' Cheyne muttered.

They found Warne there already, tight of lip, whitefaced and trembling, but after a single searching glance they took no particular notice of him. There was nothing they could do.

So they sat and smoked, each repressing his fear as best he could, each shrinking into himself with every swelling shriek that betokened a shell's approach, and then releasing again when the all-too-familiar crash and scatter told of a fresh respite. Between times they broke the silence of the cellar with low interjections like: 'Pretty bloody, ain't it?' 'Looks like the real thing blowing up again.' 'This sort of game puts years on me.' 'Wonder if he'll keep it up till dawn?' 'Can't understand people not minding this business. Beats me.'

And once O'Reilly, without any simulation of nonchalance, muttered: 'Wish I'd brought a bottle of whisky down with me.'

Cheyne said he'd a drop in the office, and screwing himself to the task—quite unnecessarily, of course, for the cellar only conveyed an impression of security which it did not possess—went up and fetched it.

The bottle was half full. They offered some to Warne, but he shook his head.

O'Reilly tried coaxing. 'I'd have a peg if I were you. Come on. Just a drop.'

Again the head-shake, but far more rapid.

'Sure?'

This time the shaking was frantic.

O'Reilly abandoned the attempt, turning away and muttering: 'That's bigger than a "five-nine," I know,' as a crash, more resounding than the rest shook the frail cottage to its foundations.

'Near the men's billets too,' thought Cheyne.

Ten minutes later the bottle was empty, and they were sufficiently composed, or drunk, to embark on a strained discussion about the Pemberton-Billing Case. They forced themselves to a semblance of normality. They knew that on these occasions sanity hung by a thread. Cheyne had seen strong men gibbering, palsied with unchecked fear in circumstances less exacting than these. So had O'Reilly. As bombardments, could go, it was not particularly heavy. It was the relentless inhuman power of the thing that got men down.

Then the cellar rocked and heaved as in an earthquake. The candle overturned, plunging them in darkness. A gasp forced itself from Cheyne. O'Reilly breathed the one pregnant invocation: 'Oh, God!' A cry broke from Warne.

Cheyne struck a match, picked up the candle and relit it. In its uncertain guttering light two pairs of eyes, no longer veiled but frankly frightened, looked unsurely into each other.

'Pretty close,' Cheyne muttered, and laughed, a dry husky noise devoid of mirth.

They remembered Warne, and saw him lying face down on his camp-bed, clutching his ears in his hands, his body contorted and quailing before some invisible horror.

O'Reilly answered Cheyne's unspoken query. 'Nothing. He's got to see it through.'

They relapsed into silence. Pretence at talking was idle. Cheyne started biting his nails. O'Reilly changed his position every few seconds. But Warne never moved. The bombardment went on.

And that was the situation when footsteps raced across the floor above, came stumbling down the stairs; when a hand rent aside the gas blanket at the bottom, and a face appeared, unrecognizable beneath the grey-white powder that covered it. Then the burly Sergeant Dalton reeled into the cellar—coated from head to foot with plaster and dust, his moustache, a drooping brush of chalk, his eyes starting from their sockets.

'The men's billet, Sir! . . . A shell!'

He struggled to say more, but his voice choked and he coughed up gouts of blood as he clutched at his throat. They beheld then, for the first time, the spreading stain of crimson.

O'Reilly, who had leapt to his feet as soon as ever the man had appeared, caught him as he fell. Laying him down he called out, bidding some one fetch Redley and dressings.

But Cheyne thought only of the men's billet, and shouting over his shoulder that he would send along for Redley, he started up the stairs, fastening respirator and helmet as he went. So into the moonless, cloud-shadowed, thundering night.

The men were quartered in a house across the road, and Cheyne ran to it, heedless of a scatter of bricks and slates flung from a nearby shell-burst. A pall of choking dust hung over the wreckage of the billet, which a few minutes earlier had been a comfortable artisan's cottage. He shone his torch as he stumbled into the rubble, and its beam cut a sharp gash in the mote-filled gloom. A glance sufficed to show him what had occurred. The shell had penetrated the roof and burst right in the centre of the house, and the shell had been a big one. The place was a tangle of smashed woodwork and plaster.

Cries came to him from the blocked-in cellar below, and fearing the worst, he started to force his way towards the steps.

But he had advanced scarcely a yard when his foot sank into something that was soft and gave to his weight, rubber-like. A downward sweep of his torch, and he saw that he was standing on Bass, the driver of the '30 cwt'. The man was twisted and tortured, but saturnine even in death; and across him, horribly bent, lay Redley, astonishment and reproach written so large on his face that not even the plaster and dirt could hide it. Those ridiculous high-power spectacles had tilted forward to the end of his nose, too, without being dislodged, and his expression was more comically lugubrious than ever.

It was not even necessary to bend down. Cheyne forced his way onward—only to encounter the most hideous horror of all. The faint reek of burning wood suddenly assailed him, telling him the cottage was on fire. It would burn like tinder. There was no help at hand. Unless he could reach those imprisoned men——

He tore at the splintered wreckage, ripping his hands, his uniform, without heed; gasping for breath under the stress of frantic exertion, and nearly howling from a sense of impotence and thwarted endeavour. And he called to the God he so frequently denied, praying for another pair of hands.

Then, as if in answer, something lurched up behind him, and he paused just long enough to switch his light over his shoulder to see who it was. Warne stood there, white as chalk, quivering in a palsy of terror, and yet, Cheyne felt, triumphant. The spirit was stronger than the flesh. Or the Faith was. Cheyne didn't know, and there was no time to think.

Another shell, detonating in the garden behind the house, shook down plaster and odd pieces of furniture upon them. Smoke, adding itself to the dust, began to make their eyes smart so that they could hardly see. A red flickering glow crept from the back of the house. And against its coming the pair tore their way to the imprisoned men below.

(4)

The bombardment had ceased. Sheltering by the door of the office, O'Reilly dressed Cheyne's hands in the light of the burning house across the road. Warne's had just been done, and Warne himself had gone below to the cellar.

Nodding after him, O'Reilly remarked: 'There's some of the Faith that moves mountains in him. But——'

Cheyne laughed, a nervous, effervescing sort of thing. 'I wish to God I had a little. A man in his state who can force himself...'

And so they waited till dawn.

But when dawn came there was no thunder of massed artillery, no flooding of the German wave; and it subsequently transpired that all the scouts had seen on the previous night was a German Divisional relief. The bombardment had been no prelude; merely incidental to the front. But it promised more, and this fact led Colonel Metcalfe to shift his Headquarters, lock, stock and barrel, to the ridge to the west of the village before he sustained really serious casualties.

They started soon as they could conveniently see, and Warne, rendered homeless, could only stand by and watch and keep out of the way as best he could. To make matters worse there was rain in the early morning.

At breakfast-time Cheyne noticed him, and calling to Dalgith, said: 'Take him with you round Villers Bret. He's only in the way here.' And he nodded in the direction of Warne's lone figure.

'Show him the War, eh! Time he saw a bit.'

'Yes. But for God's sake keep an eye on him. Fritz was gassing round there during the night.'

And Cheyne honestly thought he was doing Warne a good turn. O'Reilly was attending some wounded at 679. Keller was shifting a telephone exchange. Dalgith had to go round Villers Bretonneux, and the Colonel was far too busy to devote hours to amusing a nerve-wrecked parson. The solution, therefore, seemed obvious.

Thus, soon after breakfast, a stand-up meal in the open, the ill-assorted pair set out, two steel-helmeted figures in belted trench-coats and respirators. But the similarity ended there. Dalgith stepped briskly along as if nothing could damp the ardour of his youth. Warne just struggled along, bending forward yet lagging slightly behind, so that to an onlooker it appeared as if every step were a hardship. And because Dalgith genuinely wanted to put Warne at some sort of ease, as far as humanly possible, he kept up a running chatter as if the War had never existed. It was kindly meant, but it was disastrous. Had Dalgith pictured disruption, maiming and slow death awaiting them in Villers Bretonneux, Warne could not have been more distressed. Such flippancy would have jarred and jangled at any time, but coming on top of a sleepless night of tragedy, it was fatal. Dalgith was unconsciously playing ragtime at a funeral.

Before they had gone a mile, Warne deliberately dropped behind a few paces in order that he should not hear. Dalgith took the hint, and after that they walked along in silence.

Beneath a leaden sky they passed over neglected fields that were thick with coarse wet grasses, or the straight green stems of half-grown corn. Raindrops, like crystal beads, still clung to them, reminders of the downpour. Ahead, the Bois l'Abbé showed up black and olive against the clouds. Occasional spots of rain fell, as if the storm were loath to give over. . . . A depressing day that would gradually get moist and steamy; and to Warne it seemed that he was walking through a country left, like himself, to die.

Collett met them as they passed through 836's position, and although the hour was but a little after nine, he pressed them to take a 'spot.'

'Come on, Padre!' he coaxed, every roll of fat on his ample face wreathing itself into a smile of welcome.

'Come on. Just a spot. Do you good. Steady the old nerves after last night. Heard you were shot up properly.'

He paused to laugh hugely, and Warne, aghast, contemplated the mountain of quivering flesh and knew rage. After all that agony, that night in hell, this man was laughing at him, was enjoying the thing as a joke.

Collett wound up with a gurgling apology: 'You Headquarter wallahs so rarely get strafed, you know, that we poor devils can't help laughing when you do. Now come along. Just one!'

Lightly Dalgith answered for him, saying: 'No can do, Sir,' and slipped his arm through Warne's. 'Seeing that it is but the third hour of the day'—he started to draw Warne away—' we simply daren't!'

A grin, a glance over his shoulder as he withdrew, an eyebrow cocked for a second—Warne saw nothing of this, but Collett, for whom it was intended, did, and said to himself: 'Poor old Joe.' As he set off to his mess he softly hummed the tune of the song the words had suggested.

RETREAT

Dalgith led Warne through the row of squat ugly six-inch howitzers that glistened darkly beneath their absurd garment of rag-and-netting camouflage, and clambered up the small bank in front, explaining: 'We'll go through the wood and work north from there. I want to have a look at some stuff we've got to salvage.'

Warne made no demur. He was indifferent to destination.

So they went, and soon the wood, with its wet earthy smell and dripping branches, shut them in as if they had suddenly entered a many-pillared vault. A cold hard gloom encompassed them. The silence was oppressive. There was moss on the tree trunks, and the ground underfoot was still soft from the winter rains. A dismal place.

For several minutes they trudged on, and then, without warning, they struck a glade littered with shells and cartridge boxes. The sky showed grey beyond the further trees, for they had reached the far side of the wood. Dalgith stopped here, thoughtfully surveying the shells he had, one day, to remove. (They had been abandoned by a British Battery driven from the position at the end of the retreat.) And Warne looked round too, indifferently, without interest.

The pair drew slightly apart.

'How the devil we're going to cart all this stuff away,' Dalgith suddenly observed, 'I'm blessed if I know.'

But Warne did not reply. He was staring at the sodden twisted corpses of men in grey uniforms and deep bowl-shaped steel helmets. Some were stretched out as if sleeping; others were doubled up as if winded, or were set rigid in the last convulsions of their agony. Waxen faces looked up at him, some already dark with approaching putrefaction; and their eyes were open —horrible sightless eyes. But no, they were not all blind. A young fellow, little more than a boy, *he* could see. His death mask was not like the others. There was no surprise, no terror, no impress of death's reception here. The boy's expression was quite calm, in a way serene. Only the eyes were unquenched, and they were filled with *reproach*.

The sight of them wrung a cry from Warne, sharp, pitiful. It brought Dalgith hastening to him. Warne clutched at his arm, pulled at him and gulped: 'Oh, God! Look!'

'Oh, those!' said Dalgith, quite forgetting that Warne was seeing for the first time the ultimate ravages of War, and also thinking far more about the problem of salving those shells and cartridges from beneath the German nose. 'This is the high-water mark of Jerry's advance—as far as he got before the Aussies biffed him back. Lucky it's a cold day.'

The answer, given off-hand with all the indifference of callous war-worn youth, pushed Warne beyond the limit of endurance. He began to babble wretchedly, incoherently, saying that he could not stay there. No, not there. That dead boy's eyes. And Young Wood too, following behind his shoulder.

He broke into a staggering run, and Dalgith, thoroughly alarmed, ran with him. Warne's helmet fell off as he crashed through the hedge that bounded the glade. He did not notice it.

But there were more dead lying beyond, and Warne cried out and covered his eyes. Dalgith seized him, shaking him roughly and beseeching: 'For Heaven's sake, man, pull yourself together. They won't bite. They're only stiffies.'

Stiffies! God's creatures were stiffies, left there to rot, A low moan escaped him.

Dalgith pushed him into the shelter of a sunken lane, urging him to brace up, saying that he would soon get used to them, and concluding: 'You can't break down here! The outpost line is just on top of this slope.'

He ran back to fetch Warne's helmet, and when he returned he thrust it on Warne's head, cautioning: 'Keep it on tight. Strap at the back. You want it here.'

But the command, though Warne mechanically obeyed it, carried no significance. For the remainder of the trip he could have been counted out as a thinking being.

For hours he seemed to be picking his way round and over the whirlwind wreckage of Villers Bretonneux, over its riven walls, its splintered rafters, and its crushed and broken furnishings. Shops and houses were crumpled and smashed. Cottages stood gaping, their sides ripped completely off. And into some of them Warne was taken. He climbed precarious stairs and improvised ladders. He perched himself in various fragmentary roofs. And in each he was called upon to study a flat vista of rain-soaked country which Dalgith and other officers assured him was Hunland.

'That's our outpost line down there, see?'

'That bit of chalk couple of hundred yards further on is Jerry's.'

'That middle hangar is in no-man's land.'

'That broken chimney over there's in Marcelcave,'

'Careful! Don't expose yourself unless you want to be shot up.'

'Look! Couple of Fritzes over there, to the right of that clump of trees.' (And looking through borrowed binoculars Warne made out two black dots moving slowly across a background of green—all he ever saw of the living enemy.)

These and similar exhortations assailed him continually,

but they passed above his head. Only the jagged ruins of the Church awoke any reaction in his consciousness, and that he beheld with a sort of bewildered protesting sense of personal loss. He could not make out why it should have happened.

He felt himself weak. He knew himself to be growing weaker and weaker. His brow was on fire. Every bone was an ache. But Dalgith hurried him on, saying that Villers Bretonneux was no place for idle loitering. Several shells crashed into its ruins as they went. Pink clouds of smoke and dust shot up. But nothing fell near them.

Once or twice they encountered Australians lounging outside the entrances to cellars and dug-outs. Several had bottles of looted wine sticking impudently from tunic pockets. And occasionally they came upon brown-faced men, also in khaki, and from the French Moroccan Division, engaged in looting for looting's sake. One was pushing a battered perambulator piled with stuff he could never use in a trench.

'It's their own, or at least French,' Dalgith commented.

And once they passed the wreck of a cottage where Dalgith unthinkingly explained the faint, sickly, obscene smell which had suddenly greeted them, by pointing to the huddled corpse of an old woman lying just inside the doorway, and remarking: 'There's another of the last ditchers. And she's going to stink like an unflushed sewer when the weather gets really hot.'

They went on. Warne never knew how.

It was tea-time before they arrived back in the new headquarters, and Cheyne met them, deliberately. He explained that Warne would have to share a tent with Keller and the Doctor for the coming night, at any rate. And Villers Bretonneux, what had the trip been like?

Somehow Warne managed to force out: 'Quite—er—uneventful,' and then hurried away, mumbling. Uneventful! That dead German boy! Oh God, those eyes were staring at him still! And there was Young Wood at his shoulder....

'Anything really happen?' said Cheyne, his voice low with genuine concern. 'He looks properly rattled.'

'Nothing at all.' Dalgith searched his memory. 'It was absolutely quiet. He shied off a bunch of dead Fritzes, the first he'd ever seen, and burbled something about the Valley of the Shadow of Death. But apart from that he hardly opened his mouth, and certainly nothing happened.'

'All the same I don't like it. Looks to me as if he might have a fever.... Must get the Doc. on him.'

(5)

The end came about an hour later.

Keller, who had been on his feet all day and most of the previous night, went over to the tent, tired out and not a little damp. A shift into slacks, a half-hour on his back reading the latest development of the Pemberton-Billing Case, or snoozing, he didn't mind which so long as he could rest in the dry; and in his haste he was half inside the tent before he noticed the prone figure of Warne.

Warne was lying face downwards, but his face was turned so that Keller saw it and gasped: 'Good God!'

Roused by the words, Warne looked up, raising himself on his elbow. And Keller recoiled to the brailing before the two horrible eyes that focused themselves upon him. They rolled. They shone with the light of madness. And over Warne's taut and twisted features there slowly spread such a look that Keller went scuttling from the tent.

For seconds Warne gibbered, his lower jaw working up and down like a cat's when the bird is just beyond reach. And then words burst forth in a flood. Unbridled at last, his voice rose to the frenzied scream he had so long feared. And thus he denied his God,

When O'Reilly dashed into the tent, Warne lay as he had fallen, his arms crumpled beneath him. A deep flush had suffused his cheeks, and his breath came stertorously. But although his eyes were open he did not see O'Reilly or the others. He could suffer no more.

Next morning they lifted him into an ambulance.

(6)

O'Reilly stood negligently in the entrance of the tarpaulin-covered shack which served as the Brigade office, and idly watched his orderlies preparing the stretcher that was to carry Warne. Inside was Cheyne, moodily staring at the statistical riddle of B213 spread on the table before him.

'He's got this 'flu as well, I think.'

'The priest?'

'Yes. It was bound to reach us sooner or later, and in his state——' O'Reilly explained himself with a gesture.

'You think he'll get over it?'

'No. The flu's only a minor complication though....' He went meandering on, indifferently, clear only on the one point that he could not afford to distinguish between casualties apart from medical diagnosis.

But Cheyne saw tragedy where O'Reilly would only permit himself to see a nervous disorder aggravated by a germ. Cheyne saw the man, not the disease, and some obtruding pang of pity led him to remark: 'It is pretty awful, you know, Doc.'

'What is?' The Doctor turned lazily round.

'Why, when you realize that all the priest's departure means to us is a slight alteration in this, and little else.' He tapped his finger on the B213.

'I do. And so did he. That's the trouble. I used to think that nobody was indispensable in this world: some merely did the job better than others. But I'm not sure that it applies to parsons in the B.E.F.—unless you invert it and say that no parson is really necessary out here; some are merely less unnecessary than others. Warne discovered the fact all right.'

'Yes, he did that, as you say. I only wish I could feel that we were less to blame for the discovery. I don't think we ever really knew him—understood him.'

'As much as he understood us, I hope! If we didn't, we don't know much about him. But I'm certain of this much: if he'd worn his collar the right way round in 1914, he'd have been conscripted and shot by now for what is called cowardice. Yet, can you say he's a coward after the other night? You can't. Had a young fellow exactly like him in the battalion I was with before I came here. Young, all nerves and feeling. In the end he just went off his head and legged it before a stunt at Arras. He couldn't help it, but he was shot all the same. Trouble is that Warne's sort are too civilized: they can't accommodate themselves to this unrestrained indulgence in a primitive lust.'

'I know. It's a ghastly admission all the same.'

'Maybe. But in a world gone mad the standards of madness

prevail. The few, like Warne, who preserve their sanity for a while, either get shot for doing so, or lose it in another direction, as he's done. Moral is, of course, don't go mad in the first place. Failing that, let everybody go mad.'

O'Reilly's round face grew thoughtful; the gurglings of his pipe took on a reflective timbre, and when he spoke it was to utter the staccato phrasings of his mind. Then he switched back to Warne, saying: 'Nerves, of course, were his downfall. All in tatters. Never for a moment dreamed they were so bad. He covered it up damn' well. Obvious they were going wrong from the start, but this——! . . . Never ought to have been accepted for service. Wrong temperament. Complete wash-out as a Chaplain in the field. Probably taken because he was a huge success in his parish. Country one, wasn't it?'

'Yes. Cambridge way. And a great success! Booth can tell you about that.' Cheyne smiled faintly.

'Oh, that circular thing. He did send it then?'

'Yes. He sent it all right.'

O'Reilly laughed wheezily. 'And I suppose the one thing that worried him was that no inkling of the show he was putting up here should creep into that letter. Usual way with these people.'

'Don't begrudge him his pride, Doc.'

'I don't. I grudge him nothing—not even his Faith.'

Cheyne smiled again, faintly. 'I can understand that.'

'No, that's just where I think you're wrong. You don't. Faith by itself is useless without a definite and sturdy slice of worldliness with it. And the converse does *not* hold, for the very sufficient reason that man lives in this world. Warne had only his Faith. You can see where it's landed him. No, Faith without a reinforcement of sound practical good sense is like a modern battleship without engines: it gets nowhere. The Arabs learnt this years ago. They left Mohammed and his mountain to the Christians, and said: "Allah is good, but Allah expects us to fill our cartridge pouches." The nearest we can get to that is: God helps those who help themselves. And that doesn't happen to be part of our orthodoxy.'

But Cheyne thought of all Warne had told him of Bidderwill's badge-bespattered Boy Scouts, its Ladies' Guild, its Reading Circle; its Lectures on *The Functions of Liquid Air* and such-like; and murmured: 'I wonder.'

Impatiently the Doctor caught him up, answering his thoughts. 'I know. In a village parish he may have been the huge success you say, but success there, among people who approximate as nearly as any one to the medieval, is not going to save the modern world. Religion, which is the expression of Faith, has got to reach into the council chambers of kings and permeate the whole fabric of international society before there's peace on earth and goodwill among men. And it would, if the Church had only been run as Christ intended it to be run. Instead, what have we? A moribund, emasculated thing, choking to death under the frills and trimmings that generations of self-seeking halfwits have tied on to it. Present-day religion is like a woman's hat or a Deauville bathing costume: utility is subordinate to decorative detail. No, if the Church, which is the people who want it, don't forget, had done its job in the past instead of scrapping about the authenticity of this and the precedence of that, the nations professing and calling themselves Christian today would not have had to go through the farce of building up a Plague Convention. A Convention governing human slaughter! Did you ever hear of such a thing! And now old Wilson's trying to build up a League of Nations when there's been the framework of a much better one in existence for two thousand years. We're a comic lot of Christians and no mistake!'

O'Reilly chuckled and amusedly contemplated the pink-stained shell-burst even then drifting across the roofs of Glisy. A dull echoing report came to them as he jerked his pipe-stem at the spectacle. 'That's the result,' he said, 'not of our Church, but ourselves, for our infernal complacency in allowing men like Warne and our professional priesthood to run it.' He laughed again. 'There's no denying all parties have got what they deserve.'

He stirred himself and knocked out his pipe. 'I see they're ready with that stretcher, so we'll shift both the subject and the inspiration of our discourse. Surprising how easy it is to rant away on a subject like this when once you get started. I suppose it's because you're no nearer knowing anything about it when you've done. Still, it's good for the soul, a little airing of suppressed ideas. More free talk, fewer maniacs. Every man his own Hyde Park. If Warne had realized that and opened his mouth a bit more, he wouldn't be where he is now.'

For a moment his tub-like figure filled the bright rectangle of the entrance, and then he was gone, Cheyne, queerly disturbed, tried desperately to concentrate on his B213, but he could not bring himself to make an adjustment *then*. It did not seem decent. Warne had come to them and was going. He was just a mouth that no longer required feeding. It was a terrible conception. Later it would be all right. Not now.

A high-velocity shell from the railway gun by Harbonnieres rustled over as Cheyne stepped from the shack into the

RETREAT

sunlight. He watched the distant spurt of smoke by the main Amiens road.

'Better send him by Longeau,' he thought. It was all he could do for the man they were sending away, and little enough in all truth; but the will was there for abundance.

High in a pale glistening sky, exploding shrapnel flecked the blue with puffs of fleecy white as some invisible anti-aircraft battery unavailingly sought to repel a venturesome spy. Came the faint pop of the shells and the barely audible drone of the engine.

Two bovine medical orderlies carried Warne by on a stretcher, and Cheyne, O'Reilly and Keller, watching, saw a flushed, unseeing face staring upwards.

The popping went on merrily above the drone. It reminded one of corks being drawn. Only from Glisy came the harsher detonation of a 'five-nine.'

Cheyne turned to O'Reilly: 'A Nunc Dimittis?'

'I'm afraid so. He's chucked his hand in.'

O'Reilly shrugged dispassionate shoulders, as if ridding himself of further responsibility with a patient who spurned his attentions.

Keller was heard to mutter: 'Poor devil!'

Under O'Reilly's direction the orderlies lifted the stretcher into the ambulance, and then, with engine clattering in bottom gear, the lumbering vehicle crawled over the turf to the road. With gathering speed it swept out of sight towards Longeau, leaving dust to tell the watchers of its flight,

And thus Warne was taken from the War—a War in which Hope had set out to achieve so much and had accomplished so little; a War that had crushed his spirit and killed his soul without so much as revealing itself to his face.

As Cheyne remarked when the three of them turned again to their work: 'God knows what would have happened if he'd ever *seen* the War.'

No one answered.

They entered the shack. O'Reilly called huskily for glasses, adding: 'Where's the latest *Times*? I must see what's happened to Maud.'

Keller shouted: 'Bell! There's no soda in this Prana.'

O'Reilly pushed a glass and the bottle towards Cheyne. 'None for me, Doc., thanks.' But Cheyne looked at the bottle a second too long. He did not wait for the Prana.

The War went on.

CHAPTER XI
EPITAPH

There is a brass tablet in the Church at Bidderwill, and its black letters read:

To the Glory of God and in Sacred Memory of

THE REVEREND ELLIOT PETHWICK WARNE, M.A.,

Rector of this Parish
From April 1908, until June 1918
When He Died in the Service of His Country during
the Great War for Civilization

" Greater love hath no man than this."